# Cradle

### C.A. CASKABEL

# Contents

# 1. Tina: Cradle

It was far past midnight when Dr. Tina Walker stepped into her newly renovated kitchen, holding a crowbar and a claw hammer. She dropped the tools on the Italian ceramic tile floor, pulled her bloodstained t-shirt up to her face to wipe the sweat, and looked around. Two screwdrivers, one electric, one Phillips, a bottle of Hendrick's, and the sixty-inch ivory baby-cradle taken down from storage lay in front of her. Her son's Lego City stood half-assembled on the table, and she opened the fridge to hide it in there. She had no work gloves, and the "gobble-gobble" mittens would be useless. Thursday! It was Thanksgiving already.

Tina started loosening the screws of the first kitchen cabinet, trembling, giving up after a couple of minutes. She threw the screwdriver against the wall and stifled a sob. *I can't. I must.*

She downed a gulp of gin and reached for the crowbar. It was a rusty primitive thing, but it would do just fine; she had no need for precision work. She got on her feet, lock and push, lock and push, no break, not thinking twice, and proceeded to rip out the birch plywood kitchen cabinet doors one by one. When the last one had come off, she piled them on the marble island. The country-style dream kitchen—though she was never one to dream of kitchens—looked like a flayed beast. Resting with her back on the fridge door, Tina took a deep breath and two more swigs straight from the bottle. She was not much of a drinker, and it burned deep. She got back on her feet, took the first panel, and patiently nailed it on the side of the wooden baby cradle. Two hours, twelve cabinet panels, and a box of nails later, she had covered all sides of the cradle except the top. The coffin was ready.

It was far from airtight. Moisture and earthworms would have an easy time getting in. *And that may be for the best,* she thought, as she opened the garage door to face the starless night in the deserted suburb.

The soft November wind brought two distinct smells, like a footman carrying two different dishes. The vanilla scent of the angel-flowers she had recently planted to welcome autumn and the reek of the garbage that had been piling on the sideway, uncollected for two weeks. Under the foggy streetlight, next to the overflowing garbage bins, a tartan blanket covered something, someone. This third and foul odor, sweetly and sickening, left no doubts. So many bodies. No earth to rest, no priest to bother.

Tina started pushing the empty makeshift coffin on the uphill asphalt road, humming a lullaby fragment. The suburban neighborhood of single-family houses was sunk in darkness and silence. Neighbors, police cars, and ambulances, all the screaming of the previous days, had finally ceased. A birthing cat and a hooting owl were the only other sounds of life. She passed the last massive house before the thicket and continued on the gravel path through the trees. The cradle wheels were sturdy enough, and at age thirty-seven, lean and healthy, she had no trouble with the one-mile hike.

The top of the hill was flat, the size of a football field, covered sparsely with bushes and stones. Some of those stones had stood in place for the last twenty-seven centuries—what was left of the shrine of Zeus the Rainmaker. In recent years they served as benches for teenagers to sit and enjoy a smoke or for a dog to relieve itself.

Standing at the plateau's highest point, on a clear day, one could see all the Athenian provinces, south to Salamis and Piraeus, east and west to the balding mountains that surrounded the city, and between them the densely inhabited valley ending in Marathon. The city engulfed the hill from all four directions—an endless labyrinth of concrete, streams of red and white car lights running down its veins. But on that night, it resembled the surface of the Death Star, idling silently in outer space.

The darkness had blanketed everything except the blur of the city lights, and all suburbs, modern or historical, rich or poor, looked the same. Some lights were glowing brighter, and she guessed that they were the bonfires, literal "bone-fires," fed by the bones of the countless bodies cremated under the open skies.

She knew that there was a six-foot-wide and deep hole dug up at the hill's highest plateau that had served no purpose all those years except to cause injury to careless children. Maybe it was an ancient tomb, unearthed and empty, once reserved for the burial of the finest, an Athenian prince, an Olympian demigod.

*At last, it will find a use,* she thought.

Tina lowered the cradle into the hole and started descending the hill. The body was too heavy to put in the cradle, the cradle too big to fit even in her SUV. "Two trips. I must make two trips," she mumbled, and then she raised her voice, "Who's there?" her gaze darting all around. The cypress trees swayed a faint whisper in reply, and through her watery eyes, she saw them reaching closer, following her like hooded monks in a grieving procession. "Stop that. Don't you dare! I loved him," she whispered and immediately sensed the madness embracing her. Many can become murderers under the wrong moon, but few can stay cold-blooded. "I had to. And now I have to bury him," she said with more determination, trying to convince herself that she could go through with it.

She quickened her downhill pace and made it back to her garage. The body rested in the passenger seat of the SUV, his head covered with blood-drenched towels. She lowered the back seats and started loading the trunk with the sandbags. Fortunately, she had bought dozens of bags to barricade the front entrance from starving or ill-meaning intruders. That hole was too deep for her to dig dirt with a shovel.

Twenty minutes later, Tina drove her loaded car up the hill and next to the hole, swerving through stones and potholes. Trembling from the weight, the exhaustion, and the autumn breeze, she lowered the fresh corpse, holding it below the armpits into the tight space of the coffin. It wouldn't fit lying down, so it assumed a praying position. She had to get herself down there and bend the upper body into a yoga child pose so that it would fold into the undersized coffin. Aided by the pale moonlight, she continued, first covering the top with the ripped-out kitchen-table slab and then placing the heaviest of stones she could lift atop it. The dead body objected in the beginning but finally succumbed under the weight to a perfect yoga position. She opened the bellies of the sandbags with her kitchen knife and emptied them on top of the cradle, and then shoveled dirt, stones, and more dirt, filling the hole to ground level.

The unearthed cyclamens were the sole tribute to his grave. She had brought no milk or honey, no coin for the ferryman, no goodbye kiss.

Tina would go back to that place for the rest of her long life, during the most desolate nights, usually around mid-August, and always on Easter week, especially on Good Friday, when vacationers abandoned Athens. She'd always pull the weeds out, to help the flowers grow tall, to hide her secrets and her crime forever. The poppies above his unmarked grave wore the bloodiest red every April.

# Act 1: Relevant Backstories

# 2. Ella: Can't Bury a Ghost

*Athens, December 1, 2057*

Call me Ella. My grandma Tina always found Marcella pompous. I am your narrator. Sorry for the blunt and corny introduction, but I am twelve years old, and this is the first story I have ever written.

As all passions that end up consuming one's life—please excuse my pretentious wisdom, it comes with age—I started this project with the best intentions, thinking it would be small-scale, innocent, harmless. A short story. It is the year 2057, twelve years after my birth, and the beginning of the massive climate-driven migration, the one that ballooned our country's population from thirteen to thirty-one million within a single decade. That crisis also started small-scale, with a few well-off Brits deciding to relocate to Crete and southern Greece. They are still descending en masse twelve years later, as is everyone who used to live north of the Alps. But anyway, that is a different, well-known story and not worth regurgitating.

The end-of-year seventh-grade project was to interview a family member who has lived through one of the defining events of the first half of our century and report her story. Being my usual Ella the Unpredictable self, I decided to write about the plague of 2022 instead of the Migration, which I bet is what every one of my classmates opted for.

Most of the other kids gasped at the task of writing six pages, but my problem is the exact opposite. I have reached one hundred and twenty thousand words, going from laconic to herculean. I just couldn't tell grandma's story without also interviewing my two aunts, Yara and Lucia—that's how I ended up with three narratives.

Since my grandma is *the* Dr. Tina Walker, "the savior of 2022," the flu pandemic was an easy choice for me. She was reluctant at first when I visited her at her Cape Sounion beach house, a few minutes' walk from Poseidon's temple.

"You sure anyone today wants to read about a plague back when governments were run by populists and idiots who debated whether they should vaccinate our kids? The world has moved on," said grandma. She let the cookies and the hot chocolate in front of me, maybe hoping that sugar would be an adequate bribe for me to abandon my mission.

"I asked Aunt Yara and Aunt Lucia, and they said I should write it. I am interviewing them too."

"You know they are not really your aunts. You just call them that."

"They are closer than random blood relatives. And you all three share one story."

"Some parts. Each one of us has buried a different ghost."

"You can't bury a ghost, grandma," I said, my mouth half-full with the cookie.

"Right. You can't. Shouldn't stir them up either, Ella. Did the other two really agree to this?"

"Yeah, even Aunt Yara."

# 3. Yara: Loved the Water

*Manchester, UK, April 4, 2021*

Fifteen-year-old Yara Halabi knelt next to starting block number three and splashed water on her face. She repeated the move until her coal-black burkini clung wet and heavy upon her skin, and her hair felt damp under the hood. It was something all the other competitors—those wearing one-piece tight Speedos—did as well. She didn't mind the burkini; she had worn it for the last seven years, five times a week, at the same swimming pool. Once as they were changing with the other girls, Yara tried Sharon's suffocating yet revealing one-piece, but she burst into laughter and immediately took it off. It felt comical to her, like a space helmet on a Victorian Queen. What she did mind was that she was the only one wearing the burkini on that race. If only those couple hundreds of spectators, the moms and the families, her classmates, the coaches, Manchester's fans of amateur swimming competitions, and maybe that occasional pedophile pervert could stop staring at her.

Her dad was staring too, and that created a whole different level of anxiety, for she had lied to him. In fact, it was Faida Halabi, her mom, who had lied, claiming that the girl suffered from minor kyphosis, and it was recommended by the school doctor to continue her backstroke swimming regime. The truth was that the swimming coach insisted because of her talent, and to make things harder, butterfly was her true calling. And she loved the water.

A one-piece would probably improve her time by at least a second, but that was a second she would never be allowed to have. She tried to focus on

9

the race and not her outfit, but her mind was a mess. Two nights ago, she had overheard her father, Khaled, talking about "moving back." Back to where? The Middle East? Syria? Had she actually heard those words across the paper-thin walls of their crappy apartment, or was that some bad dream? She planned to eavesdrop again tonight to confirm if this was a passing nightmare or one from the future.

Yara climbed the swimming block and waited for the starting beep. "Butterfly, I swim butterfly today," she repeated to herself. "Right now, dad is asking mom once again why I don't swim backstroke, adding that butterfly is useless for my back. But when I win a medal, he forgets everything. The pride will overwhelm him." It was an unspoken deal: "Win a medal, and you can keep swimming for another term."

The Manchester Aquatics Centre was Yara's heaven on earth, featuring two Olympic-sized pools, twisting water flumes, and an asymmetric prism ceiling reflecting the weak British light. It even featured indoor palm trees, and her parents always liked to visit, if only because it brought memories of a home far away.

"Take your mark." The robotic voice gave the signal.

Starting beep. Into the water. That passion, cold as death.

Third place. Not bad. Bronze. If she could claim back that lost second stolen by the burkini, she would have finished first. She'd try harder next week in practice; she was only a few inches away from the abyss that was fourth place. As long as she was allowed to swim, everything was fine. She could never imagine a life without swimming or that there would soon come a day that she'd quit voluntarily. A day that she'd fear the water.

Just one year later, her father was finally vindicated. As he had always insisted, butterfly proved useless, and surprisingly so did backstroke. That night, when the dinghy with the Syrian refugees capsized not far from the Turkish coast and Yara had to battle the black sea to make it to Lesbos, Greece, it was all freestyle. Freestyle in an orange vest.

# 4. Lucia: L as in Lolita

*Athens, November 14, 2013*

Lucia sank deep in the shit-colored two-seater pleather couch outside the middle-school principal's office, wishing she could disappear between the cushions. She pulled the hoodie further down to cover her brow and zipped it high above her mouth. Bitten nails and fingers clenched in fists, left leg shaking.

The principal and her mom had been in there for some time, and the Religion Studies teacher had just walked in. They were about to start. *Please, don't bring anyone else, not him,* she prayed, to whom it was unclear as she was not religious. If she were, she wouldn't be in this mess. She pulled her phone out and texted her friend Maria. "NOW."

The school secretary was hiding at the desk behind the wide computer screen, three yards across, but moved every few seconds to peer at Lucia. Lucia needed her to disappear. The phone rang twice, and the secretary exchanged a couple of words with whoever was calling. "Really?" "Right now?" She jumped from her chair, grabbed her handbag, and ran out of the door, leaving Lucia all alone. Lucia spared the two seconds to text "THNX" to Maria, then sprang up, turned the computer screen around, and chose the camera that covered the principal's office. *Step one, I can see them.* She gulped down the half-full glass of water on the desk and stuck the rim of the empty glass on the principal's door and her ear on the other side. They were talking, and Lucia could listen to them barely. Looking at the camera, as well, helped her follow the conversation.

11

"Let's go over the events once again, and I expect the truth from you, madam. Did your daughter come to school with painted nails that day?" asked principal Petrakos.

The principal glanced up at her mom Nora for a split second. He then started turning the pages of what seemed like the school code by the Ministry of Education.

Lucia guessed that he was looking for the chapter: "What to do in case a school employee assaults and attempts to rape a thirteen-year-old student." The principal lifted his gaze from the book to make eye contact with the Religion Studies teacher sitting to the right, rather than Nora, as if to signal that only those two, the educators, knew what was "really going on."

"What does this have to do with anything?" Nora asked, still standing. None of them had offered her a seat, and being in the service business all her life—cleaning the toilets of the rich—she would not sit down unless somebody suggested it.

"The custodian said that it happened the other way around. He was seduced. That your daughter, well, you understand." The principal ended his sentence with a mumble under his thick mustache, his manicured fat fingers tapping on the desk, setting his gaze again on the RS teacher.

He was the educated Greek, and her mom just an Albanian maid, but he was full of shit, so he avoided her eyes.

"Seduced? Sir, what do you mean? No. That monster almost raped my girl. And you, you have three witnesses. He has preyed on kids before. How dare you?"

Lucia tried to stop shaking her leg every time the principal spoke. At least she was proud of her mom. Nora spoke with all the confidence an immigrant woman without a high-school degree could muster against the principal in his office.

"The other students saw what happened," Nora continued.

"Well, not really, they didn't. Only one stepped forward as a witness. Your daughter, Lucia, was all alone in that room during the Religion Studies hour and the custodian came in to fix the wall socket."

"And he—" Nora couldn't continue with her words.

Lucia felt the urge to storm the room and shout the truth. *And he attacked me right there. Put his hand down my pants.*

"Sir, my Lucia has been screaming in the middle of the night for three nights now. She is not lying," said Nora.

"But you haven't gone to the police."

"No, I will not go to the police. How can I go to the police? Then her father would know. And if her father finds out, let's just say he doesn't believe in the efficiency of the judicial system. He'll come in here and beat you all senseless," said Nora.

"I find it very curious that your husband isn't here," said the RS teacher.

"I'd rather keep my husband out of this, sir. He has a criminal record."

Lucia was startled at that statement; she had no idea that her father had a record. He was a gardener who listened to classical music and read novels in three languages.

The principal twitched uneasily and grabbed a sharpened pencil to scribble something.

"Just promise me that you will fire that man, and I am out of here," said Nora.

"Fire a public servant?" asked the principal, sharing a smirk of futility with the RS teacher. "That's just—even if we believed your daughter— impossible, my dear madam. Impossible, you know that."

"I am sure you can fire a pedophile. My kid is thirteen."

"If you don't go to the police, how can I? Even if you do. Impossible. It will take ten years, witnesses, newspapers. I am not sure that's in the best interest of your child. Stigmatize her for life."

"Stigmatize her? Not him? Don't you people have any decency?"

"Please, let's be civil here. I prefer to avoid labels. Your daughter came to school with tattoos, piercings, her hair colored pink, and painted nails. The only testimony we have is from her dear friend, who saw her later—she didn't witness the incident."

"This is, just. Shit." Nora lost her words again.

Lucia's head was bubbling with anger. That day she had been wearing an unzipped hoodie and a "Not Today" black t-shirt with a steel dagger on it—

chipped black nail polish, double-pierced left eyebrow, hair cut all wrong and messy. The last thing she ever fantasized about was sexually provoking a middle-aged man.

"There were three kids, not her friends—she doesn't have any friends," said Nora, "who saw her running out of that classroom, wailing and trying to lift her jeans. Her t-shirt torn. They rushed into the classroom, saw him jump out of the window, and run. Have you talked to them?"

Lucia's jaw trembled after her mom said that she didn't have any friends. Why did she have to say such a mean thing?

"Nobody has volunteered more information," the principal said. He added something else, but Lucia couldn't hear.

She looked out the glass window behind the secretary's desk. It was raining, and her mom had not brought an umbrella.

"Mrs. Masoura, I am confused," started the Religion Studies teacher. Her long skirt and the sour face screamed RS teacher. "Your last name is Mazur, but your daughter's Masoura?"

"Yes, she has officially taken a Greek version of the name. I insisted."

*My mom always wanted me to blend in, to be one of you, the respected and accepted folk.*

"Sir, I am not making empty threats here. You have to get rid of that man. If my husband finds out, he will break his skull, and I am afraid he might not stop with him."

Her dad would break someone's skull? Dad had a criminal record? Dad had trouble even walking after his car accident. Lucia had been in her mother's belly when it happened. They had told her it was a hit and run, but was this yet another lie?

"You see, Mrs. Mazur, we are far from convinced that this was the janitor's fault," said the RS teacher. "Your daughter has a profound tendency for scandalous behavior."

"A Lolita, you mean," the well-read principal added.

Lucia saw Nora bringing her hand to her mouth and biting her index finger, trying to hold back any reaction, even though she probably had no idea of the fictional character's relevance.

"Kids her age today will say anything to draw attention. They try to tempt the adults to see how far they can take their rebellion. The tattoos, the pink hair. We try to stop the drugs," added the principal. "But—"

"My girl doesn't do drugs," Nora interrupted him. The words came out instantly; she couldn't hold them back.

"I hope so. Every parent thinks so for their kid until it's too late. We are faced with severe degradation of moral values. Our society has lost its true path and purpose. No faith. You see, none of this would have happened if she had not opted out of the Religion Studies course."

The teacher was right about that one. Dad Jacek was a Catholic, and mom Nora was raised in the poorest of communist countries where a bar of chocolate was worshipped ahead of any celestial being. Lucia was not baptized an Orthodox Christian like most of her fellow students and had no interest in attending the class. She had explicitly demanded an opt-out, and that was why she was all alone in an empty classroom while her schoolmates were being taught that there is only one true God, one Son, and one Holy Spirit, and all three are one. Instead, she would learn that day that there is also one custodian, one pedophile prowler, and one employed-for-life "impossible to fire" public servant, and what a coincidence, all three were one.

Lucia ran to the water cooler, refilled the glass, put it back in the secretary's desk, turned off the camera window, removed her hood, opened the principal's door wide, and barged into his office.

Her mom opened her arms and covered her daughter.

"We're done here, mom," Lucia said. "There are other schools in this shitty neighborhood." She pulled Nora's arm. "Let's get out of here. Please, mom."

Nora gazed out of the balcony doors behind the principal's desk. The downpour had stopped, and the raindrops crawled down the glass, glinting brilliant green like her daughter's eyes.

"It's past noon. I got to cook the stew," said, turning to Lucia. "I promised him." That beef orzo took its time in the oven, and then she had to catch the bus for the northern suburbs, go clean two houses, and return in time to kiss Lucia goodnight. "You're right, Lucia, let's go."

"Ma'am. Sir," said Nora staring hard at the Religion Studies teacher and

15

then the principal. "Do me a favor. Remember this day when you burn in hell."

She then turned and followed Lucia slamming the door behind her.

# 5. Tina: Hides, Flies, Mutates, Spreads

*Baltimore, November 14, 2013*

"No, young lady."

No. Young. Lady.

*Three words. Story of my life,* Tina thought, as she continued stalking Professor Garnett down the busy university hallway. A swarm of freshmen was spilling out the auditorium, where biology 101 had just let out, and she pushed and shoved to get next to her target. "But Professor, please, let me show you the data. This virus is the real thing; we must get to it now."

She had to try; so much was at stake. Winning that argument meant a post-doctorate future at Johns Hopkins. Lose it, and she had to ship back to Greece, or worse, polish her resume to join some pharmaceutical conglomerate. Zurich? Geneva? A single woman, a scientist from abroad, aged twenty-eight, she could already picture growing old in some dull Swiss village, a spinster with cats.

Garnett led her into his depressingly small office and shut the door behind.

"Professor, this my sixth year here. We've done great research together. I really want to do this work with you."

"And in all those years, Tina, I have told you repeatedly: there are no grants for obscure flu viruses. I simply cannot support you."

"But the pharmas—" countered Tina.

"—couldn't care less about a bird flu strain," Garnett completed her sentence, already paying more attention to his computer screen than his student. He turned his gaze on her and talked slowly to let it sink in. "There is no money in flu viruses, Tina, especially new ones. Old and predictable ones, eh, some money, but the companies care only about cholesterol and erectile dysfunction. Hair loss too. I warned you on your very first interview; these obscure avian viruses are insignificant. Maybe you lost a dear grandmother to the flu, but as a scientist, you need to think with your head— or even better your data set— not with your heart. Fifty-nine died worldwide in 2007 from the H5N1 virus. You had come here claiming this would be the new Apocalypse. How many died four years later, today?"

"Thirty-four. But I am talking about a new virus. This, variant H7N9," said Tina tapping her index finger on her notebook. "They first detected it back in March in China."

Garnett was searching his shelves for something, and he didn't seem to listen to her. He continued his sentence as if Tina had never spoken.

"Of which thirty-three were in Cambodia, Indonesia, and Egypt? Is that your data? How many Americans? Or even Western Europeans. Zero. Fifty Americans die from lightning every year, zero from H5N1. They won't give you any grant to study an Indonesian avian virus. Our lab is next to DC; we should know better what resonates and whatnot."

Tina was nearly on his ear, only a few inches away. "But you are not listening. This is a different virus. Mortality is forty percent."

"Forty percent of a handful infected is an infinitesimal number," said Garnett facing her and gesturing *small* with his two fingers.

"Are you doing this on purpose, sir?"

"Yes. I am shunning you on purpose, preparing you for the reality check you will face once we stop working together. Nobody will listen."

Cynical but not irrational. Professor Trevor Garnett was a great mentor, not some world-class genius who wouldn't put a minute's worth on his student's thesis or a hack who got tenured by mistake. No one got to his level by mistake; Johns Hopkins was the top school, and she had worked hard to get a PhD. in epidemiology here. Garnett was lean and athletic, pushing late fifties, a testament that he was still interested in life and the future, not a burnout. His office desk was buried under piles of ungraded exam books—

that would be Tina's job—dossiers with scientific papers waiting to be reviewed, admin stuff, paper after paper, magazines, and data sets all stacked up. An average person would have fifty unknown words on every page on his desk. Was he really that sharp, a world authority on all issues? She was up to date with the latest on the flu virus much more than he was. He could be missing something.

"What would it take to convince you, Professor?"

*It wouldn't be my looks,* Tina thought as she caught her reflection on the glass door. The nose and posture, stolen out of an Ancient Greek vase, signaled determination, but her frizzy brown hair—she had not been to a salon for weeks—belonged to someone disorganized or even disturbed. It was too early in the morning for makeup. As inappropriate as it sounded, she had noticed Garnett's opinion was influenced, subconsciously, she hoped, by her overall appearance. Suit, make-up, and heels made her statistical data stand out. No. Young. Lady. *Keep fighting,* she thought and repeated the question.

"What would it take to convince you, Professor?" she repeated.

"A series of miracles," said Garnett. "You are after the wrong villain, Tina. I told you years ago that the H5N1 virus is never going to become anything. It is a lazy one. It does not hide; the farmers spot the sick chickens stumbling and exterminate them, never take them alive to the market, it's done. It does not mutate. Does not fly or travel, too bored to infect humans easily. That's a lazy villain. He wouldn't last three minutes in a Hollywood ecothriller blockbuster, even less in an NIH research grant review."

"But this new virus does hide, Professor. The birds are asymptomatic. And if it mutates and spreads between humans, then you have 1918 all over again, and seventy million people die."

"If. *If* is a thousand-forked road in our field. Can't work with all ifs. The Spanish flu was a determined killer, and we had no weapons back in 1918. Call me if you ever discover such a villain. A virus that hides, flies, mutates, transmits easily among humans. Look, Tina, you still have a few months left to apply for some other grant. You know where the money is. Nobody is going to put money on the flu."

*Hides, flies, mutates, spreads.*

Tina kept notes in the back of her mind. She had entered the meeting with three words and was ready to leave it with four.

"Regardless," Garnett continued, "you are still invited for Thanksgiving at my place. And bring that handsome doctor boyfriend of yours too. The funny one. You guys celebrate Thanksgiving, right?"

Tina shook her head in disbelief before answering back. Every immigrant celebrated Thanksgiving, and she was not even one.

"My last name is Walker, sir. I was born and raised half an hour from Boston."

"Oh, I wanted to ask you about that. Your last name was Damianou, until a month ago. Why did you change your name if you are not married?"

"I changed to my mother's last name, 'Walker.' You see, my father, Mr. Damianos, decided to remarry. It was my wedding gift to him."

"That's a mistake, career-wise; you've established a reputation through your publications. It is a hell of a process to retroactively change names in published papers. Hyphenate, at least."

"Defeats the purpose."

"As you wish. See you for dinner, Thursday. But no more sick turkey talk around the Thanksgiving table," Garnett chuckled.

The professor always roasted free-range. A flock of turkeys in Ontario back in 1966 were the first-ever victims of H5N1. Fortunately, nature knew better than allow turkeys to fly.

Pigeons fly. They are also susceptible to the H7N9 virus.

# 6. Ella: Four-foot skeletons

*Athens, December 15, 2057.*

"Back then on that godforsaken year," said Grandma Tina as she started reciting her story, "when the plague came, we were utterly unprepared. I had tried to warn them, Ella. Call me Cassandra, the doomed prophet. I failed. We knew it could happen, would happen years ago when I was still in college. I told them. They didn't listen, no one did until the outbreak was here.

"Athens ran out of coffins on the second week of the spread. Most funeral homes were looted early, abandoned by their owners who learned the hard way that too many customers may end up being a bad thing for business. Body-bags from morgues, hospitals, and army camps, were quickly sold on the black market. The family folk—those who cared not to throw the bodies of their own on the street—tried to find any plastic or bubble wrapping, but there were not many hardware stores in a city of cramped apartment buildings. Some used old trunks, an armoire, even a cradle. But most of us were not DIY people in those days, still aren't. Another thing that didn't follow down from our ancestors.

"Undersized coffins were the first to disappear. For many years, the municipal crews would exhume remains buried in parks or empty lots, resurrecting our nightmares. The twin girls wearing white junior-bridesmaid dresses, a boy with a Barcelona Messi polo shirt cuddled with another one on a Celtics basketball jersey. Globalization. Friends. All those four-foot skeletons."

# 7. Yara: A Lady Marco Polo

One thing about the Aegean Sea that licks the coasts of the Greek islands is that it is warm in June, not Maldives coral-reef-dies warm, yet warm enough for a little girl to survive a good ten hours among the wine-dark waters of the raging archipelago.

Five nautical miles. That was less than half an hour on the sea upon even the slowest of single-engine boats, loaded with as many refugees as it could hold before capsizing. That was it, five nautical miles from the east to the west, from Asia to Europe, from hell to heaven, from the Turkish coast to the Lesbos beaches of Greece. Her father had made sure to give her that information before he sent her off.

Yara crossing the Aegean Sea at night, holding tightly a seven-year-old sister who couldn't swim, was not her father's first half-thought-out plan. Khaled didn't share plans with his daughters, but he did with his wife. Even back in Manchester, they always lived in cramped apartments with walls far from soundproof, so Yara had no trouble hearing all his plans. He was never very good at planning, and as a construction engineer, planning was essential, so he was barely making a salary to support his big family.

"Everything has become so expensive here, Faiza. Things are getting better in Syria—they are rebuilding—maybe it is time we take the children and return to our homeland. It has been too long. It is not good for them here either. The streets, the drugs, Netflix. You see our Yara, how she behaves, she wants to go to Disneyland, she is still on this swimming team. We are in the beehive, and she will taste honey. How do we keep her away from all this? They need my skills back home, I'll make good money there. England has nothing more for us. Once they voted this Brexit deal, all changed here."

Khaled was partially correct. One can make good money when the war is over, but for that to happen, the war must be unquestionably over. Everyone referred to it as "the war," but Yara kept asking, "What war?" Wars had names in her books: World War I, War of the Roses, the Great Galactic War of the Sith against the Republic. When it came to Syria, it was just "the war." Whoever had the leverage to line up a group of young men, whatever state could spare a boat to send some soldiers, they were all there, perpetually fighting "the war." War was a permanent trait of the region, as was "the heat" or "the desert." That much was clear to sixteen-year-old Yara but not to three times her age Khaled.

Faiza, Yara's mother, replied to him: "You are the man of the house, you know best, Khaled, you will do the right thing, but maybe we still wait a bit? Promise me? Let's see how things unfold back home," which was the closest way that a woman of her culture could say to her husband: "Stay away from all family decisions and don't go near matchboxes or electrical outlets."

It was hard to argue with that hirsute man; his one eyebrow was always raised half an inch higher than the other as if he were born knowing everything.

Unfortunately, and unwittingly it was Faiza who provided the fatal match that Khaled needed to set their fate on fire. She was walking home, holding two shopping bags on the evening of the metro murders, a few hours after a male immigrant stabbed and killed two women on the Manchester Victoria Station. The younger was only twenty-two, the older three months pregnant. Faiza's family lived in Levenshulme, one of the most multiethnic neighborhoods, and they never had any serious problems.

That evening she saw the three young men standing outside a pub on the opposite side of the street. They crossed fast and shouted at her, "Oi, bin Laden bitch." Faiza quickened her step, but they caught up. One of the men grabbed her by the hijab and pulled her so hard that she fell on her back. She saw the tomatoes tumbling down the street, and then one of the men unzipping his pants, and she saw no more. Sweet-faced, always-polite mommy Faiza covered her eyes and mouth tightly as they took their turns urinating all over her. Things like that had happened before, but it is always harder to feel the cold knife or the warm piss than to hear about the misfortune of others.

The proverbial straw upon the camel's back that evening was the activist blogger vaping dragon clouds out his open window. From the first floor of the close-by building, he witnessed the whole incident, even took some photos, and called the police, who had to take Faiza to the hospital and inform Khaled. Naturally, he blogged all over the web, and because of the 12-megapixel camera of his, the image was so detailed and clear—hatred red as a tomato, fear gold as draught ale piss—that it went viral to his thirteen thousand followers and hundreds of millions more. Yara and her older brother, Sayid, had to get all the details directly from their mother; it was better than the made-up stories they'd be subjected to at school. The following day Khaled took his children to get their passport photos taken, and then he went to buy suitcases that he had found on sale. He was the man with the plan.

If only the war would end.

During the last days of May, they waited for the children's passports to be issued and the school term to finish. Yara didn't have many friends that she'd miss; she was always a loner but educated enough to understand that Syria was not the best place for her. "Can I go for swimming practice there? Is there a team I can join?" were questions she kept inside. *I don't want to hear the answer,* she thought while combing her hair in front of the plastic fuchsia mirror, her most valuable possession. She loved swimming, and swimming loved her back as it would eventually save her life under a starry Aegean night sky.

Yara never swam after that; it was all kickboxing.

She spent her final week in Manchester reading about Latakia, the port city where her uncle and grandparents lived and where her father was forcing them to immigrate. She had never been to Syria, not even for a vacation. It was not *her* homeland.

"As of tomorrow, I'll be an immigrant, the first of my kind to take the opposite route." A Lady Marco Polo of sorts, abandoning the mirror canals of Venice to consort with the Mongol tribes.

The Wikipedia stuff she read was enough to convince her that the war would never cease. It had not stopped for the twenty-five centuries that there were detailed records of the region, and she guessed that it had never stopped for millions of years. Her father scoffed at her planted questions during dinner-time, countering with: "Don't read these lies. It's all propaganda. You will finally meet your grandparents, find your roots. Ah, wait till you taste the chicken fatteh of your grandmother!"

"Dad? Do you know that British Airways and even Emirates have ceased flying there? Ten years now. You know that, right?"

# 8. Lucia: Not Much of a Fight

*Athens, May 19, 2019*

"This game sucks, sucks, sucks," Lucia said, turning to her father. He was breaking the sunflower seeds between his front teeth, his gaze fixed empty of emotion on the football field.

"It's the fifteenth minute, kid," Jacek said. "Patience. Just one goal down."

"It stinks, dad. Shit, I hate those Reds. Can't believe you tricked me into joining you for this shit."

"That's unfair," Jacek said. He needed her to come, his leg had gotten much worse, and she had to drive to the handicapped parking and push the wheelchair to the reserved seats. He didn't have to use it all the time, but there was no way he'd ever get up those stadium stairs.

"What are you going to do next year?" she said. It was a done deal. She had chosen Portsmouth Law School, two more months, and she'd be out of Athens and her parents' apartment. At age nineteen, it was long due.

"Either convince your mom to take up football or buy a large TV," he said, shrugging his shoulders.

"Looks like the latter," said Lucia, and then she turned to the game again. "Come on, guys, stop this number seven today," she shouted.

"He is a good player. Ivory Coast," said Dr. Fotopoulos from his wheelchair, next to her dad.

"Hoo, hoo, hoo!" The shaved head and meander tattoos guy, two rows up from them, was making monkey sounds as left-winger number seven, Yaya

26

Kone of the Reds, was speeding past the green defenders once again.

Lucia turned and gave him an icy stare, ready to yell, "shut the fuck up."

"You see, that pisses me off," she turned to her dad. "Why make monkey sounds? Athens! Cradle of Olympic spirit, my ass." She was counting backward the days to leave the city.

"Careful, Lucia. You don't start a fight with this sort of folk."

But it was too late.

"Hey, you!" Lucia turned to the walrus-sized man who kept making monkey sounds, now that he had the pleasure of her annoyance. "You, asshole. You think you're Arian-white, you coffee-beige moron? I cut you for Berberi. Magnusson, the center back, is white."

"Even Magnusson is cream-white," whispered Dr. Fotopoulos, chuckling. "Only vampires are really white, and even they are more like eggshell-white, not ghost-white."

"Shut your mouth, little miss," said the shaved-skull man.

Lucia gave him the finger, the man threw a half-full coke cup at her, Jacek turned his wheelchair and said, "Let's get out of here, kid," as Yaya Kone, ignoring the Nazi cacophony, stormed into the penalty box, passing slow-turning-as-a-Norwegian-Cruise-Liner Magnusson and with a masterful lobe, made it 0-2 Reds.

Time to go indeed.

They made it to the parking lot and got in their minivan just before the spring rainstorm started slamming the front window, both of them silent, listening to the sound of the windshield wipers swooshing left and right.

"Drive to the mall garage. The underground one," Jacek said. The storm was getting worse, and the roads had started flooding. "It's not safe out here with this storm."

"Safety first!" Lucia said, raising her eyebrows, mocking him.

Jacek was not a man to shout, so as his voice turned deep-toned, Lucia knew that he was boiling mad inside.

"Never pull this shit again," he said, staring at her hard. "Starting fights with thugs and criminals. Not if I am in front, not if I am miles away. Never!"

Lucia pouted her lips, shook her head left and right, thinking. *What the heck! Might as well have this conversation someday.* She kept her gaze on the road. "You know, dad, I know. About you doing time. You used to get into fights when you were younger. The apple, the tree, you know."

"Oh, you do? Really?"

"Yes, I know that a guy was trying to beat up mom, and you stopped him, broke his jaw, and that's why you did time in jail."

"And that's how we started dating, you know that?"

"No."

"Twenty years back. We were working at a millionaire's mansion, up at Kifissia. I was gardening the outside, your mom was cleaning the inside."

"Mom said you met next to a sprouting magnolia bush in a garden with manicured buxus! Love at first sight."

"Quite the opposite. The wife of the house was sleeping with the personal trainer, and she had him throw your mom out of the house. They hadn't paid her for two months and accused her of stealing to send her away empty-handed. So this guy raises his hand and slaps her, throws her down the entrance stairs. Well, I was there."

"You did what? You beat him up?" said Lucia, chuckling.

"He was all gym fluff and no legs. He was wearing Nike Frees. Me, Caterpillar steel toe boots. Wasn't much of a fight."

By now, Lucia had driven them down to the P2 Garage of the mall complex, away from the storm, and they kept talking in the eerily quiet surroundings.

"Way to go, dad! Then why the heck don't you let me fight that Nazi bastard back there? I can defend myself."

"I messed that guy up. I got sentenced to a so-called prison-farm facility, where penal labor cut jail time in half. They let me out after three months for good behavior. Some bribing the lawyer arranged, the system always works at the end."

"Even in hell."

"Your mom came to thank me after I got out. I took her out for ice cream. Pita-gyro with tzatziki the second time, proposed on the fourth date."

"Didn't know all this. Thanks for sharing."

"You still don't know *all* of it," he said. Jacek got out of the car, a process that took two long minutes, and stood against the cement column. He could walk with a cane and didn't need the wheelchair unless there were stairs or football and such involved. "Do you know how I got this?" he said, pointing to his bad knee.

"A car accident, right?" Lucia said.

"No such thing. A lie. Six months after I was released from jail, we were walking back from the movie theater, some silly comedy. You were there, kind of. Your mom was pregnant. They broke my ribs, crushed both kneecaps, this one never healed fully. Payback. You see, kid, there is always payback, whether you are on the good or the bad side. You hit them, they hit back. If you decide to fight for a living, expect to lose most teeth."

Lucia wished she could tell about her own wounds, share her story with dad, about the man who had tried to rape her back when she was thirteen. But that would be too much.

"I'll be careful," she said. She'd be out of this city by September, starting her studies in the UK. Playing the obedient daughter was a small price. "I am sorry, dad. I never knew."

Her parents had lied to her all her life to protect her, and she could lie just as well. Kids do what they see, not what their parents preach, after all. Lucia had no intention of being careful in this life. She was out to get them.

# 9. Tina: H7N9

*Baltimore, February 7, 2014*

The saxophone screamed a last goodbye, the double bass went looking for a bourbon, a heap of empty mussel shells gaped back at Tina, their insides devoured. The bar fell silent and Friday-night tired, time for quality conversation. Two ex-pat doctors at a Baltimore bar, on a rainy February night, they could discuss anything: the financial crisis back home, the future, even God. Something deep. Alexi was a master of pseudophilosophical babbling, another arrow in his full Eros quiver of seduction. He was a polymath, or at least impersonated one, rarely correct but never in doubt. He also thought he had a great sense of humor.

"Listen to this, Tina. That's a funny one. Why do the Chinese bury the—"

"Shut up, you moron," Tina cut him. "People can hear you."

"Oh yes, that's what people come here for, to eavesdrop on us. Get real!"

"Are you drunk, Alexi? These racist jokes of yours were not funny fifty years ago. And get it in your thick head, they're not funny today."

The Korean medical student sitting two tables to her left smiled at her, and Tina tried to smile back politely.

"Come on now, my girl. You are becoming too politically correct in this country. You go back to Greece, folks will laugh at you if you can't take a joke."

"This is racist and not funny."

"Ok, no Chinese joke. Canadians. Why do the Canadians" he mimed the

30

four-letter verb to joke that others were listening "only doggy style?"

"Are you for real today? You repeat this Canadian 'joke' every second day. And what makes you an expert on Canadian sex rituals? Have you ever met one?"

"A few," Alexi replied, taking a sip of his blood-red wine and throwing back his curly dark-blonde hair in a confident way.

*Valerie, his ex—was she still an ex—was Canadian,* Tina thought. Worse, French-Canadian. They separated last year, but does she care? *Is he still doing Valerie? Is he cheating on me? I know he is. God, he makes me paranoid; that's worse than cheating.*

Alexi grabbed Tina's pile of notes and papers and started reading aloud the names.

"Wang Fang. Let me check that." He typed in his phone and continued: "'Means aromatous.' What on earth does *aromatous* mean? Like a duck? Xin Chung. Chocolate Fudge Chunk. Wei Ye. Oh, ye. Hell yeah." He was laughing loud, almost in tears.

Tina's face turned to ice. She'd always liked this joint; it had an unpretentious style of service and décor but was still warm, even romantic. The jazz was pretty good too. But on that night, under the twinkling red lights illuminating the area above the bar, nothing felt romantic anymore. Under those lights, Alexi looked more of an idiot.

"Do you realize that you are reading the names of dead people? And you are laughing? Do you call yourself a doctor?"

"It is a cynical profession. And I am not much of a doctor anyway; I am pretty sure I'll switch to public policy once we move back to Athens. Did you talk to your father? About me?"

"Talk to my father to do exactly what?"

"Look, love, I've been over this with you a hundred times, this is our chance. He is in power now, you know him, and I are both members of the same party—"

"Are you a member of the God and Country Party? I thought you were a socialist."

"No, yes, anyway. Anyway, they won't last for long. The Radical Left is coming, and we must secure ourselves while your father has the upper hand. He can get us a couple of spots at the Ministry of Health now. Then we're set for life, we're in. Or that Associate Professor opening down at Crete."

"I am talking to my dad fifteen seconds a year, Alexi, and only to make him feel worse than if I talked zero seconds to him. Not gonna happen."

Her eyes darted toward the waiter, a bearded guy with a beanie and a plaid shirt. She had bought marijuana a couple of times from him; maybe tonight would be the third. Anything but sex with Alexi. She waved her finger a full circle. Another round. *At least get drunk.* Tonight was their last date, that much was certain. Only a few months ago, she would have sworn she was in love. Worse, she still could be. She wished that he had not said a word all night that they had gone straight to his apartment and spend the night naked and alive. If he had only kissed and never spoke.

Tina had spent five graduate years at Johns Hopkins before she met Alexi. During that time, she had tried a wide variety of unconventional, recreational activities to battle the mundane reality of studying epidemiology in the middle of urban Baltimore. Occasional smoking was the lowest of her coming and going habits, a one-night stand with the guitarist of a local band who stank of vodka, marijuana-Eddie Murphy movie-Chunky Monkey ice-cream combo, a couple of times.

But as her religious aunts would say, "Blessed are the poor in spirit," and the deeper she sank into her studies, memorizing the symptoms, collecting the data, crunching the statistics, the less effective the distractions proved.

Alexi arrived in Baltimore from Athens Medical School back in September 2013, while Tina was suffering through her fifth year in the Ph.D. program, and after a few days, she had already heard his name a dozen times. He was an invasive weed of a person, able to grow and spread in any place and climate. He soon made friends with everyone and led the weekend ex-pat community activities, making it a top priority to seduce Tina for the simple reason that she pretended not to be interested in him. The curly dark blonde hair of an Olympian Apollo and his smooth salsa moves on Saturday night were definite pluses. Tina soon came to admire, initially from a safe distance, his ability not to stress about anything, to fully embrace life for what it offered today with sheer confidence that tomorrow would be even better. He was designed to be like an antibody for everything that made her miserable.

Alexi deployed a patient and admirable strategy for getting to Tina, initially dating in parallel two other students Valerie, the French-Canadian, and Yasmin, the British-Indian, both of whom she considered exorbitantly obnoxious. When the love triangle became the talk of the small community, he shifted his attention entirely to Tina, making it impossible for her to refuse, if only for the sheer enjoyment of seeing the faces of the other two women. It was downhill from there and very fast, though Tina tried to play hard-to-get for a few seconds.

"Sorry, not this weekend. I am going to this exhibit on virus outbreaks at the Smithsonian. Some volunteer talk I am doing."

"Oh great, I am driving you. Let's go see the cherries blossom at the Potomac. They are quite a sight, I hear. Come on, Tina!"

She couldn't say no, if not for any other reason, out of her embarrassment. Five years now, she wanted to see the cherry trees, but she had never found the time to plan that visit. She would be in DC that week, but only because of the virus exhibit, completely forgetting to check if the cherries were blossoming. She had forfeited life and joy, worshipped and studied death, and here out of the blue came a man ready to bring the flowers to her.

Alexi didn't stop. "Why go back to Baltimore, let's head for New York? I know this great bar at Soho that serves crispy pig's ears. Bono and Jay-Z used to go there," and "I tried but couldn't get two rooms in the same hotel, so expensive, why don't we just share one bed tonight?" Four glasses of wine later. Excuses. Next morning, "I've heard of this amazing bed & breakfast at Harbor Hill up in Connecticut, let's keep going and copulate like bunnies on Viagra for seventy-two hours. Pizza! Ice-cream!"

She didn't, couldn't resist, though she should know better than to trust someone who fit perfectly the stereotype of her divorced father. Pizza. Chocolate Fudge Chunk. Pig's ears. His golden walnut coif. Even that lack of trust fueled the wild animalism under the bedsheets. She could finally be cured, embrace the opposite of herself, a man who deserved a doctorate in celebrating life while she was getting hers dissecting death.

Tina didn't do much research that year; worse, she didn't know if she even cared anymore. As far as the medical profession was concerned, Alexi was a bad influence and a trickster of sorts, a future political animal like her father. He was cruising through a two-year graduate program on Health Policy and Management with minimal effort, selecting the easiest of subjects. He kept bringing up his ongoing "many years now" volunteer work at Medecins Sans Frontiers in Gaza as an excuse for lack of time. "Palestine, now that is what it means to be a doctor where there are no borders." How he was volunteering at Gaza, given that he was in Baltimore and already knew all the bars and B&Bs up to Quebec, was something that escaped Tina, though he had many believable stories from the streets there. YouTube helps.

The next three months in Baltimore proved the most exciting of her stay until they returned to their homeland for summer vacation. It was back home during the long and restless nights of Athenian summer that things started falling apart. Alexi had options and other networks there, and his phone caught July fire from the onslaught of text messages of the mysterious Valeries and Yasmins of the local flavor.

"Hey, Tina, listen to this, it's funny. What do you call a Greek with a hundred girlfriends? A shepherd. Heheheh."

It was old and not funny anymore, but she laughed hard for her own reasons. A Greek with a hundred girlfriends, her answer was definitely: "Alexi."

He was not a man to be trusted for marriage, but she had no intention to marry any time soon. *Let's keep sailing*, she thought. He had not made it to his worst jokes yet.

It got uncomfortable that summer when Alexi started asking too many questions about Tina's father, his job, his political connections, and what a great opportunity it would be to meet him, "I have this great idea to present." How Alexi and her father, Yannis, shared the same "change the world, without letting globalism destroy it, ideology."

"I really want to make an impact, that's why I switched to Policy and Management. It doesn't matter if you come from a Left or Right background.

We need reforms. It is time. I must meet your father," he kept repeating.

Tina had read all Dune books during her undergrad years at MIT. She had memorized many quotes from the epic sci-fi saga, and her favorite Bene Gesserit saying was: *"More misery has been created by reformers than by any other force in human history."*

To the horror of her advisor, she didn't publish any papers that year but made one scientific discovery of her own during the summer: the Alexi virus was not lethal, it was a fly-by-night thing, not a "to have and to hold till death do us part."

By October, the affair had decayed, buried under the rust of the copper sycamore leaves, though Tina had to succumb now to the irreversible realization that Alexi was the first true love of her life, and like all things that were once born, death had come upon it. The occasions of Thanksgiving and Christmas kept them together on autopilot. It was February now, and the freezing rains begged for some companion. She had agreed to see him once more, and she chose the jazz bar, hoping that its ambiance would stitch things back to the good old days. Or at least she could enjoy the sex one more time. Both seemed unlikely as Alexi kept talking.

"Anyway, if you don't want to help me, girl, I'll go back to reading the Chinese names," he chuckled. "Yisheng Qiang Li, Hushi Min Wang."

"Do you have any idea what I am working on, Alexi? It's my last chance to stay here for a postdoc. This H7N9 virus, it just appeared a few months ago. I am on it."

"I am not staying here, love. Weather sucks, locals and not are boring. They have it backward, they live to work. Come back with me."

She tried to ignore his aphorisms and talk about *her* world, subtly pushing to separate herself from him for good.

"So as I was saying if you care to listen since you'll go into policy. H7N9 is a stealth virus. It *hides*. You see, the chickens and the ducks carry it but are asymptomatic. They are healthy, but once they pass it on to us, death. Forty percent of those infected die within days."

"Asymptomatic chickens. Forty percent. Wow!" He nodded his head emphatically as if he couldn't give a shit.

"Yes, you see the problem. The farmer will not know that his chickens are sick. So he'll take them to the live-poultry market, not get rid of them. And now wild birds have gotten it. Songbirds. City pigeons. Those that fly—" Tina flapped her hands fast, "—that go from one farm to another then to the city square. So now this H7N9, not only it *hides,* but it *flies* too. And it mutates fast." Tina pulled her notes away from Alexi and started reading them to him, her cell phone flashlight illuminating the dead. "March 31, it first appeared in Hong Kong, three dead, April 2 on Jiangsu, April 3 on Shanghai five deaths. April 11, ten deaths in Xinhua, of thirty-eight infected. I can go on and on. There have been more than three hundred deaths since then, fewer than a thousand infected."

"That's a lot of similar names to memorize. Wang, Wong, you might get them wrong," said Alexi and leaned over her. His hand touching hers, his teenager-strong perfume suffocating her. "Let me help you. Where were we? Hushi Min Yang."

"Wait," Tina's eyes widened at the sound of that name.

"Where is that? Hushi?"

"You know him?"

"Her. That's a she. And 'hushi' is not a name. It means 'nurse.'"

Tina looked at the names again. Doctor Qiang Li, Nurse Min Wang. She had brought earlier data to Professor Garnett about doctors getting infected, but he had ignored her remark. Maybe they were the ones doing the research, he said, could be research, not patient-related. The Chinese were confirming that the virus spreads from person to person. But the cases were unsuspecting mothers tending sick daughters believing it was a common cold, holding them tight through tears, sweat, and coughing phlegm. Then coughing blood, but by then, it was too late. The virus spread but only among family members who spent a lot of time tending each other. And even that, rarely. But nurses? Nurses knew better than anyone else.

"It *spreads,*" Tina said, talking to herself, banging her fist at the table. She ran out the door and headed to the lab, leaving Alexi to pay the bill.

# 10. Ella: Angry Emoji

*From the journal of my grandmother, Tina.*

West Africa, 2014

June 4, 2014

Ever since I landed in Monrovia, the heat is melting my mind and blurring my judgment. I am convinced that there is a global conspiracy of men against me as if they've all agreed to abandon me at the same time.

Dr. Garnett, my advisor for the last six years, was first. He said he was sorry: "Good try, Tina, but not enough. I looked at the Chinese data regarding the H7N9 virus. Nah, it doesn't spread easily. No evidence of clusters. If you ever hear an H7N9 case where people got on a bus or an airplane, and the next day half of them were sick, then, yes, call me. I wish you luck back home; your country will need a brilliant scientist like you."

I didn't return "home" as my advisor suggested; instead, I boarded a plane for Paris and from there to Western Africa. Monrovia, Liberia. I've only heard the country's name before from the sons and daughters of Greek shipowners, classmates back in high school. Their families fly the Liberian flag on most ships. Tax optimization. Liberia is known for something else now. Ebola has been rampant for the last few months here, and Medecins Sans Frontiers had a massive and desperate call out for volunteers. Alexi didn't volunteer, neither for Ebola nor anything else. He didn't even volunteer an "I am in love with you, Tina." He never uttered the words. He urged me to follow him back home, but the truth is he abandoned me. I vowed to be smarter than my mother; I am not going to chase after him.

And then there is the young pilot with the flip-flops who landed the tiny five-passenger Cessna next to the MSF "hospital" four days ago. He didn't actually land, barely stopped it on the dusty runway for us to jump out, and took off in one swift move. He was scared to death even to spend another second here.

A conspiracy of men. They all flee.


June 11, 2014

I promised myself that I'd write every day, but my words don't have the power to paint the pain I witness. Even videos are inadequate. Sure, you get to see the colors, the red of the vomit and bloody diarrhea, the pale green of the Redemption Hospital walls, the pale yellow of the bunny suits, the green gloves, the black body-bags. Those colorful long dresses of the locals, the bright yellow keke tricycles, the women carrying fruit and merchandise on their heads, the busy bazaars selling textiles, low-priced single shoes to mix and match. But there is so much more that the camera cannot capture, the suffocating heat, the insects crawling and flying up my nose and into my ear. Chlorine is the only thing that stops the virus. It has no color, just its usual invading odor. And all the other foul smells. No matter how much footage you see before you land, you are never prepared for the stink.

I am not sure what I am doing here; I am a passionate researcher, not an ice-veined medic. A hundred infected come every day to the made-up hospital, but we have no cure. Seventy of them will die, and another seventy queue fast to replace them. We just keep them hydrated and give them electrolytes.

I friended Alexi on Facebook a few months ago when I finally got an account and became certain that our affair had come to an end. Had to find a way to haunt him digitally. Looking at his posts, he must be vacationing in Crete. Her arms, whoever she is, wrapped around his neck. He has a deep summer tan and looking better than ever. We had discussed that our next vacation would be Paris, but the city of lights and eros ended up being a brief stopover on the way to Africa.

September 22, 2014

Most patients don't die violently. Vomiting and diarrhea consume them until they succumb to morbid exhaustion. A life extinguished. Children go fast.

September 29, 2014

I am not with MSF anymore, I just couldn't take it, and it was wise to take a break. It would be easier if I were fighting vampires or zombies. At least I could do something. Every day was just a Sishyphian descent to hell, all those children with eyes bleeding red, their ascent to heaven. For the first time in my life, I hope there is a heaven. Else what is the point of being born here, except to suffer and perish? What am I to do? I was always more interested in the cause of the problem rather than caring about the fate of individual patients. An excuse for quitting? Maybe. I am not writing this with pride; it is what it is.

I joined a team from London that has been here for months, called PHRST, Public Health Rapid Support Team, pronounced "first." We have left Liberia for Guinea. They are the "virus detectives" who located patient zero a few months back when it all started. Thanks to them, we know Ebola is transmitted via bodily fluids. They noticed that one of the local customs is to cleanse the dead before burial. Daughters and granddaughters wash with their bare hands the body of an infected elder. The virus gets in their eyes, their mouth. A few days later, the whole family has perished. They die because of burial customs; how ironic is that? Death is a trickster, a many-tentacled god around here, doesn't let anyone escape. We need to educate them more than anything else.

October 21, 2014

Alexi got married. I was in Siera Leone when I found out. He works for the Ministry of Health in Greece now, and so does his wife. I don't think it is a coincidence. He didn't post much about it on Facebook, but his wife did. All her girlfriends are marveling at her luck. I pity and envy her, Jekyll and Hyde, respectively. He is posting on my newsfeed about the crisis back home, how outraged he is with the IMF's policies, how the children in Athens are starving and eating from the garbage cans. I am sure that there are poor people there too, but his posts look like a bad joke from where I am. No matter how you slice it or dice it, our per capita GDP is fifty times that of Liberia. A low-income family in Athens earns as much as a village of three hundred here. And we don't have Ebola. I read an article that Facebook might introduce emojis in the future. I found an angry emoji and posted it back at him in the comments section. Outside my tent runs a brown stream of filth. A colorful pack of women and children are bathing in, washing with, and drinking the dirty waters.

October 22, 2014

A common friend messaged me about Alexi. Truth is, I was probing. He has joined the Radical Left Party back in Athens, posting about the coming revolution and how we'll refuse to pay all our loans and send the German bankers to hell. They say that the Radical Left will probably win the majority next year. Most of my colleagues at MSF support the Left, and frankly, I am closer to that than the Conservative Right, yet I know Alexi is a hypocrite and an opportunist. He'd have no scruples about joining the harem of the Sultan or the Borg Collective if that helped his self-serving cause. Still, every time he posts, he is getting hundreds of *likes*, mostly from young women. Two-hundred and thirty-four likes. One angry emoji—mine. His spell is dying out like those around me.

A last and lasting memory remains imprinted in my mind: a drizzly Baltimore night, sipping a glass of Merlot at the jazz bar next to him, a spitting image of Apollo, his apartment only five minutes away, fireplace, and burgundy fleece blankets. There is no chocolate or wine here, no guilty pleasures. I can sin for a few seconds. I shut my eyes to devour that memory once more.

October 23, 2014

It is a miracle I'm not infected yet. I heard that Marie, the girl who came on the same plane as I did, got sick, but she recovered. She was a strong and brave woman, but she had to return to Belgium; I didn't get to say goodbye. My mother called the other day, sobbing and burbling. She wants me back home. I promised I'd visit for Christmas. Selfish, but I am no good to anyone here if I lose my mind completely. I am spent.

October 28, 2014

I am writing more and more lately as if things are coming to an end. Dr. Peters of PHRST invited me to fly back to London with them and work with his group next year. They'll go around Europe to present their results. We need to visit the rich whites, tell a sob story, appeal to their progressive guilt or conservative religiosity, and raise funds before returning. We can't fight the virus with good intentions only. "Ebola is not the first or the last. We must be prepared for the plagues that will come," he said. Even though I always hoped for something closer to the research lab than the war zone, it is a great honor. We need money for bodyguards, protection, and bribing, too, they say. Things are getting dangerous. I promised to follow him to London, and I'll take it one step at a time.

October 31, 2014

Halloween. I heard that the MSF treatment center in Monrovia was burned to the ground last night. Local gangs, young men with machine guns, old shamans with their evil spirits, opposition politicians. They all blame us. The bunny suits don't help with establishing trust. I usually tie a yellow paisley print scarf around my neck over the suit. That way, I have a personality, and the others can tell us apart.

By now, many locals believe that Ebola is a hoax, a made-up story. They claim that we are trying to keep them quarantined, to stop them from voting because the government told us so. They say that we are here to steal the blood of their young, the organs of their dead. There are horrid rumors that some locals buried a doctor alive, not far from here. We are set to leave for London three weeks from today, but we may accelerate the timeframe.

December 3, 2014

I haven't bled since I landed here six months ago. It had happened before when I was under stress for my quals back at Johns Hopkins, but not for that long. My body shut down and refuses even to allow the possibility of new life in these meadows of Asphodel. My hair is like an old woolen blanket. I've lost weight, but it is all muscle and water, I am afraid. It's time.

December 11, 2014

The London drizzle reminds me of the chlorine spraying in Liberia. A necessary evil. I feel embarrassed to walk down Oxford Street, worse on Old Bond, as if I don't deserve to be here. These people around me have no idea how lucky they are to be born here. They can't fathom what the common man and woman still suffer on this bitter earth. I am forever infected with the pain and the images of West Africa and Ebola, and I walk among the living and the oblivious like a perennial angel of the Apocalypse, someone who has witnessed their distant past and their grisly future. One day a virus will sneak aboard a plane from Africa or the East, reach the West, and will spread in a matter of hours. We'll have no vaccines, worse, no time to prepare. As scientists, we know for a fact how all this will go down, but we don't know when.

London's weather has been better than the movies let you believe. Frankly, it is the fifth time I've been here in my life and never witnessed heavy rain. Boston—even New York—weather is brutal, the torrential rains, usually on weekends, the blistering cold winters, the burning steel and asphalt summers, the oxygen-sucking humidity. London is way milder; the Gulf Stream helps. Mom asks when I plan to visit her in Athens.

December 15, 2014

I unfollowed Alexi on Facebook. I unfriended him too the day the site reminded me of what it thought was our first friend anniversary. I had sex with him before I even joined the social media world. It is weird and awkward. I think this network was created by kids who got a million subscribers before they had their first one-night stand, before they had a friend, maybe. It is more likely that I'll visit Athens now that I don't have his face constantly coming up on my phone.

December 22, 2014

I met this Greek guy, a businessman, on the airplane from London to Athens. His name is Pericles, what a name! Not as wise as his Golden Century namesake but handsome; he has that trustworthy chin, looks more like a Leonidas. He owns car dealerships, but that is a big deal back here. We've been on a couple of dates, he laughs with his heart, and I can see that he admires me. He is not at my level education-wise but far from inadequate. He'll do, for now.

March 3, 2015

Global warming is playing a joke at me. We have suffered more rain in Athens than back in London. I had to write to Dr. Peters at PHRST and let him know that I can't accept his offer for now. With heavy heart blah, blah. In other news, I have a job! I was elected to the National Agency of Public Health executive committee, the Greek disease prevention agency. That was a month ago, and yesterday I made Head of Epidemiology, though I think there are a couple of candidates who were more qualified, at least on paper. It is under the Ministry of Health, and I am sure my dad had something to do with it. My dad's God and Country Party has joined forces with the Radical Left Party and formed a coalition government. Doesn't make sense to me, but I guess opposites attract if it is to overthrow the establishment. It won't be good for our country, but it did turn out well for me, or so they let me believe. I am afraid that my mom forced my dad to pull some strings and keep me here. She is all excited that I am close to her and that I've been seeing Pericles for a couple of months now. After the first meetings, I can safely predict that I'll have a miserable time in the agency. It is all politics and zero substance. The refugee crisis, all those poor families coming from Syria, that is real, but I am not sure I can help with anything there.

I am staying because of Pericles. He is a steady vessel in the sea of my mess, a man to rely on.

Some of the meetings took place inside the Ministry of Health, but I haven't come across Alexi yet. I am sure I will, sooner or later, we are too close to avoid each other.

## Copying from the News

On 9 March 2015, the National Health and Family Planning Commission (NHFPC) of China notified WHO of 59 additional laboratory-confirmed cases of human infection with avian influenza A(H7N9) virus, including 17 fatal cases. Onset dates ranged from 21 January to 25 February 2015.
Of these 59 cases, 44 (75%) were male. The majority (49 cases, 83%) reported exposure to live poultry or live poultry markets; the exposure history of six cases is unknown or unavailable. Three family clusters were reported, each comprised of two cases.

## May 3, 2015

Pericles is self-confident, straightforward, someone who could punch Alexi in the face. He has money, and that means that I'll never again need my father's connections. He is like an Alexi antibody, ticking all the boxes once left unchecked. It could be love; it could be life.

## May 5, 2015

*It will be our honor and pleasure to invite you to our Wedding, which will take place on Wednesday, July 22, at 7:30 p.m. at the Holy Church of Panagia Faneromeni, Vouliagmeni.*

### *Pericles - Tina*
*The Families:*
*Nicholas and Helen Aggelou*
*Yannis Damianos & Lisa Walker*
*A reception will follow at the Island Club & Restaurant*

January 4, 2016

"Today, the World Health Organization declares the end of the most recent outbreak of Ebola virus disease in Liberia and says all known chains of transmission have been stopped in West Africa. But the Organization says the job is not over."

January 11, 2016

I just bought a pregnancy test. I already feel it inside me.

On 18 March 2016,
the National Health and Family Planning Commission of China notified WHO of additional laboratory-confirmed cases of human infection with Avian influenza A(H7N9) virus, including 11 deaths.
Onset dates range from…the exposure history of 5 cases is unknown…no clear exposure to poultry…three clusters were reported.

October 27, 2016

All our friends got the same message from Pericles Aggelou. I got it from Peri-Love-RedHeart:

"There's a new baby in town, and his name is Demetri Aggelou. He arrived weighing 3.5 kilos at 9 am today, featuring his father's great smile. The elated parents, Tina-Pericles."

On 5 January 2017,
the Department of Health, Hong Kong Special Administrative Region (SAR) notified WHO of a case of laboratory-confirmed human infection with avian influenza A(H7N9) virus and on 9 January 2017, the National Health and Family Planning Commission of China notified WHO of 106 additional laboratory-confirmed

cases of human infection with avian influenza A(H7N9) virus. Three family clusters were reported, each comprised of two cases; four of the six cases had exposure to live poultry or live poultry markets, one case had no exposure to poultry, and one is still under investigation.

# 11. Yara: Laodicea Combusta

*Latakia, Syria, June 2021-June 2022*

Summertime in the city of Latakia—that was once known as *White Coast* to the Ancient Greeks—exceeded Yara's wildest expectations. There were cool-water beaches and even beach clubs, little girls wobbling on the balls of their tiny feet upon the sand in their pink bathing suits and matching mermaid floaties. Youngsters, very connected to the reigning establishment to hold a soldier's rifle, resting languorously on the sunbeds, opting for an apple-flavored shisha. A serene swarm of sea-goers stupefied by soft sounds, smoke, spices, and the scintillating sunlight, oblivious to the alliteration of shotgun, shrapnel, not to mention the word Syria itself. It was a fifteen-minute walk to a nightclub that she would never be allowed to go anyway, a three-hour drive to the carpet-bombed city of Aleppo.

By late September, the beaches were empty of sunseekers, even of seagulls. As she continued her research—school was a sad joke and a waste of time—Yara found that to the Romans, the city was known as Laodicea Combusta: "The Burning One." That should have been enough of a hint for the false optimists. Her parents didn't seem worried about the riots that had broken out, but Yara and her sister had changed school buildings two times in a month due to updated safety policies and what they called "regional reshuffling."

Every morning, she walked past the armored policemen at every major intersection. They wore black protective pads and black helmets over their black hair, though they were so skinny that they induced more pity than fear.

In October, she forgot everything, overwhelmed by her grandmother's chicken fatteh.

"She goes to the souk early and chooses the best ingredients," said grandpa Farid.

"Her secret is the pine nuts," added Khaled. "She knows how to bring the flavor out of them."

Yara asked her grandma instead for some woman-to-woman advice.

"There is only one secret in all cooking. Put twice the olive oil and half the water."

"But there is no olive oil or water in the dish."

"Yes! No water."

"What do you mean, grandma? To drain the chickpeas well?"

"There is water everywhere, *hayati*. We live in water, it flows in us. Man is death, God is life. Man is fire, but God is water. Remember, my child, it is not the fire that will undo us, no matter how long they keep fighting. Fear the water!"

Later that night, Yara combed her hair, whispering to her mirror: "Maybe I am exaggerating. How could there be a problem if the food is so much better here?"

During a mild November evening, Yara encountered the first dead body of her life, lying a few blocks from home on the pavement. She hoped that he was dead; the thought of crossing the street to check the pulse of the bleeding man was beyond her. "He wasn't moving, not your fault," she whispered to the mirror. She decided right there that her next mirror would not be fuchsia; the color was too close to the bloodstains on the cobblestone pavement.

Faiza was now pregnant with a fourth child, another boy, and the overjoyed Khaled was still trying to prove to everyone that his plan had legs. But there were no reconstruction projects and no jobs in the city, and he had been away so long that his old connections proved useless.

"We are not going anywhere with you pregnant, Faiza," he insisted. "My parents deserve to see their grandson." Their first son, Sayid, was a short, plump kid, a bit slow on the head, who spoke Arabic with a stutter and usually repeated the same two or three sentences for months.

December and January were peaceful yet veiled by the silence of a scared, scattered community. Yara noticed that they still hadn't visited anyone but close relatives in Syria, and many times she wondered if all families there were as poor as theirs. Spring brought gray, robust clouds that rose from the ground to the sky out of the neighborhoods that were getting bombarded. In March, she had the chance to see the interiors, what was left of them, of many blown-up apartments, and as she had guessed, they were poor. This was the least of their problems.

During Ramadan, Faiza gave birth to Yara's baby brother, and Khaled fixed a smile above his peppered handlebar mustache. He even convinced himself for a moment that the war was about to end, but that was only a brief interlude between the screaming of the bombs that grew closer with each milk bottle baby-brother Omar gulped down.

Yara's grandfather implored them to leave for England and never return, though he was quite old and didn't even own a passport. The old man had seen too much, first at Izraa and then at Latakia. He still believed in benevolent gods, but he trusted them a tad less.

One day in mid-May, as they were returning with Nahla from school, Yara saw a mob of hundreds of men, not a single woman, crowding the street of their usual route. They were moving against the armored policemen, throwing stones and holding sticks. "We turn left and walk fast," she whispered to Nahla. "Walk fast now!" she repeated. After a few turns, they came to a crossroads she didn't recognize immediately. She had seen it before, but now the buildings were destroyed, and nothing was the same. The streets were deserted and covered by glass and debris.

Fifty yards to her left, she saw a row of white sheets spread on the ground like napping baby ghosts. Each one covered something, someone, she guessed. One sheet was two meters long, and the other three about half of that. Wisps of black smoke escaped among the ruins of the apartment buildings, rising to meet and paint a sooty sky.

A bearded young man crept out of the rubble like a djinn conjured out from the dust. He strode toward Yara slowly, wailing over a still child he held in his arms. His hair was white from dust, not age.

A female figure in a black abaya holding a girl in a red sweater appeared at the corner of her eye and ran toward the man and the child. The woman in black and the girl in red contrasted violently with everything chalk-white around them like witches who had sucked up all color from earth and sky. Yara scanned the surroundings, but all she could see was a white-powdered field with white-washed skeletons: the bare bones of the buildings, the skeletons of the cars, and the school bus that had burned down to their frames.

Yara grabbed Nahla's hand and ran until they were stopped a few blocks farther by one of the riot policemen.

"I must take her home. She is sick," Yara said with a commanding voice and gave her address to him.

The young man escorted them all the way home and up to her apartment. It was only within the building when he removed his helmet that Yara figured that he was a beardless boy, at most three years older than her.

She couldn't shut an eye that night, so she got up and grabbed a fat black pencil and white paper. There was no red paint, so she got the kitchen knife, careful not to cut herself deep. Yara never had a passion for drawing, as she did for swimming, though she had the hand for it—her Year Eight Arts teacher back in England had said. Those first sketches, pencil on paper, were the seed of her first successful graphic novel series.

Her first drawing was an angel on one knee. She liked angels, though they were not of her heritage—the wings, the freedom, the independence, the gender ambiguity. This one had olive-oiled straight raven hair, brown skin, ashen wings, and black armor. A boy and a girl with silver-bladed halberds riding giant white wolves on her side. They were charging to battle on the banks of Thames against an army of crawling, climbing pale-white vampires. The angel was so fast that she appeared at three distinct places in the first sketch, kneeling at the leftmost side of the drawing, flying sword-first in the middle, running on icy waters farther down. It was a black and white sketch except for the carmine-painted ornaments on the children's wolf-rider armors. On the following drawings, the battle raged on the tallest structures' tops, labeled the Eye, the Shard, the Axe. The streets were all flooded and mostly ice-covered as if London were a New Frozen Venice.

"Fear the water!" Yara wrote at the bottom.

Yara lost all those sketches a few days later when they had to run. She eventually repainted them from memory, many times again in the future.

Finally, God made decisions for Khaled. The only legs that his plan had were their own, and that plan was to run fast.

The city had been divided into two once more. All had gone wrong a month ago when the police shot and killed three student protesters. The anti-government supporters retaliated, an invasion from the north was imminent, Russian and American forces were gathering fast by sea and air.

Yara heard that the shells were coming from ships outside the port. She had no idea who was firing, why, when it would end. War was a hungry sea-monster, and it was breathing down her neck until it finally decided to taste her skin. Mother first, father last, all in a row, they ran out of their building, and they ran fast, the night when the bombs roared so near that the vibrations rippled under her skin. At least they had suitcases, brand new ones, and British passports. All they had to do was get to the British Embassy, she thought, naively ignoring that no such thing had existed in Syria for quite a few years. They reached her uncle's house, which was only two blocks away on foot, and waited to hear the next step of Khaled's plan. Khaled conferred with his brother Hassan, a balding man with bat ears. Her uncle was quiet as the wind in a Latakian July afternoon, so Khaled was speaking to himself most of the time before he decided to let the others know of his new plan.

"I met this American businessman," Khaled said with the required pause and the hushed voice of a puppet-master way ahead of his puppets, "a Syrian-American. He came a few months ago, and like us, he regretted it. They are leaving tonight. He knows two men who can cross the border to Turkey with a small bus, we'll fit, they know whom to bribe. They'll stop at Adana, at the US Consulate, and we can tell them to take us to Antalya."

Khaled stopped as though that word should mean something to them.

"And what is there, father?" Yara asked as if she had become an adult at that very moment. She needed to know, to vote.

Her father didn't reply to her but turned to Faiza and his older son and said: "The closest British Consulate. It is a good plan."

Yara trembled with gooseflesh again, and that time it was not from the distant sound of bombs.

# 12. Lucia: At the Zoo with the White Tigers

*Athens, July 16, 2020*

"Do you go out, Lucia? Socialize?" asked the bespectacled doctor. She was sexy, about thirty-five, perfect legs, crossed under a black skirt, Mont Blanc pen, Ferragamo bow pumps. Comfortable with her body, her clothes, herself. She was selling exactly that, a future. If Lucia continued with therapy—this was their fifth meeting—one day, she could be like her. Normal. At least on the outside.

"Sure. All the time. I go to night school for English classes, the A-Levels prep—I stopped that now—the gym, I work at the cafeteria— I quit that now too, can't work two jobs and study."

"I meant for fun, not work. Go out for things you love to do. What does a nineteen-year-old girl love to do these days?"

"I go to the zoo. I like to see the tigers. They are white," answered Lucia.

"The tigers?"

"The tigers, the rhinos, the visitors. All white. Mostly whites at the zoo. There are many Nigerians now in Athens, especially in Sepolia and Kipseli, where I live with my parents, but I never see Nigerians visiting the zoo."

"And that's your answer about 'you socializing?'"

"I used to go with my dad to the football games. Not anymore. His leg and all."

"You feel sorry for him."

"In many ways. He still doesn't know. It's been, what, seven years since that pervert tried to rape me, but my dad doesn't know. Only my mom and you."

"Do you want to talk about the assault again?"

"Nope. I'd rather go to the dentist. Whatever you want. Shoot!"

"Any relationships? Flings?"

*The truth, dear doctor, is that not even you or my mom knows the whole story. It was Friday. That man didn't put his hand in my pants just for a second. He was there for some time. Strong hands, his breath stinking retsina. He pressed a screwdriver, the pointy end against the soft of my neck. Slid his fingers inside. Back and forth, back and forth. My only memory of "touching" was that for the next three years. Eleventh grade, I made an effort, I had a couple of flings. Two of them tried to touch me there. Not together, different dates, one was autumn, the other one spring. I kneed the first one in the chin. He tried to get rough; he thought I am into punk, karate, so that was my thing, what I liked. Sent him to the hospital.*

"Lucia? Boyfriends? Girls?" repeated the doctor.

*The second one who touched me, I ran away crying. Oh, forget it, you won't understand, and I don't want you to. Don't want you there.*

"No time for that now, doc. I am studying, saving money for next year. Tuition, room, board, airplane tickets. I checked the train, but it is more expensive, you know. Makes no sense. It would be good if we wrapped up this therapy here soon. My mom, she doesn't have this kind of money." Lucia made a full circle with her index figure to point at the walls and the office furniture.

"*This therapy* is not helping you?"

"I don't know. It might. I am not that thick to pretend that therapy doesn't ever work. I guess it works, especially if you believe it will, placebo and such. Maybe I am the problem, I am not committed here, I didn't come by myself, my mom brought me."

"What would help?"

"Justice. Ever since I learned how my father became crippled, how he met my mother. That's all I think about. Not vigilante stuff. That's for TV. I mean real justice so that I can rest."

"Is that why you decided to study law?"

She was a beautiful woman, dark straight hair, gray-blue eyes.

"You are playing doctor with me again. Dissecting me, opening me up. I guess so. Not sure what I want to be. I am glad my father is happy. He was worried about me. He doesn't know why, but he feels that I've got a screw loose."

"Do you wish that you were a better daughter?"

"I wish you were my friend, and we could go out and talk about this trivial stuff. Then my mom wouldn't have to clean stairs eight hours to pay one hour of counseling so you can take her money and buy six-hundred-euro pumps."

The doctor let some seconds pass, then continued.

"Do you believe it was your fault? What happened back then?"

"Oh, yes, it was."

"Listen to me. It wasn't."

"Yeah, got that, read it a million times. Now listen to me. It was my fault and my choice. Being too rebellious, all alone, demanding that the principal let me opt out of the Religion class. It was bad luck too. Sarah wasn't there. Passover week. The only other girl who had opted out of RS was Sarah, Jewish, so she wasn't at school that day. He wouldn't have attacked me if there were two of us."

"That's not your fault."

"You don't understand. The zoo. Did I tell you about the tigers?"

"You did."

"No, I didn't—different story. When I was eight, dad took me to the zoo. Not the first time, but the first I remember. They have the flamingos and the mud turtles up front, but if you go past the monkeys, further inside, it gets eerily quiet. And then you see them. The tigers. Caged or not, you know primal fear the first time you eye them. Immigrants, especially those from Eastern Europe, take their kids to the zoo all the time. There are so many theaters in Athens, but the shows are all in Greek. Dad, mom, they never took me to the theater, didn't know what to choose for me, what was good, kid-friendly. Ballet was an option, but how many times can one watch white and black swans going at it. The zoo is universal. So, there I was, first time looking at the white tigers and one of them, her name was Bianca, I remember that, had given birth to two baby tigers a few weeks back. I saw the cubs stumbling next to her. And I ask my dad: 'Dad, what happens if one of the cubs dies?' He just stopped, frozen, you know, couldn't answer."

"You asked what happens after death? A pretty common question even for an eight-year-old."

"You are making the same mistake with my dad. He stares at the dirt for a while and then starts telling me a story about 'animal heaven.' I was eight, so he thought that was okay for Barbie age. And he begins that there is 'animal heaven' the same way there is 'good people heaven' and all baby cubs or puppies that die go up there—he points to the clouds, it was a partly cloudy day—and hop around without ripping apart each other at the throat I guess, and they are oh, so the happiest. Don't grow up more, I guess, do they even see their mom tiger, not until she dies, will they recognize her when she does, does she go to them immediately, or does she visit *her* tiger mommy first. I mean, it is a mess if all your relatives are alive in heaven, those family social obligations must be draining. 'Oh, let's visit zombie uncle Kosta, first.' All the right questions I had but didn't ask. But anyway, dead cubs are happy, 'definitely happy,' he says. Now that I think about it, if their mom sees them never growing up, she won't be happy at animal heaven. She'd send them to tiger-shrink probably. You understand, he hadn't thought it through. And I turn and say to him, 'dad, this must be the lamest story you've ever made up'—you know, he used to make up children stories inspired from Polish folk culture, golden-braided Anuszka at the river Vistula and such, sounded exotic, to put me to bed. 'Lamest story ever,' I repeat."

Lucia ended her words with a smile; it was the first smile she had offered after five sessions with the psychologist.

"You were looking for a different answer."

"Nope. You see, I didn't care about the cubs. I knew they are dead. Their spirits float around and enter peanut butter cookies shaped like unicorns and all that, no, I didn't need that. Here is an interesting question. Do they bury them, cremate them, maybe skin them and keep their skeletons for the veterinarians, the museums, and the luxury resort lounges? Tiny tiger rugs with baby canines? That's a good question, but that was not my question either."

"What was your question? You really remember now what your question was after eight years?"

"I do. I wanted to know that day is how on earth the zoo guards will get in that cage if one of the cubs dies? The tiger mom would be mad, you don't want to be near her? Do they leave the corpse out there for days? Try to pull it out with a stick or something. Sedate the big cats and then run in with bag and shovel? Do they leave a surrogate stuffed cub for mom?"

"I don't get it, this story. Why are you telling me this?"

"Because, doctor, it was my fault that I was there in that classroom alone. I got on the wrong side of religion early, never had that spiritual need. Don't know why. My dad goes to church occasionally, he is lukewarm, never tried to push me on the left or right side of God. I did it to myself. I had attended the sixth-grade RS course; I suffered through that, actually enjoyed it. Laughed a few times hard. That old spinster was reading stories about a prophet swallowed by a fish, not Geppetto, a man walking on water, then on air, fish and more dead fish multiplying out of nowhere. Jason Momoa meets LSD type of stuff. I burst out laughing, and the teacher kicked me out of the class. And then one day she starts reading about Noah's Ark and the Great Flood, and I am like 'Jeez, I know that one, it is from Gilgamesh, first epic ever written, a thousand years before Homer,' I offer my knowledge. I thought I was active in class, and I thought, 'Wow, this is fascinating. Did these cultures borrow myths from each other, or do we share common wiring, something that makes us human regardless of where we were born, if we are black or white?' I mean, that would be kinda godlike, right? If we are wired so that the same story can arise in isolated environments, captivate and mesmerize every one of us. Could be the secret word that aliens control the simulation. Then I guess that *is* magical, divine. Because nine out of ten believe in a god from above. So perhaps there is God. Or nine out of ten are idiots. Now it gets interesting, I am all excited in RS class. And then she expels me again when I bring the Gilgamesh myth up. I was shocked."

"For being treated unfairly."

"Yeah, that too. And that no one had heard of the Epic of Gilgamesh, they actually thought that Noah's Ark was an original story. The other kids were shocked by my comments too, no one had read Gilgamesh, like when they learn that LOTR and GOT are not the first fantasy novels ever written."

"That would be Harry Potter?"

"Funny. I like you, doctor."

"So, you'd read Gilgamesh back then?"

"Well, it is exciting stuff, the guy was probably gay if you ask me, and he made up Enkidu to come out in whatever was an acceptable ancient Babylonian way. It was powerful. I had fast-read it online when I was eleven, sure. Googled 'What was the first story ever written?' and it came up. Thought I should start from the beginning. Oops!" Lucia felt the phone vibrating in her pocket and sighed, faking disappointment. "My time is up."

"You never drank your tea, Lucia."

"Makes me want to pee, and it is a long bus ride to the gym."

"I want to see you again."

"Sure you do."

"I can't make you come. But I hope you do. Are you doing the breathing exercises?"

"Oh yes, they were mega help." *The one time I managed to do them.* "No, really, they were."

"They take discipline."

"Got that right."

"See you next Wednesday, same time?"

"You never asked me. Why the Nigerians don't go to the zoo."

"They are afraid that some asshole would start making monkey sounds, and they don't want their kids to become traumatized."

"You got it, doc. Making progress. These sessions have really helped you, in more than one way," said Lucia and offered a second smile, thinking of the sixty euros that her mom had shelled out over this exchange.

She turned on her phone again, and it flashed an alert of a lowered price ticket for Heathrow. Three weeks away. It was time to hit the gym. Then the road.

# Act 2: The Godforsaken Year

# 13. Tina: Nairobi

*Athens, March 17, 2022*

For those gullible souls who still believed in benevolent gods, state pensions, and coiffed-hair politicians, it was the year 2022. For the disheartened—the nihilists, the bourgeois fathers of anarchist sons, the mothers of lazy private-schooled daughters, the recently divorced, bankrupt businessmen with a residual taste for Cuban cigars, occasionally the terminally ill—and in general all those who had figured out that God didn't believe in them anymore, it was Year 13. The thirteenth year after the eruption of a slow-moving, hope-shattering financial crisis that the people of the tiny country of Greece just couldn't shake off. It was as if some mutant virus had invaded this land of ancient glory and modern amorality—Left or Right, east or west, pious Christian or Porsche—and the poor indigenous tribe had no antigens to fight it. Whatever IMF elixirs or "radical-left" silver-bullets, the aspiring magicians and charlatans tried, just failed—the virus spread every year, making things a bit worse every month, though every day seemed like the one before it. But it added up and as it did, hope diminished.

One didn't have to be an epidemiologist to come up with this analogy; he just had to live in the city, turn on the radio, turn it off quickly to escape reality. But Tina was Head of Epidemiology for the Ministry of Health, with a husband out of a job, for the last couple of years. To make it worse, a husband who owned car dealerships in a country where no one could afford a new car.

She had chosen a man of thick, dark hair, British education—in business and finance, but still, it kinda counted as education—six-feet tall, with a resolute chin and a name for the ages, Pericles.

But after seven years of marriage coinciding with the worse part of the Sisyphean financial crisis, she preferred to call him Peri—more relatable, more believable, a sign of lower expectations. She could easily correlate the length of that jobless period inversely to the duration of his erections on the rare occasions they had sex. But sex with Peri was still enjoyable; as a student of death and plagues, Tina could appreciate and celebrate life, however weak or limp.

It was past 11 p.m. when the "By the Seaside" ringtone melody debouched out of the smartphone and pulled Tina from her random trail of thought about sex, Sisyphus, and IMF, raising her stress level instantaneously.

Athens was a city of unhealthy habits, dinner at 11 p.m. was normal. But a home phone call? Never. It had to be someone close, someone, who had the nerve or was desperate; an old friend had died, a close relative needed to borrow money, an estranged business partner was dying unless you lend him money. Tomorrow. No promised date of repayment, no reasonable hope of that. And in any of those cases, he had already ceased being a close friend; either he had died, or the old proverb would become truth: "there are two certain ways to lose a friend: borrow from him, lend to him."

Tina thought the whole financial crisis thing was just bs, at least for her middle and upper-class compatriots. They still had piano teachers, steaks—not wagyu or Argentinian, mostly Bulgarian antibiotics-pumped pork, but steaks—and vacations in sun-bathed islands. Syria was a crisis, Myanmar was a crisis, even half of Mississippi was a crisis. Greece was a crisis with a splash of champagne—some local cheap five-euro acidic brand called "Rose Bubbly" or worse, but still, champagne. Her generation was used to more though, they had tasted everything early, courtesy of the wasted European Union subsidies, and to their demise, they were kept protected from every chore and hardship, courtesy of a familistic society model that had also acquired a distaste for any blue-collar work, so now that they couldn't afford much anymore, they had trouble lifting themselves by the bootstraps, given that they owned Italian loafers and Nikes but not a single pair of work boots, thus no bootstraps.

Tina hesitated; call it female intuition, male intuition, collection agency mail intuition. *If I answer this, I am going to lose another friend,* she thought.

"Are you going to pick this up?" asked Peri from the kitchen table without turning his head away from the tablet.

"It is a +36 country code. I don't know anyone in," she paused, "wherever +36 code is," Tina replied.

"It is probably a Viber call, rerouted through a random country," Peri said.

"Or a marketing call," said Tina.

She pressed the side button to make the thing shut up.

*"TINA PICK UP ITS ME MARY,"* the text message flashed on the black mirror of her phone.

"It's Mary!" said Tina. "Aren't they on vacation? South Africa or something? Did you talk to Yorgi?"

"What?" said Peri and crouched even more toward his screen and his plate, mumbling. "These *fasolakia* string beans, this woman just doesn't know how to make them. When is Floribeth returning?"

"Another week. Her mother got sick, and she must take her to a hospital at Manilla. She texted me," said Tina.

"Shit!" He turned his head toward the old limping Filipino lady who was temporarily helping with housekeeping during Floribeth's departure. "More olive oil next time," he rasped in English, adding a chuckle that was supposed to coat his rudeness with civility. The lady nodded and smiled back, all Filipino housekeepers did, and no one would ever know if they meant it, no one but them. Tina suspected.

"Swimming in olive oil next time," repeated Peri. "This is Greece, in the name of Christ."

Peri was not much of a Christian; those who were wouldn't pronounce the Lord's name in vain or in want of more olive oil on their fasolakia-tomato stew.

It was at times like this, the banal, the insignificant, that Tina wanted to grab a baseball bat and smash Peri's head in. He had still been sleeping when she left for work that morning and spent the whole day at home, wearing the national attire of the affluent-unemployed—extra-virgin-olive-oil-stained hoodie, moth-eaten Calvin Klein checkers pajama bottom, and an iPad always running low on battery—except for a meeting at a café under the sun and the pines with a venture capitalist impersonator character that Peri declared as "do or die business, and 'this was the big thing' thing." And now he was complaining about the ratio of olive oil vs. tomato sauce on his string beans.

"Can you please keep it down, hon? It's Mary calling. Didn't they go to South Africa? Kruger or something?"

"Mary who?" mumbled Peri, combing his full hair with his fingers, not even looking at her.

*"Mary who?" Smash his head with a baseball bat.*

Mary's son and their son had been in the same class since kindergarten until a year ago when Mary and Yorgi decided that they couldn't afford the twelve Ks for private school anymore. However, they could somehow afford a Kruger National Park safari. Tina and Peri had dinner with them "somewhere casual but upscale, quinoa and ceviche, just half a glass please," almost once a month, they had even vacationed in Paros together the past July. *"Mary who?"* he dared to ask.

"I can't hear you, Mary. Where are you?" shouted Tina, holding the phone with one hand, waving with the other to everyone in the kitchen to keep quiet, and for the Filipina cook to shut off the kitchen fan. "What? Nai-what? Nairobi? Text me, can't hear you, Mary."

"Nairobi is not in South Africa," Peri said, lifting his gaze for two seconds toward Tina.

"She was screaming," said Tina, and she stayed glued on her screen, waiting for a message.

A few seconds of silence. Death or tragedy never came by text. Texting was reserved exclusively for the funny and the unimportant, never for the tragic. The tragic was becoming tragicomic through texting.

One had to call when danger or worse, Charon himself, came knocking. But the texts from Mary to Tina started coming, without the self-awareness of their creeping insolence and their comical grimness. The first text from Mary set the tone.

Mary: *He is dying, Tina. HELP*

Tina: *Who? Where?*

Mary: *Yorgi. We r at the Nairobi Hospital. Can you please call our insurance? APA p# is DX-61233478.*

Tina: *What?*

Mary: *The hospital. Nairobi.*

Tina: *Where? How?*

Mary: *Rerouted our plane. Some disease they said. Quarantined everyone.*

Tina: *What disease? Calm down.*

Mary: *He collapsed before we landed. He was bleeding. Tina. God!*

Tina: *Bleeding? What disease? Is there a doctor I can talk to? What do you need?*

Alexi: *Babe, I can't get your scent off my mind. Yesterday was perfecto. After work? Same place?*

That last text brought her back to her disturbing reality. She was cheating on Peri with Alexi, her old flame and new colleague at the Ministry of Health of all people. She had an excuse somewhere, a bunch of them, but now was not the time.

Tina: *NEVER text me again on this number. Talk tomorrow.*

She deleted the messages, blocked his number, peered at Peri for a second, and then switched back to Mary.

Mary: *The insurance. Send a plane. Make them send it. We must get out of here.*

*Send a plane? About zero chance of that happening.*

Tina: *What do you mean bleeding? Ebola?*

Mary: *Bleeding everywhere. Out of nose ears eyes omg his hair is falling out!*

Tina grabbed the phone with both hands and walked away from the kitchen. She tried to call Mary's mobile number, but all she got was an automated message. She texted again.

Tina: *Call me.*

Mary: *I can't. It's mad. Screams.*

Tina: *What did the doctors say? Did you talk to them?*

Mary: *They dont know. They say influenza viral this and that. This morning. Can you believe it? We r in hell.*

Tina: *Influenza? Flu? U sure?*
Mary: *Tina. Save us. The insurance. Call them!*
Tina: *Calling them now.*

APA's global emergency number was just a Google search away. Forcing them to do anything that would mean anything to anyone immediately would probably take all night, and Tina knew that was because she was a seasoned medical bureaucrat herself. She could talk the talk all night, but she wanted to kiss Demetri first. The glow of her phone guided her down the dark hallway to her son's room. Two email messages showed unread in her inbox, both from Alexi. In his first, he repeated his recollection of last evening's affair, while the second was a calendar invite mentioning "same place" as the location.

She stopped at the bathroom and took a long look at the mirror before entering Demetri's room.

"How the hell did you allow yourself to get on this mess? For a lousy fuck?"

Back when Tina started working for the Ministry, she knew that it was only a matter of time before she'd meet Alexi again. But there was no chance or planned encounter, not until a few months ago when the political landscape shifted. Alexi became overnight a high-ranking employee at the Ministry of Health, too close for comfort. She didn't want to say the word, but he *was* her superior, and she couldn't avoid him anymore. They came close again, but he was very polite, never indicating any interest to rekindle the affair. It was a strategy once again. He lurked stealthily in the shadows, a confident predator. He made his move when Tina opened up, and he sensed the vulnerability, Peri's depression engraved on Tina's face. "It is not *really* cheating. He is my first love from the past," she told herself, but that bullshit excuse could hold only for a few seconds.

The forbidden affair had blossomed a month ago, and the last couple of weeks, it lingered like a foul-smelling flower dying on a murky vase. *Heck, that was more like a virus,* she thought. It fed on her, it gave her blush cheeks and a fever for a few days, and then it had nothing more to do than die. At least for her. But it was mutating into something else now, something dangerous and annoying. Something that threatened her family and had to be uprooted and buried deep. "Do it, get rid of him," she said to the mirror and entered her son's room.

Demetri was sleeping, breathing quietly, both hands above his head in a starfish position. Confident, strong, Demetri, growing bigger every day. A Magnificent-Hulk pajama, its fluorescent green glowing under the phone's light. She tucked him under the blanket, but his naked feet immediately kicked it away as he stirred in his sleep, his eyes closed. How could he be so warm? An icy chill had crept into the room. Gooseflesh. At least that's what Tina felt as she dialed the APA Emergency number.

# 14. Ella: Blue Bus

*Regarding the story of Mary and Yorgi Angelou, I stitched up a version of what happened based on the faint memory of Mary herself and public accounts of flight SAR678 from Dubai to Cape Town on March 16, 2022.*

Nairobi, One day earlier

"Just take a Xanax, honey," Yorgi said. He offered Mary a one-eye glimpse as he lifted the corner of his Lufthansa eye mask. He was wearing a rival airline eye mask on a Sky Arabia flight, a silent protest for not being upgraded to business class status. The days he could afford business class to Cape Town were long gone for him.

"This thing is wobbling like a walnut shell in the ocean," Mary said, clutching his arm, claiming even more of the little space the economy class allowed.

"This 'thing' is a Boeing 777, Mary. It is one of the safest planes ever. If you are afraid of some turbulence, I wonder what will happen when you face the lions, not to mention the mosquitos, tomorrow. Are you sure that a safari is really your thing? We can stay in Cape Town, drink the wine, enjoy the views."

"Okay," said Mary and popped another Xanax. At least she was smart enough to buy her own cold water before they boarded the ten-hour flight from Dubai to Cape Town. She continued shaking her leg, holding tightly at her husband's arm.

"Listen, honey," Yorgi said, not even lifting his eye mask this time. "It's turbulence. It's nothing." He looked like a blind pagan seer preaching in a dark cave. "I've been on hundreds of flights. Only once was I worried since the moment we took off. New York to Athens. You know why? The flight attendants were edgy. I knew something was wrong. Two hours later, emergency landing, some trouble with the landing gear they had figured since take-off. Simple rule: watch the stewardesses. If they are fine, you are fine. If they run like chickens with their heads cut off, wake me up. Ok now? Gotta sleep. I am spent. My bones are killing me. These seats."

Yorgi went back to sleeping in a quick minute, trying to dream that he was already in the savannah and that the high-pitched screaming came from a pack of hyenas rather than the baby right behind him. The smell of the overheated chicken curry strolling down the aisle invaded his nose. He dreamt of a rack of lamb, a glass of Cabernet, a herd of zebras walking in front of him. He slept for four hours straight, and then he dreamt of elephants. A parade of them charging. The ground was trembling. Mary was shaking his arm again. He took his eye mask off, and before he could focus his vision, he asked loudly: "What now?"

"The flight attendants. They're running like chickens," said Mary. She was sweating, and so was he. He mumbled a complaint about the stuffy atmosphere and the AC not working, but he could feel the air-stream coming down his face. It was working fine, but he was burning. He coughed again and again, his chest hurting worse each time as if he had swallowed white-hot coal, and before he could ask for water, he grabbed the bottle from Mary and drank two sips. Hardly.

"Am I warm?" he asked Mary, feeling like his throat and skin were on fire.

"You are," she said, already signaling to the flight attendant. The smiling young lady didn't even stop for her, and she wasn't smiling anymore. She ran past Mary, the long white headscarf of her uniform stained with red blotches. Blood?

The pilot's announcement interrupted their thoughts:

"If there is a doctor or nurse on board, please report to the main cabin immediately."

"They need me. I must see what's going on," Yorgi said, the pain in his chest cutting his breath as he squeezed over Mary to take his first step down the aisle. He felt so dizzy as he got up that he had to support himself with both hands on each aisle seat. His knees trembled, but he kept moving.

There was an Indian man, three rows ahead in stress, hyperventilating. A couple of Brits he had seen before—how did he know they were Brits—the woman coughing, the man panicking, farther ahead. Yorgi was trying to make it to the bathroom, throw some water on his face. A black guy, his name was Bokamoso, he knew him—how did he know all these people? He met them before. Where? The blue bus. Yesterday. He had seen these people a day ago, they had all missed their connection, and the blue bus transported them to a hotel—an airline courtesy.

Bokamoso's eyes were red, and he was sweating as if he had come out of a sauna. His lunch napkin was pressing against his bleeding nose. The passengers around him had abandoned their seats and had left him all alone. The stewardess was pleading with them to take their seats, there was turbulence again, and the "fasten seat belts" sign was on, but they refused, pushing their way to the back of the plane. Each passenger's face painted a different image of horror as they squeezed past Yorgi. "Please, let me pass. I am a doctor," he said. Most of them were covering their faces with their hands. His belly was hurting now; he had almost made it to the lavatory. A woman was pale on her knees, vomiting outside the locked door. She was the stunning blonde he had eyed a day ago. Where? The blue bus. Screams came from the front and back rows, business and economy, the flight attendants were running up and down the aisle, their white scarfs covered their mouth and nose like surgical masks.

"Ladies and gentlemen, please take your seats," announced the pilot. "We have been rerouted to Nairobi." He paused for a few seconds, two-hundred and fifty passengers sighing with despair, asking questions. "Twenty minutes to landing. Ambulances and medical personnel have been notified."

That's the last thing Yorgi remembered as he went down to his knees, vomiting next to the beautiful blonde woman.

He wouldn't remember the landing, the green bunny suits guiding them to the bus, the stretchers rushing him to the quarantine area of the hospital, one of the doctors trying to revive him.

He would come to his senses, and only for a few seconds many hours later in a room with white walls, white sheets, men in white uniforms. That woman in white could be Mary; he could only see her eyes. Could be a nurse, his head was pounding hard, his vision was blurry. They had two kids together, boy and girl, he had insisted that they were too young to come to a safari. They had left them behind in Athens with the two grandmas. Couldn't afford the extra cost either. Mary's gloved hand touched his head and his forehead. His hair on her glove. Too much hair. His lungs burning, he tried to say "water." He was thinking too fast, struggling to make sense of where he was; he was breathing even faster. Why? He heard some words of what Mary was mumbling. "Quarantine. Terrorists. Maybe, virus, weaponized, Nairobi. Rest."

There was a man on the bed next to him. Brown skin, red eyes. Bokamoso. He knew his name.

Yorgi turned to Mary holding her wrist with his weak, trembling fingers. "Blue." was his penultimate word. "Bus."

# 15. Yara: The Wrong Sort of Folk

*Turkey, June 2022*

"Please, dad! Can we go to Eurodisney this summer?"

No Santa letter—it was not a thing—no clothing sprees, no toys, not even a one-piece swimsuit. Eurodisney was Yara's sole wish since she was a little girl. She loved the (idea of the) thrill, the (idea of the) crazy rides; she had watched everything on YouTube, and never stopped talking about it. Dad wouldn't even reply, and her mom usually stepped in with a smile and said: "You will go, someday."

In some perverse way, her father had finally succeeded. Their return to Syria threw Yara into a hellish park that no Disneyland Imagineer nor horror novelist could ever conceptualize. What was next? A crazy bus ride through Turkey, a water-world adventure in the Aegean? The thrills.

The bus with the American family—that would also have been called brown-skins by some in Manchester—stopped at her uncle's house at 3 a.m. Yara's family boarded quickly, carrying a few suitcases that made the smugglers laugh. They were two slim men, the driver, and the talker, dressed identically in white shirts, and two buttons opened up. The talker's expression revealed that he had done this too often to care about whether he was carrying children, fruit, or meat across the border.

The ride to Adana took fourteen hours though they spent seven of them waiting idly at rocky off-highway dirt roads to avoid inspections and to pray. Yara didn't understand how and when they passed the borders. She spent the better part of the night awake, a thousand unwelcome thoughts invading her head. There was the fear of the journey, the excitement of returning to her swimming pool.

Some other thoughts were subtler. Yara was trying to make sense of why people always migrated west. The weather was always worse; it was no coincidence that ancient civilizations had all developed in the east. It made no sense to abandon the Mediterranean sun for rainy York or even New York, yet the departing always dreamed of going farther west. Were humans an east-west-bound virus that wiped out a promised land and then moved to find meat in the next one? Was it the sunset? The last light of the sun, the final hope, still gleaming in warm color and spectacle when the darkness swallowed the East of yesterday?

"Sleep, Yara. Pray and sleep. Don't be scared," her mother whispered.

Yara passed her fingers through her little sister's hair. Nahla, the seven-year-old, was dreaming and giggling with eyes shut, her head wresting on Yara's shoulder. Yara had told her that they are going back to their home in Manchester, and their first job was to visit the Giddy Goat Toy Shop.

*Yes, Nahla. Grandma will come and visit us. When? Soon.*

Nahla was shielded from any of the slithering snakes of anxiety that burdened her older sister; she slept carefree as a giddy goat among toys.

"The toys," Yara said, talking to herself in the beginning. "The toys, mother. The toys."

As her train of thought ran wild on the Asia Minor asphalt, her mind got stuck on the word. "Toys" was the magical trigger word, and it unlocked a river of guilt that drowned her.

"We didn't say goodbye to them," Yara said, turning to her mother.

"What? Who? Sleep, child," Faiza replied impatiently.

"We left them behind."

There were two kids, Nahla's age and younger, who used to play with them at their apartment in Latakia almost every afternoon. A girl and a boy, Rasha, and Samer, would come two floors up to bang at their door after school. Faiza always opened the door to give them bread and invite them in to play. Rasha marveled at Nahla's dolls and all the toys she'd brought from England.

Princess Zoe of Avalor, the baby unicorns; those were Samer's fixation. More often than not, Yara was on duty to watch over the young ones, precisely at the same time when swimming practice started back in Manchester. The only thing that would shake up her boredom was her anger. This was the first trigger for her sweet, polite face to crack and reveal the steel below.

But as the bus was cruising over the potholes of southern Turkey at the first hours of the night, all Yara could picture with eyes shut was Rasha's pigtails and gray-green eyes, and Samer's brown beach-waves hair on top of his big round head. His head was not really that big; his skinny legs and torso made it look that way.

"How could we leave like that? They'll come at four in the afternoon," Yara mumbled. "Zoe's tea time. They will bang the door. Rasha will keep banging until her parents find her. We left like fugitives, didn't say goodbye."

"We didn't even say goodbye to grandma and grandpa," Faiza said. "We couldn't."

*But grandpa Farid will understand. Rasha won't.*

Rasha kept banging the door inside Yara's temples all night, weeping out of her friend's eyes for the departed Zoe of Avalor.

Later in life, Yara would add more to her guilt, thoughts about why she could leave the country, while Rasha couldn't, why she survived when all perished, why a paper with ink marks claiming that she was British, the girl in front of her American, Rasha none of the above—though they all looked like first cousins to a foreigner—really meant anything, especially to people who claimed to be civilized and highly educated. She could understand race, religion, culture, and custom dividing people. She was raised to be proud, or rather aware of all that diversity, but what on earth was a passport? How can it hold truth or justice if you can never explain it to a child?

Truth be told, she fabricated these elaborate thoughts and memories later in life; she added them as lawyers add crap to a simple argument. That first night in the bus, the only truth, the only image, was Rasha and Samer's tiny fists knocking on the door.

The driver took the American family all the way to the Consulate at Adana, and after half an hour of negotiation, without guns or knives—though Yara was certain that the smugglers could produce them at any minute—they continued for Antalya. Khaled's wallet was now light as a feather, but at least this time, he had a plan: a second and a third wallet fat with fifty-pound notes.

Yara finally got some sleep when the sunlight invaded through the thin fabric of the orange-brown bus curtains. Like a vampire in her sketches, she woke up thirsty with a heavy head when the sun had fallen west.

She heard the first words from Khaled as she saw the first sign with the name of the city: "We made it! Everything will be fine now, inshallah."

They stopped for dry supplies and water as they entered the city but did not sit down for hot food. Khaled didn't trust the smugglers and wanted to get to the consulate immediately. They made it to the exact place before sunset, but it was too late, and they had to return the next day.

The sun was scorching from early morning when they all woke up. Khaled made three phone-calls to the Consulate number, but all he got was an automated message that led nowhere.

"We're here! Get ready," he said when they came a few blocks from their desired destination. At the same moment, Yara noticed the teargas clouds rising like angry trolls among the buildings ahead. A blockade, and policemen in full riot gear.

The smuggler who wasn't driving got out of the bus to scout the surroundings. When he returned, he ordered everyone: "Shut all the curtains and keep your heads down. They're four hundred people waiting to get in the Consulate. Three queues. Turk, Syrian, British. But no Syrian made it in today."

"We have British passports; we'll go to the British queue," Khaled said.

"They won't let you. You don't look British. Trust no one, those policemen will confiscate your papers and sell them."

"We are going," insisted Khaled.

"You think I am dishonest, huh? But I brought you here. Didn't rob you, didn't steal your passport, respected your family. I tell you now for the sake of your children. You go out there, you'll get hurt."

"Our passports are not fake."

"Even worse. They slaughter you like sheep for good passports here."

Yara turned to her sister on the adjacent seat: "Sing me a song, Nahla.

Anything you like. Please. I'll buy you candy. Promise," just to distract her. She kept one ear to the men arguing three rows ahead.

She caught the word "Latakia" repeated a few times.

"Yara, come here now. Put this on," shouted Khaled.

"Why, father?"

"Take off the hijab, wear this, and follow me. The rest wait here," he said.

Khaled gave her one of her older brother's jeans; they were about the same height, though too loose for her. He guessed that Yara, with trousers and no hijab, was as close to a British as anyone in the family. Going to the gate with a girl on jeans, maybe he'd have more luck convincing the guards.

He was mumbling to Yara as they tried to make their way toward the British queue.

"Manchester was getting too hostile for Muslim folk who want to keep the traditions," he said. "That was no place to raise a family, Syria was recovering, and it was time for us to return. I couldn't stay after what happened to your mother that evening, such dishonor. I didn't know what to do; I was blinded by rage."

Yara realized that her father was apologizing, maybe to her, maybe to himself. Under the blazing hot sun, his shirt had become one with the sweat and his skin; his creased forehead was sparkling from the moisture that remained trapped above the bushy eyebrows. There was nothing British about him.

"If they ask you, you speak to them, Yara. English. Don't freeze. You say where you go to school in Manchester. Your teachers' names," said Khaled.

She struggled to remember the names, *Mr. Hornbuckle, Ms. McDougall, what was the math teacher's name?*

"We get in, and it is all over. I'll grant you any wish," Khaled continued.

"Open the door, you bastard," Khaled shouted at the guard as they both heard the dragging and the thud of the iron gate shutting.

The guard had refused to even look at the passports, showed them the Syrian queue, and turned his back. Though Yara wouldn't learn that detail for some time, more than twelve other men with fake British passports had tried to get in that day. Theirs were genuine, but they were the unlucky thirteenth.

Never before had she heard her father curse—a devout Muslim and a good man with half-thought plans. It was the first and the last time.

They tried the next day again, and they found the same queues, and a stubbornly shut gate, behind a thick man-made wall of riot police. And a third day, and a fourth. On the fifth day, a large convoy of black sedans entered the Consulate's front yard and exited a couple of hours later. After that, the police boarded on the two buses leaving only a handful of their own behind.

The note posted next to the iron-gate read something like: "By Her Majesty's blah blah, a global health directive issued by the WHO blah blah to contain the deadly virus outbreak…all Consulates in Bangladesh, Pakistan, and Turkey will shut down indefinitely…personnel recalled…blah, blah Ankara…"

No one who read it believed a word. *White men building their walls,* everyone thought and mumbled. It was still early.

Khaled and his family were stranded. Sleeping or finding a toilet, even feeding the baby, was getting more difficult by the day, and they were running out of supplies.

"I am not driving you to Ankara," the smuggler said.

"You are not taking us back to Syria," Faiza countered, standing up to the men.

She was a mother of four; the smugglers should respect her.

"I can't take you further, okay?" said the one who did all the talking. "But I know Turks here, who take Syrians to cross. I make connection. You cross to Greece, you go to your Embassy there."

It all happened too fast after that. Time was running against them, the smugglers left on the evening of the sixth day, and Khaled was now negotiating with a new group of traffickers from Turkey.

Three men came to the bus: a young one who did all the talking in English, an imposing bald, bearded giant behind him, and a quiet man in his sixties who looked like a history teacher. The giant drew all the stares, but Yara fixed her eyes on the bespectacled "history teacher," he was the one counting, calculating.

Khaled introduced himself as Syrian—he didn't mention the passports, they would be a liability.

"My friends said you could take us to Greece? To Athens?"

"Getting you to an island is one thing. I don't know about Athens. But…" They fell in silence.

The traffickers were very good at negotiating. They employed the smartest tactic, never talk about price, only about demand and supply. The man just kept saying no, "no more seats, no way, all boats full, come next week, maybe we can take this girl here only, no this, no that, is that her sister?" and the more they said no, the more Khaled would raise the offering bid.

After some long-drawn impasse, the "history teacher" who had stood quiet, proposed the most expensive plan.

"My friend," he started talking in Arabic, resting his palm softly on Khaled's shoulder. "It is too dangerous, impossible to do this with four children in one boat. All our boats are full. And the weather turned, it is going to be rough tomorrow. Maybe you split up the family in two. Maybe I can squeeze you in two separate boats. I take the girls north to Lesbos, and you try for Samos for you and the rest."

"Hassan comes with the girls," Khaled insisted.

"No, no!" Faiza screamed, pulling Khaled from his sleeve.

The "history teacher" turned to leave, raising his arms slowly in pretentious dismay.

"No, please, wait!" Khaled said.

The negotiation was over at "please."

"Listen to me. All do the same," the *teacher* said. "They split, send the children alone, easier to get asylum. One lone child gets asylum, it can bring others. That's what all do."

*Please, father. Tell me you don't have enough money to be suckered by him. Don't send us alone,* Yara prayed.

"We are not sending the girls alone," Faiza said.

But Khaled had already succumbed to the inevitable. He rushed to stop the history teacher from exiting the bus. The bald giant was too smart to let him by.

"We split up, you go with your uncle Hassan, easier that way. If one makes it, then the others can get in by invitation, they say. Hold your sister's hand tight," were her father's parting words.

"Girls go to Lesbos. Money now, they leave in five minutes," rasped the younger smuggler. He exited the bus without waiting for another argument.

Her mother kissed them both, Yara on her long shiny hair, Nahla on her black medusa-sweetheart curls. Yara had stronger, healthier hair than Nahla, and yet she knew already that she could never compare in beauty to the young one. It didn't help that until then, she had to cover her head, so no one would know she had better hair. The French nose, the big bright eyes, the ruddy cheeks were all Nahla's traits. Yara was just plain, and even that was a slightly generous way to put it. If it was not for the love she had for her sister—they had shared a twin mattress the whole year they'd spent in Latakia—Yara could have been jealous.

"Mother, I beg you, let us come with you. I'll obey, I'll never talk back again," she turned during those last words to her father.

"You have a better chance this way," Khaled said.

"I have to carry your brother all day and night, he is still breastfeeding. You'll be better off with uncle Hassan," added Faiza, her voice trembling.

Uncle Hassan had not said a word to Yara during the entire journey; he'd only talk to Khaled and Sayid, the firstborn.

"Mother, no! Please!"

Yara tried to raise more arguments about this being total madness and how could they ever find each other again, and she spoke no Greek, none of them did, and she asked why her uncle had not spoken a single word since they left Latakia, and that she had felt warm blood running down her panties a few minutes ago, but she had brought no pads, and mother's were not right for her, and a lot more, but it was too late.

"I want you to be safe, Yara. All of us. Only one of us needs to make it there, register at the camp, show the passport, make it to the Embassy, and then bring the others. If we stay together, the chances are worse; you heard them."

But Faiza was weeping as she was talking, and she couldn't hide it. She didn't believe her own words; this was all Khaled's doing. He should have insisted on keeping the family together.

Did he care just for the newborn boy? Could he be that thick?

He was intoxicated with joy after her brother Omar was born. "Allah's gift because I honored my parents," he used to say.

Uncle Hassan and the girls boarded an off-duty taxi with the younger smuggler. Yara had to give the bag with the simit, the nuts, and the water bottles to her sister because her uncle insisted: "You hold my hand, listen now." She had to hold Nahla with the other. Yara had pleaded with her mother one last time from the taxi's back seat, wailing to convince her, but everyone was waving back at her.

"Keep Nahla, at least," Yara cried. "She is barely seven, too young, too old. What am I gonna tell her? She needs you, mama."

It was only then that Nahla understood that mama wasn't going to get in the taxi, and she started screaming, but uncle Hassan shut the window fast. As the younger one sank in her arms, Yara wished her sister was a newborn baby. Or sixteen like her, a twin to share the ordeal. Not seven. Seven is the worst age.

Later in life, Yara had to suffer many dinner parties where the other couples talked mostly about their children's uniquely extraordinary adventures at grade school or daycare. Yara would enrich and change the conversation in a consistent manner: "Oh, really? Is your daughter seven? Seven is a bad age for a girl. They understand too much, can do so little. I lost my sister when she was seven."

She could swim in the silence that fell afterward as if the whole conversation had sunk in the cold ocean.

And she'd have a story for every age. "Two months, you say? A tiny baby, such a dangerous period. You must carry him around, need a crib, he can't walk. I lost my brother when he was two months old."

The faces of all those choked-up young mothers. No wonder they stopped inviting her to dinner parties after a couple of times.

"Sixteen? Worst age for a child. She won't agree on one thing with her parents. I lost my mother when I was sixteen."

Every age was perilous for a child, so naturally, Yara had made it to her fifties without giving birth to one, not even trying to have one. None of her ex-husbands proved okay with that, despite the promises they'd all made before the weddings. But she had no regrets on that front, she had followed her heart, or whatever was left in its place. Her only regret was that she never kissed baby-brother Omar that night before leaving—she only had five minutes to prepare for her journey—that was her lame excuse—but deep inside, there was that lingering realization that she was jealous of him.

We get jealous of all the wrong sort of folk sometimes. If we could get in their shoes, their routine, their beds, their coffins, our jealousy would be swept away like grains of sand on a breezy night at the beach.

The beach, the night, the stars, the rough dark-wine sea were all waiting for Yara and Nahla.

# 16. Lucia: L as in Lucifer

Lucia's father was proud as a Royal Garden peacock whenever the discussion came to her, and he always made sure it did. "Our Lucia is studying law in England. It is not Cambridge, but believe me, she will make it there one day. That girl has drive. A professor! Or a judge. Can she be a judge in a foreign country? Unless she decides to go for the money at a private firm. You know, lawyers these days make fifty pounds every two minutes! You can't beat that!"

In reality, Lucia was secretly back in Athens and about to make her first fifty for a single minute's work—beat that, daddy—for sucking the dick of the Albanian (he didn't look Georgian) mobster whom she had picked up earlier. And she was proud of it; one day she hoped to be able to tell that story to everyone, even to her father. It would be too much for her mother; there, she'd need some PG version.

As for the fact that she had dropped out of law school almost nine months ago, that she didn't dare to disclose—there is only so much naked reality a father can take regarding his one and only daughter.

Her parents didn't even know she was in Athens; they didn't know her real job or anything else for some time now. It would take some artful storytelling to explain her decision and what brought her from law school to her knees at the Royal by-the-hour Hotel in less than a year. She had rehearsed the script in her mind a thousand times, optimized and even written it down to read and flow uninterrupted because it was the kind of story that parents tend to interrupt:

"Listen to me, dad. There are so many undergrad kids studying law these days, but I did it for a year, and it sucks. TBH it's a brain freeze. They go through the motions reading and memorizing like robots, and even the work is so robotic, and you know what? Plus, Portsmouth, nice weather, etc., but it is a so-so law school, ranked 70th or something in the UK. So, I made a switch, the department was just literally down the yard from my law school. Drop the wig, get a microscope instead. The microscope is real, those wigs are relics. Criminology and Forensic Investigation, yes, I started last autumn, this is my second year in the program, yes, sorry, I kept this secret too long. And I love the program. No, I didn't drop out of college, just out of law school. It is savage, Daddy. Sorry, wrong word, you won't get it. I am the best in my class, there are a lot fewer of us, I stick out like a yellow poppy, and I can go back to law anytime. You know they suggest three books. I go to the library and borrow thirteen. As I said, I love it, dad."

She'd probably get a typical question-statement without a question mark about whether she had gone crazy to believe she could be a cop or a detective and how dangerous and corrupt the Greek system was, etc., but Lucia would repeat her last sentence. "And I love it, dad."

The internship at the prestigious office of Sedulous and Universal Private Investigators firm followed a few months later and lasted for eight summer weeks. She was not their first choice but became their extra choice when she offered to join the firm as a volunteer. That was not really a thing, more of a trick to signal commitment, they had to pay to employ her, but Mr. Langsford had become fond of her from the first exchange. Her passion, her eyes of green sparkling with excitement, determination, and foolish youth, the irresistible stuff of magic all the Langsfords of the world wished they could still reclaim, or at least observe, in their older age. A cynical youngster who would suffer anything for an internship was a common species, but a smart girl who could bring lattes and sort folders and digital photos with a smile of appreciation, that was a rare find.

Langsford was a tall and lean peppered-hair man. If he were twenty years younger, Lucia would probably have a crush on him; if she ever had crushes on older men, that was. But a young Langsford could have been a crush possibility if there ever was one for her, primarily because he was a private investigator. He had promised her a renewal of the internship for the coming summer, and it was already June, so when he called two nights ago, Lucia thought she knew what the call was about. He certainly caught her by surprise:

"Lucia, my dear, are you free this weekend?"

Lucia froze at the proposition. If Langsford, a man in his fifties, had a thing for her, that would destroy everything. She was allowed to have a secret platonic thing for him, but if it was the other way around, all was lost. She prayed to all and no gods in particular: *Please don't #metoo me, Mr. Langsford. I love Sedulous and Universal. I want the job. Don't do this to me, please fall for some other girl, please no, I am certified anti-Lolita, I haven't even told my dad, and they live in a shithole in downtown Athens, sending half their pension to me. Dad thinks I study law. I save most of it in the bank; I'll repay them, but please don't, Mr. Langsford. I want the job. I'd do anything, but not this. Please!*

Fortunately, she didn't say any of that on the phone, no time to even think of it until she replayed it later in her head. All she mumbled was, "Yes, I am free, I think," followed by a "Maybe, you know it is exams period, sir," to cover all angles.

She was done with exams and only had to deliver a written assignment.

"Look, kid. Sorry for this. I thought the exams were over. I was expecting you to start the internship in a week. If you are free and want to make two thousand fast, there is a job for you. And it's the real deal."

"To do what, Mr. Langsford?" she asked, hoping that this had nothing to do with the obvious. But no man would offer her two thousand pounds to bring lattes.

"You must leave tonight, my dear. Melissa sent the plane tickets to your email, London to Athens. Get on a train from Portsmouth immediately if you are interested. There has been a kidnapping, a nine-year-old son of a man who shouldn't have to deal with such things at this point in his life. But the rich are careless down there, and now he has gone to the other end and hired the best. And we are the best. I have my Dubai team flying over to Athens, but they can't make it until Monday, they have some business to take care of there, and that's two days too late. I am gunning for a win on this one, a good first reference for business down there. Many loaded folks from China, Turkey, Saudi, etc., are moving to the Athenian Riviera, and when they see what they are up against, no functioning police or law down there, it will be good business for us. I need someone who speaks the language and is a local, that's why I hired you for the internship last summer. Never told you that, I didn't want you to presume anything but to earn it. The client has retained an ex-Mossad team as well, so I want one of ours there now. Not someone flashy and with an opinion, just someone to watch, take notes, collect information until my guys are there. Can you?"

"Yes, yes, yes, sir. I can go. I am going," Lucia caught herself jumping in front of the one full-size mirror of her tiny student room.

She barely made the late-night flight for Athens, stuck on a middle seat between two study-abroad boys her age, snoring four hours straight in stereo-surround. The cab dropped her in the middle of the night at Mr. Papalias' address, located at Filothei, one of the few Athenian neighborhoods that resembled a wealthy westernized suburb. The night was windless, a sweet 23 celsius, the ideal setting for philosophers drunkenly debating under the Acropolis and tourists sipping resin wine at the taverna, not for dealing with kidnappings and guerilla militias. She had no problem identifying the house. It was surrounded by police cars, black cars, black cars with black windows, muscled men on monster motorbikes wearing helmets, ready to move if only they knew where they should go. She gave her credentials, but they let her in only after they called Langsford himself. He had to identify her through the phone camera.

Papalias was around fifty with the hands of someone who might have actually worked as a sailor at a younger age. He was into sailing—she had done her googling—his second wife and his football team. His pink-gold Rolex was the epitome of the generation and values gap between him and her.

"You are Langsford's girl," he said.

"I am not his 'girl,'" Lucia replied in Greek. She didn't look Greek, and she could fool anyone with that. "I am Lucia Maas, P.I. at Sedulous and International," she continued.

Another thing her father didn't know. She had legally changed her last name to "Maas" a few months ago. Maas was a German name, she could have opted for Mason in England, but that was just too plain and expected. "Lucia" could be from anywhere, but most would take it for Spanish. She was Polish-Albanian, but born and raised in Greece, so that made her Greek. She had a Polish passport under Lucja Mazur, her father's last name, and a Greek one as Loukia Masoura, the official Hellenized name her mother insisted on if she wanted to blend with the rest of the kids back in grade school. She had gone through school as Masoura, and all her friends, half a handful, called her Masu, not Loukia. Loukia in Greece would be a mustachioed nun's name, and she didn't want to be any nun. Now she had become Lucia Maas, studying and living in Portsmouth, UK, growing up with American detective miniseries, budget Chinese, and Indian food. Her roommate was a Pakistani medical student, and those guys behind Papalias were definitely the ex-Mossad agents. Earth was too small, and global warming was Lucia's top concern and her only voting criterion.

As for the ancestry DNA test she had taken, her saliva had revealed that she was quite Polish and Balkan Albanian, yet there were two-digit percentages of Russian and Italian blood going back three-four generations. Dad and mom respectively, she guessed. Retracing back eight generations and more, there was a Western Asian ancestor and a North African one. A Saracen pirate, an Ottoman pillager, a princess of Venice. Yeah, right, stick with pillager. Take your pick, better take all of them, put them in the blender, turn it on high for thirteen generations, and out comes Lucia. Definitely a German ancestor as well, but that was another thing she'd never reveal to her father. He hated Germans as much as he hated communists. The only thing that never appeared in her DNA was Greek, yet she had lived, played, read, wrote, learned, loved, and hated in her Athens birthplace, so she was very Greek in head and heart even if her saliva had other ideas.

The DNA ancestry report she had received in the app started with the text:

*"If every person living today could trace his or her maternal line back over thousands of generations, all of our lines would meet at a single woman who lived in eastern Africa between 150,000 and 200,000 years ago. Though she was one of*

*perhaps thousands of women alive at the time, only the diverse branches of her haplogroup have survived to today. The story of your maternal line begins with her."*

It would read exactly the same for Al the Albanian, Elon the ex-Mossad agent, Langsford the P.I., and Papalias, the tycoon. They all shared one common grand-grand-you-get-the-point-grandma, and she would have exactly the same cautionary tale to tell her grand-grand-children in front of the hearth as she was roasting chestnuts. "Please, be nice to your brother, child. You share blood with him. That flag of yours, I know you think it is old and sacred, but I am older than it, and you should listen to your grand-grand-you-get-the-point-grandma. Back when I was boiling mammoth broth, I had all those flags of yours as kitchen towels at my cave. As for those religious ideograms, they were first painted by half-monkey Neanderthals."

In summary, Lucia had no patience for white-supremacists, Nazi-right-wingers, or any such morons who had made her immigrant parents suffer for decades now.

"Mr. Papalias," Lucia said, offering a cold handshake and omitting the "good to meet you." "Before I proceed, I need to know if you are financing those Nazi thugs. If you do, I am sorry, can't work for you."

Papalias raised his eyebrows and stared at her, stunned. He expected anything the last two days, but not that. He replied immediately, too surprised to polish an answer.

"Where did you read that? All men with money here are nine-headed Hydra monsters, dealing drugs and financing Nazis. That's what the pests and the extortionists would have you believe."

"So, is it true, sir?"

"If it is true, I am no sir, but no, it is not."

"And how do I know that you are telling the truth?"

She had gone too far.

There was a smirk on Papalias' face, probably the first in the last two nights of hell he had suffered as he replied:

"Well, young lady, if you want the whole truth, go hire a P.I. Sedulous and Something are good, I heard. Need their number? Now, go do something useful or get out of my house."

Truth or lie, Lucia decided to take the man on his word. She had already broken any semblance of professional oath to Langsford, prioritizing her values over her job duties. Maybe it was the elegant sadness of the lady, who she recognized as the mother, weeping silently in the library room, sitting on the smoke-leather Chesterfield, wearing a smoke-colored Prada dress, a thin wisp of smoke rising from the ashtray. The effortless classiness, the filthy-rich humility. If that woman had gone for a Dolce and Gabbana leopard dress on a red silk sofa and a cosmo cocktail, Lucia might have quit right there.

As she dawdled around the house, she kept counting shelves packed with books, not walls covered with expensive paintings. An endless display of silver and Chinese knickknacks as well, but those looked cheap, some collection fetish, rather than a waste of good money that could feed the poor. Lucia approached one of the built-in libraries, and she browsed at the novels translated into modern Greek. Among others, she spotted Picoult's *Small Great Things*, Padura's *The man who loved dogs*—an odd choice for a shipping tycoon's mansion library—*The Shadow of the Wind* by Zafón. *The Mockingbird* and *the Kite-Runner* didn't really count; everyone might have received them as a gift, a two-for-one, or drop them in the bag because of their popularity, but there was a copy of *The Hate U Give,* and as she ran her fingers through the pages. It was underlined; someone had read it recently. That was quite a surprise. Who would read that? Her? Him? Not the Filipina housekeeper. Papalias had two teenage daughters. Occam's razor cut a path right to them.

There were other books, coffee-table stuff such as *The Ultimate Cigar Book*, and another one about Armagnac that she frowned at, but she knew enough.

*At least one person in this house is not a racist,* Lucia concluded. She could work for that person, a sister missing her little brother, withholding final judgment about the rest.

"Bored? Would you like some tea and biscuits with your books, dear?" the shaved bald man whispered next to her in rough English as she was flipping through the paperback.

"I am looking for the XSI team-head," Lucia replied.

"You are Sedulous, right?"

"Have to be."

"Sedulous *and* funny? Are they on such a tight budget to send just you? I am the one you are looking for."

Elon from XSI was the typical middle-aged guy, Mossad agent, Maccabi Tel Aviv basketball coach, tech-startup CTO, or New York financier featuring the same clean head, eggplant nose, and slightly cross-eyed icy stare. He briefed her on everything they had uncovered so far, but it wasn't a lot.

Papalias had five children aged between five and twenty-one, an ex-wife, and a younger wife. He'd need close to thirty soldiers of trust to provide 24-hour security detail for everyone, and he didn't want his children to grow up that way. So he opted for the plain mortal lifestyle for everyone except himself. He couldn't trust anyone else to work the ropes if they kidnapped him, but he was arrogant enough to believe he could solve any problem if they harmed anyone else. A control freak, a self-proclaimed sun shining down at his offspring planets. His younger son took the school bus because Papalias had done the same as a kid, and he had fond memories of it. The bus dropped the kid off around 4:30 p.m. each afternoon, a few yards from their mansion. The housekeeper, a lady around sixty, would pick up the boy unless the mother happened to be there and not at the usual hairdresser appointment, charity meeting, or cappuccino with her friends at the country club. It had been hairdresser duty that afternoon.

The kidnappers had parked their van on a side road about fifty yards away from the mansion. The boy hopped out of the bus, dressed in his school's summer uniform, red t-shirt and indigo shorts, carrying his backpack. Two men jumped out of the van as the boy was crossing the street with the housekeeper, grabbed and carried the sixty-pound package from the armpits to the van covering the thirty yards in a flash. Isabella from Manila was not much of an athlete, and the school bus driver valued his life. The two ski-masked men were caught on video from a neighbor's security camera. It showed them running and shoving the boy into a black van with grayed-out plates.

"We don't have much," Elon said. "We are going over all the people and personnel who had visited the house for the last few months to try to see if someone is a suspect. One of the masked men was limping as if he had a serious problem, even a prosthetic leg, I'd say. He is our best hope."

"Did they make contact?"

"Yes, they want twelve million by tomorrow."

"And Papalias?"

"Well, I think the twelve million is third on his priority list. And his son is second. His first is to see them at the bottom of the river, cement boots and cut-off balls in their mouth. He insisted that each one goes down with a different set of balls, not his own."

"Not many rivers in Athens," Lucia said.

"It is an expression. How many cases have you worked so far?" asked Elon.

"A few."

"Really? Me too, and I've been doing this forever. Where?"

"I am not allowed to—"

"None. Thought so," said Elon.

The guy was well-trained at spotting liars.

"Anyway, I don't know what you are doing here. If you need anything, let me know, or even better don't, because we are quite busy as it is," he said, turning on his heel.

Lucia figured that there wasn't much to do in the house other than drawing suspicious looks from everyone else. She opened the door and went around the front and back porch, walking between the tall blossoming magnolias and the heart-shaped pool. Two Vilebrequin trunks—identical pattern, one boy, one adult—were drying on the lounge chair. The moonlight stream on the water was interrupted by a rainbow lollipop floatie, barely moving among oversized water guns. A one-foot plastic action figure of The Flash was resting on the sunbed. The sun would rise in a few hours, and the only thing missing was a nine-year-old boy to play with his toys.

The security guard at the semi-concealed booth came out and warned her:

"You shouldn't waltz alone in the dark, girl. Everyone is going crazy, and there are too many nervous strangers here."

She approached the security booth and looked at the guard's computer screen, the nine camera windows next to each other.

"Is someone analyzing the video?"

"Which video? There are so many of them."

"Are they uploaded in the cloud or stored physically?" Lucia asked.

"I don't know this tech gibberish you speak," said the guard.

No wonder those kidnappers had such an easy time.

"Where do the service people come from?" Lucia asked.

"The front door. There is no separate service door," said the guard.

Lucia looked at the front door camera that was showing the policemen walking out of the iron gate. The camera followed them for a while. Kidnapping by a total stranger was less than a quarter of all cases globally. There were no reliable statistics in her country for anything, but one had to check the service and security personnel before anything else.

"I'll be back," she said.

That was a long shot, but Lucia was bored, and she needed to do something. Anything, even if it was a one in a million chance, it was better than sitting idle like a bored, coffee-making maid. She thought of calling Langsford first but decided to take action.

It was 8 p.m. on the US West Coast, the guy she was looking for, Seth, was probably awake. Seth was the founder of a cybersecurity startup. That being the modern West Coast, though, he wouldn't answer a call from a foreign number or answer a phone call, period. But she had him on Messenger, they had kept in touch, and he had friended her a few days ago.

"Seth, this is Lucia from Sedulous. We met last summer during your presentation."

"Hi, Lucia. You are my Facebook friend. I know you," Seth replied.

She exchanged a couple of texts with Seth, the last one reading: "I'll call you in a few minutes. Answer it."

She interrupted Elon talking with the head of the Department of Forensic Investigation and asked him for permission.

"I need access to the security tapes."

"There are no tapes. It is all digital."

"I hope so. I need access. To that and the kidnapping footage. Now, please."

After some more questions that Lucia didn't feel obliged to answer, Elon had to grant her access.

Seth was the CTO of the Silicon Valley startup that had presented at Sedulous London offices last summer. It was an embarrassing presentation done on a hot Friday after a Team England football game. The meeting had moved from 3 to 5 p.m., which actually meant it was dead and not really happening. Lucia was the only mandatory courtesy attendant; she didn't have a choice. His whole service pitch was rather blue-sky and sci-fi for the traditional folks. Lucia loved it.

Seth's little startup was a bunch of buzzwords stitched together to give confidence to the geeks inside the company but quite far from making a dollar.

"We are disrupting the biometrics market by addressing the gait recognition from motion capture data issue using disruptive—sorry, I said disruptive already, he he—machine-learning technology. Human recognition via estimated 3D positions of the main anatomical landmarks, using principal component analysis shows in early trials a success rate of—"

"Come again?" asked Mr. Ross, Langsford's partner. "What do they do in plain English?"

"Seth has a biiiig computer," said Lucia "and it can analyze any video you give it and tell you if that dark shadow walking there was John Wayne or Marilyn Monroe. Most of the time."

"I can do this every time."

"But you couldn't if you didn't know John and Marilyn in the first place."

"You don't make sense, young lady," said Mr. Ross.

Anyway, she never got to test if Seth's algorithm really worked; it was not Sedulous' priority.

"What is your current success rate, Seth?" Lucia asked.

"Depends on if you have a reference subject, if it is a cooperating subject used to train the system, that you can use for analysis. And then it's the learning rate."

"English, Seth."

"Do you know what you are looking for?"

"A man with a limp, probably a prosthetic leg, who kidnapped a boy. I have video from an okay-quality security camera recording 24/7 for the past three years."

"All from the same camera?"

"Yes, I think so. Well, I haven't watched three years of video, more like three minutes of it."

"Well, that seems doable, but it would take us a couple of weeks. I'll send you a quote for services, and you sign it back. We accept Paypal."

"What quote? You are hired, start tonight. Not tomorrow. Now! I pay you Monday if you deliver," Lucia said. She spotted the mother of the child pacing out of the living room, approaching her. Lucia extended her hand, and the manicured Mrs. Papalia held it inside hers.

"Any news, my dear?" she asked with watery eyes.

They haven't even been introduced yet. Gray suit over a black jumpsuit, a backpack and black boots, just a hint of makeup, Lucia looked the business.

"We'll find the boy," Lucia said confidently, reassuring the mother. She turned to her phone call. "Two hours? I don't have two hours, Seth. This is your chance for fame and proof of concept. It's a kidnapping, every minute counts. I have Mossad here. Mo-ssad. Get it?"

"Funny girl. Two weeks, I said. Not hours. Minimum."

"Eight hours, Seth."

"If I can get access to the university resources here, I could run the first days of data tonight."

"Write down the username. I'll send you the password separately. Call me back."

Seth went silent until the next afternoon, texting and apologizing that she was asking for the impossible. Lucia spent the day in Papalias house, talking to people and cataloging all information and timeline carefully. It was late after 11 p.m., and the Athenian night was warm and cloudless. She could be having fish meze next to the *sea*, paying a surprise visit to her parents, or working on her final paper for the semester. Instead, she was watching the TV news to see what they were reporting about the case.

The Papalias kidnapping was first in the lineup, even though it was far from her country's most severe problem. The rest of the news was about the new proposed pension cuts—that budget surplus once again proved an elusive target—three boats of refugees sinking in the Aegean, one outside Lesbos, two near Samos, in a resurgent wave of massive immigration from Turkey, Syria, Bangladesh, you name it. Some were heading for Sweden or Germany, the others for the dark depths of the Pelago. Nobody opted for Athens. There were even more remote catastrophes like a few hundred people who had perished during the past three months across the world from the same strange avian virus, including a Greek doctor who was on a flight to Kenya, one of the first victims. The UK had shut down its consulates in Turkey and Pakistan, and that caught her attention, but she pushed her mind away from all that; she had to focus on the Papalias case. Lucia called her mom and dad casually to discuss the news—sometimes they knew more than any agent because they heard more than they wanted to about the Athens underground. Her mother had quite a few nephews, and not all of them were Cambridge or even Portsmouth material.

"Yes, my child, we heard. How are you? Did you put on any weight? Please, don't eat only those candy bars."

"Who kidnaps children still?" Lucia said. "They always get caught."

"Ah, my child, they always say it is us Albanians, but you know, it is everyone," her mom replied. "We are becoming Chicago."

That was a favorite of the Greek people since the Al Capone years. Whenever there was some violence, Chicago came up. Albanians invading Chicago, even better.

The viewers were more interested in Papalias than any global plague. Most of those still caring to watch network TV in 2022 were pensioners or unemployed; rent, electricity, and beans were their whole check. They could not afford a vacation or even dream outside the realm of the lottery jackpot. But they got a reminder of their good fortune through the misery of others. Papalias, a filthy-rich man with a blonde wife being struck by a catastrophe, was God's rage and justice. It provided a shot of guilty relief, not even guilty, nine parts of "see how the rich suffer like us?", one part of "that poor little boy." A muffled chuckle by the unemployed when Papalias's headshot from a lifestyle magazine filled the TV screen.

"Seth, finally," Lucia replied as she heard his voice on the line. It had been fifteen hours; he had failed her. "Give me something."

"Well, we cranked it up here, but we're nowhere near done. We just completed the first month of camera footage, and I couldn't find your limping guy."

"Damn!"

"But I have a high probability on the second kidnapper," said Seth.

"How? He wasn't even limping."

"Well, if my algorithm worked only for limping folks, I wouldn't have a business. Look, we didn't find your limping guy because he had never been to the house before, at least not that last month. But I have a tag on the second guy. Not certain, I am close to ninety percent, not sure how you want to use it. You can't convict him, and the police can't go with that as evidence as we are not approved and certified yet, but it is a good lead. If it were life or death, I'd take my chances. My screen here says that he is the same man who entered the house three weeks ago, May 27, 2022, at 10:23 am and stayed inside for almost an hour. I am sending you the link, someone should know him."

'Thank you, Seth."

"It's ninety percent."

"I'll live and die on your ninety percent. Keep working."

"About the bill."

"Send it to London, Seth. You'll be paid. Gotta go."

Lucia searched for Elon, but he was away with his team investigating a lead, and Papalias was nowhere to be found. The two junior policemen who were there wouldn't be much help. One of them asked Lucia if she had any surgical gloves because she shouldn't be touching things. Lucia thought it was a joke but instead said, "I am going to the pharmacy to get some," and headed for the security guard. Fortunately, it was the same guy.

"Costas, right? Question for you. Who entered 10:23 am on May 27? And why did he stay a full hour in the house?" asked Lucia.

"I don't work morning, lady. And we don't keep a log."

"You don't?"

"You know this is not the Pentagon or something. People come and go all the time."

"Do you know this man?"

Costas was observing the video on her smartphone.

"I'll send it to Thanos, who covers the morning shift weekdays. He might know him," he said. "He looks like a handyman, not a piano teacher."

A few minutes later, and after a conversation with Thanos that went like, "Ela, malaka, malaka, who is this? Think, re malaka," Lucia had a name.

"Babis, first name. Soutouhakis or something, surname," he said.

"Is that a real name?" It sounded like the translation of "Bob Squarepants" in Greek.

"Something like that. You need to find Papalias, he'd know him. He paid him."

"Paid him?"

"I hope he paid him. Your man is the elevator maintenance guy. Comes once a month for inspection."

A few minutes later, Soutouhakis had become Sourouhakis, but between the misspelled name and the elevator connection, Lucia had a definite work address. And it was his own small private business, not some big firm.

Lucia looked at the policewoman yawning a few yards away, staring at her bad manicure, and instead decided to go on her own. This was not common sense nor the right thing to do. She was young and reckless and looking to let the world know she was alive and rising.

"May I borrow your car, Costa? I'll be back soon."

"You know, I need the car to get home. I work a day job."

"Two hundred. You bill London."

"I don't bill anyone. I am Air Force security working the night shift to make some extra black euros. You know what they pay us. Eight hundred euros. They hire their nieces and the other 'nieces' at the parliament for four big ones net, and they pay the Air Force peanuts. The hell with that. I can't bill anyone, or I go to jail. But I love Mr. Papalias. Tell him that I need the job."

Lucia thought: *But you are falling asleep at your day job. They overpay you by eight hundred.* It was an accurate but not time-appropriate comment.

There was a reason this country was going down the drain, and it was that everyone could justify breaking his oath because the other guy broke it first or made more. But it was her country, so Lucia took two hundred out of her pocket and gave it to him.

"Be careful, kid," he said, giving her the keys.

Around midnight, she made it to the seedy neighborhood near the train station, where the elevator maintenance company was. Her first instinct was to break in, but the lights shone brightly on the second floor of the building. She waited. Elon was not answering her calls. It was almost three when the two men exited the front door. They had shut off all the lights and locked up. Her best guess was that the kid was not there. One was close enough to the figure to be Babis, the elevator guy, and the second man had a problem walking. Lucia could choose to follow any of the two or try to break into the building. She opted for the limping man because the body language indicated that he was the boss. She had Babis recognized, and he wasn't going anywhere, so she started following the stocky one, texting Elon to check the building they left. She kept her distance as she followed his car until he parked at the service road next to Syngrou Avenue, across from the Angels at Athens Gentlemen's Club. Then she was quick on foot after him.

A twenty-year-old girl on an adrenaline rush, a super-heroine of absolutely no power other than her smarts, aiming to crush the whole world of "gentlemen" in one night.

As the man was crossing the street, Lucia hoped that he was one who would go for a little Albanian devil vs. a bunch of Athenian Angels, most of whom were sex slaves from Uzbekistan and Moldova anyway.

Two nights ago, she was worried that handsome Langsford, who actually looked like a poor girl's Richard Gere, was making advances on her. Two nights later, she was ready to offer her services "suck, fuck, etc." to someone who looked like he just walked out of Mordor, and he was armed as if he did.

Her mom always said: "You were always such a little devil, from when you were in your crib."

Maybe she had named her after Lucifer, she joked back. "L as in Lucifer, U as in umbrella," she used to joke with customer service reps who kept her on the line for more than five minutes.

Her father always added: "That girl has a lot of drive."

# 17. Tina: AI Airport

*Athens, March 31, 2022*

On the first brutally blinding-sun, pollen-heavy, African-desert-sandstorm day of Athenian spring, Tina witnessed a miracle, unlike anything her experience of fifteen years in the world of medical insurance responsiveness had prepared her for. Only one day after her furtive midnight request, the APA insurance company sent a plane to Nairobi to bring Yorgi back.

After a one-day stopover at Geneva, Yorgi finally made it to Athens in a transparent hard-plastic coffin-type box filled with ice. Inside the box was a black and glossy body bag, and inside the bag, in babushka nightmare fashion, was Yorgi's frozen-black body. The only request of APA was that they perform the first autopsy at Geneva. The unofficial offer was that if the family allowed that, they'd cover the total cost of repatriation. Still, it was never officially described in an email or document, only on a phone call between Tina and a Mr. Daniels of the Birmingham Emergency Support Center.

She had gotten the email a day ago, and the Geneva results were reconfirming the story.

```
On 21 March 2022,
the Kenya Medical Research Institute notified WHO of 22
cases of laboratory-confirmed human infection with avian
influenza A(H7N9) virus. 20 of the cases were passengers
```

of flight SAR678 from Dubai to Cape Town that was rerouted
for an emergency landing at Nairobi Airport on 16 March,
4:25 p.m. The other 2 cases were local personnel, a nurse
and a bus driver who came in contact with the patients
possibly without adequate protection. 41 of the cases
developed acute viral pneumonia and Acute Respiratory
Distress Syndrome. Autopsies performed on several bodies
in Geneva and London were consistent with the diagnosis
of the Nairobi hospital.

Tina skyped Dr. Garnett, her former advisor, immediately after she got
the report. It was 6 a.m. in Baltimore.

"You are late." He smirked. "I thought you'd call yesterday."

"I wish I'd never have to call you again, Professor."

"No, you don't. You feel vindicated. But it's too early. You know this
makes no sense, Tina. How can this be a flu virus? Passengers who met a
couple of hours ago. How do they become symptomatic so fast?"

"I know." Tina was the first to admit it. "This makes no sense. They
cannot get sick in two hours. So what is the current hypothesis?"

"Anything. Everything. A weaponized virus?"

"Seriously? You believe it is a Chinese weaponized virus?"

"I didn't mention 'Chinese' or 'North Korean.' Did I? But H7N9 doesn't
spread so fast, doesn't spread via droplets, and no way that the virus could
cause these symptoms in a few hours. I understand the rest of the passengers
who got sick a day or two later, but how did these twelve people get sick *inside*
the plane? Works for zombie movies, not for the real world. Nah. Makes no
sense," Garnett said.

"A friend of mine was on the plane. He is dead now. Let me know if you
have any news," Tina said.

"Will do. There will be an emergency meeting in Geneva in a few days.
I'll make sure you're invited as a leading expert."

"An emergency meeting? You mean, all nations," Tina said. "Is it that
serious?" asked Tina.

"Coming from you, that's a redundant question. I wish we could have the meeting tomorrow, but we need some answers first."

It would be another two weeks until Mary arrived at AI Airport—the AI standing for Athens International rather than for something intelligent— released from quarantine and allowed to return to her home country. Mary's parents, Yorgi's parents, and their two children, each holding one grandma by an arthritic hand, were waiting with Tina outside the baggage claim. Both grandmas wore black dresses; one was satin, the other matte. The dresses were both brand new—this was the first of their young they'd have to bury during the next months.

Mary hugged Tina for a long ten seconds and then insisted on driving straight downtown to her lawyer friend's office. She was convinced that she had some great case against the airline, those super-rich Arabs were going to pay for sending her husband and everyone else to die in goddamn Nairobi.

"You had no right to let them do that autopsy, Tina. This is a big-time coverup. Now they messed everything up. We don't have a good case. Can you believe that they claim he died of the flu? The stupid flu? The nerve of those bastards. They couldn't even make a decent excuse. I am going to—"

"Mary, please get some rest. Your kids need you now. We have time for all that."

"The flu? Do you believe them? You know, huh. Liars!"

Tina didn't have to *believe* them.

As the National Agency senior epidemiologist, she had insisted on joining the team that performed the second autopsy. She took a liver sample, and she looked at what should be the lungs and the brain, but they had been destroyed. All that didn't make her any wiser.

The WHO had given her access to the results of the original autopsy. Photos, results of the viral tests, everything. When she saw the first photos, she smirked and thought someone was playing a joke on her. Maybe they had sent a native Kenyan man instead of Yorgi on that body bag to Geneva. This was not Mary's husband; the body was dark-skinned, not chestnut brown, more like blue-black. The explanation was in the report, yet it looked almost as ridiculous: "the subject's discoloration of the skin is due to acute cyanosis."

To a Greek and an epidemiologist, cyanosis was not some obscure word of medical book texts. An eight-year-old could guess its meaning. It literally meant "to turn blue" from the ancient Greek word for blue. To turn blue because the lungs were failing to oxygenate the blood.

But this was the 21st century; hospitals could give the patient oxygen. For somebody to suffer cyanosis to that extent, it would mean that many things went too wrong too fast, including that the hospital ran out of space at the ICU. Yorgi had died nineteen hours after he collapsed in the plane. He had shown no signs of illness before the flight. Whatever had infected him did so during those few hours after they took off from DXB. And that made no sense. *A weaponized virus.* She was never one to go for conspiracy theories. This was not the movies; there had to be a simpler explanation. He was bleeding from every orifice and capillary. Eyes. The Nairobi Hospital didn't have time to write everything down, but the Chief Doctor had made sure that photos were taken every hour, and he had sent everything to WHO. The autopsy had revealed extreme concentration of blood at the cranial meninges, which explained how Yorgi had lost most of his hair in a matter of hours.

It was creepy and shocking in the way that the first zombie apocalypse movies were to unsuspecting moviegoers. Tina usually frowned when her eye caught a few seconds of a zombie movie on TV, not more; she hated them. It was supposed to feel like "sci-fi horror and sick fantasy stuff," but she wondered if the screenwriters realized that most of the symptoms were accurate and very real. It was all a matter of size. In a plague, and even a flu strain could cause a plague, the skin of the infected as they were dying could turn much darker, not brown and healthy but green blueish and morbid due to cyanosis. Have you seen a zombie on TV? Something like that. There would be bleeding from mouth, nose, and ear, even from the eyes. The one thing that a zombie shouldn't be able to do is run with maddening speed at you, as in the movies. He wouldn't have to; all he had to do was exhale or sneeze. You just needed nano-level vision to witness the onslaught, a hundred-nanometer-tall army of zombies rushing to infect, spread, feed. Every sneezing, breathing, infected patient was releasing millions of crazed viruses to find new hosts. Once they did, they started their gruesome feast, devouring the internal organs, liver, lungs, heart. The brave antigens ganging up to fight against the zombies, they tried different weapons, shotguns and all; most failed, a few succeeded. Zombies or flu, the cinematography, and the casting of nature were different from that of Hollywood, but deep down, deep down within the lungs of the infected, it was the exact same action sequences, the same horror.

"Who dies of the stupid flu, Tina? What are we going to do now? The kids. He left us with nothing," mumbled Mary, turning her head to look out of the car window as she spoke the last sentence. In the passenger pick-up zone outside the arrival terminal, a mob of middle-aged taxi drivers was beating up a younger guy who had bypassed them. *Uber*, Tina guessed.

"Let's get out of here," said Tina.

She wished that her husband Peri had joined her at the airport, yet he had claimed that today was the "really important" venture capital meeting. Tina sensed that he was not indifferent, just someone who couldn't take the drama. Peri was devastated by Yorgi's death and all the details. He had conjured many conspiracy theories involving Sky Arabia Airlines, the Kenyan Government and the relationship to the Chinese, the Belt and Road Initiative, WHO, the Americans trying to frame the Chinese, a new theory every morning. He had become very fond of any variant of conspiracy theories after his auto-dealerships went bankrupt. In the process, he had borrowed and lost a lot of his father's savings, but fortunately, they stopped him before he drove them all to the ground. But the only thing that mattered to Tina was that Peri had proved a coward who had left her to deal with the tragedy all alone.

Her mobile phone flashed again with a message, this time, it was Floribeth, sending word from a remote village a couple of hours away from Manila.

Floribeth: *Madam sori. Cant fly back soon. My mama died yesterday. Flu. Must make funeral.*

Tina: *God rest her soul*

It was the only message that might mean something to Floribeth.

Peri would have to live without Floribeth's cooking for another month, it seemed.

"This is impossible," Mary continued. "The flu? No way. It was the bus. Yorgi was right."

"The bus?"

"The blue bus. The day before. They put some radioactive shit in it. This is the Arabs' fault."

"What bus Mary? What day before?" asked Tina.

"We were supposed to fly out of Dubai the day before. But we missed the connection, and so did a bunch of other people. They had us waiting for four hours at the gate after the plane left, then put us on a blue bus to take us to a hotel. Those were Yorgi's last words, 'Blue bus.' He knew there was something wrong with it. Everyone who got sick on the plane was on the bus. The blonde girl, the couple from Edinburgh, that man from Cape Town next to Yorgi at the hospital, the Bangladeshi guy, who died before we made it to the hospital. Everyone we talked to."

"You mean everyone who got sick in the plane was together for many hours the day before? Was there anyone Chinese-looking on the bus?"

"Chinese? No, I don't think so. Don't remember. Yes, we were together with the others on the blue bus. That's what I am telling you."

"That would do it. The virus had more than a day to work its way."

"What virus? Do you listen to what I say, Tina? Yorgi figured it out before he died. It is the bus. None of them were sick before we got on the bus. There was something inside that bus. Radioactive maybe."

"Maybe not."

"Yorgi was losing his hair in the hospital. Have you seen *Chernobyl*, the show?"

"They did lab testing, Mary. It was H7N9. An avian flu strain, one I happen to know too well. One person on that bus was infected. He spread it to everyone. Well, almost everyone, not to you. He didn't have any symptoms, but that's when the patient is most contagious before the symptoms start. It makes sense now."

"Bullshit, I am suing. It was something radioactive, I am telling you. A dirty bomb or something, that's why we landed."

"Okay, we'll talk more. I'll drive you home to rest now."

Tina stopped the car in the emergency lane and texted Dr. Garnett: "Figured it out. They were all waiting in the same room, then on a bus together a day earlier. Asymptomatic. Missed flight. Makes sense. Not a weaponized virus. It's H7N9. Antigenic drift probably, droplets."

There was no conspiracy. It was nature, the ultimate villain.

"Those bastards," repeated Mary with red-rimmed, sleep-deprived eyes. "They thought they could trick us. As if you can lose hair from the stupid flu."

"You can. If it causes acute respiratory distress syndrome. ARDS could—"

"Oh, shut up, Tina. It is 2022 already. Who dies of the stupid flu?"

Tina had spent the last twenty years of her life asking a related yet diametrically opposite question: *How had the human race even survived for so long against an enemy so formidable and indestructible as the flu virus?*

Against the undead.

# 18. Ella: First-Person, Present Tense

*Athens, December 23, 2057*

Yara says she has no kin left, but I always call her "aunt." Given the story I've heard about her parents and husbands, I've done better than most of them.

We recorded her story twice, the sessions a week apart. I wanted to check for consistency and what was fact or passing thought. Both times, when the story reached the shores of Turkey, Yara switched her narration to the present tense. And I decided to keep it so on my version, first-person, present tense. I know, I know, that's how I felt too; it is pretentious, especially in print, cheap storytelling, YA sentimental BS, in theory.

But the truth is that both times Yara switched to present tense, she removed her oval shades, clenched her fist as she was holding a loved one tightly, her knuckles turning paper-white as she was narrating slowly, then fast with those awkward run-on sentences, then not at all for a while.

As she dove deeper into the dark waves of the events, her jaw trembled with a repeating twitch, her wiry arms shivered, and the words started coming out slurred, as if hypothermia was consuming her all over again, even though we were sitting in a warm and dry Athenian loft, miles away from the Aegean Sea. And then I knew that my "aunt's" present-tense storytelling was many things, but pretentious was not.

# 19. Yara: Surmah

*Turkey, June 13, 2022*

From the back seat of the taxi, I turn my head to see if my father changed his mind if he runs to stop us from leaving like in the happy-ending movies, but I see only the cloud of dust raised from our car. We are speeding away, and I'll never see them again. To my left, the fire-gold hemline of the distant west is darkening rapidly.

"Look! Beautiful!" says Nahla.

"Yes, that's where we go."

*You are beautiful, little sister.*

Bulut, the heavy-set smuggler, one of the three who negotiated with my father, drives us from Antalya to Babacale. After half an hour of driving, we switch to a van with spray-painted windows and pleather seats. It is a long and bumpy night-ride, cruising through central Turkey for twelve hours, stopping only twice to pee and breathe fresh air. The van smells of hashish, and there is no air-conditioning. I wrapped the plastic bags with the passports and the money on my belly before we left. By morning, they are one with my skin, I fear that my sweating has destroyed the passports, but I don't dare to undress and check. Bulut insists that we keep our windows closed, so no one sees us, but his is a hand width open.

At noon Bulut says that "we are very close to the beach," and we stop at a shop to buy life-vests. It is a little bakkal, a kitsch, red-yellow tented hole-in-the-wall, selling the basics: cigarettes for the locals, beach balls for the tourists, life-vests for the refugees. My uncle buys us ice cream, and he steals a slurp from Nahla's. The white cream crests his thick mustache. I register this as my best memory of him.

There is a sign next to the doner-kebab turning-thingy, in English and Arabic: "phone-charging: ten-minutes/five liras."

"It is a bargain," Bulut says, pointing at the sign, "the Yunani will charge you ten euros when you cross the sea." Bulut shows us the good vests and the fake as if the bargain price was not a big red flag. "This one will not hold you above water. Not even her." He points at Nahla, who is licking her vanilla-flavored, kebab-scented, ice-cream cone. His English is okay. "It is seven miles," he continues.

"I thought it was five, my dad said so."

It is 4.1 miles, to be exact—I had watched a documentary with the same name a while ago. I remember crammed boats, the fear carved on the faces, CPR on naked babies, gleaming silver emergency thermal blankets.

"We are crossing by a different route, not the usual. They don't guard that one. You swimmer, your father said? If the boat capsizes—"

"Capsize? Why?" I ask.

"If it does and you are close to the coast, swim, don't stop, don't wait for the rescue boats, they are late. They say to stay in H.E.L.P. position, you know it?"

I shake my head in ignorance.

"Better that. Don't listen to them. Swim. You seem strong woman."

*I am not a woman. I am barely sixteen, and I must hold the hand of a seven-year-old. Swim?*

"You promised to my father that we'd be safe. You said nothing about boats capsizing," I say.

"Crazy now. It is crazy. A thousand cross every day now from the coast." He points somewhere west, but I can't see the water yet. "More try. Not enough boats. Some bloody disease from the East. Flu, cholera, the plague, they say. Bangladesh, Pakistan, they closed their borders. And when they do, everyone tries to get out. Those Yunani are useless, they have no boats to help people. They don't care to save you, Europe don't care. What do you think you'll find there?" he chuckles. "Have you ever been there? It's not what you dream."

"I…" *I was born at St. Mary's Hospital in Manchester.*

"Why don't you stay here?" Bulut continues. "You stay with me. Listen. If your father crosses, we find him then. Huh? Yes?"

I make the same silent negative gesture, smacking my lips.

"I say you stay," he repeats. "We are close to the beach now, last chance. I care, I take all the burden for you."

*The burden and our money.*

"Why will it capsize?" I ask.

"You cross on a rubber boat."

My uncle doesn't join in the conversation, he stares somewhere upward at a fixed point, as if he is smoking his shisha pipe back in Latakia, transfixed to another dimension. I have started wondering if there is something wrong with him. Occasionally, he turns and urges me to stop talking to Bulut and asks when we'll get there.

"A dinghy?" I ask.

"You know nothing of the sea, huh?" says Bulut. "Some of those dinghies are big rubber boats. RIBs. If they tell you to go on fish boat, a wooden one, don't. They are bigger but rotten and can't move a bit. The Coast Guard stops them. Don't go in the fish boat, you listen?"

I nod.

"It is trick to take money twice from you, to bring you back. You have money with you, huh? A rubber boat only. RIB. They put thirty people there and children, they're made for fifteen. You hold tight, sit in the middle, keep your mouth shut no matter what you hear and see, cover your head, bring it to your knees and pray. You have a Book? Here, take mine." It is a two-inch book with black and gold ornaments. "They go fast those RIBs, if it is a calm night, you'll cross before you know it. Do not get up. If it capsizes, well. Stay here with me, Yara."

"I have my period, Bulut. You have to stop at a pharmacy."

"*Eczane.* Yes, we stop. I'll get it for you," he says. "We find."

Bulut checks his phone, and then we drive for ten minutes before he stops the van again. He returns with tampons and a pair of grey slacks.

"Put these on, take off the dress."

*In case I fall in the water.*
"I want pants too, Yara." says Nahla.
"Don't worry, sis. I am here for you."

Bulut parks in front of a deserted warehouse, and he orders us to get out quickly. The building is out of place, nothing around it but dirt, bushes, and a small sand dune to the west. The damp wind climbs the dune and brings us the scent and the roar of the sea. We run to the top of the dune—I am holding Nahla's hand—a few more steps, and I see her vast dark blue; see her whitecaps.

"Little sheep," says Nahla, pointing to the white cresting the blue, and her words send shivers down my arms.

Bulut and my uncle are waving to us to come back down, to keep quiet. Three more men have come out of the small warehouse entrance and stand next to them. Bulut begs me for the last time to join him, but I refuse. With sunken spirit and brooding eyes, he delivers us to the next set of smugglers. They are nothing like the folks who brought us all the way from Latakia here; these men wear vests with many pockets, the ones that hide guns, knives, and bullets. They seem to be in a hurry; they remind me of herders guiding animals. Nahla squeezes my hand with all her strength to agree with me silently.

"Run, you two. In there," they shout, but when they see uncle Hassan embracing us, they turn quiet. I turn to search for Bulut—could I still stay with him? He is gone, not looking back. The smugglers are holding large sticks and use them to push us inside the high-ceiling warehouse. It is a decrepit chicken farm or something that had to do with animals not long ago; it reeks of chickenshit and chicken guts. There is only one thing in the world that smells worse than a chicken farm, and that's an abandoned chicken farm on a hot summer afternoon in Turkey.

I don't know it yet, but I will never have chicken fatteh again. I'll try on two different occasions, years later, only to puke and cry the name of my sister.

We walk among the others already waiting there to cross the sea; I count maybe a hundred and twenty refugees, I guess at least six different nationalities. Afghanis, Syrians, Moroccans, Burmese, Bangladeshi, Cape

Verde, we don't look the same, no matter if they put us all in the same boat. We find a corner with Nahla and uncle away from the stench. The right side is an open toilet; men and even some women come and go urinating and defecating there.

"We've been here three days," says a man to my uncle. He is Syrian, his family has crossed already, or so he hopes. "I can't breathe anymore," he says.

It's over forty Celsius in the warehouse; the heat brings tears to my eyes. I smell the vomit; I hear the retch, but other than that, the crowd remains quiet, even the babies. The smugglers and their sticks make sure that the mothers keep them quiet.

A few years back in Manchester, I used to be a pool girl, a volunteer during the Olympic swimming team qualifiers. I remember all those young women, coming out of the dressing rooms, staring at the water. The tension in their eyes as they were heading to the starting blocks; you could cut it with a knife. But these faces here in the chicken farm are overwrought; the term "life-and-death" finds its true meaning in their eyes.

One of the smugglers goes from family to family and talks fast, pointing fingers and giving orders. Eventually, he reaches us. He argues with uncle Hassan that we didn't pay the full amount, we should at least give him whatever Turkish liras we have, they won't be good where we go. They speak in Arabic, and uncle Hassan objects and bargains. Five minutes later, he gives him whatever change from the bakkal he has in his shoe. In exchange, we get a bottle of water and a stale simit. It tastes like the rotting-wooden leg of a chair, but Nahla devours it. She is a gift from the heavens, for I have a reason to keep looking into her eyes and nowhere else, to make her feel safe, to hide from her the images of the filth and the men around us, to remind her that everything will be fine.

"It ends tonight," I say as I hug her frail frame. I don't lie, it is the last night. I feel her ribcage against mine. I curse my father that he never let her take swimming lessons.

My uncle Hassan has remained peculiarly silent, darting his eyes from the smugglers back to me, grunting from time to time.

I was stupid to think earlier in the van that I'd find a toilet, and now I must insert the tampon in plain view. I have a hunch, and I ask him in English.

"Do you mind letting go of my hand so I can change?"

He doesn't reply.

"Or I'll slap you in the face, you, ugly oaf."

Again, he doesn't reply.

How could I be so stupid? I assumed everyone in my family spoke some English, but my uncle doesn't. It is now that I realize what is going on. Uncle Hassan is not my guardian; I am his. Oh, father!

I repeat my request to him in Arabic, and now he understands but fumes with anger. I put the tampon in place, hiding between him and my sister. Hassan is stirring embarrassed, keeps waving silently to those taking glances to turn their eyes away from me.

There is one man who doesn't obey, he is watching us for some time now, not me, his eyes fixed on little Nahla. He was the first of the crowd who caught my attention. Nahla pointed at him as we were walking among them when we first came inside.

She said: "Look, Yara, a clown."

He is no clown, not in a funny way, but he wears eyeliner. It is not eyeliner. My friend Sunita back in Manchester had told me about it, they call it something else in India, in Afghanistan. *Surmah*. Yes, surmah. Coal-dark soot painted all around his sockets. It brings out the wolf-yellow of his eyes. He wears a black beret and a worn-out military jacket, but he looks more like an actor than a soldier. There is a fixed polite grin on his face—it could be madness—broad lines across his brow, and his beard is dark as coal except on where it meets his skin, it becomes a soft brown-red. His upper lip hides under his brown mustache. I haven't seen his teeth, and I don't want to; I keep picturing him opening his mouth to reveal the fangs of a vampire, the cloven tongue of the asp.

# 20. Lucia: Syngrou Avenue

*Athens, June 16, 2022*

Lucia had followed the suspect on foot. He waited at the pedestrian crossway, and she guessed he was heading for the neon lights entrance of the "Angels at Athens" strip joint. If he got in, all was lost. She raced him, crossing the busy avenue about fifty yards before the red light, hoping that he wouldn't look north. He had to wait—limping leg and all—for both lights to cross each of the three-lane sides of the avenue. When he finally made it across, Lucia was already there, leaning on the metal bar that separated pavement from asphalt.

Her gaze rose high in an effort to look careless and bored, like she had not noticed him. The glimmering sky of her homeland unnerved her for a moment; she stared, unable to fathom what she was getting herself into. Deep inside, it was the same trip as doing hard drugs, base jumping, or other crazy stuff that only an unpopular, unloved twenty-year-old would dare. She had no cigarettes, never did, so she opted for gum, chewing it hard and fast, pretending to be someone who used to be very active with her mouth always. Lucia had thrown away the top of her suit and even managed to rip out most of her jumpsuit pants on time to show some flesh. The black lace-up ankle boots would do just fine, and her make-up was professional but of the wrong profession. There was no lipstick on her small backpack, but where was that Chapstick? Anything to look cheap and eager. She looked more like an adult version of a potato head doll, a sorry assembly of a hooker, a business-woman, an angry teenager, and what else, a basketball player? *Lose that ponytail fast,* she said to herself and let her long hair fall down her shoulders. She waved them under the streetlamp, hoping he'd notice.

Lucia was gazing away from him, not to signal that she was targeting him. When her eye got a glimpse of his limping figure, it was too late; he was already moving away too fast. Maybe she was due for a miracle because just at that moment, he turned his head and fixed his stare at her. Was it her height, her reddish brunette hair that had caught his eye? Showtime.

"Don't go in there, tough guy," she said, mouth full of chewing gum, striding toward him. "Fifty, suck, fuck, anything you want. I have room across the street."

She burst a bubble and followed with a quick full-lip kiss from a distance. The man tried to touch her, but she stopped him.

"Pay first. This is fast-food, not a restaurant," she said.

"No. Pay later," he said, and from his accent, she guessed Albanian.

"Whatever. Follow me," she said.

She was not in for the money anyway. The man—by now, she was already tired of thinking him as "the man," and she had named him Al, Aleksander if Georgian, Almir if Albanian—darted his gaze between her and the picture of a Jenna look-alike attached outside the club. The girl on the poster looked way more promising and experienced, but Lucia was live in the flesh.

Lucia went for broke, pulled her sleeveless t-shirt on the side, and touched her nipple with her two fingers in front of the man. For a moment, she wished she had painted her nails red, black, or something, but then again, she had not painted her nails since her early teens.

"I am right here, baby. She is just a poster," she said.

Al gaped at her, forgetting the paper angel.

As they crossed the street, she frantically searched for a hotel by the hour on her phone and reserved a room only a couple of hundred yards away. This was Syngrou Avenue, across from the historic district, and such establishments were abundant. Mr. Syngros was a 19th-century banker and philanthropist who had achieved obscure immortality, as the red-light district of modern days carried his name. If only the poor—okay, super rich—man who died childless could imagine how many unwanted children would be born under his name, he would have been so proud. Or ashamed.

Lucia knew there was no escape when they entered the room and faced the avalanche of pink sheets and red pillows, drapes and dimmed lights suggesting a bloodbath rather than a passionate night. That tawdry lustre of cheap luxury over everything turned her stomach around, and Al unzipping his jeans with a grin wasn't making it any better. She had no plan yet, and time was running out, as she was pushed down on her knees already. Whether it was her mother's upbringing or her sharp memory, she remembered that there was no word for "foreplay" in Albanian. Al had placed his hands on his waist, like a football midfielder waiting to take a free shot at the goal once the referee set the man-wall, staring down at the brunette-hair girl.

"Ela, ela. Tora!" shouted the stocky man, anxious for his missile to make contact with the target landing. "Come on, come on. Now!" He looked like a sorry excuse of a statue, chiseled down to a single neckless slab of concrete by a lazy first-year sculpture student at a communist university.

"A jeni shqiptar?" asked Lucia, but the man just grunted and pushed her head closer to her fifty-euro trophy. An inch or two at best. Maybe closer, but this is not that kind of story, so we'll never know. Fact is, Lucia never told anyone how close.

She was certain that Al was Albanian from his accent; if he were Georgian, that would be a bigger problem. Not that she knew much about Georgians, but there was a reason nobody wanted to know much about them; ruthless, military-trained, packing a knife in addition to a gun. Not to mention that she didn't speak any of the Georgian dialects.

Albanian, she hoped. From his built, she guessed that he was some retired weightlifting champion. Her Muay Thai Khao Tat kick would not do much damage to him. Maybe a dozen kicks, but she wouldn't get that chance. Lucia had to know if his hands were close to a knife, but she also had to take care of business before the customer was out the door. *The hell with it, it's all for a good cause,* she thought.

"Kapota," she said and pulled the condom out of her purse, showing it to the man.

"No kapota," said the man.

"Herpes," she pointed to her lips that had no sign of herpes, but the word was too international and too ominous to be ignored, almost onomatopoeia for the wacky twin brother of an Olympian God attending a gay pride parade. Short skirt, feathered sandals, bleached blonde, the works.

That condom was waiting patiently there for a couple of years, just in case, and the case had finally appeared. Being a geek, Lucia wondered if these things had an expiration date. She took her time to unroll the rubber on—she was touching that other unnamed thing, this was real—and she caressed his legs with one hand, looking for that knife. Nothing. She tried to pull his jeans further down, below his knees, but he stopped her. When her hand escaped and reached below his left knee, Lucia touched his prosthetic leg. The man pulled back, almost embarrassed, and instinctively for that split second, she was embarrassed as well because she had offended a disabled man.

"Leave, bitch," the man said and pushed her away. He bent to pull his pants back up, and Lucia sensed that the game was almost over. She quickly covered the two yards between them, brought her lips next to his ear, her left hand touching his cock that was silently watching all this, hoping its time would eventually come. The poor little guy was erect and on high alert, sharing the same iridescent pink color with the drapes, the bedside tables, the sheets, and the lighting.

Time to switch to English, Lucia thought.

"Come on, baby!" Lucia made her best imitation of a raspy voice. "You are not a peacock at the Royal Garden, but you are my baby piggy at the Royal Hotel."

The man didn't understand shit, but that was not the point. She had gone with her sexiest Hollywood accent, surprising him, drilling on his thick skull another cavity of opportunity, the fantasy that he could ejaculate inside a foreign trophy, a brave new world of male conquest. Al was lured in again.

The kisses right below the sandpaper-hard stubble of his neck were effective, and Al pushed her down to her knees. As Lucia knelt once more, his pink thing jerked up for a moment and then succumbed to the weight and the poor circulation of the smoker host. She could smell the dead cigarettes on his clothes.

Lucia traveled his inner thigh with her unpainted nails hoping that the sensation would loosen his tension and lessen his strength.

*This is your last chance, girl,* Lucia whispered inside her, "For Queen and Country!"

She then put all her weight in a deadlift move, thrusting herself upward and pulling the jeans of the man toward her. Despite her strength and determination, Al didn't fall, but his atrophied left leg lost the ground for a second. As she came face to face with the stunned man, she pushed with both hands on his chest, opting for brute force vs. her fancy kickboxing training. Al hit the floor hard; he was dazed only for a second but incapacitated between the pulled-down pants that locked his legs and the prosthetic. Lucia had the few seconds she needed. She jumped over him, avoiding his move to trip her, and ran for the coat hanger before he got up. Searching his cheap leather jacket, she found his other gun, the real one.

It was small, black mate and the best friend she could hope for. Al was on his knees, the roles had changed, and he would not get up.

"Don't move. Not if you want to live. A Glock 43," she announced, knowing that the instant recognition would legitimize her as a threat to him. 'Thank you, Al! That's one of the few I know how to use," she said. She ignored all the "you bitch, I'll kill you," and all the expected blabber coming fast and furious out of Al's mouth.

"No, no, no, my friend," she said. "Lie down, hands high and away from your head. Be careful now. I am scared shitless, you see, and if I know my guns, this thing doesn't have a safety. Be careful now, it can go off any moment, and I am aiming for your good knee. Or is that your chest? Hell, I am not much of a shooter."

"Take the fifty and run," he said.

"The fifty? Oh, the fifty. Forget that. You got a freebie. Now, talk to me about that boy you kidnapped, and I'll give *you* a fifty."

Al's brow furrowed as he looked out the window, around the room, back at her. If he could travel back in time, he would have opted for the Angels strip joint—that was a certainty now—one should always go for official establishments with ISO quality certificates. It took him a few moments to utter a word. "You fucked with the wrong people, little girl. They'll skin you alive," he grunted.

Lucia went quickly through his wallet, a bunch of fake IDs, and a prepaid card, yet one of them had an Albanian name.

"A compatriot! I knew it," she said in Albanian. "I'll call you Al, no matter what's your name."

"You, stupid girl, will—"

Lucia stopped him, pointing the gun closer to his thing and her index finger to her lips. She had lost patience with all the expected, third-rate TV show dialog exchange.

"Now, now, I have no time for clichés. I'll speak to your mother tongue, we may be from the same village for all we know. So, shut up and listen to me carefully. I am Sindi, from the Albanian Interpol branch."

That brought a chuckle on the man's face; she hadn't sold it well at all.

In reality, Lucia didn't even know if Interpol had a chapter in that country. She was half-Albanian from her mother's side, had spent just one sorry weekend of her life in the motherland's capital, and had learned the language more casually and verbally, rather than formally. But she hoped the Interpol cover would do its magic. She continued:

"Okay, I am no Interpol, but I am the one with the gun. Now, the one thing you got right was what you said about fucking with the wrong people. You kidnapped a boy two days ago."

She paused for a reaction, but Al was looking toward the faint night light coming in from the single window. Lucia glanced at her smartwatch; it was 4 a.m. already. There was no time.

"Don't. Don't waste my time, Al, with your grunts, you just listen. We know you kidnapped the boy. Well, not you alone. That guy, Babis, who does elevator maintenance, was with you too."

She paused again, and Al's peered at her, almost impressed.

"But you are not the big guys, right?" she continued. "None of you two is the boss. See now how this is gonna play. The father of the boy is crazy-rich, and you think you hit it big, but he is also a bit off the rails if you know what I mean. Papalias, you know him. He got XSI, ex-Mossad, here in a day. You know Mossad, Al? May I call you Al? And Papalias is not looking for arrests, etc., his directions are straightforward, and you can guess them. So, here is what happens. You are dead already, you and your friends. You died when XSI landed here. I landed five hours ago, and I already caught you with your pants down." Her gun pointed toward his depressing limp thing. "Mossad may have found all the others already. So here is the deal. You tell me where the boy is, and you take the easy way out. You cooperate. At XSI, we have a simple rule. First man to talk, lives. Others, ah, not so lucky. But time is against you. If Babis talks first…"

"If I tell you one word, they kill us both. You die bad," Al said.

"Yes, yes, I am sure you are scared of your mysterious boss, maybe he has a scar or a beard, even a hook, and seems like some really bad-ass to you but try to forget him. He is an angry Albanian goatherder, and I am talking ex-Mossad here. Scale tips. The world is full of bad motherfuckers, most of whom you haven't met. For the last time, here is the deal. You give me the hideaway now, I send my men, I let you go. Free!"

Al made a sudden move to grab her ankle, but Lucia jumped back.

"You have one minute, Al."

One minute later, Al had not said a word.

The sound of a passerby police car approached and faded away out the window, and Lucia let the man think about that.

Lucia pointed the gun at his waist; she knew that the embarrassment of the nakedness would get to him eventually. Al would give up anything only to pull his pants up again. She added some compassion to her argument.

"I know you don't want to hurt any kid. You have been hurt yourself, you know pain." As she kept smooth-talking him, Lucia had taken one of the pillows and put it over his ankle, pressing the Glock's muzzle against it. She turned on the TV and the volume, and that brought some fear to his eyes. "So, I know you want to do the right thing here, just don't move now, this thing may go off and no more good ankle, what do they give you fifty K? They asked Papalias for twelve mil ransom, you know."

Al mumbled a curse that she had heard from her cousins from her mother's side quite a few times. That had worked too. Baby steps.

"So, Al, you see, you are the stupid here so far. They took advantage of you. But you can be the smart one by morning. Last chance. The kid. Location. I promise you are free."

Maybe that was what finally did it. The fact that Lucia said, "I promise," in his mother tongue, as if she meant it, and that was because she did. There was no way she could kill him; she had never even shot a living being in her life.

Al turned serious, like a boy apologizing to his mother.

"Give me your cell phone; I'll give you a pin," he said.

"Turn! On your belly," Lucia said and gave him the phone.

Al opened Maps and tapped with his fat index finger a few times.

"I am watching what you're doing, no funny shit, Al," Lucia said.

She got the phone back and called the number, talking clearly and making sure that Al heard her.

"Elon, I have a pin, sending it over to you. Koropi village, close to the airport, an abandoned plastics warehouse, it seems. Move your men. I have the guy here. They might suspect he is missing." A pause. "No, no, trust me, this is legit. I'll get you the bosses' names. Move now!" Silence for a few seconds and she continued: "Royal Hotel, Syngrou. Doesn't matter where I am. I am fine. Go for the boy. Call me when done. Godspeed. He says they are—" she paused, "How many of them you said, *Al?*"

She pointed the gun to him, and her eyes begged him to hurry up with an answer.

"Al, they are coming here, after they get the boy, give me names, last chance."

Al talked some more.

"Four of them, he says, not heavily armed. I am waiting for your news, Elon. Go XSI!"

Lucia shut the phone and turned to Al.

"So, now we wait, pal. Face down, and you shut up unless you want to give me names. You heard how I protected you. Names and you are free."

It became silent for a while after that, and the silence worried Lucia. She had not slept for two nights straight, and she was afraid of collapsing at the spot if she didn't keep the conversation going. The last time she had eaten anything was on the British Airways flight two nights ago. She opened her backpack and popped an energy drink bottle, fearing that it was half of a good idea.

"These things are crazy-caffeine, Al. Like a whole cold coffee pot rushing down your veins. Never drink them holding a gun."

She had to break that man, but her only experience was the Introduction to Psychology for Criminologists course at the University of Portsmouth. She had also taken a course on Wildlife crime: Threats and Responses, and Al looking like a wounded bear was closer to that subject. She needed more experience, but that would take years, and she only had minutes. Lucia saw her phone flashing with a text, but it was not Elon. No matter how good those ex-Mossad guys were, they couldn't be that fast.

It was her father, Mazur senior.

"Can't talk now," she auto-texted.

He called, ignoring her text.

"Later, dad. Working."

"That late? It is almost 3 a.m."

*Why are you texting me then?*

She thought of sending him a picture to prove that she had a watch, but that would reveal that she was in Athens time, closer to 5 a.m.

"Exams! All-nighter. Love you," she texted back.

The night was almost ending, and her time with Al would end with it. It was a lot to swallow for two nights' work, and she was glad that she didn't have to swallow anything else as she was watching Al lying down on the stained beige carpet of the Royal Hotel. At about 5 a.m., the time when the fisherman's harbor comes to sight, and the farmer packs his bread and feta for the long day, and the birds are chirping the new morning, next to the Athenian garbage trucks making their rounds, Elon finally called with good news.

"We have the boy," he said. "And the police arrested the men."

# 21. Tina: The Pakis Desecrate the Parthenon?

*Athens, June 14, 2022*

There he was, Pericles Aggelou, the love of her life, the man to have and to hold, the father of her child, the joint beneficiary of all her bank accounts. Rheumy eyes, messy thick hair, and cheeks puffy and pink as strawberry-vanilla donuts. Right eye barely open, the left definitely closed. He was sitting on the bed half-asleep, like a mummified ancient god who had just woken up for the first time in eons, trying to decide whether this century was worthy of his reincarnation. His hand reached to the bed-stand and grabbed the smartphone, the one organ of his to always wake up first. He squinted at the screen and fell back on the pillows, heavy as a bloated stock market index on a gloomy November afternoon.

"What on earth are you doing, Peri? You have to drive Demetri to school today," Tina shouted, trying to dry her hair with the towel at the same time. "Hey, have you seen my passport? I can't find it."

Peri collapsed on the pillows without replying, and Tina walked to him and shook him repeatedly.

"Please, Peri, not today. I have an 8:30 flight, I'm late, must leave now. You promised."

"Flight? What?" he mumbled.

He seemed, or pretended to, not remember anything.

"Geneva, today, it is the WHO conference. Listen to me. You dress little Demetri, make sure he gets his gym clothes and his snack bar. No, two snack bars, he gets hungry after football. Alexandra will pick him up for a playdate, and he'll bring him around six. You got all that, okay? Oh, and give him fifteen for the charity bazaar. The teachers push them to outbid the other classes. God, I hate when they do that. You remember all that? The plumber is due to come by at ten. Make sure you are back by then. He needs to replace the—"

Peri shook his head back and forth while texting, not even looking at Tina.

"No can do, today, hon. I have the meeting, can't drive the kid. Calling a cab."

"We're not putting a five-year-old on a random cab alone."

"He is almost six. Cab is my regular, not a stranger. No problem," Peri said, walking away from her.

"I guess you're not preparing his lunch bag either?" Tina asked, but the bathroom door was open, and Peri was pissing and couldn't hear her.

She spent the next half hour dressing Demetri, preparing lunch for him, and searching for her passport. She rushed frantically out the door, wearing a dull gray suit suitable for a health summit in Geneva, and jumped into one of the two cabs waiting there.

"Are you my cab?" she asked to make sure. "Please, step on it. I can't miss the flight. Fast!"

"You know what my grandmother says, my madam?" replied the taxi driver, skipping the "good morning." "The bitch is in a hurry, she births blind puppies."

It was one of those mornings when the first word a stranger greeted her with was "bitch," and it would go downhill from there. Her screen flashed with a text message.

"We regret to inform you that flight A3854 to Geneva is delayed. New estimated departure—"

"Oh, no. Too late, too late," she mumbled, and the taxi driver felt like he should interject.

"I can't go faster, madam."

Tina ignored him, already calling her mother. The family house that Tina had grown up in was only two blocks away.

"Mommy, it's me, that coffee I promised, can we do it in the taxi instead."
A pause. "No, there is no coffee in the taxi, but we can still talk. Sorry. I need
to talk to you." A pause. "Yes, you can bring your coffee."

Her parents' house was a minimalist architectural marvel of the seventies
acquired in an auction of estates repossessed by the government where her
father happened to be the only bidder—a bargain. The sharp lines of the ashen
structure cut the horizon with a brutality that reminded her how this family
had fallen apart: their divorce, her decision to stop talking to her father.

"Stop, next to this lady, we need to pick her up," Tina said to the driver.

Tina's mom was slow to open the door and get in the taxi. She looked like
someone who had run out of her bedroom, oblivious to the benefits of
makeup and a brush, yet Tina could see more. Lisa hadn't been to a hairdresser for months, and for Greek suburbia standards, she was dressed worse
than a homeless lady.

"What is the rush, Tina?" said Lisa. "You are going to age very fast if you
are always in such a hurry."

Her mom was channeling the taxi driver, slightly more polite.

"Mom, I can't take this anymore. Peri has just shut down on me, can't get
him to do anything. He is still in bed sleeping. Had to send the kid by taxi to
school. Can you please go there in the evening to check on your grandson? I'll
be in Geneva tonight, there is an important conference I have to attend."

"And you represent your country, huh. Maybe you can stay back, it is not
like you will save the world."

"I won't save it, but I can seriously fuck it if I don't do my job."

The taxi driver's gaze met her through his rear-view mirror, "fuck" been
the only word that he could follow from this exchange.

"Don't talk like this, Tina. I know your work is important to you. I am so
proud of you," said Lisa.

"Well, I am not, mom. I can't even put my house in order."

"Tina, you know how I feel about you repeating my mistake and marrying
a Greek man, but you have to cut Peri some slack. It is a terrible time for
everyone here. You see this crisis, never ends, this kind of situation makes men
weak. I was reading the Journal of Integrative Medicine—"

"Please stop, mom. Not the mindfulness thing again."

"It is true, my dear. Every disease, ailment, it is the side effect of stress."

"No, it's not. There are viruses, bacteria, rat fleas, and dirty water. Please, mom, you went to college."

Her mom had turned her understanding of psychological effects on health into a religion, forcing her brain to fight everything around her with calmness, Zen, fluoxetine, a couple of gin tonics, and a belief that mind conquers over body.

"They said that the percentage of men that suffer from anxiety-related syndromes, deteriorating to heavy depression, is just out of control."

"Mom, please. Don't defend him."

"You don't have to pretend you are that strong, Tina. Maybe he should see a doctor. Get some Prozac. Depression. Melancholia, it is a Greek word."

"Melancholia is something else, mom. The word for depression is *katathlipsis* in Greek."

The taxi driver felt he should interfere once again, proud that he had figured out the words Prozac and katathlipsis. The traffic in front of them had stripped him of other productive options.

"Listen to your mom, young lady," he started lecturing the "young lady" in Greek. "Everyone suffers from depression in this shithole. Don't you see what's happening? They are after us,"

"Who is?" replied Tina instinctively before she had time to regret it.

"All of them. Those Europeans, the Freemasons, the Jews. They all conspire in Brussels."

"You just ran the stop sign," Tina replied, without luck of shutting him up.

"It is a global conspiracy, I tell you."

Both continued talking past one another.

"That kid was about to cross the street. Did you see her?" asked Tina, leaning forward to make him listen.

"Everyone is out to get us. They want to snatch away the oil fields in the Aegean. And this city, everyone packed like ants without a job, man eats man, what do you expect? All my friends are on sedatives, they have burned a fuse or two up here, I say."

"Earthquakes," Tina said.

"What?" asked the taxi driver eyeing her again through the rear-view mirror.

"There is no oil in the Aegean, sir. And no one wants our oil. Even if there were any, there are so many earthquakes, a bubbling volcano, no one in his right mind would drill there. It is an active mountain formation region."

"The Germans—" he started.

"—couldn't care less about you and me," Tina finished his sentence.

The taxi driver's fingers played on the radio "seek" button, and he shut his mouth. Men talk to feel smart, to impress, to compensate for the lack of the feathers of a rooster or a peacock. The moment they sense that the female is out of their league, they switch to Supersport FM.

"You should take some time off work, Tina. You are just a consultant to a broken Ministry, it is not that stressful a job. Take it easy."

"We have a global health crisis, mom. I should have made it to Geneva last night, but the Ministry doesn't have any hotel budget. And my flight is late. Take it easy?"

"Don't worry. I'll go tonight to your house and stay with Demetri, but I'll leave in the morning. You see, I am moving out tomorrow."

"You are? Seriously? Already? That son of the bitch!"

"Please, don't speak like that, after all, he is your—"

"Yeah, my father. He is a derelict piece of crap,"

Tina continued ranting. "Oh shit, there goes the makeup," she said, unable to control the watering of her eyes.

The taxi driver kept talking, bringing her back to reality.

"Look at the stop signs, the graffiti on the walls, madam. I am telling you, ladies, this country is done. Over and out. Only a dictatorship would fix this now. Hang three guys at the square, save a million lives."

"Please, sir, it is too early in the morning," Tina said.

What made her mad was that the taxi driver was right. Not about the hangings, but this was surely a failed state, the one where her husband had no job, her son was growing up into, and the only one getting some was her father. The stop signs were spray-painted with "G7" and "G13" the entrance gates of football hooligans, others with As for anarchy or whatever other gibberish.

"Did you see that statue back in the square we passed? That's ancient, you know," the taxi driver said.

*No, it isn't.* Tina thought. She had been to the inauguration; the Mayor was a friend of Peri.

"I am telling you, two more years like this, and they'll spray-paint the Parthenon. Punks! It is the Paki illegals who do that, you know. They rob the churches."

"The Pakistanis desecrate the Parthenon? Is that so? Have you seen them?" Tina mocked him while her mother was putting her index finger on her lips, begging her to stop talking to him.

Lisa interjected, trying to change the subject.

"You get Peri to see a doctor, dear. Depression is a serious condition. I shouldn't be telling you this, you are a doctor."

Depression. Tina had been angry with Peri, refusing to accept the obvious. Depression was not a virus labeled based on its hemagglutinin and neuraminidase proteins. It was not visible through a microscope, and one could not vaccinate against it. At her younger age, she would scoff at such a Lisa Walker diagnosis. Even now, Tina would prefer to think of Peri as inconsiderate, selfish, lazy, even a loser, but she didn't want to accept depression. But her mom was right; even the taxi driver was right. Not about the poor Pakistanis, but for Peri for sure.

Her phone flashed with a message again.

Anna: *Dr. Walker, please note that Dr. Vardis will lead the Greek delegation at Geneva. He is flying there later today.*

Alexi was joining her in Geneva, and Tina doubted that he was very keen to learn about the pandemic. Worse, Anna, who was both the Minister's executive assistant and Alexi's wife, was informing her. She clenched her jaw and held her mom's hand tight, pushing time thirty years back.

"I'll call you tonight from Geneva, mom," said Tina as she was exiting the cab. "Please be there for Demetri. And Peri."

# 22. Ella: My Great Grandma, Lisa Walker

It was the May of 1999 when her parents announced to Tina that they had decided to return to her father's homeland, Greece.

Tina remembers listening to them and replying, "oh, ok, but I need a new swimsuit, guys," thinking for days that they'd simply go to Greece earlier than usual for the summer vacation. What else was there? Was the country even inhabited in winter?

It took Tina some time to adjust, a good two years of doubting her parents' sanity for moving her to a foreign country at age fourteen. It was a lot longer for my great-grandma Lisa.

Her mother Lisa, was the one who sacrificed herself for family, as she never adapted to the local culture, though she also never relocated to the States, no matter how many years passed. She made a formal but lackluster effort to learn the language and the grammar, but the pronunciation was beyond her. "Once I tried to pronounce five Greek vegetables in one sentence, but my tongue turned into a French braid. It took a long and painful operation to untangle it," she'd joke. Lisa settled for pointing at stuff for the grocery man and located the one ex-pat supermarket that carried Ben & Jerry's and Aunt Jemima syrup, though as a constantly dieting, newborn-vegetarian and no-gluten mom, she had no use for them other than to reminisce about Sunday mornings at grandma's kitchen in Wellesley, Mass.

The social imbibement had not proved much smoother. Her unwillingness to learn the language hadn't helped, but there were other cultural forces at work. Friendliness-for-foreigners, in local-speak "filoxenia" was a trait Greeks were proud of, but the proof of that was inconsistent, a bunch of fs, at best. The locals expressed exuberant warm hospitality for those they chose to befriend but monumental rudeness for the rest of the common citizens. For an American girl always playing by the rules, navigating that proved as hard as a mainland goatherder sailing the Aegean through the August winds.

For Elizabeth (Lisa) Walker-Damianou, even her own name changed with every person she met in Greece.

In the States, she was always known as plain vanilla Lisa, and the problems started right there with her first name. For "lisa" in Greek is the actual word for rabies, literally synonymous with a yellow-eyed hound foaming from the mouth, metaphorically referring also to a bitch-in-heat, clearly not a very flattering name for woman or animal. The locals would always call her Leeza, pretending that they didn't hear right, which was a different name altogether to her. Her husband, Yannis, had always opted for Liesel, for reasons unknown to her—was that his elementary knowledge of German, or the first backpacking pigtail chick who took his virginity back when he was a camping teenager at the island of Corfu? Anyway, she found Liesel a name more suitable for the mistress of a Luftwaffe General. "Elizabeth" was unheard of in such a tiny, rebellious, socialist-at-heart, yet consumerist-in-mind country, unless one claimed to be the Queen herself. Eliza, Liza, Betty, she had tried everything, changing names like dresses every season.

Her surname problems were equally severe. It all started when she took her husband's name, Damianos, but not exactly. The female version of the name was Damianou, and with horror, she realized one afternoon at the grammar class for adults that this was the genitive case of the original name. In plain English or Greek, she was not a Damianos but the property of Mr. Damianos. Moreover, this was not a choice; it was bad taste to keep a male surname, almost as inappropriate as naming herself Sophocles or Jerome. Soon that became less of a problem as the socialists came to power, and by law, all women had to keep their maiden name, which for Greek women was the genitive case as well, so she never understood what the point was. Thus, she became a Damianou-Walker. The final nail to the coffin of switching names came after Tina left for college, and Lisa became Walker, period, ending the sentence as her marriage ended. For Yannis in his early fifties started making tons of money, mostly tax-free, as the General Secretary of Transportation and Telecoms of the succeeding far-right-wing government, a low-paying, in-theory, public servant position. Tina's daddy traded the family Volvo for a screaming-red Alfa Romeo, which Lisa now found ridiculous and unfit for him. Her disapproval meant nothing, for a month later, he decided to trade in Lisa herself for that marketing assistant.

Lisa was stunning in her younger years, the epitome of the Hollywood-fragile American beauty, rather skinny than fit, with sunflower blonde hair and gray-blue eyes that Tina didn't inherit. A face hinting of Farah Faucet or Michelle Pfeifer at their beauty prime. Yet she carried the curse of all Anglo-Saxon beauty—in her late forties, her skin had lost all the fat, warmth, and patience, in brief, all ingredients that kept it firm—and she rapidly turned into a vegetarian bleached golden Sultana raisin viciously desiccating under the Athenian sun.

Her father had aged much better, at least until he decided to leave. Tina never thought of him as old until she saw him once in his brand-new Alfa Romeo with his brand-new girlfriend. Comical and sad, that image invaded her body as if a shaved-head pagan hierophant had ripped out her childhood and her bleeding pumping heart.

But that was all in the past, the vacations and the family dinners all three shared, the Christmas presents, the open-air summer movie-theaters surrounded by bougainvillea flowers and tiger mosquitos.

# 23. Yara: On the Boat to Lesbos

*The Aegean Sea, June 13, 2022*

Deep in the starry night, they herd us out of the livestock warehouse. I smell the open air again, the brine, and the tamarisk. The joy of being away from the chicken shit, the terror of the vast blue roaring in front of us, those feelings I add later to my story. I have no time to worry about anything other than the sensory, certainly no time for feelings. I smell, I hear, I hold Nahla tight, I struggle to see.

They separate us into a group with the young men, away from most families and babies—I don't know why; maybe it is my slacks. We wait for another couple of hours, sitting silently on the sand, watching the stars come alive.

About halfway through our wait, I get up and walk to the sea to meet her, greet her. I squat right where the backwash leaks the cold sand and splash water on my face with my left hand, the right still touching Nahla's fingertips, always keeping her close. The mistral picked up, and my little sister is trembling, wearing only a long sleeve pink cotton shirt under her orange vest.

Back at the Olympic pool in Manchester, I'd always kneel and splash water on my body before I climbed on the block. It is a habit of mine to meet the first water on my terms, sooner rather than later. It gives me a jolt and makes me fearless. But I am not fearless, not tonight.

This is not some practice or even a race, and I fear that no matter what those smugglers promised back in Antalya, I'll be battling Homer's wine-dark sea before the sun rises again. The belly of the sea is growling; the murmur turns to words:

"Come inside, girls. I am waiting for you."

A dinghy approaches the beach, and the smugglers signal to the group with the families to board it. They push the first ones into the water. The families stay together, walking like six or eight-legged sloths, taking small steps, praying, holding, and encouraging each other. The water is up to the waist of the women, the mouth of the children. They don't shout or cry; the smugglers make sure of that.

The flashlights dance around, and one of them falls on the man with eyes of soot, standing alone a few feet away from us and staring at the dark sea. He has no family, no brothers or comrades. The smuggler orders him to embark on the second boat, but the man in soot whispers to him, takes something out of his camouflage jacket, and passes it to the smuggler—money, magic, a human finger bone, I can't see. He points to my sister. I am trying to tell my uncle.

*Uncle, that man is staring at Nahla. Since we came here. He is no good. I don't think he is man but evil, his eyes flare. I think he is a djinn, one of those who live and prowl around the desert dunes.* My thoughts run faster than my tongue. I just manage a couple of words. "Uncle, look." He holds my hand, and I can feel the tremble of his knees—is it the vastness of the sea or has he seen the djinn too—and I abandon the effort. They don't take the man in soot on the second boat; he stays behind with us.

Two rubber boats have left, and we are now waiting for the last one to come ashore, but I think they messed up. They are too many of us left behind, more than thirty. Will the boat hold?

My shoes sink in as I walk toward the forty-footer. The water is not ice-cold but not welcoming either. It is June, and this is not the North Ocean or the Atlantic; this is the sunny Aegean. Bulut gave me a waterproof jacket to go with my slacks as if that would do anything. I wear two shirts underneath it; I tied the life-vest above it. The two large plastic waterproof wallets are strapped on my belly, each with a mobile phone, one of the passports, and some money. Father told me they are waterproof; I must believe him.

When we embark, the boat is already full, and we squeeze hard against the young men to find space for three together, yet half the passengers are still in the water, waiting to get in. How can they ever fit? They're all men, except a plump lady, hijab, and a newborn in her arms sit across from me. I give her Bulut's Quran, and she tells me I am blessed. Right. That I am.

It will be years later when I find out that the survival rate in the Aegean in June is between three and twelve hours before hypothermia takes over. It is a very rough estimate; a lot happens between the third and the twelfth hour, life, death, the bloating, the fish gnawing at the cheeks, and the eyes. I'll find out later that spear-fishermen don't dive these waters anymore; you find things you never wish you saw down there. I'll find out many things later, like what is a H.E.L.P. position and all the useful advice on how to avoid hypothermia.

I don't know it yet, but I will never go to the beach again; this is the last night I feel the sea on my skin, even throughout the many years I'll spend in sunny Greece. Any dinner recommendation of a taverna where the seawater licks my toes will send hypothermia chills down my spine, make me want to get drunk and cut myself. I keep trying to overcome my fear, using virtual reality and such, but it is not the same; even when I see a beach in a film, I tremble.

I will never go to Eurodisney either—neither before nor after the 2042 floods when they moved the venue to Cyprus—chasing after fake thrills and cheap scares feels to me like spitting on the dead. They don't appreciate it; they visit in your deep sleep at the first breath of dawn, standing at the edge of your bed, cold fingers and fluttering dress touching your bare feet.

We are packed like sardines in a can, roughly ten rows of four bodies each—two gun-carrying smugglers on the bow, two more on the stern, one of them pulling the cord to start our short journey. The boat is climbing the dark waves excruciatingly slow like an old lady pushing a cart over sand dunes. Even at this speed, it shouldn't take more than half an hour to cover those seven miles. I see some lights across, but I don't even know if that is the Turkish coast curving around us like a monkey's tail or the villages of Lesbos.

Everyone, including us, wears orange vests, but it is too dark now, and I see no orange. There is the black of the sea, the black of the rubber boat, the black of the sky. There is the sparkle of the sky stars, the glimmer of the village lights of Lesbos, the wolf-yellow of the eyes of the man painted with soot.

Another man, younger, not Syrian—could be Moroccan or Algerian—gets in a fight, they push him, and he pushes and shoves the rest and finally comes to sit next to Nahla. He starts rubbing his body against her, puts his hand on her knee, and caresses it. I scream, and I punch his chest, but the smugglers shout back to me to shut up.

The man in soot signals at the smugglers—they all seem to be under his spell—and they stop the boat. One of them pulls a gun, and he points it to the man who touched Nahla, shouting words at him. Before I understand what happens, the smugglers grab the young man by the armpits and throw him in the water. The sound of the splash makes me shiver. The young Algerian, or whatever he is, who touched Nahla, grabs the side of the rubber boat, but one smuggler kicks him in the head, and a second pulls the cord to start the engine. We abandon him overboard, soon lost in the white of the boat behind us.

The smuggler bows slightly to the man in soot as if he is the ruler of boats, winds, and waves. He peers toward Nahla again with the same grin, and I know now that he is a servant of the devil of the west, the fire-eyed djinn of the east. He is the ripper and the claimer, the bringer of death, he has chosen Nahla, and won't let her go from his eyes, he does not need to touch her, she will be his, before morning he will steal her, I know, and yet I cannot do anything, who will believe me if I say what and who will help me, they all obey the flare of his eyes.

The boat stops again, this time for no apparent reason.

The sea doesn't; it becomes wilder as we stall, hungry and stirring, talking vulgar words to the women who try to cross it at night.

We are nowhere close to land, the village lights haven't moved much closer, but I hear voices. I squint hard, and I see one of the other boats that left before us. We both approach a much bigger boat; its lights illuminate the skeleton of a fishing trawler. When we get closer, I see that it is old and wooden, and I hear it creaking like the coffin of a restless witch buried alive. The smugglers shout to us to board the fishing trawler, the men on top of it throw ropes to tie and pull us. Men from our boat, Syrian, Afghani, men from Central Africa, young men, escaping their country, too many men on both boats. The fathers, the mothers, the infants, scout scared and try not to move an inch, but the young men, stand up, shout, and struggle to untie the ropes while the smugglers beat them with the sticks.

They know what I know, what Bulut told me, we shouldn't board the fishing boat. The fishing boats never make it to Greece; they return to Turkey. It is suicide to board it. The plan was for the smugglers to unload us close to the shore—how close, Bulut never told me—and they'd return with the fast RIBs. Not the fishing trawler, it will find no Greek port. The young men shout the two boats collide, a smuggler fires a gun in the air twice, the sea gets mad with rage now and climbs on our boat, small waves, but they lick my skin already. The men fight, the group of Africans attacks the smugglers, and the weight shifts, and it happens. What I knew.

The man with eyes of soot snatches Nahla away from me, and he jumps with her off the boat. Immediately I follow them in the water, I swallow it, and it swallows me, and only a split second later, our rubber boat capsizes behind me in one fast move, not slowly as a large wooden would. Most of the men are trapped under the weight of the boat, a few escape and jump around us, one of them lands on the man in soot, and he loses hold of Nahla. Men wave hands frantically and scream around me, I fight them away; those under the boat I can't hear after a few seconds, they can't survive there.

"Hold me, I am here," I say, and I embrace Nahla, trying to pull her away from the man. He got to us; he is yanking me down by my hair, no, that's my uncle, he struggles to climb on my shoulders because my uncle cannot swim, Nahla cannot swim. It is cold, colder than I hoped, and Nahla screams. Why is Hassan pulling me down, he has a vest, and he should be fine, but he has panicked. "Let me go," I shout, but he keeps kicking and pulling me down, and I bite his hand hard until he lets go. I can't see much; it is the screams I follow. I try to make it to the boat that hasn't capsized, but it is crammed with people and more trying to climb on. As I get next to it, a woman gives me her hand, but I can't grab it firmly, and more bodies fall from the boat; one of them falls right on top of us, it almost crashes my forearm, and I am separated from Nahla now.

"Yara, Yara. Help!"

I swim toward her, the waves carry her away from the boat, and I must keep close to her, but I still haven't caught her hand, the sea has gotten a good taste of our skin now, and it growls with hunger, the waves rise taller, the wind has picked up, but I am only three or four strokes away from Nahla, I take four strokes and then I am still three away and is the same no matter how many times I try. And I try. God, I try. I tried.

Now I see her every second breath. I shout her name at the crest, despair at the trough. She is not drowning, but she doesn't scream either, and that scares me, I scream for both of us.

"Scream, Nahla. Scream. Here. Here!"

But she is quiet as if the djinn of the sand-dunes has whispered honeyed lies to her and convinced her to join him, and when I look again, he is there. The yellow of his eyes, it sucks all light around for me to see their flare, how can I see it unless he is the demon who brings the sea-storm, the soot still dark, no, darker around his eyes, and he holds Nahla, gently, he tries to hold her high above the water, he helps her, her hair is silken with the weight of the water, but now every second breath they disappear more and more, every third now, and then I don't see them, I just think I see them because they have to be there, they have to, and every time I see Nahla her eyes glimmer gold like his, but no, they are gone, and I cannot hear our boat, I see a faint light of the fishing trawler, but nothing else, but I keep swimming the opposite way away from it, to get to Nahla and the man with eyes of soot. It is not soot. Surmah. I forget. Men in Afghanistan wear surmah, but there is no sea in Afghanistan, I know that this man didn't come from there, he wasn't brought by smugglers or with a bus to the beach, he was always here, he is on every boat, he came from the depths of the sea.

It will take me another two years to have my evidence. One night with howling rain, I am alone in my room, and I browse pictures and videos on the internet. I find a short documentary back from 2016, and I see a rocking rubber boat at mid-afternoon, and the faces are clearer; women, children, their fathers, trying to cross the same straits and in that boat, six years before ours, I see the same man, soot and eyes of ember, he is there among the living, same clothes, same grin, not a day younger or older, holding another girl gently, and I know then and now, years later, though I really knew it from that fateful night, that he is not one of us, he is not one of flesh and warmth, he is a creature of the deep, a djinn servant of the sea god, or the sea-god himself. He chooses the youngest and most beautiful of each boat, and carries her down to his dungeons, imprisons her in his lair where her fingers turn to black seaweed and her tears to pearls, some he devours but a few he keeps alive, those who shine with incomparable beauty strong enough to illuminate the depths of the ocean. He sucks their light for a thousand years, every night, a sigh of stardust exhaled from the girls' mulberry lips, until all life is gone from their bodies.

I am alone and tired among the waves, can't see Nahla anymore. I want to shut my eyes. Nightfall stirs sea, land, and sky into the same black pulp.

# 24. Lucia: Jamón ibérico

*Athens, June 16, 2022*

"I don't know what you did, kid," Elon confessed from the other side of the phone line, "Never seen one so young pull anything like this in one night. You'll tell me. Someday."

"I'll be back in an hour," Lucia replied.

"No, you won't. You must disappear," said Elon.

"What? What about the one here?" she asked.

"You are Greek, right? If you want my advice, you have to let him go, and you have to change face, hair, clothes. Disappear."

"Say what? I do?"

"You have him at gunpoint, you said, right? You totally abducted him, threatened him, the law is fucked up here, doesn't work like in the movies. Are you licensed to do any of those things? You'll be a vigilante in huge trouble if he talks or if he gets a good lawyer. Also, you'll get publicity, which means you are dead in this business, and he'd never get convicted. Most likely, he'll walk, and you'll go to jail unless Papalias pulls some strings. Tell me you didn't get in this business for glory because there is none. I do it for the money. My kid is at MIT."

"The Turkish spy agency?"

"What? No. You Greeks are so drama and conspiracy all the time. MIT, the institute. I need the cash. Remember, you have no license to pull a gun in this country or threaten anyone."

"But you arrested the men—"

"Did no such thing. The police arrested them, brought the boy back. I am no cowboy, and this is no movie. Last time I tell you this. You did great, and you also screwed up big time, kid."

"Lucia."

"Yes, Lucia. Great name. Not Sherlock or Hercule. No glory. Just try to stay out of prison now. Listen to me, let him go, he'll never dare to go to the police. Tell you the truth, I want to follow him discreetly. My men will be there in fifteen. He has a prosthetic leg, right?"

"Yes."

"Take it with you."

"What?"

"The fucking leg. Take it. And leave him at the hotel. Don't harm him, or I'll report you myself. My men will follow him when he gets out. I need more names. That's why I don't want you to hurt him or bring him to the police. I want him free so that I can follow him. And get some wig or disguise or something, change face completely, disappear for a while. Choose a place where you've never been to before. The islands or something. You deserve it."

Elon hung up, and Lucia looked at the man who was still naked in front of her.

"We need more names, Al," she said. "Else, they will be here. Look, it's over. They caught the other guys. We have the kid. Speak before the others do."

"If they caught them, what do you need? I spoke the truth."

Lucia waved her hair; those bangs needed trimming. There was a big-time haircut in her immediate future.

"There is some guy who has the smarts to organize this operation, but I bet he doesn't sleep the nights at a warehouse in Koropi. I need his name, Al. In the meantime, spread your legs and don't try anything funny."

As Al was lying belly down on the carpet, Lucia removed the black sleeve that covered his prosthetic leg and grabbed the fiberglass shell.

"Don't you dare," he growled.

"Shut up, Al. You are almost free."

She pressed the black pin at the bottom of the shell, and the prosthetic popped out. She stuck the gun on Al's spine, reminding him not to make another move.

"Last chance, Al. It is morning. Sunshine is here," she said.

Al turned his head, his eyes red with rage, fear, and lack of sleep. She could be certain only of the latter; feelings are a messy thing to decipher.

"Give me back my leg."

"One name, for one leg."

"The Wolfman," he said.

"The who?"

"Ask around; everyone knows who I am talking about. The Wolfman. He is the one who moves the slaves from the islands these days. He did the kidnapping."

"Sex slaves?"

"Yes, you know the girls from Moria."

"Moria? The refugee camp in Lesbos, you mean?" It was a stupid question on her behalf. Al was no LOTR fan; he couldn't even read the back of a potato chip bag.

"Are you stupid, girl? Yes, Lesbos. The Syrian girls, the Nigerians. The Wolfman. He is the one you are looking for."

"You think I'll go for some bullshit nickname? The Woooooolfman?" Lucia replied, gesticulating like a boogeyman monster, showing that she didn't believe a word, hiding her excitement that she had a name before Elon did. "Tell me more. Give me something."

"About what?"

"Moria."

"They gather them every Friday. Moria to Salonica and from there to Vlora."

"Vlora, the Albanian port?" It was a stupid question on her behalf. If Al had any wit, he should have replied, "Vlora the Explorer" but that was not *her* Al.

"Yes, the girls. To Vlora. They chain them, drug them, and load them up, rape them a few days to break them and then ship the prime stuff from Vlora to Italy across," said Al. "Or from Salonica back to Istanbul, the rest. Give me back my leg now, that's all I know."

*Rape them to break them...*

"And when are they leaving? From Moria?"

"Every Sunday, the next shipment is Sunday."

"Thank you, Al. For your sake, I hope that Wolfman of yours is a real person. You did the right thing here. And the smart thing. Take your time if you decide to follow me. Sorry! I'll have to keep this as a souvenir."

"You said, one name, one leg."

"Yes, I did. One leg for you, one for me."

Lucia walked out the door holding a hollow fiberglass half leg over her shoulder. Staring at the elevator mirror, she fantasized that she was Artemis, daughter of Zeus, Olympian goddess of hunting, returning from the forest. That pig had gotten what he deserved. If only that half leg were a jamón ibérico to carry back to her lair. She was starving to the point of nausea. And the boat trip to Lesbos would make it even worse.

# 25. Tina: The Songbird and the Pigeon

*Geneva, June 14- June 15, 2022*

"No breakfast, just coffee, black, thank you," Tina said to the flight attendant and kept flipping through her tablet, going through the WHO reports that read both ominous and inconclusive.

```
WHO Influenza (A/H3N2, AH7N9)
Update 1
Influenza-like illness in Bangladesh.
The Government of Bangladesh has reported 850 confirmed
human cases of bird influenza. It remains inconclusive
whether an A/H3N2 or an A/H7N9 strain is responsible.
The Government of Bangladesh has reported 3 separate
ILI (influenza-like illness) events. In the city of
Dhaka, surveillance began picking up cases of ILI
starting 10 March. Laboratory evidence confirms an avian
A/H3N2 virus. Of the 803 people affected, 137 developed
pneumonia and 3 deaths were reported. In the city of
Chittagong, in eastern Bangladesh surveillance picked
separately 27 cases of A/H7N9 type influenza starting
March 12, and another 20 cases of the same virus in
April. Of the 47 cases, 20 resulted in deaths. The
mortality rate was extremely high for children below 12
```

years of age, where all but one of the infected, died within three days of contracting the virus.

Influenza normally affects the very young and the very old, but the first group fared much worse. Because there are human cases associated with an animal influenza virus, and because of the geographical spread of multiple community outbreaks, these events are of high concern.

Update 2
Influenza-like illness in India.
India was reporting 200 cases of influenza H3/N2 in Mumbai. Two died.

Update 3
Pakistan was reporting 12 cases of A/H7N9 of which 5 of the infected had died.

Update 4
Turkey was reporting 6 cases of A/H7N9 near the city of Erzurum of which 2 of the infected had died.

The next report caught Tina's attention as her housemaid Floribeth had lost her mother recently to a flu virus back in the Philippines.

Update 5
The Government of the Philippines has reported 73 confirmed human cases of influenza A/H7N9. All cases occurred in a small village north of the city of Floridablanca. Of the village's 189 inhabitants, 73 were affected, and 32 died, of which 21 were children under the age of 12.

The Government of the Philippines mobilized medical and military personnel to quarantine the village, and no more cases were reported after April 12.

There was one more report, and it was one she knew too well.

Update 6
The Government of Kenya has reported 22 cases of influenza A/H7N9. Of those cases, 20 were passengers on flight WAA788 from Dubai to Cape Town, that had to perform an emergency landing at Nairobi on March 16, 2022. The remaining 2 cases refer to medical personnel, a nurse, and a doctor who attended to the patients. Of the infected, 8 had died, of which 1 was a three-year-old child.
It has been determined that most of the infected passengers shared a waiting area, buses, and a hotel a day before. The fact that they became rapidly sick within a matter of 24 hours is of high concern.

"I am late," she said, pushing ahead of business class passengers the moment the seatbelt sign went off. She stormed out the jetway and into the airport halls. She noticed that they were decorated with hundreds of colorful models of birds hanging from the roof, a choice she found ridiculously ironic on her way to an avian flu pandemic assembly. Travelers from every country, the opposite corners of the Earth, gathered around the luggage belts. As far as any virus was concerned, the planet was one small village, one body. One got infected; all were in danger.

"Emergency. WHO HQs, now," she shouted and jumped in the first taxi, skipping ahead of the waiting line and leaving locals and tourists equally stunned.

The ride was brief, passing museums and international organization buildings. Asphalt and pavements, clean and immaculate, bright ironed flags fluttering against a soft summer breeze, barely a living soul walking the streets.

One would think that a virus wouldn't survive in a city as sanitary as Geneva, but Tina knew all too well that the crisp weather of Central Europe was much more accommodating to influenza. She was surprised that the virus had originated in Bangladesh, a hot and humid environment. Many things in these reports didn't make sense.

The WHO headquarters rose in front of her, a modern structure of concrete and glass, made up as if the architect had stuck seven rows of white coffins atop one other. Compared with the extravagant spaceship-like buildings that housed the banks, the pharma companies, and the tobacco firms in the same district, the natural conclusion was that the governments of this planet didn't value much the health of their citizens.

The amphitheater was filled to capacity, and without counting, she knew there were about two hundred people in there, as many as the countries of Earth. Her old friend, Dr. Antonio Canetti, wearing a checkered elbow-patch suit, waved at her from the second to last row. Tina rushed to him, and he scooted over to make some space. Nobody else paid attention to her late entry; they all seemed engaged in the presentation.

"Bella Matilda! To Greeks, time is always a suggestion, not an obligation," he whispered.

Her colleagues knew her by her official name Mathilde Walker (ex Damianou), and Canetti always called her Matilda. She was using Tina instead, if only to make her father mad. It was his mother's name after all that she discarded, and that should hurt him deeply.

"My friend, I had an awful morning so far, so, please. Give me some good news."

"You expect to hear good news today? Is that why you came here?"

"Tell me it is not the *songbird*," Tina said.

"We all came here, hoping for the *chicken*. But it is the *songbird*. Worse, it is the *songbird's* evil cousin or something they don't even know yet."

The reports she had read on the plane were talking about two different avian viruses: an H3N2 and an H7N9 virus. Among her colleagues, the first was informally nicknamed the *chicken,* while the second was the *songbird.* The chicken virus was common and well-known, quite widespread, and the second most famous after the swine H1N1. Every person getting his flu shots had H3N2 antibodies, and that virus was rarely lethal unless the infected were in high-risk groups.

But the *songbird,* that was an Asian horror myth, a needle-mouthed Chinese ghost that could never satisfy its hunger, an eerie song escaping the gates of hell, with mortality exceeding forty percent of the infected. She was one of the first to study it when it appeared in China back in 2009. It was quite unlikely for the *songbird* to spread; a mother had to stay next to the infected daughter for days and nights, breathing and touching the girl, then her own eyes, her mouth. Until now, the songbird had infected people mostly within the same family but never expanded widely. Almost no one had antibodies to defend against the songbird virus.

The presenter, an experienced Geneva-based epidemiologist whom Tina recognized as Dr. Mercier, was addressing the audience through streaming video.

"Where is she broadcasting from?" Tina asked Antonio.

"She is here, in Geneva," Antonio said.

"Then why—" and before Tina finished her sentence, she realized why Dr. Mercier was not presenting in person. "Ah. Quarantine."

"Yes, she was on the team that moved the patients from Nairobi and then from Chittagong to here to run the tests. She got infected two weeks ago but is recovering. She'll be fine, at least that's what I heard."

Dr. Mercier continued her report.

"The symptoms unravel quite rapidly after less than twenty-four hours of incubation. In my case, it started with eyes burning and a headache that got worse by the hour. Then it was shivers and weakness. The second day was one of excruciating pain that seemed to break every bone in pieces. I had a hard time walking, and I started coughing so hard that I thought my lungs would burst, my temperature reached 39.5°C. But I am lucky.

"As you are aware, we have witnessed many cases that grew immediately worse and resulted in death. The most likely symptoms that proved lethal were the development of ARDS and even cyanosis, where the feet and other extremities of the patients turned black due to lack of oxygen. Where an autopsy was performed, we consistently found that the deceased's lungs were filled with a reddish foam, the color of blood. In many cases, the patient, especially the children, died from heart failure caused by ARDS. And now, the man who has been leading the effort against H7N9 for the last few days, Dr. Trevor Garnett, professor at Johns Hopkins University."

Tina bit her tongue as her old professor moved to the podium but couldn't hold her thoughts back. She was heard at least two rows ahead and behind her.

"Hides, flies, mutates, spreads? Sure does, doctor Garnett."

"What was that, Tina?" asked Canetti.

"Oh, nothing. Everything," she sighed as Garnett started speaking.

"As you know, I will be leading WHO's special workforce on battling the H7N9 virus. The rest of the workforce members will be known to everyone within the next two days. What we know: there is an active scenario that patient zero may be a man from Chittagong, Bangladesh, who died on March 15. A second less probable scenario points to someone who boarded the plane to Dubai on the same day, and twenty-four hours a second plane from Dubai to Cape Town that was rerouted to Nairobi. It is confirmed that a passenger from Bangladesh was on that plane, he died in Nairobi. We still have many questions.

I must remind you all of WHO's strict guidelines for naming new human infectious diseases. You must refrain from naming viruses after countries, animals, or cities. 'Chittagong virus, Bangladesh virus" is not an acceptable name. We will take a twenty-minute lunch break now, and we will continue with more information about the virus and the suggested countermeasures afterward."

The delegates around her were texting and calling as Tina walked out of the amphitheater with Antonio and two-meter-tall Dr. Julian Van Hoult from the Netherlands, who was still shaking his head.

"So, Julian, what are you hearing?"

"It is a mutation of the H7N9 virus, probably an antigenic shift. They have detected pigeon DNA. They call it the Chittagong virus already."

"Well, the moment Garnett mentioned that we must refrain from naming it that, you knew what the media's reaction would be. He sealed it," said Antonio shaking his head.

"Something doesn't add up for you?" asked Tina. "Because it definitely doesn't add up for me. Can any one of you point me to the Philippines delegate? Where can I find her?"

"Him," said Van Hoult and pointed to a short, bespectacled man by the buffet. "But you may learn more from that man behind you."

Tina turned her head only to see Garnett moving toward her, with a big icy smile and open arms.

"I need a word with you," said Tina and pushed softly through the groups of delegates who were chatting and munching.

"I am so glad to see you, Tina. That tip you gave me about the bus in Dubai was crucial. It saved us a lot of wild goose chasing."

"Yeah, we're down to wild pigeon chasing now, it seems."

Garnett eyed the veggie wraps on the buffet table.

"Let's get a bite."

"Later, sir. I have questions. The Floridablanca incident, in the Philippines. Can you tell me what happened?"

"Playing detective again, Tina. Anyway, here's what I know. A female worker returned to her village from South China. She was on a flight to Manilla but didn't infect anyone there. Four days later, the ambulances were called, and they had to deal with a pile of thirty-two bodies and dozens more sick patients who recovered."

"And that was verified as H7N9 virus?" asked Tina. "The songbird virus?"

"Let's stay with H7N9 for now. Songbird and pigeon are not acceptable names. It might. We are not certain."

"It might? And how can we even have a Chittagong patient zero if your patient arrived in the Philippines before that? And you say she came from China? I am sure you have asked all that yourself."

"If you listened carefully to my talk, I didn't confirm that patient zero was from Bangladesh. I just suggested a hypothesis. Wait for the second part of the meeting."

Tina walked back to the auditorium in the process, overhearing random conversations from colleagues. Three of them, who were from African countries, talked in French, repeating the word "Ebola" a few times, while a Canadian delegate was lecturing his Norwegian colleague about obesity and how it kills a lot more than any virus. The plagues of the poor, the curses of the rich. All mortal, all real. Tina sat again next to Antonio.

"Found anything?" he asked.

"They're hiding something," she said and started scribbling a diagram on a piece of paper. She was trying to make a tree of how the virus spread based on the minimal info she had. Her phone kept flashing with messages, each one dropping like a bucket of cold water.

Alexi: *I need to see you. We must talk. Miss you!*

A few seconds later.

Alexi: *Just landed. Surprise!*

Tina put the phone in her bag.

"That's a persistent boyfriend," chuckled Antonio.

"Or a husband who can't find his socks," she joked. The wrinkles on her brow, the crow's feet hiding under her light makeup, had frozen in a fake smile.

Dr. Antonio Canetti was a man well over her age, approaching sixty. He was a respected scientist, an ancient history buff, and a deep-water fisherman who had vacationed in the Ionian islands almost every summer. A true friend, practically a father figure for her at WHO. They had exchanged emails and attended the same meetings in the last two years, but they were not close enough for her to spill her guts.

It would have been different if she were a guy. She could make fun of the naïve other sex who had fallen in love and share her secrets. She could lean over and show Antonio her phone, her Tinder account, brag about her Bumble traffic and giggle. But she was not a regular or even casual user of any dating service; she hadn't actively looked for an affair and didn't care to get a promotion by any means necessary. Alexi had already become more influential in the Ministry than she was, but that was only because he waived the ruling party flag. After elections, he'd be a nobody again. Everybody else would assume she got involved with him to help her career; she couldn't brag about an affair to anyone. Not only would it destroy her marriage but her career. The word was puttana in Italian, puta in Spanish, πουτάνα in Greek. One Europe, one language. A rotten deal.

Her phone was vibrating now, and she was certain that it was Alexi. She ignored it, yet it flooded her mind. A mother, a scientist, a country delegate attending a pandemic conference.

"I wish this could just disappear," Tina mumbled.

"Who?" asked Antonio.

"The virus. Do you think we are looking at a pandemic?"

Dr. Garnett had just repeated the dreaded word from the podium and then started shedding light on her questions:

"Thanks to the Chinese Government that helped the Bangladeshi authorities set up a laboratory in the city of Chittagong. Genome sequencing has revealed that the H7N9 virus under investigation was the result of a dangerous antigenic shift."

He kept talking, sharing more information about the scenario of how the virus mutated.

"So, let me get this straight, Tina, you are the expert in mutations," said Antonio. "A human flu virus infects a pigeon. The same pigeon gets infected on the same day by a chicken or something that carried the H7N9 virus, the two viruses mix and mutate; more pigeons are infected by the mutated one, a pigeon infects a human, our patient zero and—"

"That's what they claim."

"How unlikely is that?"

"Extremely unlikely until you put millions of pigeons next to millions of humans for thousands of years. Then it is simply inevitable," said Tina. "I don't understand this whole reference to the chicken virus cases though, that was a completely different one and just a coincidence."

Tina stopped talking as Garnett announced:

"The Governments of China, Germany, and the United States will provide immediate financial support of five hundred million dollars to the WHO to prepare the poorest nations of Southern Asia and Africa to deal with a potential pandemic. More than eighty percent of the funds will be used to accelerate vaccine preparation."

"Did he say five hundred million dollars?" asked Tina.

"He mentioned China ahead of his country. They must be shelling out most of the money. Fried squab is a bit more expensive than usual," said Dr. Van Hoult. He was using his pen like a drumstick against his blank notepad.

"What?"

"Fried squab. Pigeons. A delicacy in Chinese weddings. You will not find any restaurant serving pigeons in Bangladesh. I am guessing that this is a South China virus. Farmed pigeons, patient zero is someone who fed them, slaughtered them. I discovered a blog post yesterday that talked about more than eighteen deaths in Guangzhou from flu in March. The official report was hinting H2N3, but who can say for sure."

"That's unethical, quite an accusation," said Tina.

"Unethical but expected business practice," said Antonio. "At they are providing all the data, did genome sequencing, they are shelling out the five hundred million dollars. I'd say kudos to them. They are preparing us, while Americans want to talk about obesity and safe drug use, and we Europeans, I don't know, probably about our pensions."

"Why would they hide it?" asked Tina.

"I think it is just about naming it. Guangdong is a booming China province. GDP is, let me check. Wow, $1.5 trillion! That's almost like Italy. Wow!" Antonio was showing his tablet screen to Tina. Van Hoult was flashing a second screen, a photo of a bucket of brown-red fried whole little birds. Whole. Heads, feet, and all. Pigeons, she guessed.

"Chittagong GDP, do you want to guess, Tina? Forty times smaller. So the Chinese care about the virus not being named Guangzhou. As long as it is named Chittagong, they'll pay."

"This is ridiculous."

"Is it? A name is a big deal. What would your country be if it was not named Greece but Southern Balkania? What if Rome switched to Lazio? Tourism would be *prrrr!*" Antonio blew a raspberry, thumb down. "It would disintegrate. You name a pandemic after Guangzhou, business dies. 'Come invest in Chernobyl.' 'I'll pass.' Imagine if you named the virus 'the Greek Islands virus.' 'Cretan virus.' Your tourism economy dies. But who would ever care about Bangladesh, anyway?"

"Not him for sure," Tina pointed to Garnett as he was speaking.

"The half a billion injection comes at the most critical time. We have been caught unprepared by the H7N9 spread, and we are fortunate enough that summer is here, at least in the Northern hemisphere. Humidity and heat conditions will most likely keep the virus spread under control. We still need to investigate how easily it can spread. The case of the infection spreading on a plane so fast is quite alarming.

"I will strongly urge all the representatives of the fifty richest nations to lobby their governments to approve extraordinary funds to support the WHO. It doesn't matter from which country the virus originates or where it mutates. If it assumes a reproduction and contagion profile similar to more common viruses, it will reach your country within months, maybe weeks. We need to prepare now, and each country needs to make preparations for vaccinating the entire, I repeat, the entire population. Needless to say that the latter is the key concern of WHO and one that needs to be addressed before October is here."

Tina walked out of the conference with Antonio, busy looking for a flight to Athens on her screen.

"I was scheduled to return tomorrow morning, but I need to find a flight out tonight. Shit, there is nothing."

"I suggest we have a coffee before you make decisions," Antonio said.

They sat on the coffee shop by the lake, watching the locals strolling by, the grade school kids doing yoga exercises on the green, the pigeons swooping down to mingle with the ducks and the swans on the shore. A girl with pigtails feeding a grey pigeon from her hand.

"Aliens," said Tina. "I wish it was aliens."

"What do you mean, doctor?" asked Antonio.

"The public doesn't know anything about the flu. What damage it can do. There was a survey back home recently, most people believe antibiotics are a must against the flu. I am still trying to convince them at the Ministry to do some social media advertising, they prefer to print brochures. If it were aliens invading, we'd be okay. Everyone knows about aliens, there are a thousand blockbuster movies about them. But an obscure avian virus? They are clueless. How do you educate a country in a few weeks?"

"Garnett was talking about us," said Antonio. "We are among the fifty wealthiest nations. Italy, even Greece. We think of ourselves as 'struggling,' but we are the rich. It is hard to explain this to everyone protesting in Athens, Rome, and Paris, but we are the ones that need to carry the burden."

"The ones protesting? I will have a much harder time explaining it even to the Minister himself, down in Athens. Especially these new guys, I don't think they want to talk about ordering vaccines. They are almost anti," sighed Tina.

"Hmm, well, you'll have to persuade them for the sake of your compatriots. You know, today Garnett announced a Noah's Ark type of scenario. At best, the pharmaceutical companies can produce two, maybe three billion vaccines a year. Say you need two per person to cover the season, we are talking about sixteen billion. Van Hoult left already for Zurich to secure capacity from one of the big pharmas."

"He told you so?"

"They are the Dutch. Everything is open-curtain with them."

"I wish that the European Union did its job. That I haven't had to convince everyone separately."

"If this is as deadly as they think, infecting children and everyone, don't expect any solidarity. Noah's Ark, Bella Matilda. You act now, you reserve vaccines for your country, you are the only one who can put them in Noah's Ark. Else, come October, you may be responsible for a pandemic."

"Thank you, Antonio. In your grimness, you are helping me put that in perspective. I hope you can come to Athens and help me convince them."

"It won't take much. Show them the reports. The mortality rate of H7N9 is forty percent. Can you believe it? I don't even know how this thing propagates; it kills the host before he has enough time to infect others. The swine flu that wiped fifty million back at 1918—"

"Seventy million," Tina said. "I actually stand by the eighty million number."

"Let's say seventy. That flu pandemic back in 1918 annihilated more young men and women than World War I, and it had a CFR rate of around three percent. Imagine if this is four-five times as deadly."

"No one remembers anything about 1918. We are equally unprepared now."

"The laggards will suffer," said Antonio. "It is your job and mine to make sure our countries are ready."

Alexi was calling her for the third time in an hour. She desperately needed to talk to anyone available at the Ministry of Health, but he was not calling for the right reason. She ignored him once more. Lisa Walker texted and that she couldn't ignore:

Lisa: *Please call me right away. We have a serious health issue!*

Tina stood up and started pushing the redial frantically. Her mom didn't respond. Mom Lisa was always zen, so if she texted about a serious health issue, Tina was already going mad, fearing the worst. She finally got through.

"Mom, what's wrong? Where are you? Which hospital?"

"Hospital? We are at home, dear."

"What's wrong?"

"Oh, yes. My grandson. You have raised him to demand ketchup with everything. Floribeth was preparing chicken nuggets, and he asked for ketchup, but I insisted on steamed chicken with broccoli. He is not eating. This is wrong, Tina."

"Is that it?"

"It is serious, Tina."

"I know, but I don't have time for this now, mom."

*Good luck with making Demetri eat steamed broccoli without ketchup,* she thought.

"I am sorry if I scared you, but you have your work cut out, my girl."

She had to convince Demetri to eat broccoli, convince a politician in a bankrupt country to proactively buy vaccines for eleven million people, convince Alexi that she really meant it; she'd never again meet him at "their little hotel."

Unlike college days, this time, the sex with Alexi had been average. Maybe it would have gotten better if they kept going at it for months, maybe even worse, maybe their little hotel was just too corny and didn't turn her on, but she had no time for a relationship with another insecure man. She needed a jolt of life, fire, and joy, but all she had found this time around was a bucket of lukewarm water that had dried cold on her skin. Their extramarital affair proved to be a wine with a pretentious name and an ornamental label that tasted like a dirty sock dipped on a bottle of vinegar. She had fallen again for his blonde-gray hair and the mellow voice, but the taste, nope. If only that whole thing could disappear, along with him.

After she finished dinner with Antonio, they made it back to the hotel. As she entered the lobby, Tina squinted hard twice to make sure that her eyes weren't failing her, that the wine didn't give her hallucinations. There he was, Alexi, waiting, sitting with crossed legs on the sofa, a carry-on next to him. He waved casually at her as if they had an arranged date. He was dressed in jeans and a crème raincoat that let the eye focus on his hair.

"What the hell, Alexi? What are you doing here?"

"They sent the reports to the Ministry. There is an EU-members meeting tomorrow. We'll discuss with the other countries how to proceed with a common vaccination policy."

"I know there is one. This is Dr. Canetti from Rome, we were at the conference together."

Alexi greeted Antonio and then switched to Greek.

"Anything going on with *il professore* here?" asked Alexi.

"What do you mean? No, nothing is going on. I don't fuck every colleague I meet."

"We need to talk," said Alexi, grabbing her arm.

Antonio excused himself, and Tina stood there, shaking and staring coldly at Alexi.

"Not now, I am tired. Let's have breakfast before the EU meeting," said Tina. "Why did you come here? Are you going to stalk me from now on?"

"Darling, I just arrived. I don't have a hotel room."

"Is that so?" Tina said and then stood silent for a second. There was only one way this thing would end; egos had to be satisfied one last time. "You better come upstairs then."

Tina had a brief chat with the reception and joined Alexi in the elevator.

"Your hair smells so Italian," he said.

"So you are jealous of my old friend now? Can we just get it over with?"

Tina unlocked the door and shut it back faster once he was in. She took off her suit as if she were in a terrible hurry, got on her knees, and unbuttoned his jeans. A few minutes later, her cheek was flat as a pancake on the pillow against the mattress, her fingers were clawing hard in the bedcover, her stare followed Alexi through the bedroom mirror as he moved back and forth inside her. Why was she doing that? She was not in love, not even in lust. Power? Freedom. Sex, her face on the pillow, naked, Alexi pulling her hair, a reminder of her mortality. She was a woman of flesh rather than a grey suit at a doomsday conference in Geneva. She was sick and tired all day, from the taxi driver to the delegates, to the husbands and lovers, everyone messing up and not paying for it. Why couldn't *she* mess up for a few minutes? Do the stupid thing, say it, scream it. She was tired of being everyone's nurse from heaven. Why not be the femme fatale from hell for one moment? Come down to earth live like the common folk. Peri, taxi driver, daddy, Alexi. Screw all of you, indeed. For the last time, anyway.

"Are you up for another round?" she asked a moment after he fell with his back on the pillows, panting like a happy puppy. Despite the psychological void, this had felt unexpectedly good.

"Need some time, darling," he said.

"Time is the one thing we don't have, *darling*," said Tina, already waving goodbye to him mid-sentence. "Here is your key. You are three floors down. You are not sleeping here."

"Seriously?" said Alexi.

"You can't imagine how seriously. Can you tell me before you go? How the hell did you get the name of the hotel I stayed? I booked it myself last night when I learned about the meeting. Didn't tell anyone at the Ministry."

"I called your home."

"You did what? Called my home? My husband?"

Alexi stopped for a second and found his words. "I had Anna call."

"Anna, your wife, you mean?"

"Only way she wouldn't suspect anything."

"Are you mad? You are trying to get caught, make her divorce you. Is that it?"

"It was your mom there, I think. Or she called your husband. Anyway, I think it is time we let him know, love. Let Anna know too. We are destined to be."

Alexi and Anna didn't have kids. Tina was by the desk, holding the heavy black table lamp with her fingers so her hand would stop trembling. If only he were not the boy, the man she'd once fallen in love with, she would have smashed it down his head and let him bleed to death.

"Alexi, this is over."

"Doesn't look this way," he said, getting back into his white boxers.

"But it *is* this way. This was our farewell performance, our swan song. It was great *knowing* you once, not as great the second time around. You are the skunky odor on my clothes, my house, my family. I screwed up, but no more. If I smell you again, especially near my family, I'll report you to the Ministry, better yet, I'll start with the newspapers."

"You don't have to be theatrical now," Alexi said.

"You got what you came here for. From now on, it is work and nothing else between us. Get out!"

Tina shut the door as he was walking toward the elevator.

She slept alone but not as alone as she hoped, drowning in a restless nightmare, in which she was running down the endless corridors of a manor, its walls strangled by burning ivy, blackbirds flying away from it, she was gliding with them, blackbirds nibbling on a cow's carcass. It was sick and senseless, and she woke up every half an hour. She showered, she peed and drank more water, then to bed, then up again.

Antonio was at the breakfast buffet, and he greeted her with another penetrating question.

"Long night?"

"I just want to focus on the day, my dear doctor. It is important what happens today."

"Maybe not so important. They canceled the EU delegates' meeting. It will be a conference call instead," he said.

"Why?"

"Well, there is no consensus. Germany and Spain want to move fast even by themselves, France wants a common decision for all Europe, my idiot of a Minister doesn't trust anyone and wants to wait, Poland and Hungary won't show up at all, and they are not willing to give a dime for this, it is unclear if the British should still be in the discussion given the special border status with Ireland, some countries like yours haven't responded yet."

"Well, it is the weekend."

"The virus doesn't know what's a weekend," said Antonio. "Anyway, I booked a small conference room on the mezzanine. We can dial in from there. Dr. Hofbauer from Austria is joining us too. He is staying here. And there is an espresso machine."

She had to invite Alexi too against her personal preference.

Moments later, she was listening to the German representative dictating several guidelines that everyone should follow:

"We have concluded that a common decision will be a prolonged and ineffective process. Therefore, we encourage all countries to act as they see fit, under the following guidelines. Expedited approval of an extraordinary national emergency item outside the government's budget. Prepayment of eighty percent of the cost of the vaccines before delivery. A nationwide campaign to vaccinate everyone and possibly enforce it on antivaccine groups, at least on all children. You must also take into account that the insurance agencies of any supplying pharmaceutical company will require complete indemnification, and any possible legal costs and damages from citizen lawsuits will be covered by the state."

"Excuse me, sir," interrupted Alexi with a hard accent and the confidence of an unjustifiable superiority complex. "Who is paying for all this? The pharmaceuticals, the insurance. Is it the EU?"

Hofbauer was shaking his head, and Tina guessed the answer.

"Every member state has to make own arrangements, sir." A pause. "Please announce your name next time. This is a matter of security, too critical to strip control from sovereign states."

The phone call was soon over, but Alexi was still mumbling about whose fault all this was and who needs to pay.

"How do we know this story is not made up by the pharma industry itself?"

Tina pictured Alexi driving to the airport with the same conspiracy-theorist taxi-driver of yesterday and giggled nervously. What if he had killed Alexi and now used his skin as cover? She kept laughing alone, very alone.

"Seems like everyone is on their own," said Antonio.

"I don't understand what kind of Union this is. If it is something irrelevant about feta rights or frying the guts of the sheep, we have Brussels dictating ultimatums. Still, if it is a global pandemic, everyone is on his own?" said Alexi.

Hofbauer was quick to confront him, standing up and in a hurry to go, but still with words to say.

"You see, mister, if we Europeans—"

"We are all Europeans," Tina stopped him.

"You know what I mean."

"I don't have the slightest idea what you mean."

"If we of the North vote on a common policy, a mandate, the South will defy us. You won't even care to enforce it, and you will start all about Ancient Greece this and Ancient Rome that, and you don't take mandates from anyone. But when it is time to pay a bill, you act like a lost Amazon tribe, naïve and oblivious to such matters that just need saving, aka cash. We are sick of babysitting you and paying the bills. I am sorry, but on this, you are alone, and you better get your act going fast." The lanky, mustachioed Hofbauer exited the conference room, and Tina could breathe again.

Tina was chuckling nervously as she was keeping notes. She had about zero chance of getting a result, dealing directly with her own Ministry of Health. Alexi would be able to help her with how to go about it, but she preferred to deal with Ebola than with him. He offered his opinion anyway.

"Make sure that the Germans send these guidelines in writing, darling," he said. "Directly. It will cover your ass, and the Ministry will not aim at you."

"Aim at me?"

"If you communicate these guidelines yourself, anyone who reads them back home will assume you are on the take," said Alexi. "Paid off by the pharmas. If you delivered them verbally only, they'd be sure. Hell, even I would think so if I weren't on this call. You are lucky I was here."

Now she had to feel obliged to him.

Alexi stopped and peered at her persistently and silently. The left side of his face twisted into a smirk. "Or are we?"

"Are we what?" Tina asked. Next to her, Antonio was waiting for the two of them to finish their conversation in Greek, though Tina suspected that he could pick up a few words and maybe even the whole meaning.

"Are we on the take? I need to know."

Was he suggesting that they take a bribe? *Loneliness*. She'd be very lonely in this fight the next weeks, that much was certain.

"My God, Alexi, don't you get it? This is a race for survival. They left us alone. Survival of the deepest (pockets). Global production cannot push out more than two billion new vaccines a year. We need sixteen for the whole world. We are the only hope of everyone you know back home. If I come out ahead, our people live. If we finish in the second half, we die."

"You're being melodramatic. Again. You are right only if this becomes a pandemic. What are the chances it will?"

"I don't know, small."

"You were at the conference yesterday. Like five percent?" Alexi asked.

"Less. But can we risk it?"

"If you tell them back home to buy twenty million vaccines for a maybe one percent chance, they'll assume you are on the take for sure. Good luck with that one. Maybe if it is that bad, we two should leave. Go to Miami, Montevideo, or something, my brother is there."

Loneliness.

"I am going to check out," Tina said. "I don't know what flight you are on, and I don't care. I am out of here, alone."

"Oh, oh!" said Alexi, staring at his phone screen. "The Ministry just emailed. Better read it."

Tina read the email, got up, and rushed to her room to pack and check out. On her way to the airport, she called Antonio.

"Antonio, I am afraid you were morbidly accurate," she said.

159

"About what?"

"That Greek islands virus, you mentioned jokingly. I am not sure if you are a prophet or something, but they just emailed me from the Ministry in Athens. There were three deaths in Moria in the last forty hours. Flu-like symptoms."

"Moria, Lesbos? The refugee camp?"

"That one. Worse place to control and contain. They have quarantined some cases at the infirmary, but they don't know what to do. I am going there tomorrow."

"Be careful, Tina. I'd recommend BSL-3 equipment until you know what you are dealing with."

"Yeah, right. A biosafety level 3 laboratory in Moria. I'll have to buy my own gloves and masks from the airport pharmacy if I am lucky."

"Arrivederci, bella Matilda. You are the best scientist and the most diligent one I've known. You'll be fine."

A pigeon virus. A populist, anti-science, anti-pharma government that would need convincing. An overcrowded refugee camp. Three dead. Peri's depression, Alexi's teenage type infatuation, Demetri's broccoli with ketchup, her father evicting her mother, she had a worse time handling the men than the virus. The phone vibrated silently.

"Mrs. Walker, the Minister asked for a plan of action." It was Anna, her stringy voice unmistakable. "By Monday."

"Three deaths, right?"

"They just confirmed four."

"May I talk to him? Monday is too late."

"I am afraid he is unavailable now. He is at the Awards—"

Loneliness.

"Tell them to shut down the camp; no one gets in or out," said Tina. "You shut down the airport."

"No need for that. There was a ground personnel strike planned anyway. No one flies to Lesbos today or tomorrow."

"You must get me in a flight to Lesbos tonight, as soon as I am back in Athens. Military helicopter. Anything."

"Alone? What good will that do? The Minister requested a meeting at his office Monday morning to consult with the team that will go to Moria. We are sending about twenty people, and I understand you'll need equipment. You will all be taking the high-speed boat tomorrow night, Mrs. Walker."

She searched for the name and the itinerary of the "high-speed" boat: nine hours and five minutes from Piraeus port to Lesbos. Most likely eleven hours in winter weather.

If only she could scream in a Swiss taxi.

# 26. Ella: Something Fishy

*Athens, January 15, 2058*

"How do I start a story, aunt Lucia?"

"Why are you asking me, Ella? Your grandma is the protagonist. Yara is a writer. They know better."

"But, *you* are the Chief Inspector."

"And? Do you think this is a murder mystery?"

"No."

"You don't?" Lucia was staring hard, trying to tease and intimidate young Ella, and with her sharp tone, she had succeeded.

"Huh?" Ella paused for a few seconds. "I just thought, you know, you have solved so many cases, maybe you can help."

"Sorry. Yes, I can. Make a *crazy wall*," said Lucia.

"Like in the old crime movies where they connect pictures and names with string?"

"We still use walls. I mean, the detectives do."

"But, the detectives are software agents."

"Still, the AI bots bring up a wall real-time with all the facts to pitch me, every time they figure a crime out. They draw a crazy wall with all the facts. Also, draw a tree."

"A tree?"

"Yes, the names, the birthdates. Always helps."

"About those bots. Do they have an account of the events I can use? You know, from the police side?"

"Yes, but the case is still open. You can't access it."

"What do you mean it is open? After thirty-five years?"

"Beats me. Crime, fraud, something fishy. Has to do with your grandma and that idiot Alexi she was dating back then."

Ella shrugged.

"Sorry, I thought you knew about this," Lucia continued. "We agreed with Tina to be truthful to you. You are twelve, after all, not a kid. If you can do trigonometry at ten, you are mature enough. There is no story without him. If she is not going to talk about Alexi, there is no point continuing a bullshit story."

"I do know. But what do you mean the case is still open? Like an unsolved murder case?"

"Alexi disappeared right on the night the crisis ended. Thanksgiving. As if the earth swallowed him, which is quite unlikely in today's world."

"But you just can't disappear anymore."

"Promise me something. If your grandma tells you anything about Thanksgiving, 2022, you come and find me before anyone else. Ok?"

"I promise."

"Look at me! Promise." Lucia stared into Ella's eyes, stiff-lipped.

"Got it. Thanksgiving. I'll come to you first once I am done."

# 27. Yara: The One Who Kisses You Sweetly

*The Aegean Sea, June 14, 2022*

I am alone now, a tattered bag of bones in the vast darkness of the sea. I am shivering, and when I tried to scream a while back, my voice came out as a slur. It could have been an hour since I lost Nahla, it could have been an eternity. I hear no sound but the sea, I am not in the H.E.L.P., but in the starfish position. My vest has failed me, and I took it off to swim faster to get to her. I longed for the freedom of my body, of swimming, the freedom of death. So many stars above me, why can't I be a fairy to ascend at will and reach to them, reach to their heavenly worlds, find her, find Nahla.

I've held on to the starfish position too long, and it is time that I rest now, I let myself go, just let my head rest inside the water. Maybe I'll see where the palace of the soot-eyed man is, and I can sneak in there in the quiet of the deep sea and steal Nahla back. But I can't see a thing, that palace is way, way down in the dark, too far for mortals to reach. I take another breath, the last one, and then as I turn my farewell gaze to the sky to curse my father before I drown, the gods decide to save me, for I have not suffered and they haven't tortured me enough, and I see a castle, or is that a church, floating among the clouds, no it's on top of a rocky hill, bathed in bright light, brighter than all the tiny speckles of the distant stars. It is a white palace, its glow illuminating the hilltop, and I swim to it, I must steal Nahla back from him.

I have lost the sense of above and below, of east and west, I truly think that I dive down to the palace of the sea god. It will be much later when they tell me that I swam toward the village of Petra, and my palace was the church of the Holy Mary, the One Who Kisses You Sweetly, *Panagia Glykophilousa*, in Greek. That is her actual name and the name of the church. I am born a Muslim, and the Holy Mary saves me only for me to become an atheist. Worse than an atheist, someone who has seen the demonic djinn of the sea and believes in his existence, in the ember of his eyes.

"How far can this palace be? A couple of miles," so said my father and Bulut. Much less now, I am not far away. Not that I can make it, it is less than two miles, or so I think, but I am too tired to swim, even though the wind has died now. I could do this back when I was practicing in a pool, but those last days have been nothing but torture, and this is the cold open sea. I just cannot.

I took off my slacks a while back when I realized that the passports were gone. Only the money-bag remains strapped on my ribs. But I've lost my passport and Nahla's. What if she is at the beach, waiting for me? Will I fail her again? I will need her passport once I find her. I keep swimming, more to punch the sea that swallows my life, her life, to hurt her, rather than to make real progress. Once back at school, I've read that the Persian King Xerxes had the waters of the Hellespont strait whipped and branded with iron to punish them for crushing his fleet. I had laughed then, misjudging his rage and grief for stupidity. I can't laugh anymore.

I may have covered some distance, but I will never reach the shore. As I turn my head out on the side to take a breath, I count the stars dying one by one—they are dying the death of the morning light, and only Venus remains alive, the star of the goddess who rose from the froth of the sea and washed out on the coast long before this world became ugly and vile and undeserving of her beauty. *Beautiful Nahla.*

I see the luminant white castle up front and Venus in the sky erased by the early daylight, and as my last strength drains away, I see them, here they storm out the heavenly gates, the angels in their chariots, they circle and gather around me blaring their trumpets of joy, a beautiful illusion viciously destroyed by dawn, those are no chariots, no angels, no smugglers, those are fishing kaiks, buzzing their horns, flags striped white and blue with a cross, they stop next to me, and barefoot fishermen in shorts pull me up, I am ascending from the sea, descending from my cross, my head falling to the right side, blood from my parched lips, blood from my underwear, they pull me up, and I am the image of a female Jesus, long black hair and pallid face, sent to death by her father. *Apokathelosis.*

I am lying on the deck among the fishing nets, the flies circling the buckets, buzzing a dull threnody. A young boy, my age, skin darker than mine but born European, I guess, throws water to my face after I lose my senses for a moment. Staring with his bright honey brown eyes, he gives me sips of juice, but the citric acid burns my lips of salt and blood. I keep repeating her name now to him, but he doesn't understand what I say. No one does. They think *my* name is Nahla.

"Okay, Nahla. You, safe now."

*No, she is not.*

They wrap me in a silver mylar blanket, and we sail softly toward the land. The sea sleeps serene and quiet now, and the only sound is their shouts on the radio, "an ambulance, a doctor, now, re malaka."

We are cruising close to a rocky cliff, its lower boulders white from the spume, all white, except for the empty orange vests that amass by the hundreds there, floating on the water, resting on the sand, grasping the rocks, one for each soul rescued or lost. Lost. So many orange vests, spreading across the rocky coast behind the boulders, fighting to stay afloat, some struggle to climb up the cliff, but it is a steep one, and the waves pound it hard, and not one of those empty vests will make it.

And I realize then that for each orange vest I see, there is a body I don't, and that trembling gold upon the water, may be the first dance of the dawn and the playful sunlight, or is it the skeletal fingertips of the dead reaching up? I realize that I will never step into the sea again, and I am wailing, shaking my head up and down, a living image of madness, begging the shocked fishermen to dock the boat now. "Faster!"

I stumble and fall once my sea legs meet the wood at the pier. A mustachioed policeman, the spitting image of my father, and a younger man in civilian clothes stop a few inches from my face; they look into the white of my eye.

"Help me," I cry. "My sister." I raise my palm to show how tall she was. "Is she here?" *Four feet.*

For a moment, they look at each other startled, maybe because I speak with a perfect British accent, though my voice comes out slurred and otherworldly.

"Did you swim across? Alone?"

"No, the boat. Smugglers. My sister. Nahla. Did you find her? She was on the RIB. Surmah. The djinn. Help me! I am a citizen of the United Kingdom."

"Is that so?" asks the man in civilian clothes, sneering and holding his chin with one hand to pretend he is puzzled. He turns to the policeman—it is early morning, he just had two smokes, and his iced frappe coffee with two sugars, and why not, a good joke will really kickstart this new day, put him in a jolly mood. "What a coincidence! I am the Queen of England," he replies.

# 28. Lucia: Denver on a Sunday Afternoon

*Athens, June 16, 2022*

Sugar-glazed carrots dipped in hot butter. A Hooter's waitress carrying a tray of tequila sunrise cocktails in the sunset. Paintball with fire-bullets on a field of pumpkins. Denver on a Sunday afternoon, during a football game. Mila's Fifth Element hair. Lucifer's eyes as they set ablaze the fires of hell on a July weekday.

Lucia had used all these—save for Denver and Hooter's—to describe the hair color she wanted to Rita. In the beginning, she had just said "orange," but Rita, her friend since grade school, working the family hair salon now, wouldn't get it.

"You mean light brownish? Golden brown? Auburn?"

"Nope, carrots in hot butter. Get it?"

"Are you sure, girl? Even that Mila looked so and so with orange hair. I mean, your dad will have a stroke if he sees you like that."

"He won't see me. I visited already. I am out of here tonight."

Earlier that morning, around six, Lucia had stopped at the bakery across from her parents' house, greeted the baker who she had known since childhood, and waited for the first pies and the fresh bread to come out the oven. She got a cup of hot coffee, spanakopita, and *tsoureki* and rang the bell of her parent's apartment.

She carefully hopped over the heroin junkie who had passed-out right at the entrance of the apartment building, opened the entry-hall closet where the doorman hung his coat—it had been twenty years since the tenants could afford one, so she never remembered seeing a doorman even as a child—and hid inside the fiberglass leg of Al the Albanian. Lucia took the elevator up to the third floor, spending her few seconds reading instructions printed and posted on the elevator mirror: "Always keep the outside door locked. Burglars!!" Somebody had forgotten to follow those instructions, obviously; she had found the entrance wide-open.

Her mom greeted her with a short scream of surprise as she opened the door, and Lucia kissed her one too many times, reserving as many more for her father.

"Why did you bring all this? Your father doesn't eat that stuff anymore. The doctors won't allow it," said mom, the second half of the sentence in a whispering voice.

Lucia was eating already without remorse as her father made it to the doorway.

"Is that you? How? When?"

He looked disoriented, like someone taking one too many pills, blood-thinners, pre-diabetic, blood-pressure, statins, and more, someone who wakes up every half an hour at night to pee his medications away.

"How is your leg, daddy?" she said.

"Well, I am not going to play for Arsenal any time soon or any of your British teams, little Lu. How is law school?"

"Oh, yes, law school. Great! I have a summer job in London, but I am going on vacation today, leaving tonight."

"Not staying? Even one night?" her mom opened her eyes wide.

"It's a big group of friends, mom. We have tickets for tonight. Corfu. I'll be back Saturday."

In Greek geography terms, Corfu was as far away from Lesbos as it could be. Lucia wanted to make sure that if anyone asked her parents, they would send them west to the Ionian Sea, searching for a girl with long brown hair rather than one with a short blood orange crew cut in the northern Aegean.

She spent the morning eating and eating more, watching the breaking news, and telling stories about a fictitious law school in Portsmouth. Her parents looked happy, and that was all that mattered.

"I am going to leave at noon," said Nora, "but will be back at six."

She wore work clothes.

"Mom, tell me you're not cleaning stairs again. Not with your heart condition."

"Oh, it's nothing tough, just babysitting."

Those clothes were the same she wore back when she cleaned houses.

"You promised me you'd stop."

"And how will we pay for all these medicines, Lu? Don't worry about me. Work is good. I get out of the house, so I won't go mad in here watching the news and arguing with your dad. He is so stubborn."

"You cannot do this shit-work anymore, mom."

"Sure, I can. Half the TV programs are people cooking, the other half jumping around to lose the weight."

"The men do the cooking, the women pump the iron," her dad added from his armchair, still staring at the TV.

It was just the thing she would expect Mazur Sr. to say.

"People pay, you know, to do what I do," mom Nora. "Go up and down the stairs, push a stick back and forth. They call it a 'healthy lifestyle.' At least I am getting paid."

This time her dad shouted from the living room: "They found the boy! Come, Nora, they found him!"

The Papalias case.

"Oh, thank God," said her mom, visibly relieved.

Lucia spent the next ten minutes glued on the TV, and there was no mention of her or Al. The TV channels didn't know anything.

Mom cleaning stairs in her sixties, mom taking two buses to get to the nice neighborhood where they paid her enough to justify the four bus rides, mom without a pension because the landlords paid her black money forty years, never social security, mom spending her quality time at home worrying about all the Papalias shipping tycoons of the world. Lucia's militant leftist side sprouted back to life whenever she visited Kipseli.

The next news story kept Lucia in her chair. Three young girls had died of what appeared to be a novel and very dangerous type of influenza at the refugee camp in Moria, Lesbos, and the Ministry was advising everyone to stay away from the island. All flights had already been canceled.

"All those immigrants swarming here. They bring this disease. Who is going to feed them?" said her dad.

"*You* are immigrants, dad. You are from Poland, mom from Albania. What are you talking about?"

"It's different, we came to work."

"I don't think they came to die."

Lucia checked her app, the high-speed boat was due to leave at midnight as scheduled.

"Got to go, mom. See you at six?" she said, kissing her father at the same time. She was not coming back, and if she delved deeper in explanations, the questions would only get worse.

Lucia grabbed the empty khaki duffel bag from her room, the one from her anti-establishment riot days back in 2015. Thanks to her mom, she had clean underwear, the extra-baggy camouflage sweatpants, and two purple tank tops. She ran down the stairs, retrieved the fiberglass leg, shoved it in the duffel, jumped over the heroin junkie still there. *Time for a hair makeover.*

"Extreme makeover. Orange. Carrots in hot butter," she said to Rita. "And very short, number two on the clipper. Nope, I don't have an appointment."

"We'll squeeze you in!" Rita joked.

She never needed one with her best friend.

Five minutes later, she was still trying to convince Rita that she won't blame her after the haircut.

"I need a complete change, going for a vacation," said Lucia.

"Where?"

"Corfu."

"Romantic. A boyfriend? Don't tell me you have a boyfriend."

"Better that you don't know."

"Okay, if you insist. Look, I am not going a crew cut and out. A side buzz cut on the left, leave the crop thicker and the right a longer, pixie cut to touch the ear. We cut most of the hair first, then color, then the finishing touches.

It's gonna look stupid ugly until I finish, don't be scared."

*The uglier, the better,* Lucia thought.

"What's in the duffel bag?" Rita shouted hard over the blow dryer.

"You know, the basics, bathing suits, beach towels, fins."

"Fins! Yeah, right. You are not back with those malakas, again? Those Red Dawn brigades."

"No, I don't play games anymore. I am past puberty, girlfriend," said Lucia.

"I see your father all the time, passing through here to go to the bakali. He stops to greet me every day, tells me your news. I think he makes up most of it. I caught him telling me the same things months apart."

"It's the pills."

"And you never call, you piece of shit," Rita punched her hard on the arm.

"You know, uni, I am way too busy," said Lucia, but her friend was right. She was a piece of shit, trying to sever all ties with her old neighborhood. It was getting worse, with each visit she felt further away than before. The pavements with the rotting-black chewing gums of the teenagers and the thick yellow spit of the smokers, the idiotic graffiti smearing each wall and traffic sign, the sawed exhaust pipe roaring scooters going the wrong way, when they weren't blocking the pedestrian crossways, the overflowing garbage cans, the cats and the old ladies fighting inside them at the first daylight for scraps of soiled food. How she had escaped the neighborhood of Kipseli, literally translating to the "Beehive," how lucky she was. Whether she was studying law, criminology, or bovine proctology in Portsmouth, it was still a huge upgrade.

"Is he limping more now?" Lucia asked.

"Your dad? Well, I won't lie. It takes him a full minute to appear from the left side of the salon window and disappear to the right. He drags the leg." Rita was holding the mirror so Lucia could see the back of her head. "You are going to cry in the morning, but I warned you. A new you. Lucia the Luminous."

"Love it! How much?"

"Buzz off! Oh, and don't go into the pool for two days unless you want the chemicals to give you a cool frog-green color."

*Lucia the Luminous.* Another name to add to her changeling identity. Lucia hugged her friend, called an Uber taxi, and jumped in the back seat before neighbors or even her mom passed by and saw her. It was still 5 p.m., and her boat wouldn't leave until midnight.

"The nearest quietest hotel, you know, sir," she said to the driver. He was polite, helpful, and went out of his way to help her choose one. Maybe it was her new pumpkin hair that did miracles, maybe it was the fact that taxi drivers called through the app were rated and pretentiously polite. She crashed on the twin bed, the back of her shaved neck cooling against the soft pillow.

# 29. Tina: About that Moussaka

*Athens, June 16, 2022*

"I have only one question for you, Dr. Walker," said the Deputy Minister sitting across the mahogany conference table.

Alexi and two other younger lackeys had joined in the meeting and chosen sides next to their DM, opposite Tina.

The slipper-size smartphone was dark and silent in the grip of the DM's fat fingers but covered his ear and one of his bulldog cheeks as he pretended to hold a parallel conversation to showcase his Napoleonic multi-tasking skills. His eyes were fixed in a persistent alert mode, the face of a man who had forgotten when it was the last time he spoke the truth. The flag pin attached on the plain charcoal suit's lapel signified that he was from the Patriotic side of the government alliance, not from the Radical Left one.

The Patriotic Party was another excuse for simply disseminating conspiracy theories and surviving on the votes of the hardline ten percent who didn't just believe those theories but were convinced that the survival of the human race depended on them. One in four of Tina's compatriots were certain that airplane condensation trails visible in the sky were proof that foreign intelligence agencies were spraying biological agents to sedate the population and prevent it from revolting. Another one in ten had answered "maybe" in the same survey, an answer that seemed more dangerous to Tina. Some of those had gone as far as to make this belief the one issue that would determine their vote and thus voted for the "Patriotic Party," which had

174

formed an alliance with the "Radical Left Party." They didn't share an ideology but rather one common and effective belief: for one to become the god of the people, he simply had to show them a devil responsible for all their miseries. Performing the occasional god miracle was optional; the devil bit was mandatory.

Moderate parties and candidates had been squashed repeatedly in recent elections. Their loyal followers were dying of old age, their weak sympathizers were getting radicalized, and their pessimistic supporters had emigrated en masse to some country still resembling a functioning Western society. It hadn't helped that "moderates" also stood for the "old, failed establishment," the captains who had led the country to bankruptcy, in a boat named "nepotism, corruption, and self-serving policy." The end effect of their moderate governing was not that far off from the ludicrous conspiracy theories.

"Shouldn't we wait for the Minister, sir?" said Tina. "There is a lot of crucial information here, and he would have more questions."

"Are you trying to say that I am not qualified to understand your arguments?"

"It would help if we had a fellow medical professional in the room. Epidemiology is very sensitive and difficult for people to grasp in a few seconds."

"Try me, doctor. Because a few seconds is all that the public is going to give to our Prime Minister if you are wrong. The gentlemen here *are* medical professionals," said the DM, pointing to Alexi and his two colleagues.

They continued to enjoy the exchange passively while wearing the matching grins of unjustified moronic confidence. The DM was the only one wearing a tie, a clear sign that everyone else was from the government's radical left side, as was the MIA Minister of Health.

"Dr. Alexi Vardis, here, was in Geneva with me," said Tina. "Why don't we ask him what he thinks we must do."

"I have my own view on this, which I'll share with the Minister only," said Alexi, maintaining his icy grin.

*Damn you, coward.*

The DM's flag pin caught a brief ray of sunshine and sparkled before Tina's eyes, reminding her that a scientist's ego should play second fiddle to the eleven million people out there.

"It is not a matter of wrong and right," said Tina. "I am presenting the guidelines provided in Geneva by the German delegation who has taken a leadership role in coordinating efforts. If we don't act, we may be responsible for genocide."

The Deputy Minister put his phone down—though Tina was certain that he was not talking or listening to anyone for a long time now—and brought his massive frame closer to the table, one of his tits clearly visible in shape stretching the poor shirt and resting on the mahogany.

"Germans should be more careful talking about genocide," he said. "The last time I put the two words together was at the Memorial for the execution of three hundred of my fellow villagers by the Nazis. Children too!"

"Seriously, sir? Are we going to talk about Hitler now? It is 2022. Can't we move forward? We should have been to space already."

"But we are not in space. We are down here. And I suggest you stop waiting for the Minister and answer my question."

"Please, go ahead."

"You say here that we must turn our budget upside down and order twenty million vaccines asap. I will bypass the question of whether you know anything about the criminal charges against the previous government's officials who erroneously ordered sixteen million vaccines for the 2009 H1N1 crisis."

"Erroneously?"

"Let's not go there. The judicial system took care of them. Are you suggesting we actually use those twenty million vaccines, or are they just for backup?"

"Backup? What do you mean? We buy them, we use them, we vaccinate the whole population. They are to cover us against the virus, not to cover our ass."

The DM shook his head in disgust and disagreement.

"You are aware that thirty percent of the population does not want to get vaccinated, not against a fictitious flu virus, not against anything."

Probably the same thirty percent were convinced about chemtrails, but Tina didn't offer that. It wouldn't be constructive.

"Is that the question? Can you just tell them that 99.999 percent of the doctors in any civilized country will get vaccinated and will vaccinate their children? Don't the doctors know better?"

"But that's not my question. Here is my question. How many people will die following the vaccinations?"

"You mean, how many will die *from* the vaccinations?"

"That's not what I meant. You know what I meant."

Tina looked around the table and the room, her eyes stopping at the outdated medical brick-heavy encyclopedias that decorated the cherry wood library, the Greek flag, the EU flag that had taken a beating that day, the den of cables sticking out of the TV and the projector like the ripped-out guts of an alien beast that had been blasted to pieces, the oversized photograph of a younger version of the missing Minister shaking hands with Fidel Castro during a "cultural" trip to the golden-eighties Cuba.

Nobody was going to help her.

"Four hundred and fifty people, sir. Give or take a dozen."

"Come again?"

"Assuming we vaccinate the entire population, four hundred and fifty people will die within forty-eight hours of getting the shot."

"That's, that's ridiculous," the saggy bulldog cheeks of the Deputy were trembling in disbelief. "You are joking, right?"

Tina was fast-typing and Google-searching through her tablet while talking to the Deputy.

"A hundred and three will fall dead from a heart attack, a dozen as they walk out of the vaccination center, ten will have a stroke a few hours later at dinner, five will commit suicide the next day, one—not sure about him—will die from encephalitis, one from something exotic like Guillain-Barre syndrome."

"What are you trying to say, doctor? Are you mocking us?" said the vested Minister confidant, who was dressed like a wildlife photographer returning from a safari at the Serengeti.

"I stand by these numbers."

"Based on what?"

"Based on the fact that so many people die every forty-eight hours in Greece from those causes, no matter what. Whether we vaccinate them against a deadly virus, give them a glass of lemonade, or make them eat two blocks of moussaka, the same number of people will die. That's what four hundred and fifty people, divide by two, give or take a dozen, do every day. They die. Two thousand vaccinated toddlers will be diagnosed with autism within a year. Do you know how I know that?"

"No, we get it," said Alexi.

Tina had her doubts whether the one who mattered most, the Deputy Minister, got it, but she soon found that he shouldn't underestimate him. Scientists always confuse a politician's ruthlessness with cluelessness. They just cannot imagine how deep in shit one has to dive to become a government Minister. Worse, they can't imagine that he may like it there in the deep, an evil replicant of Yves Cousteau filming himself incessantly, swimming in the brown.

"You understand the issue this creates, doctor," said Alexi.

Tina was struggling to keep up with this exchange, taking furtive looks at the door, hoping the Minister, who had a medical Ph.D. degree—albeit in the Comparative History of Medicine, rather than on virology, or anything hard-core—would show up and save her from this band of idiots.

"Yes, I understand. See, I have dual heritage. First the banshees and then the harpies, they'll come for all of us. Mothers with children who died or stopped talking after the shot—if they ever talked—will wail, wives who lost husbands to stroke on the same night will be cursing you to hell as they peel the skin off their faces in front of open graves, the craziest of death-cases will be the ones monopolizing the evening news and the headlines at the newspaper kiosks, you will be grilled and condemned even by the moderates on every open-line radio station, you'll fire me just to save face. Criminal and civil lawsuits to eternity. I will end up defending myself in courts for fifteen years. I may go to jail, etc., etc. I understand."

"All of us."

"All of you. Anyone who ever mattered in this land, the last three thousand years, died in some dark prison or was assassinated. Congratulations, you'll be worthy of your office."

The DM stirred in his chair like a pig in the slaughterhouse alley.

"That is why the insurance agencies demand the indemnification for the pharmaceutical companies," said Tina. "Nutcases and grieving parents will sue them. The pharmas will lose to court. Guaranteed. Unreasonable doubt and such."

"And the Greek taxpayers will have to pay twice the pharmaceuticals to reward them for the death of their brothers," said the DM.

"As a tear-jerker statement as you make it sound with your immense rhetorical talent, yes, sir. The government needs to cover the lawsuits. Else no pharma will give us vaccines."

"You seem to know a lot about those pharma companies. Do you work for them as well?" asked the advisor to the DM.

A question long due had finally come.

"No," said Tina.

"But you're an American, right? US passport."

"Yes, and a US education, and a mother. I also like rock n roll, and I watch American football. What's your point?"

"Have you worked for a pharma company before?"

"I have done consulting work for a couple of Swiss ones, years ago."

"Here in Greece?"

"In Greece, in Spain, in Congo, in whatever. Does this interrogation lead anywhere?"

"Have you spoken to them recently?"

"No, I haven't. This will be your job if you make the right choice today."

"And that's all you wish to share with us?" the DM interjected.

"You are asking the wrong questions, sir. Everyone, American, German, is telling you the same thing. We must get the vaccines because we don't know what we'll face. It may be a thousand times the numbers I mentioned. And you must order a complete blockade of Lesbos right now. We are too late."

"That would take at least five Ministries to coordinate."

"Do it! We can't lose another minute."

"We are only setting a quarantine on the Moria camp."

"No, sir, that will not be good enough."

"We are not condemning an island of Greek citizens to isolation and tourism death, at the beginning of the season, because some illegal immigrants got sick in a guarded camp."

"Too many people go in and out of that camp, sir. It is barely guarded. We need to block the port and the airport."

"Back to the vaccines."

"You must order the vaccines now, sir, or we might never have a chance."

"The consensus here is to wait. We'll form a five-member committee and investigate the progress of the virus outbreak if there is such an event."

"You will be late, sir. And, and..."

Tina couldn't find the words to continue. She was thinking of her son Demetri and no one else at that point. How could she save him? Leave the country? Back to the States? New Zealand? Then she thought of Peri, her mom, her best friend who had just thrown a party to celebrate the baptism of her twin girls, Mary's children still mourning their dad, she thought of Demetri's soccer team buddies, the Apokries Carnival (Mardi Gras and Halloween all-in-one) children parade at Demetri's school. All the children. She couldn't stop thinking and counting; she couldn't just take Demetri and run, not more than the pilot can take the first parachute and abandon a passenger plane in trouble.

Tina tried another angle.

"Indonesia, gentlemen."

The second minister counsel, the one with the cheap blue suit, was drinking his ice frappe coffee from the ecological paper straw, putting out the fifth cigarette in the last twenty minutes on the ashtray. At least he didn't use the hardwood floor.

"What about it?" he said.

"Can you guess its population, Mr. Deputy Minister?"

"I don't know. Eighty million. More?"

"More. More. Two hundred and seventy million."

"I am certain that's not correct, but why is that relevant?" asked the DM.

*He was certain. Too lazy to google it. Our elected official. State of Greece. Birthplace of democracy, the cradle of Western civilization.*

"I just heard from a colleague in Italy that they have gone ahead to reserve vaccine capacity."

"Good for them. We are not a dictatorship here. We answer to voters."

"To citizens. We answer to citizens, sir. I don't know if they are a dictatorship, but there will be only three billion vaccines. Noah's Ark is filling up, and you'll be the mammoth that forgot to buy a ticket. Make that two tickets. We better hurry. Or pray."

"That will be all today," said the DM. "You will be invited to join the committee as an observer, Mrs. Walker, and we are sending you with our best team tonight at Moria. Dr. Vardis will lead the team."

"Unless you don't need me," added the *Serengeti Photographer*, hoping for a yes.

Alexi opened his palms in a presumed innocent manner, leaving the impression that this was not his doing. The memory of having sex with him two nights ago made her feel weak and inadequate suddenly as if he had the upper hand or surely thought he did.

"An observer. Right," mumbled Tina. "I have to go coordinate the team and pack. You'll excuse me, gentlemen. But hear me out, I'll find a way to talk to the Minister himself, one way or another."

"That will be it, doctor. Unless you want to reevaluate any of your previous colorful statements about the death of innocent people, please don't make any effort to share such rambling factoids with the media."

Tina's back was already facing the Deputy, but she stopped cold and sighed hard before opening the exit door. She turned and peered right into him, faking her most solemn face.

"You are right, sir. I am renouncing my previous statement. About that moussaka. I think it would kill more than the vaccine."

Interlude

# 30. Nahla, the Luminant Sea Maiden

*A short story by graphic artist Yara Zed*

*Deep in the unholy straits of the Aegean Pelago, near the rock-barren island where the primordial gods of the sea bore their monstrous children, sleeps the forsaken god, the one who has no name in the scrolls and the myths, known only to those who have served him as master and suffered under his reign of terror.*

*He is the last son of Phorcys the red-scaled merman, and Ceto the Mighty, brother of Echidna the serpent-bodied and Medusa the snake-haired, of Graeae, the three gray sisters who share one eye and one tooth, of the man-eating Sirens, of Ladon the Drakon Hesperios, the dragon of sunsets, and of Scylla the once beautiful nymph who bathed in the poisoned water of Circe and turned into a six-headed sea hound. Those heinous offspring of Phorcys and Ceto are the monster gods of myth and song, the ones who Odysseus, Jason, and Perseus fought, but their youngest and most abominable unnamed brother lives in no story, for he was rejected by his mother right after birth, and sent to exile. Fifty slaves rowed the penteconter that carried the son with no name to the deep to drown him, but they all went down, their skulls and ribs and chains surround him still as he sleeps in the bottom of the sea upon the soupy black sand.*

*He once had the power to summon the vilest of beings to do his deeds by invading their dreams. He called first his Siren sisters to fetch him man's meat, and when the old gods died, and the Cross rose on their place, he called the dark angels of hell, and when the star and the crescent moon ascended, he called the djinns of the desert and the spirits with eyes and hearts of soot. All those demon slaves came when he summoned them to the darkness, and they knelt with eyes shut and ears opened, for they dared not see, for they dared not disobey and asked the same question.*

*"What should we call you, master?"*

*"You will call me Maulus, the Last One, for you will know of no one and dream of nothing after me," he said, with a voice that still stirs their nightmares.*

*They say he is a gigantic monstrosity, a hundred-eyed cephalopod head with a pulsating purple mantle, and the mouth of Charybdis. It opens up to reveal lines of teeth shaped like the ulnae of the dead. Mile-long tentacles, their poison-oozing sucker cups line the underside, the sharp teeth of the Acanthias on the other.*

*"What do you wish for, master?" asked the servants because they dared not pronounce his name.*

*"Bring me your youngest," said Maulus, "and your most beautiful, the brilliant sun-bathed maidens of the earth above, for I have been banished to the deepest darkness of the waters below, and I need them to illuminate my kingdom and this desolate palace."*

*In ancient times, the Sirens would lure the adventure seekers and the sailors and crush their wooden ships on the rocks, sending young boys down his mouth. But if they found a worthy girl aboard, princess or slave, they'd snatch her and lead her down to Maulus alive. As the eons of glory faded, the old gods weakened, and Maulus dared to capture Olympian goddesses and demigods and even his sisters, the Hesperides, the Nymphs of the West, and Daughters of the evening, the ones who gave birth to the fire-gold lights of sunsets.*

*Then came the age of medieval darkness, broken only by liquid fire. For a thousand and more years, there was no song or poem in the seas of Homer, only men praying to gods and dying under a holy sign. It was the age of the Roman Centurions and the Byzantine Emperors, the Saracen pirates, the Crusader Knights, and the Ottoman askers—kingdoms rising by feeding on the ashes of the fallen. Countless princesses and virgin girls were sailing against their will for the harems of the Sultan, and Maulus salivated with hunger and lust, the foam of his mouth becoming the spume of the angry waves. The meat was plenty for the monster to devour, the beauty for him to enslave.*

*But man's greed kept growing until his power surpassed even that of Maulus. Eventually, man became God himself; he mastered the seas, the skies, and the superstitions, conjured iron ships, and metal birds, and armed them with tentacled mouths that spewed fire and lead. Navies and armies grew mightier and deadlier, so fearsome that soon man stopped fighting like in the old ages, for he realized that he had become slave to the God of War. And there were no more shipwrecks, no more virgin girls for Maulus to add to his collection. Only monster merchant ships crossed the straits, and they battled the waves effortlessly. And Maulus almost perished from starvation, his name erased even from the minds of his demon servants.*

*But man trusts peace only for a breath, yearns for war the rest of the time, so he was lured to his doom once again. At the young dawn of the new century, Maulus regained his lost vigor as the millions of refugees, the hopeless and the weakened, cross the straits from east to west. They come in wave-ravaged dinghies and rotting kaiks, and these are easy prey to the waves. And the sea god called again to his servants, the soot-eyed djinns of the desert, and ordered them to handpick and bring down to him the most luminant maidens of the kingdoms of the east, of Damascus and Bactria, of Parthia and Indoscythia.*

*Most refugee girls are weak and have no light in their eyes, so Maulus pounds them to a pulp at sight, and he devours their meat and marrow. But some are made to shine even at the depths of the oceans—it is not always the rosy light of beauty, some shine with the red of passion, the orange of bravery, the gold of warmth, the violet of mystery, the forest-green of wisdom or the lime-green of fertility; so many lights each one unique to the careful eye.*

*Maulus lines them in homocentric circles around him, chained to his tentacles, and with time the girls' feet turn to shelled mollusks, the shell steals the color of their beauty, their pearls, always two, shining radiantly. Other sea creatures are attracted to the myriad of lights, and unknowingly they run to their doom, the mouth of Maulus, all serving and feeding him.*

*But alive the girls remain, some for centuries, some forever, tattered skin bags of bones, they talk to each other through the motions of their seaweed-spawning arms, the older ones speaking whispers of hope to the younger, and the younger ones—Nahla, the Luminant Sea Maiden of Laodicea, the younger of them all— wonder when they'll be free again to ascend and reunite with their mothers and sisters, their friends, the light of the sun, and the scent of the chrysanthemums.*

*"One day we will," says Aphrodite, the ancient one, the first one who Maulus captured when the gods fell from Olympus, "One day we will grow a million strong and Maulus won't be able to keep us in chains, we will all turn together and shine as one, our light will blind his hundred eyes like fire, and we'll set the sea ablaze, powerful and unstoppable and condemn him to ashes. We will ascend again.*

*"But I fear, my sisters, that no one will accept us like this, with feet turned to mollusks and fingers dark as seaweed, with eyes pearly-white and hearts ashen-black. I fear no one will care to hear about the horrors and the suffering we've been through. These days people long for summer to splash their toes in the shallows, take a dive from a boat, and laugh at the sea's beauty, ignoring the skeletons further below, the fish-torn cadavers of the refugee children, the girls who didn't make it to "civilization."*

*And to all them, I say, so what? Who can dare judge us? Didn't we serve, against our will, an evil master for too long? Why should we care who accepts us and what they think of us? Why can't we just be free for ourselves, ascend and take in the earthy scent of the chrysanthemums once more, listen not to the voices of those who dare judge us but never dared to save us, listen only to the waving whispers of the seaweed among us? We will smell the chrysanthemums again."*

# 31. Yara: Pleasure Island

*Lesbos, June 14-15, 2022*

Yara opened her eyes to meet the darkness. Her fingers touched the bed, then her body trying to make sense of the surroundings. She was lying on a cold creaking camp bed, wearing a gown—no buttons, probably a hospital garment. The sheet was plastic and thin, not cotton, and the sensation felt familiar—mylar blanket. Images were flashing through her mind one by one. A bus leaving Latakia, a taxi to the Turkish coast, her uncle, the dark sea, an abandoned chicken farmhouse, Nahla, a man with eyes painted with soot, surmah, the boat, capsizing, another one saving her, a fisherman wrapping her in a plastic silver blanket, orange vests everywhere, Nahla, two men, one policeman, making fun of her. Nothing after that. No memory of how she got there or where she was. The room around her was vast with a high ceiling, more like a hall, and barely lit. As her vision acclimated to the weak light, she saw a figure emerging.

A girl in a white gown, her age, was standing still at the end of the camp bed, her knees a few inches away from Yara's toes. Messy, Exorcist-style hair, head bent down in a kyphotic posture of misery and omen. Hollow black eyes, like two shotgun barrels staring back at Yara. A bright light was flowing out of her palm. Two more girls, shorter, her sister's height, on identical robes, sleepwalked in the aisle separating the two rows of camp beds. Their airy gowns were cutting through the darkness, absorbing the light that came from the open door and the girl's hand.

The white gown of the close-by girl moved and touched Yara's toes, sending chills down her spine. Yara crouched and brought her knees to her chest, frozen with terror, unable to run away. The girl protruded her hand, the beaming light, toward Yara very slowly. She was holding a mobile phone, offering it to Yara. If she didn't look white as death, pale as a ghost, Yara would have taken it.

This was hell, Christian hell probably, given the wooden hanging icon of an apathetic Jesus observing the girls from the right wall. Hell reserved for older sisters who let their sisters drown.

It was not a mere metaphor. For months after she woke up in that room, not knowing how she got there, Yara remained convinced that she had descended to hell. None of what was happening to her anymore had any resemblance to life. Afterlife, afterdeath, something like that. Did she drown in the sea, did she leave her last breath at the port, or in this hospital of ghosts and no nurses? She had no recollection of dying, but from the moment she awoke, she entered a choreographed ceremony of evil, exceeding her worst nightmares. The hollow-eyed girl at the end of her bed, neither moving nor speaking, was enough of a clue. Yara lifted her blanket to cover her eyes so that she'd stop staring back. She got on her feet with the slowest of moves, still covering her eyes, and walked toward the light, the open door, escaping the lair of the zombie girls. They didn't follow.

As she stepped out to the corridor, she saw a bright white light at the end of it and, based on Christian tabloid pop culture, guessed that it was the path to heaven. So close to hell. If only she had saved Nahla. It certainly didn't smell like heaven. The chlorine odor invaded her nostrils, but there was also another foul smell like someone had defecated very close. Distant screams and nearby sobbing came from the rooms she was passing. Other than a numbing headache and a burning thirst, she was okay, not bleeding, or hurting, no wounds, but then again, all that probably proved that she was dead already.

Back when she lived in Manchester and had a decent broadband connection, Yara had taken a free online film course offered by RISD without her parents' permission. As part of the course, she watched an old movie called *Siesta*. The protagonist, an athletic blonde with a raspy voice, had woken up somewhere in Spain, not remembering anything, and then went through incomprehensible ordeals, some of them lethal, but no matter what happened, she wasn't dying. As Yara watched, she figured that there was only one simple explanation. The blonde was dead from the beginning. Yara never watched *The Sixth Sense* because she guessed the plot twist even from the trailer.

She felt light on her bare feet like a spirit levitating down the corridor. When she reached the end and pushed the screeching door, she entered a kitchen bathed in bright ice-cold light. It was not her grandma's kitchen, nothing warm in there; steel worktables for cutting and cooking, cold tiles, dirty and greasy as she tiptoed barefoot on them. She imagined more girls in bloodied white dresses cut up and stuffed in the freezers.

There were tables and on top of them chairs upside down. Two figures were sitting at the table farther away: a man in a jumpsuit uniform and a lady on a doctor's white coat, both of them smoking, whispering. Yara moved toward them, and they turned their heads. The lady doctor got up, put out her cigarette on the floor, and rushed to Yara. Before speaking, she hugged her softly with her nicotine-smelling arms and guided her to the table.

"You are up. Poor girl! Do you know where you are?" She touched Yara's hand softly, like a mother. Her fingers were yellow.

Yara nodded; she thought she knew.

"My name is Dr. Maria Armandou. I am a volunteer here at Moria." The lady doctor talked in some form of broken English that Yara could barely follow. Not French or Russian accent—those she had heard before—but something else, Greek-English, she guessed. "You fainted at the port after the police found you. Hit your head, chipped a tooth. You are dehydrated, and you'll probably need a few stitches."

Yara passed her tongue along her gums repeatedly. One of the upper teeth was broken, the canine next to it was dangling. She tasted blood as her tongue kept pushing against the tooth and the lip.

"Inside, in the lip," the doctor continued, "I'd rather stitch you up in daylight. A couple of hours, don't worry about that. We have a dental surgeon volunteer, but he can't operate until we remove the stitches. One thing at a time."

Yara felt her canine dangling again and tender. Dental surgery was too much, even for hell. Her mother's face and touch came to her mind, and she collapsed in tears, burying her head in the doctor's arm.

"Shh now, shh. What's your name?" asked the doctor. "We must do the processing here to register you officially at Moria. Thomas here will ask you some questions; I'll help."

"What is Moria?" asked Yara, two long pauses between the three words.

She had heard the name "Moria" before, but that was a different hell, a fantasy movie with orcs, no dental, and dwarf skeletons in armor. She repeated the question.

"This is the refugee camp of Lesbos. You are in Greece, in the European Union. All illegal immigrants are brought to the Moria camp. Are you seeking asylum? Not that it will make any difference any time soon, with what is happening in the last few days. But I have to ask. How old are you? I need your name and nationality, please."

"Yara. Yara Halabi. My mother is Faiza. Is she here?" Yara actually did look around, hoping that her mother would appear from the door.

"Are you seeking asylum?"

"What? I have a United Kingdom passport. Here," said Yara, reaching for her ribcage where she had strapped the passports before they left Turkey.

"They brought you here naked, little lady," the man intervened. His voice was strict and louder. "In this mylar, you are covered with now. No papers. Tell me you fell from the skies, I'll believe. But no Kingdom, they are not even cooperating with us anymore after Brexit. Wrong choice. So please, no lies."

"I am Yara Halabi. I am from Manchester."

The way Yara uttered "Man-cheh-stuh" was quite convincing. The doctor and Thomas looked at each other wide-eyed, eyebrows raised and curved, thinking, "can't be, is she really from Mantzesterrr?" It was obvious that they had started believing her. Either she had the best ESL education Syria could offer, or she was telling the truth.

"Do you have relatives in England? Trying to get to them? Father? Mother?" asked the doctor.

"No, they were in Syria."

"Figured. Please stop lying! You are not helping me or you."

With the corner of her eye, Yara caught the man snorting dismissively.

"Syria?" the man asked, putting the emphasis on the "i." His accent was different, something brute like the spy movies.

"My sister. Have you found her? Nahla. Nahla Halabi. She has papers."

"Naya Galabi?" asked the doctor. "Spell it here. I will check. But she didn't come through the infirmary or registration today. Did she travel with you? Can you please write the names here?"

Yara's hand was trembling, but she tried to scribble the names as clearly as possible.

The man left with a paper that had both names.

"If what you say is true, we'll know. Do you want to call someone?" asked the doctor again and offered her a phone.

"Yes," Yara said and grabbed the phone in front of her.

She tried her mother, then her father, and got the "unavailable" message once again.

"Please, tell me the truth, girl. We can help. Are you seeking asylum? Did you come here from Syria?"

"I am Yara Halabi. I am a British citizen."

"You called two Syrian numbers," said the doctor looking at her phone screen. "If you are from the UK, please give me a British number to call. Your English is excellent, but I've seen all kinds of tricks here."

"I was born in Manchester."

"Do you remember your passport number?"

"No. 107 something."

"You are not helping me, Gianna. Look, you need to rest, drink some water. Eat. There is rice and bread." She pointed to a tray sitting on the metallic bench. "Wait here. I need to go and tend to a couple of patients, I will be back."

Yara ate slowly and alone, keeping a watchful eye around to make sure that none of those girl ghosts had followed her in the kitchen. The first light of dawn was flowing through the eight-feet high small windows. She climbed on a table to look outside; she had no idea where she was. It seemed like a barbed fence surrounded the building, and she spotted two men who looked security. Farther back lay an olive grove, the tree trunks visible against the morning haze. A mob was moving among the trees, gray and black figures, night creatures trying to hide before sunlight. They seemed to be arguing and fighting with the security guards, but their voices were too far to reach Yara.

About half an hour later, the doctor returned along with a man dressed in a plain white dirty shirt and blue pants. The man had gray hair, a beard, and a darker skin tone, probably Syrian. The lady doctor looked different, exasperated, even frightened.

"Did you find my sister?" Yara asked, running to the doctor, who pushed her back softly.

"No time. Look, Gianna, you have to go," said the doctor. "Follow Mohammad here."

The man greeted her in Arabic.

'Go? Where?" Yara asked.

"You're Syrian, right? We established that," the doctor said. "You need to get out of here and to a tent now." She emphasized the *now*. "They are bringing some very sick people here, and then we are shutting down the hospital. Quarantine. You don't want to know. If you don't leave now, you'll both be stuck here. Here! I brought shoes and a bag of clothes. Mohammad will take you to his tent. He is a family man. Go. We'll continue the registration after this quarantine. Or go to the asylum office."

"No more asylum office. They shut it down two days ago," said Mohammad, switching in English.

"Five hundred arrivals per day, what could they do?" said the doctor. "Dress. Now!"

Yara rushed to the corner, hid behind a table, and put on the underwear, no bra, a typical home dress her grandmother would wear, and sandals. She hated sandals. Dr. Armandou was gesturing to her to make haste.

"Go, now! Take the blanket too. You'll come back for the stitches when the quarantine is over. Take these. Antibiotics. Two a day, morning, night."

Mohammad grasped Yara's hand firmly and dragged her out of the kitchen, then the building, then the barbed wire fence. As they stepped out of the hospital, the air felt wet and cool—it had rained during the night.

She wrapped herself again with the mylar blanket, and like a silver winged angel among a swarm of demons, followed Mohammad. They were crossing a different canvas now, a hell that Jackson Pollock would have painted if he had no paint but just blue and silver tarpaulin, wooden pallets, mud, and desperation.

"Syrians, Afghanis, Algeri, Blacks," Mohammad said, switching to Arabic and pointing to the four signs of the horizon to Yara. "The hospital back there is camp center. We always stay on that side," he said, pointing west. "Only west side for Syrians. We have to cross, move fast, and don't stare or talk to anyone until we are there. Follow me! You'll stay with us, my wife and children."

Yara obeyed, her borrowed sneakers squelching on the fresh mud, following Mohammad through a labyrinth of made-up tents. The dwarf-sized tents were cramped, randomly spaced, and stitched together, thronged with grim faces of all ages. Babies crying, mothers soothing them, men from the four corners of the Earth staring at her.

If Dr. Armandou had more time, if it were not for the quarantine, she would have explained more to Yara, maybe even made it a priority to check with the British Embassy the two names Yara had written down. She would tell Yara that Moria had been a refugee camp since the migration started back in 2015. It evolved to a barbed-wired fenced hellhole on a paradise island, capable of hosting five thousand refugees on temporary container homes. It had reached twenty thousand in 2020 when it was described as "the hell of the west" by the media worldwide. Eight thousand of them children, half under the age of twelve. After last month's pandemic eruption in Bangladesh, Pakistan, and Turkey, the numbers had changed abruptly. The dozens became hundreds, and they were coming daily, a massive migration—the shocked locals would call it an invasion and react with fear and sometimes rage. It was mostly fear for the refugees, true terror for the children. There were no toilets, food, supplies, no tents to hide from the summer sun or the winter rains. The government was one step away from throwing the towel and succumbing to sending the military to control the situation. It could not go on for another week, not at that rate. Moria had been the devil's favorite playground for a decade now, but if Dr. Armandou had time to explain to Yara, she'd say that this morning, June 15, 2022, was the culmination of hell, the day the devil had decided to throw his apotheosis party.

Mohammad was about her father's age, svelte, and much shorter. He insisted that Yara cover her head with the blanket.

"The doctor had no hijab for you. My wife will give you one. Stay close. There, you see!" he pointed at the tents. "Afghanis, bad trouble, you stay away. We are all separate here. Stay with your own. Police, doctor, they guard the fence, the hospital, the food, and water. They don't come further in. You want to ask?" Yara didn't want to ask anything. All she cared about was to look carefully at all the little children around her, those around four feet tall. Mohammad continued. "The woman doctor is good. She saved my girl. She called and asked me to help you. I ran here. That place you were, the hospital, all they can do is stitches and medicine, but it is safe. Until today. They quarantine, she said. A plague, spreading. Out here, not safe for young girls. You stay with us, we help you. You have money? You don't, uh?"

Yara let go of Mohammad's hand and ran toward a curly-haired girl. "Nahla, Nahla," she shouted, tried to get a response. It wasn't her.

"Follow me. Don't speak to anyone," Mohammad repeated and pulled Yara by her arm.

They crossed on a wooden plank over a river of rubbish that was separating two sides.

"Made it. Syrian here," said Mohammad. "We're close now." The Syrian side was a grotesque puzzle of tarpaulin blue tied in pallets over pallets to make tents, shelter, bed, baby crib, pavements over the mud. The crowd was getting dense now, smells and voices were multiplying, bedraggled figures waking up, slow movements, and watchful eyes, staring at her. They walked for another ten minutes, Mohammad exchanging nods and greetings with most of the other men on his way. "My niece, here," he said a couple of times, introducing Yara to the bystanders.

He stopped next to a woman on her knees who was tending a fire. The woman was heating a pot, but there was no stove or wood, just cardboard she was trying to set on fire.

"My tent, your tent," said Mohammad. "This is Jamal, my wife."

Jamal turned her covered head and nodded only for a second. "Tea. You want some?" she offered Yara, still kneeling over the fire, holding the pot. Two girls, one boy, were waiting at the mouth of the tent, peering at the newcomer.

"Please, do you have a phone? I must call my father," Yara asked Jamal.

Mohammad gave her his phone reluctantly. His face was fierce and wrinkled like a cartoon villain, yet he had been nothing but helpful and protective so far. The screen was broken, and the battery was at seventeen percent.

There was no answer from the other end, just some voice, first in Greek then in English. "Subscriber's phone. Out of coverage. Call back later."

Mohammad asked for his phone back before Yara could make a third call and then ordered the older girl.

"Fatima, go with the new girl here for water. Don't stop anywhere. Give her," he pointed to Yara, "something to cover."

He threw two garbage bags full of empty plastic bottles at them. "Fill all of them. You are two; you manage to carry them back. Don't go anywhere else," he said.

Fatima got hold of the bags and silently signaled to Yara to follow.

The younger girl, Fatima's sister, was sitting on a palette reading something, and that by itself caught Yara's attention. She was about seven, like her sister, but she was not *her* sister. The book was a few pages thin, some grade school level illustrated version of Pinocchio. The letters were Greek. The little girl showed with a conspirator's seriousness to Yara the page with the wolf and the fox—or was that a fox and a cat—who were trying to lure innocent Pinocchio away from school and to the Pleasure Island.

"What's your name?" Yara asked.

The little girl didn't reply to the question. She just showed Yara the fox, or was that a wolf, and waved her finger, whispering, "We don't go there."

"Where?" Yara whispered back and caressed the girl's hair.

"And get a diaper for her," said Jamal speaking to her daughter Fatima. "If she has to."

194

Yara didn't understand that last order; she thought Jamal was talking about the little girl. She wrapped the borrowed hijab around her head and started following Fatima, who had stuffed the diaper in the plastic bag.

As the sun was getting higher, the summer heat was returning, erasing the coolness of last night's rain, and Yara decided to take off her hijab after a few yards.

"What are you doing? Put it back on," said Fatima, pulling Yara's sleeve.

"No," she said. *I must stand out, Nahla must see me. She will not recognize me if I am one of the thousand hijabs.*

"Stupid girl," said Fatima. "Stupid."

The two girls kept swerving and jumping over pools of mud, babies, and women, garbage piles. A man kneeling on a prayer rug, a woman taking a shit behind a tree stump, a kid playing with a yoyo, five more watching him.

"Hey, princess, here, come to me," a young man called at Yara.

Fatima showed her the hijab again, making an angry gesture that she should put it on immediately. "You are bringing the men. Trouble," she said.

The whole thought of attracting a man, her body stinking like a pig, her teeth broken and crooked, dressed in Syrian grandma clothes, was ridiculous to Yara.

The young man whistled to her. "Hey, princess," he shouted again, gesturing. "Come here, have some tea with me."

Tea, princess, for a split-second, Yara's mind combined the two of them. Disney World. "Tea with the princesses" was supposed to be quite a party experience in Orlando, USA. Back when she was in Manchester, she dreamt of going to that one day. She'd take Nahla. Promise. She started calling Nahla's name again as she saw three little ones kicking a can around. There were so many children here; it was a matter of time. One, two, five more tents, and she'd see her.

Fatima stopped at the tail of an endless queue of hijab-covered women, all of them waiting with empty bottles.

"What is this? I must go to the police," Yara said. "Can't wait here."

"Asylum? Office closed," said Fatima, and the frail toothless woman in front of them turned her head and nodded to Yara to verify the statement.

Yara ran her tongue over her broken teeth again. "Epidemic," said Fatima. "All closed, everything except food and water. We must get water, or we die. You stay here with me. I can't carry all those bottles. They'll steal them if I am alone."

"How long?" said Yara. *I have to search for my sister.*

"Four hours yesterday, but looks worse today. Maybe five."

"What? Hours? For water?"

"And five evening. We two do water all day. My dad does food, another five hours wait. My mother stays with my brother and sister. They cook, she protects the tent too. We all work here. You help. Or you leave."

The skinny body, steely-eyed Fatima, had no love and patience for Yara.

An hour passed, and Yara saw that they had barely made fifty yards progress in a line that was three hundred yards and more. She couldn't see how long it was stretching. Two men argued, one pulled a knife, the women screamed, and more men ran to separate them. They were all Syrian; that was the sole reason to feel safer.

Another hour passed, standing in the queue, the sun scorching more as it was almost noon. "I must go," she said to Fatima. She had not been to the bathroom for four days.

Fatima gave her the diaper. "Here!"

"What? No, not my period, I have to go, not pee. Other."

"Here!" Fatima said once again, extending the hand with the pull-up.

"Do you understand what I am saying? Where are the bathrooms?"

Yara was turning her head around as if she expected to find a sign in English with a female icon pointing the way to the WC.

"No bathrooms. Never. There are bad men waiting there. Not safe. They hurt you. You want to go, you go here, we all do," said Fatima and threw the diaper to Yara. "Only men go to bathrooms."

Yara let the pull-up fall to the mud and turned her back to Fatima. To the rest of her days, she'd be ashamed of that act of stupidity and ungratefulness more than anything else that had happened to her in the Hell of Moria.

She broke away from the queue and started wandering in the opposite direction, searching for the toilets. Fatima kept calling her back, "Hey you, come back, help me," but Yara had enough of those stupid refugees. She was a British citizen, after all. And Nahla was still missing. What if the little one was all alone in the camp? All she had to do was find a policeman, a doctor, an office, and a bathroom. What was the worst that could happen? Shoot her? Yeah, there it was. Had to be somewhere. "WC." Gray portable toilet booths. How bad could they be? She'd use the hijab for sitting. Not even a line of waiting. Her raven hair flowed with the wind as she rushed toward the bathroom. She was uncovered, alone, sixteen years old, sweating, and shivering. She had left the mylar blanket, her guardian angel wings back at Mohammad's. Broken teeth, period, stinking; the opposite of attractive, the thought not even crossing her mind.

A young man was resting with his back against the wall across from the women's toilets. Shaved head, tall, athletic figure. Clean, no beard, tanned skin, Algerian, or something. She tried to avoid his eyes, but she couldn't. The brightest jades she'd ever seen. He greeted her silently with the grin of a fox, or was that a wolf?

# 32. Lucia: On the Boat to Lesbos

*The Aegean Sea, June 17, 2022*

The Lesbos Star ferry was almost two hundred yards long, with double-deck car loading, and could carry a village, about fifteen-hundred people. As a result, it was slow, scheduled to leave the port of Piraeus at 10 p.m. and arrive at Lesbos eleven hours later.

It was the transportation of choice for locals, commercial trucks, and vacationing families with kids, cars, and baggage. The sleep-in cabins were all booked ahead, so Lucia settled for a first-class ticket.

The wind was slapping her hard as she queued behind a dozen passengers to board. She had thrown everything into her duffel bag, laptop, one change of underwear, and the fiberglass leg, the only evidence of last night's adventures. Once she was alone, she'd make the evidence disappear at the bottom of the sea. The line wasn't moving. The usher was trying to check-in a large group ahead of her, and he kept counting, one, two, seven, fifteen, again and again.

"We are from the Ministry. Yeah yeah, we are one ticket short. Let us in. We'll pay inside," said the man who was leading the group.

Lucia started pushing through the crowd to get ahead. "Sorry, sorry, I am with the Ministry too," she whispered and made it to the beginning of the line.

She tapped on the shoulder of the man in front to ask what Ministry they were from. As he turned, she saw the nametag on the lanyard: *Dr. Alexi Vardis, Ministry of Health.*

"What is it, lady?" the middle-aged man asked.

"Nothing, forget it," Lucia replied in English to confuse him.

She followed them all the way to the second-class seats, despite the ticket inspector pointing her to the first class, and she kept close to see where they were sitting.

*Pick one, pick the right one,* she said to herself, and her eyes focused on the lady in her late thirties who was sitting down by the window. The seating was three by three, the same as in a Boeing 727, and Lucia needed both empty seats.

She pulled out the prosthetic leg, dropped it in the middle seat between her and the lady who looked like she had jumped out of an Ancient Greek vase painting. Dark hair falling straight on her back, a Greek nose that neutralized the innocent beauty of her olive eyes, dark circles under them. A mom, a scientist, or both. She'd do.

"Oops, made it," Lucia said in Greek, slipping into the aisle seat.

"I don't think this is your seat," Tina said, looking at Lucia, then at the fiberglass leg, then back at her.

"Yeah, well, I don't know. You see, my brother, his leg, they are bringing him up, with the elevator, in his wheelchair, he is sitting there, you know he needs me." Lucia pointed to the adjacent three seats on her left, separated by the aisle, "I need to be next to him, you understand. I am Luka, by the way."

"Luka, strange name. Where are you from?" asked Tina. Strange name, hair, a fiberglass leg, she twisted uneasily. "I am Tina," she offered a brief handshake and turned bleary-eyed toward the darkness of the window.

Lucia had managed to steal the seats of a couple of Ministry officials; now, she had to keep them.

"I am sorry, lady, you are at my seat," said Alexi, now him being the one tapping on her shoulder.

He winked to Tina, Lucia registering every exchange.

"I don't understand," Lucia switched to English again, trying to avoid a long conversation.

"My seat! Here."

"I don't think so, sir," she said, pointing to the leg, "You know I am waiting for my brother. He is disabled."

Alexi showed his ticket. "Well, you are wrong. Inspector!" he shouted, raising his hand, but there was no one at close distance.

"Well, sir, please, can't you just go back there? I'll give you a first-class ticket. Here. Half the hall is empty. They don't care."

"I do care, I'm afraid—" he started saying.

"Seriously, Alexi? Did you book our seats next to each other?" Tina was fuming.

Alexi leaned over Lucia, his previous century fashionable perfume suffocating her, the casual sweater over his shoulders tickling her. He caressed Tina's arm for a second until she pushed him away.

"I'll go find us a cabin," he whispered, confident that Lucia wouldn't understand a word.

"Get away from here, or by my word, I'll report you. The girl is staying here, she has to be with her brother," said Tina.

"As the lady says," said Lucia switching in Greek, and Alexi backpedaled, shocked from the embarrassment. He disappeared down the aisle, throwing a couple of looks back at the women.

"Thank you," sighed Tina. "You were in the right place, right time." Without knowing it yet, Tina had summarized the next year of their lives in that one sentence. "Sorry, I need to get some rest," she continued.

"You going to Moria?" Lucia asked, just making sure that she hadn't gone through all this charade for no reason.

"Huh, yes, how do you know?"

"I guessed, from your nametag. Health Ministry etc. I am going there too. I am from the press."

"Really? The press? What press is that? The camp is closed to anyone but emergency personnel."

"The…the independent press."

"Right! Well, goodnight and good luck getting in," Tina said and pulled a beige sleeping mask over her face.

The behemoth vessel sailed out of the port and into the Aegean. Both women were fast asleep, touching the prosthetic leg that separated them, dreaming a different dream, and fighting a different villain under the same undulating rhythm.

Lucia woke up at 6 a.m., and she watched a rerun on the TV screen across from her, waiting for Tina to wake up.

"I've seen this one," Tina said as she woke up near the end of the episode. Soft voice and puffy eyes, she was looking at the screen rather than at Lucia.

"It's stupid. Why is she helping that man?" said Lucia, referring to the thriller. "He is a criminal. He abducted her."

"It's TV. And he is handsome, in a *brutal* way," said Tina.

"He is a psycho. An escape convict. He could rape her. I'd kill him with the rolling pin back when he fell asleep on her couch. There was a rolling pin in the kitchen."

"The rolling pin? Wow!" said Tina. "You don't live here, Luka. Is it Luka, you said?"

"Lucia, for you. No, I live abroad. Berlin."

"Berlin! But no German accent. Freie Presse, der reporter?"

"What?"

"Yeah, forget it, you are not very convincing. Where is your disabled brother, by the way?"

"They gave him a cabin, all good," Lucia countered quickly.

"Right! But you stayed here instead to watch TV with me."

"I'll go get some coffee," said Lucia. "Maybe I'll get on your good side. We must talk. It's serious."

"I don't think so."

"Please, I know about your husband," said Lucia, hoping that fear would be a motivator. "And he doesn't know about Alexi."

Tina jumped off her seat as if she had been hit with a rolling pin. "What the hell? Who are you?" she asked.

But Lucia was already walking down the aisle toward the coffee bar, confident that Tina would wait for her.

She was back a few minutes later, holding two papers cups. "How do you like your coffee? Black, I guessed, but I brought sugars, stevia, and milk."

"Who are you? How do you know me?" Tina leaned toward Lucia, her patience exhausted, tapping her clenched fist nervously on the drop-down table that separated them.

"I don't know you, doctor," said Lucia. "But I need a favor. You must get me into the Moria camp. It's life and death."

"It is more death than life, and even if I could, I would never let you in, not this week. You heard of the influenza crisis."

"Yeah, but it is the flu, after all. No big deal. What I am after is really big. Much bigger!"

"Really? Bigger than a potential flu pandemic? Do you know anything about a flu pandemic?"

"We need to stop the sex-trafficking ring. Moria!"

"The sex what? Are you on drugs, girl? Partying too hard? Your eyes have that haze."

"I didn't sleep much, and the truth is I was in a strip joint last night. Research," said Lucia, and Tina just shook her head, mumbling a curse and starting to get up. "Please, listen to me," Lucia continued. "One minute is all I ask. I represent an anti-slavery NGO, Berlin's Freedom First. I heard something in that club. There is a big sex-trafficking ring in Moria. They will ship out a group of girls in two days. Sunday. They do it every Sunday. I must stop it."

"I've never heard anything about this."

"Of course, you haven't. You have your cushy public servant job, the humble Gucci sunglasses, the cute XS phone, your husband, your son. Why would you know?"

"My son?"

"Okay, calm down, I am not stalking you, just listen, doctor," Lucia said. She held the laminated catalog listing the cheese-pies and the coffee types at the ship's canteen and started going line by line. "Pretend with me that this is a sex-trafficking catalog, I'll give you some facts about this world we live in. Here is your ordering list:

"Refugees in camps around the world: ten million.

"Sex slaves, most of them children. Twelve million. I mean slaves like back in the old days and the movies that win the Oscars and such.

"Five thousand rupees buys you a boy at Varanasi—do you know where Varanasi is? Eight thousand a virgin girl. Not for one night, that is a hundred rupees, less than a burger, I mean buy the girl for good, flesh and soul, exploit her for years, if she lasts that long. Fathers sell them. Every time somebody puts their thing in them, a quarter goes back to the father at the village. They're like slot machines for the village."

"And how do you know all this?" Tina asked.

"I am a reporter. That's what I do," said Lucia. The truth was that this was her research for the term paper she had to submit in the criminology class a month ago. She continued: "Nepalese girls. Nepal's per capita is hundred eighty dollars. Get it? Once you're sold, you never escape. That's Asia. Ten-billion-dollar industry a year in America, free market and all. Here, in Europe, or whatever we are, the same. Moldova, Turkey, Romania, Greece, Albania, the refugee camps, all those girls from Syria and Nigeria, from there to Italy and farther. Would you like to order a blonde, maybe? Eight hundred euros buys you a girl from a Ukrainian village. You keep her for a couple of years. Here, let me take your order, doctor?"

Tina knew where Varanasi was; it was in the WHO report. There had been deaths from H7N9 there. She knew too well.

"Are you saying that you have proof that there is a sex-trafficking ring operating at the Moria camp?"

"First-hand testimony. Obtained the hard way."

"The police? Go to them."

"You are joking, right? Go to the police to stop a crime! That's a new one. I go to the police like this," Lucia pointed at her carroty hair, "what do you think they'll say?"

"My son. How did you know?"

"Will you get me in the camp? I know nothing, dear doctor. You have a photo of a kid on your phone screen, you wear a wedding ring, you called your husband earlier, but that man who came here before, Alexi with the metrosexual teenager perfume, he winked at you, and the way he touched you.

He suggested in front of me that you two share a cabin. Look, I don't need to be a detective to add one plus one. I need your help. Else…"

"Else what? You tell my husband?"

"Else, you are not doing your duty as a scientist and a decent human being. I am half your age, and I am."

"I am thirty-seven."

"I am twenty-one, about right. Look, sorry to come out strong like this. I don't have many options. Please, help me! Get me in the camp."

"We don't know what we'll find there. People are dying. I cannot allow civilians in and out. Do you understand what a pandemic is? Everything can go too wrong too fast."

"Look, I need to stop the trafficking ring. Else, if they smuggle these girls out and send them to the brothels, the epidemic will spread. What if they are sick already? How about that? We help each other."

"No, I can't, I don't know you. It's not right."

"Let me tell you what is not right. Watch this."

Lucia gave Tina her laptop and tapped on the video to start playing, the images changing fast before Tina's eyes. Cities and villages from Romania, to Ukraine, to India and Thailand, all poor to the level that brought Tina back to her senses about how lucky she was. Narrow streets and decrepit buildings, bordering filthy rivers in India, nuclear wastelands in deep Russia. Cernavoda, Romania, a teenage girl doing cartwheels in front of her friends, stopping to tell a reporter about her experiences at the massage parlor where her school boyfriend had led her to for work, Ukraine girls sold and bought six different times from Istanbul to London, twenty men with cameras bidding and surrounding a frightened kid hiding under a dupatta head-scarf in broad daylight in Benares, an Indian woman, red bindi on her forehead, barefoot with anklets, confessing that she worked twenty-hours seven days, abducted from Nepal when she was thirteen, Russian girls describing the extra menu of no condoms and anal at a London massage parlor. The whole thing went by very fast, like a silent slideshow.

Tina rolled it back to where the kid was sold at Banaras, surrounded by the bidding men. A pack of wolves on a baby deer. The little girl managed to avoid everyone's eyes, starring down at a corner with her left eye, terrified, as if she had seen the gate of hell opening, its maw ready to swallow her.

"This is just the menu, the table of contents," said Lucia. "If you click 'Show More' below, you get all the hyperlinks, then you can select a country and find all the documentaries. You can spend the whole weekend watching. Or you can do something about it. I am."

"You will stop them? The global mafia rings? *You* alone?"

"I don't know. I am not talking about teleological grand designs and stopping all crime across all womankind. But I'll stop this Sunday. The girls will be shipped out Sunday. I'll stop that. A dozen gang rapes, a thousand nights of rapes. A start."

The carrot-hair girl was getting to Tina. "But I can't. Our mission is too dangerous to add a teenage vigilante to the mix."

"I am twenty-one. You can, and we will."

The drop-down TVs were all playing in unison the updates on the Papalias abduction, talking about the boy's return home. Lucia caught a glimpse of the villa and the security cars at its entrance.

"They found that poor boy. He was at the same school as our son. Thank God!" said Tina as she was getting up to escape Lucia's siege. "See! The police. You should trust them. Sometimes they do their job."

"Yeah, thank God and the police. Both were a hell of a help last night," said Lucia, and then sold out, sensing that this was her last chance. "God doesn't save anyone, doctor. We do. I tell you what. You get me into the camp, I'll tell you how I saved the Papalias kid, alone. It might happen to yours someday, and you should know who to call."

Tina chuckled dismissively.

Lucia's phone rang from a number, and without thinking much, she answered.

"Ms. Lucia Maas?" the voice on the other end was professional and spoke in English with a Greek accent.

"Who is this?"

"I am connecting you to Mr. Papalias. Wait on the line."

Lucia turned toward Tina and whispered. "That's him. Mr. Papalias."

Tina blew a raspberry and threw her hand in the air.

Lucia turned on the speaker, and "John Papalias here," were the next words coming out of her phone. She quickly put the phone on her ear, cutting a dumbfounded Tina from the rest of the conversation.

"Sorry, business, doctor," she whispered and then removed her hand from the phone. "I'm listening, sir. Everything all right, I guess, send my best to your lady."

"Ms. Maas, I have a rule I live and do business by, and I call it the rule of three."

"And it stands for 'three million?'" Lucia giggled.

"No problem if that's your wish. My rule is that I repay everyone three times what they bring to me. Somebody brings a euro to me, he'll make three. He brings me trouble, I bring him three times the trouble. Somebody takes my kid away. Anyway, you get it. I want to thank you."

*Is he going to thank me three times, and that's it?* Lucia thought.

"Just doing my job, sir," said Lucia, winking at Tina concurrently. "Our firm will send the bill."

"You did more than your job, and it cost you personally. I heard you are in hiding, Elon told me. But after the dust settles down here, and we get them, there is nothing to worry about. And listen to me carefully. You have three wishes. Anytime, anywhere in your life, if you are in trouble, you call this number we just called you from, you talk to Roula, my PA, and ask for anything you need. Three wishes. Use them wisely."

"Thank you, Mr. Papalias. I will be in touch with you soon."

Lucia turned off the phone and grimaced a "I told you so."

"You don't expect me to believe that," said Tina.

"Do you want to call him back to confirm? It will cost me of my three extra lives, but I'd do it if it gets me in your camp."

Lucia didn't glance up to the right, didn't blush or sweat or touch her face. As far as anyone, even an FBI agent, would say, based on facial expressions, she wasn't lying.

"May I have your attention, please," an announcement came over the ship's speakers. "Ladies and gentlemen, in a few minutes, we'll arrive at the port of Mytilene, Lesbos. All passengers are kindly requested—"

Out of the window, the port of Mytilene had opened its maw wide, ready to devour all who dared enter, saviors or vigilantes.

# 33. Tina: On the Boat to Lesbos

*The Aegean Sea, June 17, 2022*

Tina sank in her seat by the window on the premium economy hall, knees pushing against the front row, cursing all the world's engineers that they still couldn't find the secret to Star Trek's teleporting technology. Ships always made her uneasy, and modern ferry cruisers gave her that feeling of spatial disillusionment. The seats were identical to an airplane's shape and configuration, three together, aisle, four in the middle, aisle, and three more. The windows were wide and tall, resembling a bus, but the rolling motion was definitely ship-like, signaling that the night would be long and wobbly. She was already chewing her travel gum, hoping that the dimenhydrinate would help her fall asleep even faster.

Lesbos was ten dark and nauseating hours away, and the Ministry's budget did not allow for a cabin. The mouse-colored neck pillow matched her slacks; comfortable clothing was the only weapon she had to battle her distaste for a long journey.

Out of her window, the Piraeus seaport at night gave the illusion of a Gothamesque cosmopolitan setting rather than the overcrowded shithole it had become due to cheap over-construction and lack of elementary urban planning. Tina was wearing gradient sunglasses, though the sun had set an hour ago, using them as a loud warning sign that she had no interest or strength to talk to anyone. The Geneva conference, Alexi, her desperate attempt to convince the Deputy Minister to buy vaccines, an epic fight with Peri, who might have even figured out that she was having an affair. Her father throwing her mother out of her birth home to sell it—had she inherited his infidelity gene, she'd never thought of that before. Silence, that's all she wished for.

She took the sunglasses off as she caught the strangest of things approaching her. It was a scene out of a "new-weird" movie played out in front of her, just for her, as if she were the weirdo director. A leg, a naked human leg, detached from the body, was moving down the aisle, floating above the headrest level of the airplane-style seats. The leg kept getting closer, and suddenly, it came to rest on the middle seat next to her. Tina realized just then that it was a transfemoral artificial leg, a genuine relief given any of the possible alternatives. The girl who carried the leg had bright orange hair, orange as in Finding Nemo and chrysanthemums in September.

The orange-hair girl had sat down before Tina mumbled that the seat was taken. The girl's spread arms claimed the space, marking it and surrounding it with her youthful perfume, a subtle river of jasmine, grapefruit, sandalwood, and wild strawberries invading Tina's nose. The girl was wiry and athletic, not doll-beautiful but with a disarming smile that pushed Tina to switch her similes toward carrot cake and away from Disney fish.

"I am Lucia," she introduced herself.

In the next swift moments, the girl Lucia had already proved her worth and uniqueness as she managed to get rid of Alexi, the pesting-going-to-sleazy flirt that Tina was trying to avoid.

It took only a couple of sentences from Lucia for Alexi to disappear, and soon after that, Tina fell asleep at her seat, leaning peacefully against the window. She didn't even manage or dare to thank the girl; she didn't want to give her familiarity rights.

Tina claims that she dreamed of Lucia that first night, or so she'd convince herself afterward—she knew very well that dreams are a tricky thing to rely upon—in retrospect, we spin their blurry images like yarn to weave the missing threads of our incomprehensible life.

If this were a cliché-shocking type of TV show, the screenwriter would add a crypto or chili-hot lesbianism angle—and who would blame him, given the two of them sailing toward the namesake island. But sexual attraction, let alone consummation, obvious or subconscious, was never implied or expressed by any of the two women.

When Tina woke up, she quickly realized that the girl with the orange hair was probably psycho. Lucia was making up stories about being a German reporter, an NGO, knowing Papalias, rescuing his child (that took the cake), a sex-trafficking ring in Moria, even knowing about Alexi and Peri.

Tina held the line until the end of the conversation: "I really wouldn't know how to help you."

"I am going to sneak into Moria, whether you help me or not," Lucia insisted.

"Is that really so important to you? Do you understand what's at stake? Know anything about a flu crisis?"

"You ask any of these girls if they prefer catching the flu and sneeze for a few days or being sold as sex slaves and been raped by fat-ugly fifty-year-old blue-pill-poppers up the ass day and night, what do you think they'd answer?"

Lucia's green eyes peered at Tina, demanding an answer. *Answer me. Answer.* Tina got up from her seat. She needed a few minutes to switch out of this conversation, stretch her legs, change to a professional suit, brush her teeth, and freshen up. They were maybe an hour away from the port of Mytilene, and the sun was rising, thankfully, on the opposite side of the ship.

She returned to her seat, looking to talk some sense into Lucia.

"Sneeze for a few days, huh? Let me explain it to you, young lady. Let's play a game," Tina said.

"No time."

"It's a fast one. I say the year, and you tell me the event. The first that comes to your mind, okay?"

Lucia shrugged her shoulders.

"1940."

"World war two," said Lucia.

"1821."

"Greek independence revolution."

"490."

Lucia stood silent.

"490 BC," Tina continued.

"Battle of Salamis? No, wait, battle of Marathon."

"Good! You are good. 1789."

"French revolution."

"1968."

"May, France."

"1969."

"Man on the moon."

"Good! Last one. 1918."

"World war one."

"1918."

"I don't know, Red October?"

"Off by a year. 1918."

Lucia shrugged her shoulders again.

"Nothing else? 1918. Come on, Lucia. For fifty euros."

"Nothing."

"Nothing you learned at school, heh? It is only history if a mad man is storming with troops and fire. As if we are alone on the universe, even on the planet," said Tina.

"Enlighten me?"

"Yes, I will. 1918. A flu pandemic breaks out in the USA, most likely in an army camp in Kansas. They'll call it the Spanish flu—"

"I've heard of that."

"—though it didn't have much to do with Spain. Long story. Within a year, fifty million people die; others say a hundred million if we count all the Asian victims that no one counted accurately. I'd give you a seventy million researched and personal estimate. About as many as in World war two. But in a year."

"That can't be right."

"But it is. Tell me, how many movies have you seen about World war two? A hundred? Two hundred? Out of the thousands available. How many books? Countless. There is no movie about the Spanish flu. The flu is dull as death, no story to remember. Half a billion were infected, a third of the world, back then. An unusual number of the dead were between twenty and forty years old because the stronger the immune system was, the faster it would kill the patient as the antibodies kicked into overdrive. These were not the old and the sick, those you expected to die. They were deaths that were not supposed to happen. A young son, a young mother, it is devastating. Elderly parents destroyed by sorrow, children starved to death. The death that kept on killing. Every family lost someone. All in a year, three waves, spring, autumn, winter. Rings a bell?"

"I can't say that I've read much about it."

"Do you know about the plague of Athens? Hippocrates?"

"Yes, we read about that at school. Peloponnesian war."

"It ended Athenian civilization, tilted the war toward Sparta. One-third of Athenians died. The Antonine plague?"

"No, what's that?"

"Measles. One-third of the Romans died. Two thousand died every day, it raged unstoppable for nine years. It ended the Roman Empire as you know it. Not enough men left to man the armies. The Black Plague?"

"You try to scare me?" Lucia asked, unnerved.

Tina knew that she could not scare a young person with such stories. Lucia had probably binge-watched zombie movies since she was eleven.

"And this thing at Moria, you think it is the Black Plague or something that big?"

"This thing, this outbreak. No, I hope not, I don't know yet. I am not trying to scare you, just to educate you and give you some perspective. Once we dock, half an hour from now, it is a race. I'll run out the ship faster than anyone in here. No time for goodbyes. I am an epidemiologist, I know nothing about sex-trafficking rings or how to neutralize them. Sure, you know karate and all and think you can stop them with your bare hands, but I am not your age. Family," Tina showed her ring.

"Karate or not, if you asked me to help you with your mission, I would. At least get me in the camp," Lucia insisted.

"I wish you could help me," Tina sighed. "We'll need all the help we can get. But I can't."

"I am resourceful," Lucia said, tapping her fingers fast and repeatedly on the fiberglass leg that separated the two women. "You know we are coming to this island by ship," Lucia continued, "but every night, kids and families drown trying to cross those straits from Turkey. Imagine a young girl, younger than me, who survives the sea. Maybe she loses her mom along the way. Imagine that. And then she ends up in a camp and from there smuggled in the back of a truck, only to be gang-raped and be sold as a sex slave. In the first weeks, they rape them to break them. That's their words, verbatim. I heard a man from the ring yesterday. Tell me you don't give a shit, doctor. Just tell me that."

"May I have your attention, please," the ship's speakers announced. "Ladies and gentlemen, in a few minutes, we'll arrive at the port of Mytilene, Lesbos. All passengers are kindly requested—"

Out of the window, the port of Lesbos had opened its maw wide, ready to devour all who dared enter, avenging angels or teenage refugees.

Interlude

# 34. Anaya, The Mouth of Hell

*A short story by graphic artist Yara Zed*

*Deep in the holy streets of the city of Varanasi, India, upon the sacred land where one of the five heads of Brahma rests unseen, sleeps the prostitute Anaya, the one who was born to a different name in the poorest of Nepalese villages, her true name remembered only by her mother and known only to her friend Shefali, forgotten even by her malik, the brothel boss she has served as master for nine and more years.*

*She is the last of the seven daughters of Baburam, a goatherder from the mud-villages of Jethal; daughter of Bilhana, who was forced to marry her mother's brother at age twelve and bore his eleven children and three more stillborn, all in April; mother to Chimini and Sanani, twin girl and boy, born by a miracle five years ago, refusing to die in her womb despite the pills forcefully fed to her by the malik; sister of Dhonu the one named King and Kwina the one named Queen, who were both sold before her to the same dalal, who trafficked them across the mountains and down to the most violent streets of Varanasi to be auctioned off at the market, albeit at a low price and a lowly establishment after he had stolen their virginities for himself.*

*She once was known to her mother as the girl with the smile of a thousand flowers, before that night, her father interrupted her innocent dreams and woke her up at the first sign of dawn. "Daughter," he called upon her, "you must follow*

214

*this man who will take you to a rich and important city. You will obey him, and he will help you find a job and a man to serve and to care of you."*

*And thus, Anaya departed the rhododendron-stained slopes of Nepal, trembling from cold and fear equally, following a man who wouldn't talk or reply to her until night fell over the steep mountains, and they stopped at an empty hut that the dalal called "home."*

*"What should I call you, kind master?" Anaya asked the dalal, the first night they stopped to rest. The Nepalese girls are known for being meek and obedient, thus have a reputation of becoming "manageable" slaves.*

*"You will call me 'kind,' and you will call me 'master' for you will know of no one and dream of nothing after me," said the dalal.*

*He grabbed Anaya by her frail arm, and when she screamed in utter surprise, he took out his belt and welted her until she silenced her to a muffled sob, and then raped her repeatedly, for three days and nights until Anaya couldn't scream anymore as she felt her ribs, spine, and spirit broken to a thousand pieces and begged for his kindness to stop and knelt in front of her master willing to do anything for water or a piece of stale roti.*

*The dalal took her to the city of Varanasi, and she marveled as they passed by boat the Ganges river and saw the red and ochre-colored ghats, those shrines, with concrete steps reaching the river banks, where the pilgrims come to find water and fire, in ablutions or cremations, heaven and hell. For it is a great fortune to die in this holiest of cities, thousands and thousands of pious and devoted men and women come to do so. Anaya would see nothing more of Varanasi, the city also known as Benares, except for those ghats on the first day she arrived and the street she'd be forced to slave in as a prostitute every day for the next five years.*

*It is a fact that even in this sacred place, there are more men of ill-intention and vile instincts than kind-hearted ones. A salivating pack of them, more than a dozen, came to bid for ownership of twelve-year-old Anaya in the market, and the malik who won her, a gigantic monstrosity of fat, filth, and greed, locked her in a pinjara, a four by ten foot street cage, it's front side visible to locals and tourists eyeing the merchandise, the child, the prostitute. He forced her to sleep with men day and night, some days as many as twenty of those who paid no heed to the holiness of the city.*

*On the third day, she begged, "Let me go," and the malik told her that she was a fortunate one because she was destined to die in Varanasi, a sacred place where everyone prayed and even paid to come and die. He promised that he'd never let her go.*

*The opium erased everything in her mind after the ninth day, and from then on, she was a servile broken wooden doll, a female Pinocchio, a slave with rattling joints, but no fairy godmother, among thousands of Honest Johns.*

*It was a spring sun-blinding day when Anaya turned seventeen. She didn't know her exact birthday, other than it was spring, had to be. The rays and the sun's warmth fell from the sky down to her street and cut through the cage's bars. One week had gone by since her second abortion, induced by swallowing the malik's poisons. On that self-proclaimed birthday, they brought Shefali to the pinjara next to her. Maybe Anaya was dazzled by the newcomer's name, reminiscent of flowers and happier days, or by the motherly sweetness of Shefali's voice, for she was some years older than Anaya. Shefali would talk to the younger girl day and night, between the customers' visits, and whenever she felt Anaya suffering under the weight and the wrath of a brute. That woman was an indomitable spirit, unbroken and unwilling to accept the fate that the world had reserved for her, and she tried to pass her message of hope from her cage to Anaya's.*

*"We will escape, Anaya, one day, we will, I will help you, I have escaped before. My true Nepalese name is Binsa, the fearless one. Last spring, I escaped slavery and made it to my village in Jethal. Yes, we are both from the same villages, and it is a sign of the gods to be together."*

*Shefali, whose true Nepalese name was Binsa, did not tell Anaya the whole story, how she made it back to her village and told them about her tormented life, only to be scorned, ousted, and refused by all known and not to her, her mother first. For the village's convenient story was that she had married well in Mumbai and was cleaning houses of noble people, and every time she would clean a house, her husband, that would actually be the dalal, would send twenty rupees back to the village, for every house she cleaned, but she was not really cleaning houses, in fact, she was a slot machine that swallows the filth and spews out coins for her father and her village, day and night. And no one wanted such an unclean and untrue woman—one who smelled, looked, and talked like a whore, and that was the only schooling she had ever had—to settle back at the village and corrupt the men. And as the night fell cold and Shefali wandered alone out of her village, somebody messaged the dalal who worked those villages, and he caught her and returned her to the brothel boss, a wronged businessman in rage.*

*Shefali never told Anaya what her punishment was, how the malik almost beat her to death, and how he inserted—four men holding her down hands and feet— a broomstick dipped in lemon juice and chili powder inside her, and how she screamed as no human being had screamed before, the pain so maddening that she could not even faint from it. The nights of pain that she could not sleep or even crawl to the bathroom.*

*But a woman like Shefali obeys her master only for a breath, yearns for freedom the rest of the time, so she is poised to escape the pinjara of the malik once again.*

*"Promise me you'll come with me, Anaya."*

*Anaya is not so brave; the thousands of rapes had twisted themselves around her spine like a braid of paralyzing fear, and she cannot promise Shefali. She can only tell her of her fear; because she has already accepted that there is no other life left for her.*

*"I fear, my sister, that no one will accept us like this, with bodies broken from venereal disease and minds broken from the opium, with eyes pearly-white and hearts ashen-black. I fear no one will care to hear about the horrors and the suffering we've been through. These days our parents and brothers enjoy the spoils of the sold children who bring back rupees, a handful but enough to buy some rice and bread, maybe to have another child at their old age, one more to provide, ignoring the skeletons of the lost children of Varanasi, the slavery-torn cadavers of the sex-slaves, the girls who made it to "civilization.""*

*Shefali tries to change Anaya's mind.*

*"Come with me, Anaya. Do not fear them. Even if it is so, to all them, we say, so what? Who can dare judge us? Didn't we serve, against our will, an evil master for too long? Why should we care who accepts us and what they think of us, why can't we just be free for ourselves, ascend and smell the heavenly scent of the rhododendrons once more, listen not to the voices of those who dare judge us, but never dared to save us, listen only to the waving whispers of the home mountain winds embracing us? We will smell the rhododendrons again."*

*And so did Shefali escape one night, she crossed mountains and deserts and made it all the way to Europe, selling her body again and again along the route to earn each mile of freedom. But Anaya did not follow her, for she was again pregnant, and moreover, she had forgotten how to walk miles and miles under the sun, convinced that she would burn to ash if she tried. She had accepted that her ashes were destined for the waters of Ganges, and she prayed to the goddess Parvati that she protects those unborn and brings them to life. The goddess listened, and next April, Anaya gave birth to the twins Chimini and Sanani. After that miracle, the malik couldn't have her at a pinjara anymore, she was bad for business, so he moved her to a less busy brothel, a massage parlor where she got her own one room to work, live and raise children. "You ruin me, woman," he said. "That debt you owed me for buying you from the dalal was almost paid, but now it is big again with all those extra costs you demand. You owe me for giving you a room and for the medical. Eighty thousand rupees."*

*Anaya doesn't worry about that; she knows that there will always be a debt to the malik. She is happy to have a room; she got the one with the cerulean-colored walls to hide the children inside. When they are asleep, she waits downstairs by the doorway, wearing her "Wet'n'Wild" bright red lipstick, uncaged and able to turn up her head and see the sky above. Yet, she rarely gazes at the sky unless she prays for Shefali or her children. She is an old woman of twenty-one years of age now, and the sky has no magic for her. The malik keeps bringing younger girls to upgrade his massage parlor, but most of them are weak and don't survive, and the ones that do cannot speak much from the opium and the disease and communicate through the rising smoke rings of their cigarettes. They spend their hours of freedom smoking and spitting—Anaya sees them spitting and spitting again, and so does she—for the filth inside is so much every day that they can never be clean, no matter how much they spit.*

*She still needs to work—there is no escape from slavery—but business is slower here. Her children are only four years of age, but they have already learned to hide, the boy under the bed, the girl in the closet in her tiny room when customers come. They think it's a game; she told them it's called "hide and never seek."*

*She prays to the goddess Kali, the Slayer of Raktabija, Raktabija, the demon who kept giving birth to clone demons, Raktabija, the demon reincarnated in her malik. She prays for revenge and justice.*

*It is an unusually cold mid-March night, the year 2022, the godforsaken year when the goddess will hear her prayers. A young boy, hungry for lust and money, ill-spirited, not over twenty of age, visits Anaya to enjoy her services. He has just returned from China, where he works in a pigeon farm in Guangzhou, and on that cold night, his bones are aching, and he sneezes for he has been infected with an unknown curse, a virus so vile that spreads faster than the clones of Raktabija.*

*And as Anaya's rage, her hate for all that is man and world and civilization, becomes one with the seed of the poisoned man, as her desperation and misery swallow his greed and lust, the gods and the demons unite in their rage and decide that this world has become undeserving of life. Enough. Time for retribution. Divine justice.*

*The epidemiologists would have called that boy patient zero, but no one will ever know his name. Inside his body, the goddess unleashes her deathly curse, the antigenic shift of the H7N9 virus, on his last day at the pigeon farm, a few hours before he takes the flight to India. It is a mutation that can happen only once, a massive change to the nucleotides of RNA, it forms a new virus subtype, and on that day, the obscure H7N9 avian flu virus turns into an unstoppable pandemic. It was known to have a 40 percent mortality rate back from 2009 when Tina was studying it, but it could never spread easily. "Not a viral virus," the experts joked. It will change with the pigeon farm boy, and that day the mutation results in efficient and rapid human-to-human transfer.*

*Still, nobody would probably know about that, as that boy dies next to his mother three days later, blue from cyanosis in a pool of his own bloody pink froth. His mother is too religious to care about doctors—she knows that this is the work of gods and demons—and the virus mutation would have died, claiming only those two victims had he not visited Anaya before. But he did. If it wasn't an unusually cold week with a high of 20°C. But it was. The mantra. She listened.*

*And it will be Anaya, the Mouth that will Unleash Hell, the one responsible for all that will follow in this story—it is always the woman's fault in these streets—for she will (be forced to) sleep with fifty-four more men the next five days, hallucinating from fever and pain, cursing them knowingly and unknowingly, and she will infect all fifty-four of them, and in turn, they will infect thousands who breathe the air on the overcrowded streets of Varanasi.*

*The malik stops sending customers to her after the fifth day because they won't touch her; they can see that she is sick with death.*

*She will be finally left alone; with her last strength, she pushes the crying children away. Anaya dreams of the goddesses as the disease spreads inside her, she feels it. In her agonizing sleep, she is Kali, wearing the skirt made of the severed arms of the demons and the necklace with their fresh-bleeding decapitated heads. As her last dying wish, she calls on the goddess Ganga, the one who in the times before time came down to sweep the earth with her waters after she was insulted by Brahma.*

*"O goddess, Ganga, unleash my rage and my revenge on all demons around me. Drown them in your purifying waters. Spare my children, unless they're bound to follow my destiny of slavery, then kill them first."*

*The goddess listens.*

*There will be no escape for anyone, evil-spirited or kind-hearted, poor or rich, pale or dark-skinned, believer or not, as Anaya's curse ripples to the four corners of the earth, raging wild in the months up to the summer of 2022, succumbing temporarily to the July heat waves, and resurrecting in October, to end the lives of men, women and children, so many that no goddess would ever dare to claim as retribution.*

*Within a week, no more, Anaya and most of the brothel neighborhood's population is devoured by the mutated virus. One of her customers on his way to Cape Town through Dubai will spread the disease to twenty airplane passengers; others will do so by foot, bus or train. A man who visited her for pleasure right after she got infected will travel to Chittagong, Bangladesh, the same night, and he'll lead the spread to the West. Guangzhou, Varanasi, Nairobi, Chittagong, Karachi, Izmir, Lesbos. Varanasi to Mumbai, to Baku, Moscow, Nairobi to Paris, Paris to London. London to Reykjavik, Mumbai to LA, Paris to Rio de Janeiro. The rest is known. It is a fire, many of these clusters will die fast, others will rage uncontrolled.*

*The Red Cross volunteers will find the four-year-old barefoot twins crying next to an overflowing toilet and a rotting body. In the year 2058, when this story is written, the girl Chimini is leading another Indian mission to Mars, the boy Sanani is a high-school math teacher in Milwaukee, Wisconsin.*

*Shefali will make it to Turkey and from there to Lesbos, Greece, and finally to Hamburg, Germany, where she spends her last days in a drug addiction clinic.*

*As for Anaya, the girl with the smile of a thousand flowers, she will never smell the rhododendrons again.*

# 35. Yara: Loverboy

*Lesbos, June 17, 2022*

"Toilet? This door," said the young man with eyes of jade and warm tan skin tone. "The other ones are dirty."

Yara hesitated, turned her head to see if there were any other girls around. This refugee camp was a busy hornets' nest, yet she had suddenly entered the quietest of spaces, the lair of a spider. The young man seemed to own this spot, no other living creature, not even a cicada making a sound. She couldn't see the rest of his gang securing the space around.

"Toilet is free. Clean. No problem," said the man. "I leave, don't worry, to be all alone."

"Thanks," Yara mumbled and ran into the toilet. She couldn't wait any longer; she had no time for debates.

It was clean and even had toilet paper.

When she got out, the man was about twenty yards away, his back on Yara, and talking on the phone. He had kept his distance, ignoring her, and Yara sighed in relief, wiping the sweat from her brow.

"Thank you," she mumbled again and continued walking, trying to remember which way she had come from.

"Are you here all alone?" the man asked her as she started distancing herself from him.

Yara didn't reply and opened up her pace.

"Want to make phone call? I have phone," he said in English with a flowing French accent. Yara turned to realize that he was just a breath away from her, almost touching her. "I am Nassim," he said. He offered his phone, but Yara refused and kept her pace, head down and faster.

She covered another thirty yards before she turned around. Nassim had turned his back on her and taking the opposite direction. How stupid had she been to refuse help? She found the strength to shout.

"I am sorry, yes, may I make a phone call, please?"

Nassim turned around and smiled, showing a set of clean white teeth. He pressed some buttons, grimacing in distress before showing the dead phone to Yara.

"Sorry, it is out of battery. Come with me, I'll give you a phone to keep. I have a spare. You can't survive here without one. Do you have money?"

"*No*," Yara shook her head.

"It's ok, you'll pay later, whenever you can. Where are you from? You speak good English," he said, already striding next to Yara, with hands in his pockets.

He had muscular arms, showing through his tight t-shirt. He was the most handsome man Yara had talked to for more than a few seconds in all of her sixteen years. Still, there was something wrong with him. That smile was too fake, a trickster, or too real, a hunter too happy with how his hunt was going.

An overwhelming sensation grew on Yara's belly as the two of them passed among the refugee crowds and the tarpaulin tents to get to his place. An unmistakable feeling that she was the Red Riding Hood, the Pinocchio, entering the ugliest part of the story. She had a guttural desire to turn around and run, yet she was embarrassed at the thought of how stupid that would look. He wasn't threatening, holding, pushing her. If her mom was close, in one of those tents, even that family man Mohammad who had offered shelter, she'd run to him, to mommy, without a second thought, but she was all alone.

Nassim's tent stood next to the barbed wire fence, oversized and brand new, surrounded by smaller ones as if he were a local chieftain. Young men, his age, just men, no women, were standing before his tent. They greeted him silently, taking head to toe glances at Yara, their hands busy with neck chains and cigarette packs.

"Hey, Omar," one of the men greeted Nassim. Her companion made a signal to stay quiet. Yara pretended that she didn't hear that, but her legs were trembling already as Nassim or was that Omar, entered his tent, signaling to her to wait outside. Omar! That was the name of her little brother; it had been only a few days since she was holding him in her arms.

"Here, phone is yours. Keep it," Nassim said as he came out of the tent a very long minute later.

Her mom and dad's phones were "not accepting calls," as in the previous days.

"I must leave to find my sister," she said and turned around to walk away.

"Where are you going?" asked Nassim.

"The hospital."

"Oh, the hospital? Hospital is shut down. Quarantine. Not safe there. You go there, you die. Are you in pain? I have pills. Here, come inside."

He was telling the truth. The lady doctor had rushed her out of the hospital because something terrible was going on.

"My sister, I must," said Yara, repeating her story.

"Come inside, I'll make a couple of phone calls. I have friends in the police."

The ogling men made her uncomfortable, and Yara entered the tent, the spider's lair.

Nassim was not lying; he made phone calls and even had Yara speak to a police officer or somebody pretending to be one, with elementary English. He circled her as she talked to the officer over the phone, or most likely to one of his gang buddies.

Yara burst out crying after the fruitless phone call, frustration and fear overwhelming her. Nassim was now behind her and placed his strong hands around her neck, massaging her.

She stood frozen for a few seconds, a sliver of excitement, a river of primal fear before she jumped away abruptly and rushed out of the tent. She was trying to escape. It was late in the evening. Too late.

The physical torture was brief yet shocking; she'd never thought sex, what every teenager fantasized about, could be that painful. The embarrassment stung worse than the pain, everyone had warned her, she couldn't even scream or fight back, it was pointless, and the one time she tried, Omar slapped her that hard that her ears were ringing for half a minute as he pushed himself inside her. What is the point of being more graphic about the shit that followed? A wooden doll, a bleeding doll, a teenage body ravaged, a spirit broken.

Two men carried Yara and threw her inside a cargo container after she passed out. As she regained her senses and tried to make the other figures in the dark, she started hearing single words. Someone, soft and female, touched her in the darkness for a brief moment, but Yara screamed and crawled away to the front end of the container. She had no idea where she was if she was buried alive in some mass grave or abandoned in a dark cave for the beasts to feed. There was light coming through the bullet-sized holes of the metal walls. This was only her first day in the world of Moria, the underworld where she had descended to.

"Loverboy? You met Loverboy?" asked softly the woman who had tried to hug her.

"Poor girl! How old is she?" a second voice.

"Sixteen?" a third.

More women speaking, young voices, but in languages Yara couldn't understand. She didn't say a word. She wouldn't speak another word for weeks.

"It was Loverboy, huh? He sells love and flowers to the girls and gets them here."

"I am Shefali. From Benares. India. What's your name?"

Yara didn't offer one, couldn't.

"Ekemma, Lagos."

"Fatima, Idlib."

"Naomi." Naomi didn't know where she was from.

More names, about a dozen. The light invaded stronger now; fire bullets through the container holes. Yara felt her heart pounding like a hammer on the metal walls. Tears were streaming down her cheeks, but among the ocean of sorrow, there was a tear of bliss for Nahla. Her little sister didn't have to suffer any of this—whoever, whatever took her, didn't bring her to this hell.

Nahla rests at the bottom of the sea, in silence and darkness. Quiet. Peace.

Hours passed, maybe a day. Yara cuddled at the corner of the container, closer to the doors, wearing only the sweater and her bloodied underpants, refusing, unable to talk to Shefali. The smell of urine invaded her nostrils. Shefali whispered in her ear stories about rhododendrons, she told Yara not to worry, they would soon start a new life in Europe.

Visions consumed Yara; it could be the shock of the rape, the first time she felt a man inside her, a wolf devouring her, she was shivering.

"Those girls are sick," said Shefali pointing somewhere in the darkness, "stay away from them."

Yara was starved, her body and mind breaking from pain, an animal driven by fear of torture and hunger. Hallucinating. Visions of angels and saviors came back to her, like two nights ago when she was battling the waves. The dark of the sea consumes her again.

And then comes salvation, the most beautiful and terrifying vision. The doors open wide, and the sun invades unstoppable, a river of warmth and splendor. An angel, a young boy, emerges from the blinding light, embraces Yara, and kisses her on her lips. A first kiss. Warm, wet, suffocating. The angel's hair is orange, her lips are soft, and she smells of sandalwood; she is no boy. So lucid, luminous, her name is Lucia.

# 36. Lucia: Ninety-Six Percent

*Lesbos, June 18, 2022*

Lucia watched as Tina and the team of fifteen were getting dressed inside the bus. Filtering Facepiece Respirator 3 masks, goggles, rubber gloves, the water-resistant gowns covering the whole body, mobile phones, and shoes wrapped in plastic. Tina insisted on the adult nappies, but most of the team members were not convinced. There were two kinds of people on her team, doctors and nurses who were getting ready for hell and bureaucrats who thought this was a thirty-minute field trip.

"We are not gonna stay here that long," said Alexi, validating their ridiculous decision.

"No suit for me?" asked Lucia.

"You are not getting in. We'll take you as far as the Moria gates, and you can discuss your case with the guards there. That's the best I can do," said Tina, wearing her strictest grimace.

"Discuss?" asked Lucia. *Just get me there, and I'll find a way in,* she thought and gazed out the window.

An African woman carrying a baby girl on her back, walking barefoot in the same direction the bus was heading, four men, Moroccan or Algerian behind them wearing Nikes and colorful t-shirts, a car with beachgoers driving past them, a child waving from the rear-view window. Another ten minutes of winding uphill roads and the bus slowed down, stopping a few yards away from what looked like a prison camp, encircled with three-meter high chain-link fence crowned with barbed wire.

Guards in blue jockey hats and armored police in helmets stood at the gate, modern centurions making no effort to greet them. Lucia wore her purple tank-top, cargo pants, and boots. She covered her orange hairdo with a bandana to keep from drawing attention as she followed one step behind Tina.

"Here we are. District Nine," Lucia said.

"What's district nine?" asked Tina, getting no answer. She put on her face mask and proceeded without another word.

A guard stepped forward with palm raised. "You, lady. No further," he said.

Tina stood four meters away from him.

"We are the EHT. We need to get in the quarantine area," said Tina, without removing her mask and gave her name and Alexi's. The sound of the two names pronounced next to each other brought her instant stomach sickness.

"Don't know any EHT, nobody gets in and out, I have strict orders," continued the guard avoiding Tina's eyes.

Lucia glanced at the far right, about a hundred yards away. Two men climbed swiftly over the fence and disappeared into the orange grove. Anybody could go in and out of that camp without questions.

"You are damn right. Nobody gets out, seal this camp now," said Tina, "but we are the Emergency Health Taskforce, and we need to get to the quarantine area. I am running things here until further notice. You report to me."

"We had five dead already," said the officer, unfazed. They are in the hospital; we isolated the sick and the dead there. My superior said nobody in, nobody out."

"Where is your superior?" Tina demanded.

"It is Saturday."

"Tell that to the virus."

The guard shrugged his arms. "I don't report to you. My orders are that no one gets in until Monday."

"Step away," said Tina, raising her voice. "We're not gonna wait forty-eight hours to get in. Every minute counts."

"We are on minimum personnel. I have four of my men sick. I can't protect you, guard the camp, and isolate the hospital with nine officers left."

"Sick with what?" asked Tina. "Get all your men here, healthy or sick, and lock down this camp. I want a full *cordon sanitaire*."

"Cordo what?" The guard muffled a roaring laughter, and Lucia imitated him and tried to enter the conversation. She kept her amused face on to relate to the guard.

"Sorry, I am from the travel agency," Lucia jumped in, Tina and the rest of her team staring, "I'll take here the *space shuttle crew* back to the hotel, Officer. A. Pa-pa-da-kis," she said, leaning forward to read the name on his uniform. "A is for Andreas? Antonis?"

"None of your business."

"Yeah, right, give us a second here, Officer. A. Papadakis," Lucia said and stepped away. She took off her mask and goggles and dialed a number three times until she got an answer.

"Hello, who is this?" replied the female voice on the other end of the line.

"Are you Roula? Mr. Papalias told me that I could call you anytime, and you grant me three wishes. Write it down, this is wish number one. Papalias calls the Minister of Public Order, and the Minister calls the Chief of Police, and he calls Officer A. Papadakis at the Moria camp gates. A. Papadakis, the officer in charge of the camp. He must let the EHT team get in now. EHT. Yes. It must happen now. Got it, Roula?" a pause, "No, no. I don't have his number. They do. Find it. A. Papadakis. Moria, Lesbos. ASAP. Oh, and give the officer a strict order to help us with clamping down the sex-trafficking ring, else it is his last day in the force, and he is off to big trouble. Yes, s-e-x trafficking. Got it?"

Lucia rushed back to Tina, who was debating how to navigate the situation with Alexi and the rest.

"It is a delicate one," one of the bureaucrats said, scratching his unshaven chin.

"I am sorry, Tina," said Alexi, "I cannot find the Minister. Let's get to our hotel, get some rest and a coffee, and try to resolve this later tonight or tomorrow. Everyone needs to rest."

"What hotel? What coffee?" Tina shouted. "Are you out of your mind, Dr. Vardis? We have no hotel reservations. We are all going in and staying in. In the hospital. For good. Till death do us part or the last one of the infected is clean. Get back on the bus and put your nappies on. All of you."

"You can shout all you like, Dr. Walker, but they are not letting us in," said the man next to Alexi, who had removed goggles and mask and was puffing on a cigarette. She was the chain-smoker in the Deputy Minister's office meeting two days ago.

Tina exhaled in despair and headed to confront the guards again. Lucia ran to intercept her, grabbing her arm.

"Hey, doc, listen to me. Fixed. We are in. Any minute now, they'll call him."

"What?" asked an exasperated Tina, ready to slap Lucia. "Can you please leave me alone? I have no time for your antics now."

"You are not listening. It's done. Give it a couple of minutes. I fixed it. Under one condition. You get me in too," said Lucia to Tina and then turned to the officer. "Hey, Papadaki. You have a call. Incoming. Athens calling. Ten, nine, eight," she counted down as he walked away, ignoring her. She repeated the countdown, following him getting closer to his ear. Another ten seconds passed until the mobile phone in his pocket vibrated suddenly and cheerfully, streaming the "Que te la pongo" ringtone.

The officer answered the phone and "yes-sired" repeatedly, staring at Lucia, who was giving Tina the thumbs up again.

"We are in, doc. Told you!" Lucia tried to high-five Tina, but the doctor was stunned.

Tina's motto was always "follow the protocols, never improvise during a medical crisis," but the situation had quickly overwhelmed her. Four of her colleagues had taken off their protective uniforms and refused to join her in the camp, especially after getting more information from the officers. "No way we are going in. We didn't come here to die unprotected." Refugees who should be in lockdown were walking in and out of the unguarded fence in what was a mockery of a quarantine. But her EHT team could not get in until Lucia, a kid with a punk hairdo, made a phone call. Tina succumbed to the surreal, unable to control the situation or even grasp the sequence of events. The bus was making a U-turn to leave with half of her team. Lucia was undressing a few yards away in plain view, putting her nappies, uniform, and the rest of the gear on. The young girl kept the skulls-bandana on to separate herself from the others.

Enter, Moria.

Two officers accompanied them to the hospital wearing regular surgical masks without exchanging any more words. Tina led her remaining seven colleagues—two virologists, three nurses, one doctor, and Lucia being the odd seventh person. Alexi said he would join them later, but Tina knew he wouldn't. Small groups of refugees were jeering and shouting at the bunny suits, but luckily, the hospital was very close to the entry gate, and they didn't have to walk for long.

Dr. Maria Armandou and an apathetic nurse were the only ones to greet them.

"Thank God, you're here. We are three people left with thirteen infected. Four critical, they need ICU now."

Tina waved her hand in a "bring it on" gesture, asking for more information.

"Four dead, maybe five any minute now," said Dr. Armandou. "I can't even diagnose them here. The district governor interfered and said there is no way he is sending ambulances. Doesn't want to infect the hospital. They can't breathe, rapid ARDS, going into overdrive, and shock."

"Are the infected isolated?" Tina asked.

"Yes."

"You get us to the isolation ward, one of the virologists stays outside. Lucia, you don't need to be here," Tina said.

Once again, Lucia shocked her, removing her mask. She gave Tina the thumbs up. "Great, 'cause I have to take care of the other thing. I need this," she said, grabbing the backpack with the camera drone that the team had brought along with the rest of the supplies.

"What on earth are you doing?" Tina said. "We are all quarantined in here.

Nobody goes in and out. I meant you don't have to be in the isolation ward."

"The girls, doc, sex trafficking. Gotta go. I'll be back soon."

Lucia ran out of the hospital and to officer A. Papadakis, who was waiting there. "Now we go find the girls," she said. Four more of his men joined them at the bridge before they crossed toward what was the Syrian section of the camp. The guards were marching fast with heads bent down, surrounding Lucia protectively. She was still dressed in the bunny suit and eager to remove this ridiculous outfit, but the fearful looks of the bystanders changed her mind. It served as a superhero's outfit, demanding fear and respect, concealing her age and sex. She had a hunch that the guards were taking her for a ride, away from the kidnappers, so she launched the camera drone and watched the video on her phone, not caring for her surroundings.

"I am not sure what you are looking for, lady," said officer Papadakis when they reached the north end of the camp where the olive grove started. "There is no sex trafficking gang here, we would know. This is bullshit if you ask me. Tell me where you got your info."

*That's the last thing I'll do,* Lucia thought and continued. "No, not here, that way," said Lucia, glued at her phone screen and now leading the guards. "You brought us to the wrong spot as far as possible from where we should be. Look, officer, if you don't cooperate, you will receive an Affidavit for Administrative Examination before we are back at the hospital. Got it? You follow me now."

She had spotted an intermodal container, the type that could be loaded on a truck or ship, at the west end of the camp, next to the highway. There were no office buildings around it, and no gate, just tents, and that huge container. It shouldn't be there.

It took another twenty minutes, Lucia almost running in her hazmat outfit, among the tents and the refugees, some of them throwing cans and insults to the lagging officers. The faces were changing from Syrian to Afghani, then African, Somali, and finally to Moroccan or Algerian as she crossed the camp end to end.

Lucia knew once they reached the blue container with the bullet holes. Unlike the rest of the rat-packed camp, the area was deserted. She had no doubt that one of the officers informed them before she made it there. The container was about twenty feet long and locked by four manual bars from the outside and a lockbox. She took off the stupid bunny suit and started pulling the lock bars one by one. As she did, she heard women screaming, shouting from the inside of the steel box. Fists banging on the metal door, legs kicking frantically. Under the blazing heat, she felt the chills on the back of her neck and down her arms.

"Will somebody help me for a change today?" she shouted to the guards behind her.

She pulled the four manual bars open and the doors wide, the light rushing in and illuminating the frail figures, one, two, three, twelve girls cuddled next to each other or alone at the corners.

"No sex trafficking ring, huh?" she said to Papadakis, gasping for air, in the stuffy metal box, exhausted, her hands resting on her knees. "Water, bring some water," she said.

Papadakis played the shocked officer now, calling on his phone, talking to her at the same time. "May I see an ID, young lady?" he said. "Who the hell are you? This is now a police matter, please step aside, and we'll take care of this."

"I am not going anywhere until we get some real police here. You are the one who should show me some ID. Are you taking bribes from your friends here?"

"Step aside and shut up."

"Chief, these girls are sick," said a second officer who had stepped in the truck and quickly back out.

"Fuck! Get away from here," said the third man who had joined him.

Lucia heard a girl coughing at the far end of the container. The girl closer to her was barely seventeen years old, a gentle face with puffy cheeks, full lips, and hollow brown eyes, Syrian or something. She was half-naked in a torn shirt and panties and looked heavily drugged or in shock.

"Marko, you moron, don't touch anyone. You are in quarantine too, as of now," said Papadakis. "Antoni, you too. Yanni, you run to the hospital and bring those doctors here now." He then turned to Lucia. "Once the doctors are here, we two are heading down to the police station. You come with me, lady. You are under arrest. Better start explaining how you knew about all this."

Tina and the rest of her crew arrived in full gear thirty minutes later. Lucia knew what she had to do; there was no way she was going to that police station. She struggled to remember what the probability was of surviving this flu virus if one got infected. Dr. Walker had suggested a four percent mortality rate in the ship, yet Lucia's mind was that of a risk-taking pilot, wired upside down.

"Ninety-six percent survival," she whispered as Tina rushed toward her and the officer. "I'll take it."

Lucia sprang into the container, embraced the brown-haired glassy-eyed young girl, and kissed her deeply on the mouth.

It will be another forty-eight hours until Lucia feels her head pounding with a splitting ache, curled into a fetal position on a camp bed at the quarantined Moria hospital, desperately shaking off the chills.

# 37. Tina: Big Party

I am keeping a diary once again, a sign that I am deep in shit, like that time in Liberia with the Ebola outbreak. This might be the end of me, of all of us in this room. Last night, I crawled to the window and stared at the two blurry streetlamps that marked the camp entrance. They have become the beacons of salvation, illuminating the path from Hades back to life to Peri and Demetri.

I talked to my son again today.

"Turn on the camera, mommy," he said.

I had Peri tell him that the connection is terrible. "I am fine. We need to keep the camp under cordon sanitaire," I said, lying to my husband. Not that it was the first time. "See you soon, love. No, no, we are safe here."

It started yesterday with bone-crushing pain and exhaustion. It feels like five-inch midgets are within my chest, struggling to pull my ribs apart one by one. The fever started today, and it is up to 38.5°C now. I have no strength to write—haven't written in a notebook for a long time—I will record on my phone app.

There are six of us in the isolation room, Lucia, Ekemma from Lagos, Naomi from god knows where, Southeast Asia something, officer Antonis Mertzos, the no-name teenager from Syria, myself. Dr. Maria Armandou and nurse Zoe Kotopouli are the only care providers. I spared the rest of our EHT team; they will monitor the asymptomatic and the rest of the Moria camp and maintain the quarantine. If they find any infected, they must bring them here. Maria and Zoe are sleeping in the room next door. The outbreak will stop with us eight if we're lucky. Based on the odds, we'll lose three out of the eight. We sent blood samples for the six symptomatic to Institute Pasteur at Athens for analysis. Alexi sent a Super Puma copter to bring the samples to Athens, even though the state's official line is that they have everything under control.

They don't bring food or water per my orders. We stockpiled canned tuna and corn, and we have a double counter-top burner to cook spaghetti, rice and boil a can of soup. Yes, they have Campbell's even here; I can go back to my grad school gourmet diet. The tap water is drinkable, two of us are vomiting badly, but it is not because of the water.


*Tuesday, June 21: Day 4 of the Quarantine*


Three days have gone by, and there are zero mentions of us in any nationwide or local TV network. Lesbos TV is advertising beach-bars and tavernas as if nothing is going on. There are rumors that the government is shutting Moria down, and the government won't spoil the planned announcement for any deadly virus.

Current patient report:

The Syrian teenager we rescued from the container is burning with fever, and I am afraid she won't make it. Nurse Zoe brought three blankets and wrapped the girl in them. She has been soaking in her sweat there, and we try to keep her hydrated. No complaints, no reactions—she hasn't uttered a word. Dr. Armandou examined her and said that she had been raped repeatedly. The doctor offered more details that I don't want to record now. Apparently, Dr. Armandou is experienced with such incidents and examinations in Moria.

Naomi will probably succumb today. Since day one, Dr. Armandou fought hard to rush her to an ER hospital in Athens, but the Ministry won't allow me. They know that if this virus reaches a five million-person city, we might have a million dead. I conceded because it is too late for her. She is coughing blood and even bleeding from the ear. Her breathing rate is 25 to 30, and her heart will burst any minute.

We are at odds with Dr. Armandou; her job is to save everyone, mine to make sure that no virus escapes this room.

Ekemma is weak but under control. Lucia is teaching her Greek words. Lucia has a fever and a dry cough but insists that she is fine, and it's just the flu; she'll get over it. It *is* the flu.

*Wednesday, June 22: Day 5 of the Quarantine*

We have a problem with Officer Mertzos. He is becoming dangerously delusional, complaining about terrible headaches. I do, too, since day one. I made a passing attempt to explain the symptoms of the viral infection, but I don't think he is pro-science. He screams that the goblins are inside his skull, working with a pickaxe to drill a hole between his eyes. This morning, he got up, banged his head on the wall repeatedly, and then tried to jump out of the window. We had to wrestle him down. He is tied on the bed now. We used the one real bed for him; everyone else will do with a camp bed. He says we are flesh-eating Sirens and curses us when he's not praying.

There is one more empty camp bed as of tonight. Naomi didn't make it; she died in agony as if she were drowning. My best guess is she was, the lungs filled with fluid that they couldn't pump out. No way I can do an autopsy here, and I know what I'll find anyway—two red sponges for lungs. Our spirits are broken already.

*Thursday, June 23: Day 6 of the Quarantine*

Shit! I am not ready for this; I thought I was.

Officer Mertzos is suffering from subcutaneous emphysema, his lungs have burst open, and air bubbles accumulate under his skin, around his chest, back, and neck. We roll him over when we untie him to clean him up; he can't go to the bathroom. His body is crackling like a restless bag of popcorn in the microwave. He is gone mad too, making sexual advances to the girls, sticking out his tongue like a Satyrus. It's not his fault. Severe flu has been known to make people delusional.

I noticed that blood was dripping from Dr. Armandou's nose today, but she said, "it's nothing."

*Friday, June 24: Day 7 of the Quarantine*

Update on me first because I feel like I won't make it to the end of this recording: The goblins have brought a claw hammer and a box of nails and are trying to split my head open. Rib and joint pain too, my fever is up to 39.3°C.

Dr. Armandou cannot help anyone; she is lying on the camp bed coughing and breathing hard. I've seen the blueish tint on her lips and fingertips, the dark spots on her cheeks. She knows that there is nothing much to do at this point; the lungs can no longer clean her blood, and her skin is turning dark. Cyanosis. She should have been in an incubator, but this so-called hospital has only one portable oxygen inhaler, no ICU, not even an X-ray machine. If she could talk, she'd say, this is all my fault; I was supposed to help them, not lock them up here until we all die. I did try. The Ministry claims that they are preparing a special isolation hospital floor for us back in Athens and everything will be up and running tomorrow. Another two days for transportation. They probably hope that none of us will be alive in three days.

We check on the Syrian girl every hour. She hasn't moved at all, and I am not sure if it is the shock of the abuse or the virus killing her. If Lucia doesn't force the food and water into her, she'll die from starvation or dehydration.

*Saturday, June 25: Day 8 of the Quarantine*

We put Mertzos in a body bag this morning. We have taken over a second adjacent room to store the bodies there. I don't want anyone else to touch them for now unless they come in with hazard suits. That room is not airconditioned, and the temperature has gone up to 38°C. We blocked the bottom crevice of the door that connects the two rooms with towels.

Ekemma, the Nigerian girl, was recovering slowly, but today she started coughing so violently that I think she tore some muscles on her chest and maybe broke a rib. She cannot even weep from the pain.

Dr. Armandou's nose is oozing a pink froth, and I can't even help her. We are expecting the helicopter today to take both away.

Lucia's only symptom is a low fever. As the old Greek proverb goes, "the stray dog never dies." She was the most careless and yet suffered the least.

Lucia claimed that I told her "four percent" when I tried to educate her about the virus's mortality rate at the ship.

"Forty percent, Lucia," I repeated. "Forty percent. Why on earth did you kiss that girl?"

"Oops, sorry," she apologized, and she ran to help Ekemma, who was coughing. I think Lucia meant it; she is sorry.

The mortality rate of the H7N9 virus was forty percent during the previous epidemics. The results came back from Athens today. They confirmed it *is* H7N9. But I got some news from Geneva that the virus has mutated. The original H7N9 was almost eliminated back in 2017 when they vaccinated billions of chicken. What we are facing here is a different strain."

After telling me Ekemma's temperature is 39.1, Lucia asked me, "Is any of us going to live through this?"

"*You* will," I told her. Unless she does something stupid and goes out in the camp running in the heat, playing cops and robbers, and exhausts herself. The mortality rate has actually gone down with this mutation. I got some initial data from WHO; they estimate a twelve percent death rate if symptomatic. A bit better than Russian roulette. When I explained this to Lucia, she replied, "Oh, good."

It is not good. Very bad. Twelve percent is more complicated to control than forty percent.

The helicopter never came because it was sent to rescue a baby from nearby Ikaria island that needed transfer to Athens. It will be here tomorrow at noon.


*Sunday, June 26: Day 9 of the Quarantine*


Ekemma resembles a victim of a demonic obsession, with the whites of her eyes veined red, voice hoarse, and reduced to a wheezing cough, gasping for oxygen. She is vomiting whatever is left inside her. We didn't even put her in the helicopter. She has hours left at best.

I keep flipping over the pictures of Demetri and Peri on my phone screen, trying to find the strength to breathe by looking at their faces. None of them, not even my mother, knows I am sick.

The Syrian girl's name is Gianna Jalabi, I think. Dr. Armandou left a note with the nurse—probably misspelled it—before she was taken with the helicopter to Athens. Lucia googled the name and couldn't find a single reference under that name. I got the news that Dr. Armandou never made it to the hospital; they took her directly to the morgue. She was a mother of two, a volunteer at Moria, and a brave woman. Unlike her, I plan to be effective, not brave.

Lucia is begging me to help her with Gianna, but I am neither a doctor nor a psychiatrist. Nurse Zoe is convinced that Gianna is braindead, "cauliflower in a gown," she calls her. She is not very compassionate. I wish I could run some tests on her; she is entirely asymptomatic.

"How is that possible?" Lucia asked me.

"Well, her name is Kotopouli," I answered. *Kotopouli means "chicken" in Greek.*

"And?"

"Chickens are asymptomatic to H7N9." We were both laughing hard, coughing and laughing, two women going mad among the dead and the dying.

Gianna has become the sole purpose of Lucia's existence since Ekemma died. The Syrian girl is the only survivor from the group that Lucia rescued from the sex traffickers.

""I am not letting her die, no matter what," Lucia said. "She'll get better, right?"

Aggressive viruses like the 1918 H1N1, aka "Spanish flu," were known to cause serious distress bordering madness but mostly during the time of infection and high fever. In Gianna's case, it is something else because she is getting better. No fever, no coughing.

*Monday, June 27: Day 10 of the Quarantine*

The tally. We lost Mertzos, Ekemma, Naomi, and Armandou. Nurse Zoe, Lucia, Gianna, and I remain alive. Death comes at night next to our beds and tosses a coin. We save one; he keeps one. Lucia has taken it very seriously; she thinks it is her responsibility and mine that we didn't save these girls.

For the umpteenth time, I am trying to tell her that I am here to stop a pandemic, not to save everyone.

"Did you see how these young people died in here? What happens if this spreads in Athens? Five million people."

Lucia wants all the answers today, but I can't explain to her why some live and others die. Such insights need months or even years to be obtained. She now reads books about the 1918 pandemic. The "Great Influenza" by John Barry, "Flu" by Gina Kolata, "Deadliest Enemy" by Osterholm/Olshaker, whatever she can download on her phone. The reading helped her put things in perspective, and she mellowed toward me. People in a pandemic curse their fate, but this is just nature's sieve—the finest grain makes it through to the next round.

"Tina, you are right, if this thing gets out, we are in deep shit," she summarized the situation in her colorful way.

She calls me "Tina" now—we are buddies, survivors. I warned her that if she calls me "Doc" one more time, I'll call her "Marty McFly" from now on.

She didn't get the joke. I am recovering, too, I can joke.

I am checking every hour with the Ministry of Health, the National Agency of Public Health, and the local hospital in Lesbos. There are zero incidents confirming or suggesting an H7N9 spread outside the Moria camp.

The cordon sanitaire has worked at the expense of my career. That's the thing with any virus outbreak; there is no optimal policy for the policymaker. Any action is wrong. The Agency emailed me that Alexi has taken over my duties as the Head of the Emergency Health Taskforce and will coordinate the country's response from now on. Alexi escaped during the first hour of the cordon sanitaire. *"You are relieved of duty until further notice, and you have the right to an appeal in three months from July 1,"* the letter stated. We are sending the latest samples to Athens, and if everything tests negative, we should be out of here in two-three days. The endless summer vacation I have always dreamed of.

*Tuesday, June 28: Day 11 of the Quarantine*

I texted Dr. Garnett at WHO, hoping for some good news. He said they are witnessing a massive slowdown in the Northern Hemisphere, and the virus hasn't spread significantly south of the equator. The temperature is a boring 36.6°C both inside my body and outside the window. The UV rays are scorching and sanitizing even the dirt of the Moria camp. The heat kills it. We'll revert to a celestial object religion, astrolatrists praying to the Mighty Sun to save us from the pestilence, as the Ancient Egyptians and the Aztecs did.

But the sun will rest in October, and the enemy will return, I know it. Will it be a few thousand cases or a pandemic? I can't tell you that. No one will have immunity, except us three in this room probably.

The race for the vaccine is on. Garnett is back and forth with Geneva, coordinating the WHO efforts. This hit hard and fast; no government in the world expected it. Thirty-five thousand infected worldwide, about four thousand dead, all in a few weeks. He'll send me a full epi report once they complete the research end of this week, but I got the exclusive preview. Children are as likely to be infected as adults. The only thing I didn't want to hear.

*Wednesday, June 29: Day 12 of the Quarantine*

Garnett says that the cases in Lesbos are probably the last ones in Europe. Only a handful reported globally this week. He has reassured himself that this virus cannot spread easily. "Not sure what happened in Varanasi. Maybe it was a dead-end strain," he texted me.

I had a call with him because I don't agree. I recorded it for future reference and my own benefit.

"Professor Garnett, I understand you are the WHO coordinator with regard to the H7N9 epidemic crisis."

"Correct."

"Do you recommend that every country should stockpile vaccines ahead of October?"

"Recommend it? I would strongly mandate it if we could mandate it, Dr. Walker."

"I need a favor. They kicked me out of the local Emergency Health Taskforce, and I need you to contact them."

"To reinstate you?"

"No! That's not important. I want you to alert them about October in your official WHO coordinator capacity. They might listen to you."

"Will do, Tina."

*Thursday, June 30: Day 13 of the Quarantine*

The Ministry said we could be out of here tomorrow, though I am pushing for another two weeks of hospital quarantine. None of us four has any signs of infection, and the results came back negative from Athens. Apparently, the epidemic is over worldwide, and they don't want to be the last country in the Mediterranean reporting active cases. "We are in the middle of the tourism season, and all of you are healthy. No reason to drag this any longer," Alexi told me on the phone. He won't admit this in writing.

*Friday, June 30: Day 14 of the Quarantine*

The two weeks of self-isolation begin now. Lucia decided to stay here with Gianna and nurse Zoe. She is not that bad; the poor girl was frightened. I approved her request—the less anyone moves, the better until we are certain. I'll self-isolate at my mother's new apartment in Athens. She left for the thermal spas. Peri and Demetri will not see me for another fifteen days. I had to tell my husband the truth, now that the danger is over and there is less for him to worry about.

I got a job offer from Garnett. Johns Hopkins or WHO HQs, whichever I choose. Peri is out of work, Demetri will benefit from a year abroad. I accepted before asking Peri. He doesn't know yet.

The helicopter will be here in an hour or so. I am done with goodbyes; I embraced Zoe, Lucia, then I passed my fingers through Gianna's hair, but no response from her.

Peri is texting me.

*Peri: Hon, when ru back? I mean back back. Home. Are we making reservations for Paros? July 28 ok? Can you spare two weeks this year with the job change?*

Paros. Vacation. Peri's priorities. He craves the social life, the getaway, the windsurfing. I shake with uncontrollable sobbing laughter; my mind crawls back to Dr. Armandou, the young girls, and the officer who died here.

The summer is already over for me, it is October in my head. I hate myself, the rut I am in. I betrayed Peri, failed my family, lost my job. Reminder to delete this recording, it is getting too personal.

*Peri: "Demetri misses you terribly. Me too."*

When was the last time I read a book to Demetri?

I text back: "*Paros! Yes. Make it three weeks, love. And let's throw a party there. Seven years together. #7 is my favorite. Invite all our friends, they'll all be there anyway. A big party!"*

Bright red and yellow balloons explode on my phone screen as I type the words.

# 38. Ella: By the End of September

*Geneva, June 30, 2022*

**WHO Report on H7N9/22 Outbreak**

**Attn of: Dr. Mathilde (Tina) Walker**

### H7N9/22 Virus

The virus is the result of an antigenic shift of the H7N9/13 avian strain, which initially appeared in birds (wild ducks, pigeons, chicken) and humans in China in 2013. The recent reassortment of the genetic material resulted in a variant that, unlike its predecessor, is highly transmissible to humans.

### Human Cases

The search for patient zero continues with three potential candidates identified: a 23-year-old male in Guangdong, China, a 22-year-old male in Varanasi, India, and a 35-year-old male from Chittagong, Bangladesh. The latest data from China's National Health Commission points to a pigeon farm in Guangdong, China, where a cluster of human cases appeared in late February 2022. Initially, the outbreak was contained until late March when new clusters were reported in India, Bangladesh, and a flight from Dubai to Cape Town that had to perform an emergency landing in Nairobi. Transmission of the virus continued in Pakistan, Turkey, UAE, UK, France, Greece, Italy, Switzerland, and other countries. No new cases have been reported since June 20, which indicates that the virus is highly vulnerable to higher temperatures and humidity levels, and potentially sunlight

(UV radiation). Cases in the Southern Hemisphere have been reported only in Rio, Brazil, and Jakarta, Indonesia, but potential outbreaks have likely been eradicated by extreme temperatures assisted by the unprecedented temperature rise in 2022, a potential effect of climate change.

## Disease Burden and Mortality

To date, 35,149 cases of H7N9/22 have been reported, resulting in 4,208 deaths, a mortality rate of approximately 12%.

## Age/gender distribution

The male to female ratio of the infected is 3.2:1, while the median age is 58 years of age. The mortality rate was significantly higher in males of all age groups. Young women under forty without preexisting conditions who were immediately treated with oseltamivir faired very well, averaging a mortality rate of 2%. For older males without treatment, that number rose to 28%. There were 1,423 cases of children reported, and the mortality rate was an extremely alarming 6% (9% for males).

## Symptoms and Treatment

Symptoms include high fever, dry cough, and shortness of breath. In severe cases, the virus overloads the immune system, causing a cytokine storm. At least 50% of the patients became critically ill and had to be hospitalized and treated with neuraminidase inhibitor Oseltamivir, with varying responses. The major cause of death was acute respiratory distress syndrome (ARDS) or multiorgan failure. A study by a team of Chinese researchers suggests that people who had received the common flu shot in the past three months before infection showed increased immunity to the virus, and their overall symptoms were milder. More data is needed, as those results have not been reviewed extensively by the scientific community.

## Transmission

H7N9 was a particularly worrisome virus to experts since it first appeared in China because of the adaptation it shows in mammals, the high mortality rate, and its asymptomatic behavior in birds. In a previous study, the CDC determined that H7N9 was the likeliest strain to cause a global pandemic. Research to create highly transmissible and deadly forms of H7N9 has been carried out in high-security labs worldwide to study the virus and create vaccines.

Mass vaccination of more than a billion poultry by the Chinese authorities in 2017 eliminated the virus spread until recently. The current hypothesis is that the antigenic shift in 2022 is due to migratory birds. Relevant DNA traces have been identified, and genomic sequencing of the particular strain revealed that the virus did not originate in a lab.

## Human to Human transfer of virus

The original strain of the virus was transmitted primarily from birds to humans. After the antigenic shift event, the virus has acquired the ability to transmit effectively from human to human via droplets and aerosols, and fomites (plastic and metallic surfaces). Initial estimates of R-Naught, the basic reproduction number of the infection is estimated at 2.8 (range 2.5 to 3.0).

Patients are infectious in the beginning, and the end of their illness and usually show symptoms within the first three days. In 55% of the cases, symptoms developed after 36 hours, and patients became infectious after the first 24 hours of being exposed to the virus. This pattern suggests that if a pandemic were to occur, it would develop rapidly, without allowing for weeks of planning and testing of presymptomatic persons.

## Vaccine

Following the aggressive vaccination of poultry in China in 2017, the infection was almost eliminated. The risk of the virus reappearing was considered low but with a high degree of uncertainty. Efforts are underway globally to modify previous H7N9 vaccines (A/Shanghai/2/2013 (SH2) and A/Anhui/1/2013 (AH1)), as studies have shown that they provide little protection against the previous antigenic shift of the fifth epidemic. Those efforts have shown great results in 2021, and tests on the /22 are already underway.

Given the ongoing research, we expect a vaccine to be available as early as October 2022, with mass availability depending on the industry's production capabilities and the priority nations give to obtaining and financing vaccine manufacture.

## Efforts to prevent the spread of disease

Testing, monitoring, and rapid exchange of information are crucial to prevent the expansion of the infection in the Southern Hemisphere during the summer months and its resurgence in the Northern Hemisphere in October 2022. We believe the virus will not appear earlier in the Northern Hemisphere due to its susceptibility to high temperatures or sunshine.

Vaccine development and production are the global community's highest priority, but we anticipate a significant shortage if a pandemic unravels within early autumn. We strongly urge every government to prepare as if the probability of a pandemic in late fall 2022 is very high.

Suppression measures (travel bans, long-term quarantines, and lockdowns) will need to be also taken as early as possible if the weather changes. It is of the utmost importance to suppress the spread before it's too late. The extreme heatwaves of June were an unexpected ally, but we cannot rely on them for much longer.

# 39. Yara: Ypsilon

"What's RTS," asked Lucia.

"RTS, rape trauma syndrome," Zoe, the nurse, whispered. She didn't want Yara, who was resting on her bed a few feet away, to hear them. "We cannot keep her here, Lucia. They are shutting down Moria."

"They've been shutting it down since it opened."

"No, this time is real, a matter of days. The girl has no papers, no name, she didn't seek asylum, she is not even recorded in our books. All we have is the name Dr. Armandou left on this paper before she died. *'Gianna Jalabi,'*" Zoe spelled out the name.

"But there is no one by this name registered in Syria or even the UK where she claimed to be from. That's a fake name, or she is from somewhere else." Lucia went through her emails again on the tablet, hoping that some new clue had emerged. She had asked Sedulous, the PI agency, for help, but they couldn't find anything.

"Those officers came again from the Immigration Department today. She needs to be shipped back, they said."

"Where? She has no papers."

"Then, she must go to a guarded center."

"A prison? She is underage," Lucia objected.

"Not a prison. A guarded center. We don't know *what* she is. Dr. Armandou has registered her as seventeen years old to be able to apply for asylum as a minor, but we have no idea," said the nurse, sucking on her vaporizer.

Two days were left on the self-isolation period imposed, and then they were free. For Lucia, the Moria hospital was the perfect place to hide until the spotlight faded away from the sex-trafficking scandal. But the few times she had tried to step outside the room, Yara would start weeping silently. Lucia was the only one who could get close to the girl, and feed her, the few bites she would eat.

Yara was listening to the two women, the orange-haired angel and the other mean one on the light green uniform who kept vaping. She was listening but couldn't speak a word. She had tried to open her mouth a hundred times during the last ten days after her fever dropped. Every time she tried to utter a word, her jaw trembled uncontrollably for a few seconds, her eyes filled with tears that stayed there like sparkling Christmas ornaments, and the words were stolen right out of her mouth.

"*Halabi. Halabi,*" that's the only word she wanted to speak but couldn't. They had her name wrong. What would it matter anyway? All she cared about was that she never had to leave this room again and stay here with the orange-haired girl who had saved her from the dark cave.

She liked the other doctor too, that Tina lady who left a few days or was that weeks ago. Dr. Tina had a gentle face, rumpled but gentle, and a warm smile, a subtle reminder of her mother. Her English was good too, a bit American and brutish, but at least Yara could understand her, unlike the nurse. There used to be more girls in this room, but it seemed like a million years away when they carried them out covered in white sheets.

The Luminous girl was persistent. Yara knew that her savior's name was Lucia, but they had *her* name wrong, so she had decided to use made-up names for the others. The orange-haired girl stood by the window in the morning, looking out, attracting, sucking the light. To Yara, she was Luminous. Unlike here, Yara stayed as far away from the windows; she knew what was out there; she had spent a whole day in that camp and wished for no more. She had heard before the term *cordon sanitaire* from Netflix, and to her, it meant protection. Safety.

The nurse had forgotten her med pad again, and Yara started drawing on it. A sparrow feeding on a dead cicada.

Luminous glanced at her pencil strokes and asked her. "Do you like drawing, Gianna? I'll tell them to bring a kit."

The next day the nurse brought orange juice, a stale chocolate-filled croissant on a sealed plastic bag, and a drawing kit that Lucia had ordered and paid for. A sketchpad, twelve pencils, even some wax crayons.

Yara never opened the croissant bag, but she started drawing anything she could see, sparrows and glass windowpanes, gowns stained with blood, a wolf with jade eyes, camp beds, and skeletons.

"These are very beautiful," Lucia said, flipping away from the skeletons back to the sparrows. "You should name each drawing. Please, for me." The Luminous girl pushed another bite of croissant into Yara's mouth. That toilet paper taste.

Luminous brought her an even bigger drawing pad a couple of days later. Yara had no idea how Luminous could find such beautiful presents, even though she never left the room. Yara couldn't sleep much; she would get up, find a cell phone, and use it as a flashlight to draw. Angels, vampires, and the djinn with eyes of ember. She called her parents' mobile often, but there was no reply.

Lucia had tried to search for the number but found no trace or name behind it.

It was the evening of July 12 when the nurse and a police officer entered the isolation room. He was breaking the quarantine, but everybody had forgotten about the handful of dead in Moria by now. There were no more infected; the media worldwide had stopped referring to H7N9. "Happens all the time. The refugees get sick, always something," he said, to justify his barging in. "We need to take care of the little lady here, process her."

Yara ran and hid in Luminous' arms, and the orange-haired girl shushed her. "Hey girl, it is all right, they came for me, not you," said Lucia and then turned to the officer.

"This girl is staying with me until we locate her parents," Lucia said.

The officer chuckled with a bitter smile. "I doubt that. We can't locate anyone, not even a record. We must send her to a detention center."

Lucia raised her voice, hoping that Gianna would open her mouth finally.

"Sir, to begin with, I don't care if the girl is Syrian, Afghani, or British. I will help her, anyway. But the embassies care, so I need you to request a new search through the British Embassy. Send another picture of her. I am quite sure that this little lady here is from England. The first night they brought her to the hospital, she was interviewed by Dr. Armandou and a male nurse. I talked to him. He had heard her speak when she was still speaking, she had a British accent, he says. Also, look at this," Lucia said. She held two drawing sketches that Yara had made.

"What am I looking at? Kid's drawings?"

"This is Big Ben, and this is the Gherkin, both London buildings."

"I can draw a pyramid. Doesn't make me Egyptian," said the officer.

"Look at the titles. Gianna doesn't speak, but she named each one of these sketches," Lucia said.

The officer stood silent with pursed lips offering no response.

"Let me explain, Officer Antoniou." Lucia read the titles. *As if she were an angel.* The girl used the subjunctive form of the verb. *Tears, brine, and salt.* That's an Oxford comma. Now, this may mean shit to you, especially since I can't even translate it in Greek, but I'll tell you what. This is not how a refugee from Syria writes. The girl was raised in England, I'd bet my ass on that. She was an A student too."

The officer took a few seconds flipping over the sketch pad.

"What is this? Ypsilon?" he asked. "All her drawings have a Ypsilon at the bottom right corner."

A capital Y. Lucia hadn't noticed until then. She stared at Gianna, hoping for an answer, the girl's jaw twitched once again, but no sound came out. Her mind raced back to the man who raped her and froze there, how he pushed harder every time she tried to squeal.

"What did you say her first name was?" Antoniou repeated.

"Gianna," said the nurse.

"Gianna is a Greek, not a Syrian name."

"How do you know?" Lucia asked.

"How do I know, kid? All I do the last five years here is write down Syrian and Afghani names. I know. Yara. Try Yara. I bet you got her last name wrong too."

"That's why we can't find her."

"Genius! What are you, a detective?" the officer chuckled. "We need to search for a Yara girl who traveled to Syria from the UK in the last two-three years. I'll talk to the Embassy, give them the photograph too. I'll get fingerprints."

"Yara?" asked Luminous staring hard at her, holding the girl's hand between hers.

Yara nodded, and Lucia nodded back, visibly embarrassed as if she ought to have figured it out a long time ago. A Ypsilon. How did she miss it? That was a piss-poor job for an aspiring detective.

Lucia went to the corner to make a phone call to her mom.

"Yeah, mom. Everything is fine here in Corfu. Give dad a big kiss. What's that?" She paused. "An amazing time, the island is just magic. Yeah, we swim, taverna, bar, you know." She wasn't lying about the magic part.

"I bet there is a boyfriend," Nora said, amens and joy flowing through the airwaves.

"Something like that, mom."

Officer Antoniou returned a couple of hours later, holding a tablet and displaying a triumphant broad smile.

"I think we found her. 'Yara Halabi,' age sixteen from Manchester. Her family moved to Syria a year and a half ago. I have the UK Embassy in the line, and they have someone back from home who might recognize her. Anyway, whatever home is for her."

"Family member?" Lucia asked.

Yara felt a sparrow fluttering up and down her chest, nibbling on her heart.

"I'm afraid not."

The videoconferencing window opened to two faces, a bespectacled lady sitting on a desk that introduced herself as Ms. Hodson, "call me Jane," and a man with cropped hair. Yara focused on the man; his face was familiar, despite the different haircut. She knew once he started speaking.

"Yara, is that you? Oh my, golly, it is you. I am coach Murray, remember?"

For a moment, Yara's chest filled with hope, she managed to open her mouth, and after, two weeks, a year, an eon, she didn't know, she uttered words for the first time again.

"Coach. Murray." A three-second pause between each word. "Is my mom there?"

Coach Murray stood dumbfounded and wordless, searching for an invisible life-vest to save himself. The camera switched to Jane from the Embassy, who mumbled that they were trying to locate her parents, and they had some questions regarding their whereabouts for Yara. And if she could answer them now.

Once again, the camera switched to coach Murray.

"You must excuse me, but I need to get to practice. I confirm that the lady here is Yara Halabi, she was in our club till 2021, and I've known her for four years. She is a British citizen for sure, the school must have her birth certificate on file. Tell you what. That girl can swim like a dolphin! Remember, Yara?"

Coach Murray switched the camera to focus on the pool, the cold blue water, the light dancing on the surface.

At the sight of the water, Yara brought her fists to her temples and screamed so loudly that even the luminous orange-haired angel shivered and jumped up from her chair.

# 40. Lucia: A Hoodie

*Lesbos, July 25, 2022*

Yara became an adult that day. She chose what to wear without having to worry about what her father or anyone else might think. The Embassy had sent a wide variety of garments just for her. Teal high-rise fleece jogger pants, a plain white v-neck t-shirt, a matching hoodie, and white sneakers. If it was not for the river of anxiety oozing out of her body, as she was rocking back and forth, wrapping herself with both hands, refusing to open her eyes, one might say that she was ready to go out in the real world, even on prime-time TV.

This time Moria was shutting down for good. The media were having a field day, gathering by the dozens, now that the camp had been declared clear of the epidemic. It was just too good a story, not one but two and three stories together. The virus had succumbed to the heat, and Europe was reporting zero cases. The refugee camp that had been a disgrace for years now was shutting down. But the real story was Yara. The BBC, Channel 4, and the rest of British media had discovered the improbable fairy-tale of a sixteen-year-old swimming champion born and raised in Manchester, a modern-day Gretel suffering evil witches and careless parents—unable to save her little Hansel sister. Big bad wolves with a plague on top.

The media couldn't get enough of this, and they quickly uncovered the worse. Yara's younger sister, father, mother, and infant brother were all considered lost at sea. Their boats had never made it to land, and they had not registered in any camp.

Lucia had been fortunate—though that's not the appropriate word—to have an infinite abundance of resources at her disposal once it became clear that Yara was the owner of a passport with the Royal Coat of Arms printed on its cover. Rewards were promised in Turkey and Greece, searches in other Greek camps and databases. Nothing came back except for some witness stories, which proved the worse.

It would be too good a story for Yara to reunite with the rest of her family, at least one of them, on a different island camp. Alas, there is just so much fairy-tale stuff that can fit in one life. It had been a couple of days since Lucia had abandoned hope; the grim reality dawned on her that Yara was by now all alone, an orphan with no home to return to.

By now, every TV viewer in England and Greece knew that Yara was an orphan. Everyone except Yara. As the last buses of the common, "no story worthy of media" refugees were abandoning Moria, the cameras waited at the gates for the last two girls, Yara and Lucia, to make their glorious exit, seal the gates of hell, forever. Lucia had become a celebrity all by herself, the intern detective who had uncovered the sex-trafficking ring in Moria. The publicity made her a target, but it was also a shield; no one would dare touch her now. So she hoped.

Officer Antoniou entered the room, polished shoes, and civilian clothes, and announced: "It is time to go, Yara. Freedom at last," he tried to fake a celebratory smile.

Lucia made a cut-it-out signal and knelt next to Yara to talk her out of her latest fit. The problem was that Lucia wasn't sure what she was trying to convince Yara to do.

A team from the Embassy and the social worker who had arrived from London would take Yara back home, but there was no home waiting. First, they'd have to explain to her that none of her family members had been located. Her only option would be to return to Syria and starve with her grandparents, something no one would recommend, or to be placed in a foster care home in the UK. Too many families had already offered despite her older age.

"Sorry, officer, I need two secs, to update Yara. Else, she'll learn from the reporters' questions, and that's just too much."

"Learn what?" Yara asked.

She was past her mute phase and conversing with Lucia for days now but refusing to go into more serious conversations.

*"I am not leaving you. Stay with me,"* was the only answer Yara offered once the conversation moved to anything serious. She refused to talk about the past or the future and exchanged words only about the now and the fantastic: "Give me a chocolate. Read me a story. I want to watch a movie on your iPad. Together. Adventure. No blood."

Yara was the only reason that kept Lucia in the Moria hospital for so long; the cabin fever was getting to her. It would be over in a few minutes; they had to face the world. Lucia sighed long and hard to find some strength inside her and then spilled the news to Yara.

They both sat on the floor cross-legged across each other, Lucia holding Yara's hands. She looked the girl straight in the eye.

"The police think that your parents got on a boat heading for Samos, two days after you and your sister boarded. Some witnesses made it across, and they recognized them from pictures that the Embassy gave them. Unfortunately, most people from that boat were lost at sea. I am sorry, Yara. The government sent a lady from the Social Services to take you back." Lucia spoke like a robot, trying to avoid emotion.

Yara didn't cry or scream this time; she had figured as much about her parents.

"I know they are gone. I realized over these last days. If they were in a camp, the Embassy would have found them." Yara was an adult now. She tried to behave like one, so they could take her seriously. "I want to stay with you, Lucia."

Lucia turned and looked at the police officer with a "help me out here" puppy face.

Officer Antoniou jumped in, guessing that his role was to play the bad cop.

"This is not possible, Yara. There are procedures and laws. You are underage and a British citizen."

The guy was too chubby, rosy cheeks and favorite-uncle mustache to be convincing as a bad guy.

"Lucia, I am sick," Yara continued. She stood up and went to the corner window, where she could see the cameras and the buses that had gathered outside. "I am sick of myself, of everything out there. I can't make it. Jeez, it's so hot in here."

Yara removed the hoodie revealing the bandages around her wrists and why she wore a hoodie with 33 Celsius. Those bandages had to be changed again. Lucia had stopped the bleeding on time last night, the girl didn't cut herself deep enough to die fast, but she wouldn't have survived it if Lucia hadn't stormed the bathroom to find her resting on the floor, head against the toilet bowl.

"Why, why, why?" Lucia had asked her once they stitched her up. "I've been through hell to save you."

"Hell?" Yara had replied. "We're there, aren't we? I am pretty sure I won't die if I cut myself. I drowned back at sea, this is some hell we're in. Not reality."

It was mostly a show, not a genuine suicide attempt—that was Lucia's verdict—though she wasn't much of a trauma psychologist. She had convinced the nurse not to make a fuss about it. "It's an act," Lucia said, "an effort to convince us that she is serious about it."

That had happened the night before, but this morning Yara was keeping the act on.

"I am telling you once and for all, I am not going out there. You send me there, I die," Yara said. "I want to rest anyway."

Officer Antoniou moved to the next room and had yet another conference call with the Embassy. He pushed hard again and again. It was to no one's benefit to see Yara committing suicide a few days after being placed back in the State's hands. Not much came out of the call.

"Only way that the Embassy will agree to leave her here is if she has relatives in Greece," officer Antoniou said. "We can start the procedure for asylum, and then she can invite her grandparents if they want to immigrate here."

"How long would that take?" Lucia asked.

"These days? Four, six months."

*Useless.*

Lucia walked over to the window and embraced Yara. The camp was deserted, reminding once again of the summery Greek countryside instead of an arena of suffering. A stray cat, invisible cicadas cutting the heat with their song, two butterflies dancing a few yards away, circling the sunflowers of the hospital garden.

"The girl has no relatives here. But she is sixteen. What if she could marry someone. We could run to the State House now," Lucia said.

Antoniou took two steps back, stumbling and giggling. "I am sorry, young lady. I am engaged already, I could never. She is too young—"

"Yeah, I thought so," Lucia said. "Guess I'll have to do everything myself in this story. You do have a car, I hope, officer. Call the mayor."

Yara and Lucia were married the same afternoon, with officer Antoniou and the Hodson lady from the Embassy being the only witnesses. No media were present.

# 41. Tina: Sunbeds

*Paros, Greece, August 14, 2022*

A massacre.

Giant red snappers and groupers, sea breams the size of newborn babies. Fresh off the sea, and grilled whole, devoured to the fin and the cheek, only the eyes and the center fishbone resting in white platters of oil, lemon, and oregano sauce. A feast.

The Pucci and the Missoni dresses rubbing against the white open shirts showing some hair, women and men packed like sardines, dancing around and on top of the white taverna tables, between the bottles of ouzo and Jagermeister—deer blood to kill the fish-breath—the high heels masterfully avoiding the half-empty grilled octopus and crayfish risotto plates. The crowd was quite upscale and not into breaking plates—that custom had been outdated since the sixties—but the spirits were high and the music loud at 2 a.m. Tina and Peri were swinging among the other thirty-something-year-olds, some of their best friends, and a swarm of total strangers celebrating.

Tina made an effort to dance, be jovial. Earlier that morning, she received the news, all bad. She was sunbathing on Golden Beach, among hundreds of packed tourists, most of them well-off families from Athens, when the message flashed on her phone.

Garnett: *"Las Lenas. Five cases."*

Las Lenas ski resort. It was the middle of the snow season in Argentina, and she had expected one of those countries to be hit first. Australia, South

261

Africa, Argentina, New Zealand. It was Argentina, five cases of H7N9 reported at the ski resort, and as Demetri was nagging her to come to see the sandcastle he built with dad, all she could think was that it would be forty cases the next morning.

"Las Lenas." She said the name loudly.

"Never heard of it," said Nancy next to her. "A new restaurant? We can try it tomorrow; let's stick with Barbarossa tonight. You made a reservation, right?"

Tina nodded to Nancy and then texted Professor Garnett, *"Las Lenas? What's going on?"* She was in constant communication with him lately, planning her sabbatical at Johns Hopkins. She hadn't managed to sit Peri down and talk to him about this; hopefully, he would agree since he was jobless. Another fight she had postponed for tomorrow, after the party.

Garnett: *"Did u guys order vaccines?"*

Tina: *"Idk."*

Peri was asking if she wanted a Corona; he was ordering one from the beach waitress.

Garnett: *"Get the vaccines, Tina! This is no drill."*

She had pushed everything to the next day, after their party. She'd talk to Peri about moving to the US for a year and even call Alexi and beg him to order vaccines. Her ego was not part of the equation anymore. A dozen of the adults around her were friends, their kids attending the same private school as Demetri.

The beer, the heat, and the swim made her dizzy under the blazing afternoon sun, and she closed her eyes to take a brief nap. She dreamt that she was on the same beach, but it was eerily quiet, no children or music. In the silence of her dream, Ekemma, the girl from Nigeria, who had died at Lesbos, walked naked out of the sea, approached, and sat at the end of Tina's sunbed. The girl's eyes were not red-rimmed anymore but a full dull red as she pointed to her left then to her right. Thousands of sunbeds spread on the golden beach, covered by white sheets instead of umbrellas, separated by white curtains. It was 1918 all over again, young and old gasping for air and coughing blood—an endless made-up hospital of white and gray, of red and brown. Tina jumped from her nightmare, panting and sweating, drawing worried looks from everyone. She quickly faked a smile to Peri and tried to join any other conversation that would derail her train of thought. Soccer-mom talk, what time should they gather at the chick taverna by the port tonight to celebrate her birthday, anything to get her mind away from what was coming.

"This beach is too damn crowded," said Jenny, her friend on the next sunbed. "It's torture," she said, sipping her margarita.

"A massacre," Tina replied.

The whole world had changed in her eyes, and that was not some metaphor. The sunset was blurry; all things land and sea were gray, the necklace she wore last night was gray too, but she knew it used to be turquoise. Tina had been left with five colors after the viral infection—her optic nerve had been damaged, temporarily, permanently, she didn't know—and even this handful of colors were faded versions of their true tones. White of shroud, gray of ashes, brown of earth, a blood-caking red. Black, but it didn't count as a color. There was a fifth color, some shifting shade of gray that she called "blue" or "green," depending on whether she was staring at the trees or the sea, though yellow was completely gone from her vision. She had first noticed when Demetri's drawings of a happy family at the beach were missing the gold of the sun and the sand, only to realize through conversation that he had, probably, colored everything just fine; it was her sight that was the problem.

Later in the evening, they were getting ready at the Airbnb seaside villa facing the sunset when Peri asked her: "Gray? Are you going to wear a plain gray dress on your birthday like a nun?"

She quickly switched to a long white cotton dress and the summer probably turquoise necklace, refusing to let Peri know the truth. She had promised herself that the darkness, worry, and pain of Moria would not violate their Paros vacation.

They drove to the main village and walked to the restaurant, passing among the cramped white-washed alleys, the bars, and the tavernas packed to the last useful centimeter, uniting everyone into a carefree celebration of life.

"A massacre," Tina repeated the word, looking at the dinner table hours later, the devoured snappers, the birthday cake. They were celebrating Peri's latest failed business venture, Tina's birthday, and her certain path to join her husband in unemployment. Everyone, especially the women, was exactly thirty-nine years old or younger on the island of Paros. In Tina's case, that was the truth, certified with a cake that had all its thirty-seven candles, daring the other women to count them.

Tina had let herself be seduced by the wine and the kamikaze shots, surrendering her night to the DJ. If his song reminded her of old-times and carefree days, she'd get in the joyful mood instantly and twist herself for a minute or two. If he switched to a faux carnival jingle, a sleazy Latin dance tune, or something reminding her of her fake ex-boyfriend, she'd go into instant depression staring aimlessly around, like a ghost in white. She downed another shot whenever the sour mode overwhelmed her and shouted to the waiter to "Keep 'em coming! We are celebrating!"

Perri twisted her around for another dance, and she followed through another two minutes of fluid and supple moves.

"I need a minute. Bathroom," she said and pushed through the crowds, the dresses all washed out red and gray—she knew that wasn't right, Emilio Pucci rarely used gray—trying to escape for a moment to get to the seashore to feel the night breeze.

She passed by the drunk teenagers and found a quiet corner to clear her mind, stare at the sea, feel the soft sirocco. After fifteen minutes, she decided to end her "bathroom" break and return to the party when a Roma woman and a wide-eyed barefoot girl with raven dark oiled hair approached her. The girl held a red flower in front of Tina.

"Buy a rose, pretty lady. Buy one!" she insisted with a contrived smile.

"Sure," Tina said half-drunk and pulled the rose away from the girl's hand. "But I don't carry money." Even drunk, she would not finance the slave labor market for the first time in her life.

The Roma woman darted forward and grabbed Tina's wrist.

"Hey, that's not right, lady. Pay up."

"I have nothing with me," she said.

"You bring, or you'll regret it," said the woman, holding Tina's palm with both hands now, peering once at the lines and then at Tina again. "Silver me, pretty lady, and I'll help you. I lift the darkness that shadows your soul. Your marriage is cursed. I lift the curse. Silver me!"

Tina pulled her hand from the grasp of the woman and ran away. Her curse was crystal clear; no silver-seeking fortune-tellers were needed. Tina had already landed in the hell that was to come, the return of the pandemic in the autumn of 2022, and she'd have to wait for the rest of her friends and family to join her there. It would be lonely till then, and no one would understand.

It was about 3 a.m. now, and the crowd was dancing a bit more tired, a lot more drunk. She wrapped her arms around Peri to feel safe, to defy the curse of the fortune-teller, and downed two more shots.

She didn't notice the alert until the next morning; the twenty-three reported cases of H7N9 in Buenos Aires. There was an odd case in Paris, too, a flight attendant who hadn't even traveled to Argentina. All of France hoped that she was banging a pilot who had. Demetri was jumping up and down, asking for Cheerios. She sleepwalked to the kitchen to feed the kid and then crawled to the toilet, still in her underwear, to find some headache medicine for the hangover. Tina read the alert after gulping down the pills.

"Hey, Siri, call Damianos," she mumbled to her mobile the name of the one man she had sworn never to call again in her life. Her father answered on the second ring.

"Tina? Is that you, baby?"

"Yeah, dad, it's me. I need your help."

# 42. Ella: Flashforward

*Greek Parliament Investigation Committee, Greece, April 21, 2023*

"Would you like to take a break Dr. Walker?" asked the President of the Committee.

"No, Mr....Mr. President," Tina said, realizing that she had forgotten his name once again.

She sat on a plain desk, her lawyer by her side, facing off opposite three rows of committee members and the camera. A swarm of reporters filled the long room behind her, and Tina wondered whether it was the lack of AC or them responsible for her sweating. There were precisely ten parliament members per row, and any one of them could ask a question at any moment. She didn't bother, and she didn't care to memorize their names. They were all Papasomething. Papantonopoulos, Papadopoulos, Papargyropoulos. "Papa" standing for the ancestral patriarch who was also a priest, "poulos" ending signifying the Peloponnesian geographical origin of the family.

"Are you sure? Not even a bathroom break? We'll be here for a long time. We have many questions," repeated the president.

"But they are all typical 'Greek' questions," she said.

"What's that supposed to mean?" asked Mr. Second Row, three from the left. Tina kept marking her grid paper notepad with numbers a letter for each member to keep track of them. Second row, three from the left, was "2-3." She'd put a B for blue, R for red, in the box. Unlike the USA counterparts, red was for the left (radical socialist), blue for the right-wing party. There were two more colors, black for the two ultra-right, green for the odd nut. A pattern was emerging on how to tell them apart: the right-wing wore ties, the left didn't, the Green was the one John Lennon lookalike, and the black were the ones who looked severely constipated with vast necks supporting tiny heads. "What do you mean our questions are Greek? What else could they be? This is the Investigation Committee of the Greek Parliament," said 3-4 black.

"By 'Greek' question," Tina replied, "I mean that you start with a long pontificating statement, and then you put a question mark at the end, simply demanding that I verify your opinion."

Two of them, 2-5-blue and 3-2-red, chuckled in amusement. The rest didn't seem to get it. They were not there to learn anything; all the answers were long imprinted on them before the pandemic had started.

"Dr. Walker, I assume you understand the impact of your deposition here today," replied the President, 1-5-blue. "What you reveal to this committee might determine the political and potential criminal charges that will be brought against the former Minister of Health and the former Prime Minister, among others. This is a matter of life and death." He uttered the last sentence very slowly to emphasize.

He had studied law, Tina guessed. Most local politicians did.

"Death primarily," Tina said. "Anyway, we've covered all that happened last year. But if you have more questions, shoot!"

"Are you testifying that you requested and had a meeting with the Minister of Health back in September 2022, before the outbreak started?" asked 1-5-blue.

"August 22, to be exact," Tina said and continued. "But the meeting took place in early September because he was on vacation. Actually, yes, I need some water. A Coke even better."

"In fact, it was your father, Mr. Yannis Damianos, who arranged the meeting. Why didn't you go through proper channels?" Red 1-8 asked.

Red 1-8, she was the business, Tina paid a lot more attention to her questions.

"Yes, I couldn't get a meeting with the Minister, so I asked my father to arrange it."

"Your father was a high-ranking official of the Radical Left party until his recent death, correct?"

"Yes," muttered Tina, "he was a Radical Leftist." The closest to the Reds ideology that her father had ever been was the paint of his Alfa Romeo Cabrio.

"You'd already been fired from the National Agency of Public Health?" asked 3-3 Red.

"No. I was not Head of EHT anymore, but I was still a NAPH employee."

"Was the man who replaced you as Head of the Emergency Taskforce, Dr. Alexi Vardis, in that meeting?" asked 2-7 Blue.

There was an increasing murmur from the reporters behind her once Alexi's name was mentioned.

"No."

"Why not? He was a trusted colleague of yours, correct? The records indicate that he had called," Blue 2-7 put his reading glasses on and checked his notes "one hundred and fifteen times in the months before the pandemic. Wow!"

"We worked together."

Tina could hear the cameras clicking behind her.

"You are aware that Dr. Vardis has been missing since last November, correct?"

"I think the whole country is aware by now," said Tina.

"When did you become aware that Dr. Vardis was missing?"

"I guess the same day you were. He was on TV every evening, informing us about the pandemic developments until he wasn't, so I am not sure why you are asking me that."

"Because you are the last person who called Dr. Vardis according to the records of the phone company," Black 3-4 said.

Tina's lawyer whispered in her ear, though she knew the drill.

"I have testified to the police about him. I thought I was here to talk about the Prime Minister. May I take a break?"

The next question came even before the President nodded "yes," and she decided to continue since it was not about Alexi.

"Why did you request a meeting with the Minister back then?" asked 2-7 Blue, saving Tina.

"But it was not an official meeting. It happened in a cafe, correct?" 3-3 Red interjected.

"Yes, we met in a coffee shop outside the Ministry HQs," Tina replied. "I am not sure what you refer to as 'official meeting,' and I don't want to waste more time. I told the Minister that the pandemic was to return in October, and he needed to order vaccines right away," said Tina.

"You were pretty certain about that," said 3-4 Black.

"Is that a question? Well, I was 95% certain."

"Yes, it seems that some of you knew everything about what was to happen when. We had zero infections before then, and yet some of you could predict the exact date that the pandemic would strike, how many it will kill. Everything. Amazing, huh?"

"Is that a question? Yes, some of us knew that temperatures drop in October, sir. It is 'proprietary' knowledge. As the cold weather returns, so does the flu. It was spreading in Buenos Aires and Johannesburg before I had the meeting with the Minister."

"But you made accurate predictions about the death rate and the death count," added President Blue 1-5.

"No, I didn't. I just recited the predictions of the world's foremost scientists, the history of previous pandemics, and the fact that if I were wrong, it wouldn't matter."

"It wouldn't matter?"

"No, it wouldn't. The cost of vaccinating the whole population was below thirty million euros. I mean, shit, we are a small country. We spend the same amount on toilet paper for the Armed Forces. A freaking frigate costs six hundred million, more than twenty pandemics."

"Are you a military expert now, Mrs. Walker?" continued 3-4 Black.

Tina ignored him.

"You are not even a doctor, am I correct?"

"No, I am not a medical doctor. If you are in need of blood pressure or psychiatric medicine, I can't prescribe it. I have a doctorate in epidemiology."

"Did the Minister of Health tell you that the vaccines were expensive in his opinion?" asked lady 1-8 Red. Her hair was a matching washed-out lion-king red. She was supposed to be the most charismatic speaker of all the Reds, a fierce political persona that even Tina, who never watched TV, could recognize.

"The Minister spoke only one word to me, and I knew: '1976.'"

"Meaning?"

"You see, unfortunately for our country, the Minister was a graduate of the History and Sociology of Science Department from Penn. He got his Ph.D. there in 1979."

"You are not helping us," said Red 1-8.

"Are you familiar with what happened in the US back in 1976? No, you're not. Not to waste your time, I'll summarize it quickly. February 1976, an 18-year-old dies in Fort Dix army camp in New Jersey. Somehow this is overblown into a repeat of 1918. President Gerald Ford, flanked by the most trusted doctors, appears on TV and announces an imminent swine-flu pandemic and his intent to vaccinate the entire country. He overreacted. Moreover, some of the initial vaccine batches were probably defective, and a few people died, though it is unclear what they died from. It was a total disaster. Billions, 1976 billions, of lawsuits. Un fiasco grande!"

"And how does this relate to ex-Minister Georgiou?"

"The Minister was obviously not a Republican supporter—he has a photo of himself with Fidel Castro in the conference room. The young Georgiou did his thesis on the fiasco of the faux-pandemic. He was emotionally invested in overreactions to a flu outbreak and money wasted on the pharmas."

"So, when he got the news for the H7N9 last year, he probably—"

"I know where you are going with this," said Tina. "Yes, he immediately told me that he is not going to waste a single drachma of the public's money to finance some organized pharma extortion scheme. And that there was no way that he'd agree to indemnify the vaccine producers."

"You are testifying that the Minister did not act out with the intent to cause harm, but it was rather his educated decision that the evidence was insufficient to act at that point? Correct?" said 1-8 Red.

"No. I didn't use any of these words, and you are jumping to random conclusions."

"So, in your scientific opinion, was it gross negligence to his part not to order the vaccines on time?" said 1-5 Blue, the President.

"I am not vindictive, but as the results demonstrate, it was."

"The Minister fired you, correct? Are we to believe that you are not vindictive?" repeated Red 1-8. "You just admitted, a minute ago, that his opinion as a scientist was not to order vaccines. As a scientist. We could have had a repeat of 1976, couldn't we?"

"I can't teach epidemiology in here, and that's not what's asked of me. All I can say is that in such situations, it pays to 'panic early' and prepare for the worst even if you are wrong." Tina bit her lower lip and stood silent for a few seconds. She didn't have much more to say, but twenty-eight of the members—the other two were half asleep—were looking at her wide-eyed and bent forward with hands on the table waiting for an answer. The reporters behind her were hissing as if a snake pit was coming alive.

"To clarify, you don't condone any of the Minister's actions, do you?" asked Blue 1-5.

"Inactions," Tina replied. "Look, Ms. Red, Mr. Blue," the room filled with laughter, "I'll meet you both halfway. I didn't say that the Minister is a criminal. I said he is an idiot."

Blue 1-10, an eighty-three-year-old prominent figure of the Conservative party, raised his trembling hand for the first time. Until then, Tina thought that the frail man was sleeping. "Dr. Walker," he asked, his voice Yoda-faint and tired, "is there a difference between a criminal and an idiot if he happens to be the nation's Minister of Health, hmmm?"

If it were not for the dead listening, Tina would have laughed.

"But you didn't stop there, Dr. Walker," said President 1-5 Blue. "You then managed to secure a meeting with the Prime Minister."

# 43. Yara: Cradle of Democracy

*Office of the Prime Minister, Greece, October 3, 2022*

"Please, Tina, could you take her?" asked an exasperated Lucia from the other side of the video call.

"Is it the punk hairstyle? You don't feel you are fit to meet the Prime Minister like this?"

"What? No. The Prime Minister is a punk himself. I just can't stand all those reporters gathering and their bullshit questions. 'Oh, how is your other half, Lucia?' 'Was that a real wedding or a trick?' 'Is it ethical to marry a sixteen-year-old?' I've had it with them. 'Was it a publicity stunt?'" Lucia was imitating the annoying voices of the reporters who had camped outside her parent's apartment the first couple of weeks when she returned from Lesbos.

"All valid questions, I had myself," Tina teased her.

"Yeah, Dr. Tina, the thing is you didn't have to save the girl from bleeding to death so you can talk all the shit you want. I know what happened. I had to keep her here, and same-sex marriage was the only way to do it."

"So, this, the two of you, is not romantic, in any way," said Tina, with phone held between shoulder and ear, fixing Demetri a ham and cheese lunch sandwich.

"Ro-what? Please," Lucia started walking and headed for the bathroom where nobody else could hear her. "Yara is a kid," she said after shutting the door with a bang.

"Sixteen-year-old kids get romantic, you know. A kid that the Prime Minister wants to chat with."

"No way I'll be part of this circus act," answered Lucia, shaking her head firmly within the six-inch screen.

"I thought you were *for* the Radical Left. How come you don't want to meet the Leader?" asked Tina.

"You thought that? Tell you what. I am leaning left, but all the people I respect from there won't even talk to *this* Prime Minister. The guy is a fake. An opportunist. And those around him."

"You know my father is Secretary of Transportation and Telecom. Appointed by our Prime Minister."

"Sorry, that doesn't change my opinion."

"Mine neither," said Tina with a grin. "My dad is a fake, too."

"So, you don't mind taking Yara to this? It is just a photo-op. A few minutes, they said, quick in and out."

"Fine, I'll take her," said Tina, her sharp tone faking reluctance. She had to meet the Prime Minister, time was running out, and that was the only opportunity she'd ever get.

Two days later, she put on her two-piece, gray-green plaid business suit, her dull brown (call it mahogany) lipstick, and got in the car that the Security Office had sent. It was a thirty-minute bumper-to-bumper drive to Lucia's place to pick up Yara.

The married couple walked out of the apartment building front door, Yara holding Lucia's hand. The teenager was wearing a midi wrap dress that she had bought online for thirty pounds from a youth fashion brand. The color had returned to her lips and cheeks, but her moves were excruciatingly slow, and there was no trace of a smile on her teenage face. She was barely more talkative than what Tina remembered from Moria, and she fixed her stare outside the window, avoiding talk with Tina. Five minutes and twenty stick shift changes later, Yara threw up, and her face instantly turned to banana yellow. She started panting hard, eyes filling with tears, repeating, "I'm sorry, so sorry." Tina felt so embarrassed for the kid's embarrassment that she didn't even dare clean her stained shoes. The driver made a U-turn and took them back to Lucia's apartment.

"Get dressed and come down, Lucia," Tina said on the phone, with a soft but strict tone. "Yara is not going anywhere without you. She thinks I am going to take her to the airport or something. And bring me a pair of heels, size nine." A pause. "Some wet wipes then."

The three ladies waited at the coffee shop across from Lucia's apartment for another hour until the Security Office sent a second car, one that didn't smell of gastric acid and cereal. Tina had another iced latte and, by the third sip, regretted it. She sat in the front passenger's seat this time, tapping her fingers repeatedly on the PVC dashboard.

"Geez, I had too much caffeine," she muttered.

The driver jumped in to help. "No worries, the Prime Minister has only five minutes for photos. You'll be in and out."

Tina needed more than five minutes.

The radio station hosts were burbling something about a "secret" EU plot to cut Greek pensions again, switching from that to the pandemic that was ravaging South America and Africa as they spoke. "This is just the flu," the radio host said in a derisive sharp-pitched tone, "man is making futile attempts to live forever," intervened his sidekick in a low husky voice.

"Here, you got your daily dose of Greek neophilosophers, kid," said Tina turning to Yara. "Remember the weeks we spent in Moria? That was just the seasonal flu. Morons!" The bendy bus outside her window was packed with people, no one wearing a mask.

Ten minutes later, the Mercedes C Class stopped in front of the Maximos Mansion.

"Look at those fuckers," said Lucia, pointing at the press waiting outside the Prime Minister's mansion. Middle-aged bearded guys, a couple of women showcasing their brightest blonde coupes, each one of them holding a microphone. "I'll stay in the car," Lucia insisted, at the same time jostling a napping Yara to wake her up. Surprisingly, this time Yara followed Tina without disagreement, maybe because she was still dizzy to understand where they were.

Tina held Yara's hand and quickly sliced a path through the mob of reporters, like a barracuda through a school of pilot fish. As a kid, she often passed by the mansion when dad would take her to feed the ducks at the National Garden across, but she was always unimpressed by it. It was neither maximal and barely a mansion, one floor and the size of a small-town library in a little US town—a petite beauty, impeccably designed and maintained, yet tiny. Marble steps, two Ionic columns rising as bookstands to the front gate, a roman post and lintel fence defining the roof's edge. A wine-red carpet was crawling up the marble steps struggling alone to add much-needed importance to the structure. The apartment buildings had risen tall around the tiny 19th-century gem and were breathing contemptuously down at it. Tina felt Yara's hand sweaty and shaking as they walked up the rec-carpet steps. The young girl stopped before entering the dark innards of the mansion, supposedly to observe the two white-washed statues that stood guard, left and right of the entrance. The Kori and Kouros facing each other, rather than those entering or leaving, the female one with legs, arms, broken, the male intact.

"Why did they choose a broken statue?" Yara asked.

"One symbolizes the future, the other the past," Tina answered, with a solemn tone that justified the totally random explanation that came out of her mouth.

"Which is which?" Yara asked while the guard was holding the door open and had fixed his stare on Tina, trying to communicate that time was pressing.

Tina shrugged her shoulders, and Yara repeated the question. "Which is which, Mrs. Tina?"

"We'll soon find out."

The Security guard led them through the metal detector and down a wide checkerboard hallway.

"It smells of lemon scent chlorine," Yara said.

"It smells like a government of twenty-five male ministers and two female," Tina countered. She peeked at the rooms left and right, all dark and morbidly serious with wooden panels covering the walls, reminiscent of a dull British gentlemen's club.

Men with suits and folders, women with coffee trays moved fast in and out of the rooms and the hallway.

"Pawns, bishops, and knights, positioning on the chessboard," Yara remarked, taking the slowest of steps on the black and white marble tiles, carefully peering at each detail around her.

"Do you always talk like that?" Tina asked.

"Like what?"

*Like an alien who landed on Planet Earth five minutes ago,* Tina wanted to add, but she carefully selected her words. "Like, an observant artist."

"Please step inside," the security officer whispered as he opened the door to the PM's office.

The Prime Minister, a man slightly older than Tina, with thick black hair and barely standing 5' 9", shook Yara's hand, offering his condolences once again, and then greeted Tina.

"Mrs. Walker. What a surprise! I didn't expect you here today. Where is Mrs. Mazur? I guess I'm not important enough to meet the couple of the year," he said.

His hand squeezed hers. It was cold and had an alien texture like mannequin plastic slathered with oily cream. It was a cautious handshake, an attempt to ice an opponent, rather than to bring two people closer.

His wife stood next to him, a lady of old money known for philanthropies and not much else, who had married socialist, to feel closer to the "common people." The lyrics of a Pulp song came to Tina's mind whenever she saw the First Lady's face on TV.

"I am very sorry that Lucia is not here. What a brave thing she did to save these girls," the First Lady said. "Please call me Dora."

Yara frowned, and Dora offered them orange juice and water to keep the ball rolling. The pointless chit-chat went on for another couple of minutes, while Tina's efforts to turn the subject to the virus were thwarted easily by Dora before the PM even had a chance to intervene. The First Lady was making a genuine effort to engage Yara in conversation, so Tina found the opportunity to talk to the PM in private.

"Sir, if I may have two minutes of your time. It is of the utmost importance," she said.

"Dr. Walker, let me guess. You want to educate me about the new flu virus."

"Yes, the pandemic," Tina answered.

"The pandemic is a non-issue for our country. It caused only a handful of deaths in Moria months ago," said the PM.

Tina had a visceral distaste for the man across from her. He was supposedly an ideologue, who had united extreme Left and Right into the most unlikely, on paper, government coalition, yet he acted like a National Socialist. A strange breed, not matching Tina's stereotypes from US politics or the country's past. She tried to remember why she hated him so much if there was something more than the fact that her father and Alexi were both members of the Party. She was never one to delve deep into politics; maybe it was just her father's decisions that clouded her judgment.

"But I believe you want to talk about the vaccines," the PM continued.

"Yes, but how did you know?" she stopped. "I must tell you that I met the Minister of Health last month about the same subject."

"I know who you met. Do you think we let anyone come in here?"

"Yeah, I guess. Anyway, then you understand. There are outbreaks in five countries now in the Southern Hemisphere and isolated incidents in Europe. A hundred and fifteen dead in Argentina last month, two-hundred and forty in South—"

"Three hundred and fifty in Greece," he said.

"What do you mean?" asked Tina.

"Our tourism industry is dying, and so do our businesses. Poverty kills people too," he said.

The man had been elected on the slogan that his countrymen would not become the waiters and hostesses of Europe.

"It is our last chance," Tina said, pointing her finger at the bright light coming from the balcony door. The day's high was projected at twenty-nine Celsius; non-working Athenians were flooding the beaches. The prolonged summer weather was the last shield the goddess Athena had bequeathed to the city.

"Please take a seat," the Prime Minister offered and pointed Tina to the conference table. Opposite from them, Yara was getting interrogated by a very polite First Lady, and Tina sensed that the girl's patience was running thin.

"Have you tried to secure a vaccine supply, sir? I am begging you, and I haven't begged anyone in my life. Your Minister of Health is wrong."

"Let's stop right here," said the PM. "We are talking about a flu virus, after all."

Tina pursed her lips and waited in the fermata until his next sentence.

"There is some evidence that the seasonal flu vaccine might provide protection," he continued.

"No, there isn't. That was a hypothesis last summer that proved false. You must procure the new vaccine for the H7N9. Sir, I've studied this virus all my life. This might be a type of flu but is *not* the seasonal flu."

"The pharmaceutical multinationals demand an arm and a leg for immunization. And full legal immunity. Greece is the cradle of democracy, doctor." He pointed the finger at Tina. "We will not be bullied by the New World Order! We won't let them seesaw governments in and out of here."

"Sir, this is not about price or political agendas."

"Half the Greek people believe that the virus was weaponized. Once our party signaled that we were leaving the EU, the cases started appearing on the island."

"Weaponized? Seriously? Sir, the virus has no idea if you are socialist, conservative, black or white. Not even if you are pig or human. To the virus, you are a host. This is not about politics and New World Order. To put it bluntly, it's about survival. We cannot afford not to vaccinate our children."

"The *children* argument is the last resort of the false alarmists. Children are *not* susceptible to this virus."

"But they are!"

"By the way, seventeen kids died in a school bus accident just yesterday," the PM said, already darting glances to his Security officer and signaling.

Time was running out for Tina. A photographer was setting up, there would be some photos of the PM and the First Lady with Yara, and all would be over soon.

"There is a rumor that you have been trying for months now to get vaccines, but the pharmas have run out of capacity, sir. Is that so? Maybe I can help."

"That's far from the truth. We have a committee of the most prominent scientists, I am sorry you are not in it, and I understand where this is coming from. They are convinced that all this is an overreaction. I will not have my country succumb to foreign money-making interests. You'll excuse me now," he said and stood up to join Yara and the First Lady in the photoshoot. He offered his hand to Tina. "Thanks for your visit. I don't suppose you want to join us. It would be awkward for both of us, and after all, you are not related to the girl."

She shook his hand for a split second and took her gaze away to hide her grimace of repugnance. As the photographer was giving directions to the trio, she glanced at the newspapers that spread on the conference table.

*Prime Minister demands emergency aid package from the EU for the virus fiasco.*

*Germans! Pay up for WWII.*

*Minister says: make China pay.*

*Antoni, the true leader, says no to neoliberals.*

*Wise monk of Mount Athos predicts: Plague and famine across Europe before Easter.*

Revenue from tourism, the country's primary industry, had dropped forty percent last summer, mostly due to the thirty-five thousand dead of the first pandemic wave. The country's budget was off by a few billion, but one too many billion for a small country. The PM had promised a lot of favors to many special interest groups. Someone had to foot the bill for him to play Santa before Christmas and the February elections. After all, there were only a handful of deaths in Greece, and his narrative was that all this virus publicity was an overreaction, an attempt to sabotage the country's economy. He'd do anything except acknowledge Tina's efforts to stop the outbreak in Moria. As far as the government was concerned, Moria had never happened. Even Yara was there to remind the public of Moria's shutdown, not the virus outbreak.

The photographer was giving directions, *"One eighth to the right, like this, yes, not this frozen smile, try again,"* but he was not going to get much of a smile out of Yara. The photoshoot was soon over.

Tina stood up from the conference table chair and tried to steal two more seconds.

She stepped close to the PM and said: "At twelve percent mortality and a sixty percent infection, you'll be responsible for seven hundred and fifty thousand deaths, sir. Thousand. One in fourteen of our fellow citizens. I am doing you a favor here. They will hang you from the tallest tree," she said, pointing out the sun-bathed window pane that faced the National Garden across the street.

"Thank you so much for your visit and your kind words," he said. "Good luck, and be careful out there."

They were out of the office and back on the black and white tiled hallway.

"Ooof," Yara sighed. "That room was like a coffin, all the wooden panels. How 19ᵗʰ century! And Dora's perfume smelled of rotting peaches."

"And those leather books on the shelves, I bet they're bound with human skin," Tina said, making Yara giggle for the first time.

The man who approached Tina as they were walking down the corridor was familiar, the chain-smoking aide to the Deputy Minister of Health. He had been in the first vaccines meeting in the MoH before Moria and had joined her with Alexi in Lesbos, just for the first day.

"Mr. Raptopoulos," Tina said with a sigh.

"Please wait for me here, Dr. Walker," he said, never breaking his stride as he headed for the PM's office. "There is more to discuss."

The security officer pointed the two women to the armchairs in the middle of the hallway. Tina and Yara lolled back, gazing at the wrought iron and glass ceiling. A white marble Apollo bust, laurel wreath and all peered at Tina disapprovingly from the antique console table. After all, he was the god of healing and medicine, and she had not served him well in the PM's office.

"The King is shorter than all the pawns," Yara said, still gazing at the ceiling.

"What?"

"They were the King and the Queen, right?" asked Yara.

"No kings. Greece is the cradle of democracy," said Tina, chuckling.

"Unless you are making a chess analogy again."

"No, the way she talked to me, she must be a Queen or something. That man is the leader of the Isolationist Party, right? They want out of the European Union. Maybe he wants to be King. Emperor."

"How do you know all this?"

"Lucia told me everything I needed to know for today."

"They just play that tune to get to power and stay there," Tina said.

"Nah, it's more. I felt an evil presence there. One evil, one vile. Her or him, I don't know. She was weaponizing every sentence out of my mouth. Her words were chisels and rakes, cutting pieces out of me. She was guiding me on how to play it out with the reporters, what to say. She wants me to give an interview to some reporter she has in her pocket."

*Weaponizing.*

The same word again, it was clicking. The Prime Minister would weaponize everything and everyone, a loan shark robbing Peter to lend Paul.

"Are we ever going to leave this place?" said Yara, moving restlessly in her armchair.

"In a minute," Tina said.

Raptopoulos, the aide, finally stormed out of the Prime Minister's office and walked straight on Tina.

"That was no way to address the head of the government, Dr. Walker," he said, with the body language of a school principal reprimanding the troublemaker. "You of all people know that we have a committee of experts handling this. Dr. Alexi Vardis is leading it. Take your theories and complaints with him."

"Dr. Vardis? This fool will just end up being a scapegoat for this sorry office you just exited and all your Ministers. But our friend Alexi has a lean frame. I don't think a whole government can hide behind him," she said.

Tina turned to leave, quite certain that she'd be kicked out anyway, but Raptopoulos stopped her.

"Dr. Walker. Four hundred mil for eleven million vaccines. We have the budget. Do you have a seller?"

She was struck by the proposition and the number as if it were a bolt of lightning delivered by Zeus himself.

"What? You don't need that budget, pal. That's way more than the market price."

"We have the money. If you have the right seller." There was something very *wrong* in the way he said *right*. "We know you are close with the WHO and the pharmas. We can count on you, I hope? Call me," he said and gave her an old-fashioned business card with a hand-written mobile number.

"I can—" Tina stopped. She couldn't finish her sentence.

"Good luck with your relocation, doctor," said the aide, this time with an icy grin across his face.

"The what?" How did he know? She hadn't talked to anybody at the Ministry, and she had postponed the appointment because Peri did not agree to move to Baltimore or Geneva, for that matter. *"Worst two city choices I could think of. Dull as hell,"* he had said to Tina, and she was fighting the fight to convince him for weeks now. *"But it will only be for a year, dear."*

Tina walked out the doors, down the crimson red carpet, and knocked on the passenger's window where Lucia was still waiting, her eyes glued on a tablet.

"Come out, Ms. Maas. It is safe," Tina said. "No reporters."

"How did it go?" Lucia asked, her hand rubbing Yara's shoulder.

"Let's take a walk in the Garden," Tina said, already crossing the street. "I need to think."

The street was mildly crowded under the sunny Athenian sky, as it was lunchtime by now. A lanky grandpa in a sleeveless wool sweater was holding two toddlers, heading for the same garden entrance. Three *tsoliades*, the white-kilted traditional guard, were coming down the street, stomping their red leather clogs in their distinct marching pattern.

"They have pom-pom shoes," Yara said, pointing at them.

"That girl is an artist," Tina said, turning to Lucia while rubbing Yara's head. "You must take her out more often, give her a haircut, so nobody recognizes her. She looks at everything around her as she just landed on the planet."

Tourists in shorts and sandals that didn't make them look a wee bit closer to Ancient Greeks were taking photographs of the traditional guard.

"How was our Prime Minister?" asked Lucia.

"The way you described him," answered Tina. "I think I need to go to the newspapers."

"Check this out," Yara said, staring at her phone. "Those naked statues we saw on the entrance were meant to be burial tributes in the olden days. Told you that was a mausoleum."

"That's not the right time, Yara," said Lucia and turned to Tina. "Papers? Even better, I can get you on TV, doctor. There is a tycoon guy who owes me a favor. Two more favors, actually. He can get you with a phone call in any big-shot TV panel."

"Seriously, you can do that?"

"Just name when."

"How about tonight?" Tina asked.

"That's, err, may be tough. Is it that urgent?"

They were deep in the public garden now; the place was smelling of life and Mother Earth as if a shred of hope had returned. Yara was observing the tall cypress trees, ignoring the conversation. They strolled under a wisteria canopy, passing by strangers who stopped to stare at Lucia and Yara, probably recognizing them from the newspaper photos. No one was wearing a mask. H7N9 had disappeared from the news, even from Facebook, except for the typical racist jokes made at the expense of the suffering and the dead of countries too far away to care about.

"I think the government tapped my phone," said Tina.

"Oh, my god!" Lucia exploded. "We *must* go on TV."

"There is something even worse," Tina said, shaking her head in disbelief, glaring at her heels. The Yara stomach hydrochloric acid stains on the leather were clearly visible; she'd have to throw them away the moment she got back home.

"Even worse?"

"I think they are scared shitless in there," Tina said, pointing her thumb back at the Maximos Mansion. "They're on the market, trying to buy vaccines for months now, but they can't get them at the right price."

"Too expensive, huh?" asked Lucia.

"Too cheap, I'm afraid."

# 44. Lucia: The Burning Bush

*Athens, October 6, 2022*

The car with Tina and Lucia stopped at the front gate of the TV station complex. The guard, round bald head and round belly asked for their IDs.

"Dr. Walker, huh? You're not up for another two hours," he said.

"I've never been on TV before. I wanted to get in the mood, feel at home."

The guard called a number and waited, phone on ear for many rings, whistling and gazing at the pigeon flying fast and determined above their heads. He exchanged some words and then said: "I'll take you up for make-up. Mr. Kokonis will see you afterward to prep you."

It had started drizzling, and the guard gave his umbrella to Tina.

They followed him, Tina in the middle, Lucia last, like little duckies in a row. Lucia could see Tina's left fist clutching and opening repeatedly. She quickened her step to reach her.

"Hey, Tina, if I may, you were calmer when we were locked down with the dying in Moria," said Lucia.

"This might be more important. If I mess it up…"

They went up the stairs and into the makeup room.

A woman, cigarette between lips, wearing a floral Desigual blouse greeted them: "You, stay out, please," she said to Lucia. "No room, I am busy. You," she pointed to a girl that seemed to be of high school age. "I am Georgia. You, here," she turned to Tina. "Beige shade foundation. Corrector, concealer, definitely. Matte always, always matte, not shimmer. Light on the upper cheekbones. Got it?" Georgia gave the instructions to the apprentice and rushed out of the room.

*Great, I got the amateur,* Tina thought.

Lucia re-entered the room.

"Thanks for being here," said Tina, "and for arranging this."

"It was nothing, just a phone call to my friend Papalias. I told you, he owes me. Have you memorized all your key points?"

"I think so. Must buy vaccines, panic early, low mortality shows positive correlation high R0, this is not about politics."

Lucia was miming a "no no no," shaking her hand.

"Children, don't forget children!" said Lucia. "Drop correlation, they won't get it. Three children died in Argentina yesterday."

"Seven in South Africa," said Tina.

"Eyes closed, madam," interjected the make-up girl.

"They don't relate to South Africa," said Lucia "TV folk know Argentina from football. Stick with Argentina."

"I think I am going to get sick," said Tina.

"Maybe, if you stop swiveling around," said the make-up woman giggling as she stopped the rose-gold bar-stool chair. "Don't worry, you haven't even met Kokonis yet."

Another fifteen minutes passed until Tina heard the magic words "We're ready," and opened her eyes.

The excitement for the professional makeup session was extinguished as she gaped at the person getting set on the adjacent chair.

"Alexi? What are you doing here?" asked Tina, swallowing hard, as she already guessed the answer.

"I came to chat. Missed you! You look great, by the way," he said, winking to Tina.

"Are you going to be in the panel, too?" she asked.

"The *Burning Bush Show* is debating the Asian flu. Do you think they wouldn't invite me?"

Tina didn't reply and signaled Lucia to follow her as she exited the make-up room. Two more guests entered as the ladies walked out—a beardless scrawny Jesus look-alike on a red button-down shirt and a stunning blonde actress-model whose name Tina didn't remember and wouldn't dare to ask in fear of ridicule.

"You'll be all by yourself against four idiots," said Lucia.

"Maybe that Jesus guy can help," said Tina.

"No, I know him, he is some weird Green Earth, no flights, no burgers, go bees, guy. He might even be antivaccine."

"Jesus won't save us today, I guess. Keep this," she said and gave her mobile phone to Lucia.

The messages kept coming while she was getting prepared.

Mom Walker: *Be strong and truthful, dear.*

Garnett: *Tina. Need you in Baltimore. Now. Top research projects underway. Lmk if ur coming. 25 dead Spain today. 5 in Boston. This is it. It begins.*

Peri: *GOOD LUCK MOMMY! DAD+DEMETRI!!!*

Lucia gave the phone back to Tina. "Maybe you want to read this."

Garnett: *Confirmed, new variant Spain, Boston, lower mortality rate. Nine percent. Incubation up to five days. Early indications, Buenos Aires, presympomatic transmission.*

"Stop twitching your face muscles, doctor. Here he comes," said Lucia.

Kokonis, the talk show host, greeted Tina and started talking fast. Tina was just staring at his cartoonishly gigantic head, his impeccable pepper-grey coiffure. Most TV people had huge heads, somehow that was a plus on the screen, but his was out of the *Mars Attacks* movie. Her mind had frozen to the last text message from Garnett. *Incubation five days. Presymptomatic transmission.* She wanted to grab Kokonis by the lapel and cry, "Help, get the vaccines now!"

"And that's all you need to remember, Dr. Walker," said Kokonis as he pushed the bridge of his black-frame eyeglasses to the base of his nose. The frame was empty; its purpose was to define his face and add much-needed sophistication.

The air was smelling of car freshener in the cold dark studio as the technician wired Tina. The hall quickly came to life with blinding, warming light, and for the next few minutes, the guests and the audience were getting in place, waiting for the signal. Kokonis, as host, was in the middle, to his right, Alexi, and the no-name bombshell actress whose only qualification was that she has just returned from Madrid, where "people were dying, ohmygod." On the left of Kokonis sat the beardless Jesus and to his left Tina.

Lucia watched from the first audience row. She was pretty certain that Tina didn't see her, but she still gave her thumbs up.

Kokonis started fast out the gate, declaring the global situation as dramatic, showing a video with epic battle music score. Emergency rooms, doctors, and nurses in full-protective gear, fragmented sentences of random people from Argentina, Spain, South Africa, USA, Japan.

"It is spreading. That's not to be denied," said Kokonis, "and now the question for you, doctor."

Tina got ready and sighed, staring at the notepad, her palms resting on the arched studio table. *Stay with the talking points,* she reminded herself.

"Is our country ready, doctor?"

*Count to three and answer,* she said to herself.

"First of all, we must not scare the public." It was Alexi speaking. *He* was *the* doctor Kokonis had asked. "We have zero incidents in Greece at this point. We faced this before, last summer, and we lost only a handful." He cut his gaze on Tina as he finished his sentence. It was due to her that only so few had died in Moria, but his stare was blaming her even for that. "We have opened a call for the hiring of fifteen hundred doctors and nurses, increased ICU capacity twenty percent in the last month."

"But it is here, in Europe, Doctor Vardis," continued Kokonis pointing toward the table or his groin as he said the word 'Europe.'

Alexi was the worst opponent that Tina could face on a TV panel. Everything that came out fake and sleazy about him in real life transformed to lively and elegantly polite on camera.

"We are ready. The Prime Minister has entrusted our team of world-class experts with defining and implementing strategy. I must tell you that we've been expecting this for months now. I was in Geneva months ago, attending the first WHO meeting on H7N9. We've been working for a whole year on this."

*You were in Geneva to sleep with me.* Tina held the thought inside. He had managed to make Tina lose her cool by now, and moreover, he knew he was doing that. She couldn't lie like this; it took a sociopath's natural skill that she lacked. Whatever truth in science, facts, and data she could bring forward, he would obliterate with a bullshit cannon of confidence.

"We come to you, Dr. Walker. What is your assessment?" asked Kokonis.

Tina had lost her words and talking points. She was tapping her pen on the desk, and when she lifted her eyes to speak, she sounded angry already.

"My assessment is that we, you, everyone watching has hours left," said Tina, in a stiff and sour tone. She was squeezing the pen between her fingers, ready to snap it in half. "I don't know what kind of preparations Dr. Vardis here is talking about, but there is only one for a pandemic with such virulence and nine percent mortality. Get the vaccine. Now. Not now, yesterday. That's all we should be discussing."

"Hold on, doctor," jumped in Dr. Vardis. "You are not privy of our Emergency Heath Taskforce actions, but we are doing everything to assess the vaccine situation."

"Assess what? People are dying already," Tina was not looking at the camera but at Alexi, and moreover, she was grimacing a *"get lost, you idiot."* About everything she could do wrong for TV, she was doing it.

"Nobody is dying, please, Dr. Walker, don't spread panic. Panic is the worst message we can send to the audience today."

"No, panic is the only message. Panic now," Tina said, and before she finished the sentence, the host had turned to the Jesus guy, trying to save her.

"I agree with you, Dr. Walker," said beardless Jesus, turning to Tina for a split second to bless her with his twenty-seven-year-old wisdom. "Someone is dying. For years now, she is crying for help. Our Earth is dying. We have tortured Mother Nature, and she is returning the favor."

Tina was holding her chin with left hand and kept her right down so as not to punch him. He was so close.

"I must say," the bombshell blonde interjected, turning toward Kokonis. "There was an aura of anguish and fear on our flight from Madrid."

"No, no, please, everyone," Tina said. "This aura you said, it's not fear. It is droplets and the virus. You must go test yourself, you shouldn't even be here but at home quarantined."

"Quarantined? Why on earth?" said the blonde as if she had heard "guillotined."

"Did you quarantine those who landed from Madrid today, Dr. Vardis?" continued Tina.

"I am sorry, everyone, time for our sponsors' break," said Kokonis, opening his arms apologetically, while Tina was reciting how many flights had arrived from Spain that day and how many more were due tomorrow. "We'll be right back."

"Six flights, almost six hundred people," she said loud enough for all to hear, but they were already on break, sipping water.

She spent the next two minutes trying to make eye contact with Alexi, who was ignoring her. Lucia from the audience stands made a signal to drink water, and a second one, throwing quick fists in the air, like Rocky on round fifteen. "Fight back, I have to fight back," Tina mumbled. They were back on.

"What is the problem with the vaccines, Doctor Vardis?" asked Kokonis. "There are rumors that you cannot secure any because other countries have reserved all capacity. Is this a race about which nations will survive? A final solution we are facing?"

"Nothing is further from the truth," he said. "We are talking about vaccinating ten and a half million people with an unproven vaccine that at best will have a fifty percent efficacy, and we know for a fact that at least thirty percent of our citizens will not agree to do it. Do you understand the logistics involved? What do you suggest we do? Drag them to concentration camps and force mandatory vaccination upon them? These things take time."

"China is forcing one and a half billion people. They vaccinated a billion chickens to stop H7N9 years ago, and you cannot vaccinate ten million?" asked Tina.

"Exactly my point. It is an issue of human rights also—"

Tina interrupted: "You get the vaccines, or you better get refrigerator trucks and body bags. Has anyone here run the numbers? Do you understand what a virus with R0 of 2.8, nine percent mortality, and presymptomatic transmission will do to a city like Athens if it finds us stripped of defenses?"

Lucia was making a third signal, her palm moving swiftly and parallel under her chin, to cut, cut, cut, but it was too late.

"Is man going to rely on yet another vaccine?" asked beardless Jesus, marveling at his own question. "How many? Are we going to be forced to get fifty vaccines per year if this keeps going? Become the voodoo dolls of our own evil? Is this our answer? When will we understand that we have to change our habits?"

The bombshell blonde had shifted her attention to Jesus now, drinking from his fountain of truth.

"That's a great question from Mr. Jesus here." Tina had actually said Jesus—the loud laughter from the audience destroying her argument. "But it is a question for the nine million who will survive. The one million dead is what is at stake now. We can answer the philosophical stuff next year. Can we stick with what we do tonight?"

"I thought you said the mortality rate is nine percent, doctor," said Kokonis. "One million dead? Do you suggest that everyone will be infected?"

"No, but the mortality is nine percent if you have ICU beds for everyone who will. You don't. So I don't even know what the effective mortality rate will be."

"You don't know." Jesus had been insulted and was fighting back.

"Let's go back to Dr. Vardis," said Kokonis. "Is our government considering quarantining the twenty-five hundred football fans who return from Barcelona tomorrow?"

Tina was jerking her neck fast left and right; she had no idea about this. That was not her way of having a life-or-death conversation, not knowing the facts.

"This is an active scenario. Our committee is assembling tomorrow to discuss possible quarantine measures," said Alexi.

"Wait, what, seriously?" Tina said. "You'll let twenty-five hundred people who were at a football game in Spain to re-enter tomorrow untested? Might as well carpet bomb us with the Stukas like it's 1941."

"Please," said Alexi, this time turning and waving his hand to Tina dismissively. "Your comments are not appropriate."

"Shut down all the flights from Spain," said Tina.

"Only from Spain?" asked Kokonis.

"Frankly, yes, thank you, all the flights. Shut them down."

"From anywhere?"

"Yes!"

"You are the voice of panic," said the blonde, losing her frozen smile for the first time.

"Dr. Walker, I understand you are here representing the pharmaceutical companies, the vaccine producers?" asked Kokonis.

"What? No! Who told you that?"

"A Ministry source said that you had multiple discussions with public health officials about purchasing vaccines."

"No! What?"

"Didn't you?" insisted Kokonis. "What about two days ago at Maximos Mansion? Or before when you met with the Minister and his Deputy?"

"No, that man came to me, that was informal."

"So, you had informal discussions," said Dr. Vardis.

Jesus was shaking his head disapprovingly. Tina had just lost about ninety percent of whatever fraction of the audience she might have convinced.

"Aren't these vaccines completely untested? Couldn't they cause serious side effects?" asked Kokonis.

"No, completely untested, no. There was research and development of an H7N9 vaccine for years since the first outbreak back in 2013."

"But you *don't* know."

"I just said I did know."

"Are you certain that they won't cause side effects?"

"I am certain that most European countries have gotten vaccines."

"Sweden hasn't," said Alexi. "Russia hasn't."

*As if Russia would tell you what they're doing,* Tina thought.

"A heated debate to be continued. Maybe next week?" said Kokonis. "A final word. Dr. Vardis, you first."

"Our country is prepared. Our doctors and our best epidemiologists are ready."

A wide smile of perfect white teeth from the blonde.

"Remember the troubadour!" said Jesus. "If I could change the world, I would paint the sea blue and feed the poor."

"And on that note, we wish you goodnight and thank you for being with us," said Kokonis. "I thank you all for being here, and maybe we set a date to talk again in a couple of weeks about how the virus outbreak is progressing?"

"No, we won't. If we're lucky, we'll teleconference at best. Your studio will be shut down. Do you understand what nine percent mortality means?" Tina was still talking, but the talk show was over. People from the audience were getting up; the technicians were removing the microphones from the speakers. Kokonis was scratching his nose with a finger inside the hollow glass frame. "None of us will be here," Tina muttered.

Kokonis was signaling others to shush while he was listening to the producer on his earpiece.

"Damn it," he said. "We got intel that they have a positive match on H7N9 cases. Two of them, a married couple was tested at Salvation Hospital up the street from here. News just came in. We missed it. Our show is already outdated. That's TV, folks!"

Nobody spoke a word, though Alexi was already on the phone, whispering secretively. Tina turned to him but couldn't find a word or anything heavier to throw at her ex-lover.

"We must run," said Tina, turning to Lucia. "Now."

# 45. Tina: It Begins

October is the massacre. Always has been, pandemic or not. Oak and maple leaves, the colors of blood and pale skin. A swirl, a rustle, a farewell dance. Naked boughs, trembling on the wind, black against ashen skies, defeated skeletons charred to the bone. Halloween and foliage.

October was the reason Tina had become an epidemiologist. She had grown up in the Middlesex suburbs of Massachusetts. Skeletons, witches, and glow-in-the-dark inflatable spiders swaying on the front yards, peering with red eyes of evil. Did the witches bring October's death, or were they mere spectators of Mother Nature's onslaught?

The roses in their garden spent and covered with rust. Third-grader Tina had tried to save them one by one, spraying and cutting and pruning before and after school for days. The devastating thought of abandoning her flowers to move to a different country had overwhelmed her.

"When I grow up, I am going to save them," Tina had said to her dad.

She used the same metaphor when she announced to her mom that epidemiology was her career choice.

"No one, God, Nature or Witch, has the right to kill them all. I don't care what they have done or what powers someone has. I told you when I grow up, I am going to save them all," said Tina.

"The old must perish for the young to blossom," Lisa Walker replied.

Their front yard in Athens was much smaller, but mom Lisa made it a habit to plant every fall. Fragrant angel coneflowers, white, double pink, and purple stains on their petals.

On that Saturday morning, Tina woke up at 5 a.m., watered her angel flowers for what she hoped was the last time, packed two suitcases, one for her, one for Demetri, and called the taxi for the airport. "Please take care of the garden," she said to Floribeth and kissed Peri on the cheek. "We'll see you soon."

Peri had refused, stubborn as a stump, know-it-all, to follow Tina on a day's notice. "Next week. I can't leave so fast," he had insisted, even though Tina knew there wouldn't be a "next week". Not even a day. She had checked the departures status already, and the news was grim, but still, she had to make an effort.

Nothing changed for the next thirty minutes when she entered the departures hall, Demetri on the one hand, the pushcart on the other.

"DL0263 NEW YORK (JFK) CANCELED."

"I am sorry, madam, all flights from Athens to the United States are canceled. No." A pause. "JFK, Logan, Newark. All of them. We got the notice just last night. We sent you an email."

"I am a doctor of epidemiology. I am the one fighting the virus. And I am an American citizen," she said to the clerk behind the protective plexiglass.

"Please get in touch with the US Embassy," the short-haired brunette replied while signaling with her finger to the passengers queued behind Tina. "They can provide details if there is an emergency flight for ex-pats," she said, not even looking at Tina anymore.

The moment the first handful of incidents were reported in Athens, the US government had shut down all flights. She knew it would happen, but that was the first flight out she could find after her night on the talk show. Bad luck.

"Demetri, let's go. It's your lucky day," said Tina forcing a warm smile. The kid didn't want to leave Athens, he had sensed that something was wrong, and he had asked about fifteen times why dad wasn't coming with them to Baltimore.

"So, can we go to Mario's party now?" Demetri asked, with a grin of excitement, his face imitating the Buzz Lightyear's figure he was holding.

"Eh, yes, birthday party. We'll see. Let's call your dad first," said Tina and fast-dialed her husband. Plan B. "We're coming back. Can you please run to the supermarket, Peri?"

"You are? That's great. Anyway, it's for the best, hon. You are freaking out. We are better here, we know the doctors."

Everybody thought they knew a doctor who could help because they once had drinks together. Nobody "knows a doctor" during a pandemic. Peri wouldn't understand, and she didn't want to continue this over the phone. The taxi ride was short, and they were back home before eleven-thirty, about the time that her flight was supposed to depart.

"Please run to the supermarket, Peri. Now," she said as she rushed into her country-style kitchen and started throwing useless stuff out of the pantry.

"Ok, I'll go. Need to buy some Monkey 47 for Thomas's party tonight. What do you need?"

"Everything."

"Come again?"

"Buy everything you can carry. Everything. No toilet paper, we have a bidet. Food. Milk. Whatever Demetri eats. Non-perishable. Get the SUV, fill it up. Unload it. Go for a second run and fill it up again."

"I think you are—" Peri's voice had none of the urgency she needed to hear.

"Yeah, okay, just leave the car here, I'll do it myself," she said. "You take care of Demetri."

"Fine, I'll go," said Peri.

"Powder milk, flour, quinoa, lentils, canned tuna. Frozen vegetables. As much chicken as you can carry. Nescafe." Coffee was not negotiable. "Go twice and then go get an extra freezer from ApplianceMax. Don't order it online, go get it now."

"I'll get the van from the dealership. It can carry enough for the whole neighborhood. But if everyone panics as you—"

"Can you please leave now?"

Her phone was repeatedly vibrating. Someone was insistent. It was Niki, one of the moms from Demetri's class. Tina had not told anyone that she was leaving; there was no time for drama.

"What do you say I drop by, and we all drive together to Mario's party?" Niki asked. "It's a bit far away so the kids won't get bored. You know how they go restless if they're alone for a long drive."

"What? Niki? Is the party still on?"

"It's a big one! At the arcade. I heard she has gone for a mega-production."

"The arcade, you mean the one with the hundreds of people."

"Yes, the one by the airport with the roller skating rink."

"No, please don't go. I'll call Mario's mom to cancel it."

"Do what? Why?"

"Please don't go, Niki. It's this virus, it's all over Europe. Stay home for a week until we see what's going on. You'll thank me."

"I promised Hector, I'd take him."

"Niki, Hector is six, and he doesn't understand what viral pneumonia is. Please, this thing is here, it is going to be everywhere in a few days. Go to the supermarket. Buy food."

"You're scaring me. Bye."

Tina wasn't convincing, and she wouldn't be until the ambulances started screaming. She strapped Demetri on the booster seat of the SUV and dropped him off at her mom's.

He was crying for the whole ride, he had woken up early, and he insisted on going to that party.

"Worst day ever," he cried as mom waved goodbye.

"Guess what, it can get much worse," she mumbled as she drove away.

She called Lucia and offered the same advice, "food, medicine, barricade," and then continued calling those she cared most. It was too slow and painful; everyone wanted to chit-chat about this, that, and the other. The virus was still something horrible and irrelevant, like a tsunami in Indonesia or a landslide in Bangladesh.

"Get on Facebook and Twitter," two of the moms suggested, those whom Tina had filed long ago under the neurotic label. They were the only ones who took her seriously.

She stopped at the gardening shop to get plant food. *Save them all.* A truck was unloading potting soil.

"Can you deliver to this address?" Tina asked the man who had sold her flowers for years.

"How many bags?" he said, grabbing a seventy-liter one to load on Tina's trunk.

"As many as you can."

"What do you mean?"

"Fifty. A hundred," she repeated.

"You want me to deliver seven tons of soil? Did you buy the National Garden, lady?" his words ending on a burst of roaring laughter.

"Here. The address," Tina gave the paper to the man and rushed home.

The radio was broadcasting that "the two H7N9 confirmed incidents were in negative pressure isolation chambers and were doing fine. The MoH ETF is having a meeting later tonight, and the Minister will address the public tomorrow evening on a national broadcast." She got home when Peri was unloading the groceries in the basement and checked the Athens Timeout guide.

Celine Dion at the Music Mansion, Red Hot Chili Peppers at the Faliro Sports Center, Turandot, at the Opera Center. All tonight. "How many sports games you think per weekend?" she asked Perri.

"I don't know. Three thousand?"

"What are you talking about? There are like twenty teams per division, right?"

"Football, basketball, volleyball, hundreds of divisions per age and county. Thousands of games."

"How many with large crowds?" she asked though she knew that the smaller games were a problem too.

"Fifteen, maybe. Max," he answered as he opened a beer.

"Did you have to buy gin, Peri? I said essentials only."

"I heard you," he smiled. "Here, I'll make you a gin and tonic. It's early afternoon, but you need it."

"Please, run back to the supermarket. Buy more stuff."

Tina sat in front of the computer, browsed the news from WHO, the international networks, checked a couple of articles at the Lancet and the New England Journal of Medicine.

A thousand sports games. Twelve thousand international passengers landing in Athens per day. Thousands of bars and restaurants bustling on Saturday night. Hundreds of churches. Sunday service. It was the busiest time of the year for the city, no long weekend, no vacation period. Everyone was there. A thousand child birthday parties across the country. Easily.

She walked downstairs to the kitchen and poured a gin tonic, slightly cutting herself as she tried to slice the lemon. A tiny drop of blood slipping down the rind.

"What social media do I use?" she asked Lucia on the phone.

"Insta if you are in the market, Twitter if you are a celeb."

"What if I want to convince mothers?"

"Facebook, maybe."

Tina logged into Facebook again for the first time in years. Two hundred and forty-seven friends. Was that a lot? Things were getting out of control in Spain. AP was reporting twelve hundred cases already. Four hundred in Belgium. It was everywhere, but most countries were not up to speed with their testing. People were posting about the outbreak, but no one sounded alarmed in the comments.

Just in, a report of a quarantined flight. Bucharest, Romania to Salonica, Greece—two passengers bleeding from the nose and falling seriously sick. Ambulances and an epidemic response team on the scene.

"What's on your mind, Tina?" asked the little window on her screen. She started typing her first Facebook post since the annual "Thank you for your birthday wishes. You made my day."

*Everyone. Please, listen to me. You've known me for years. I was one of the first scientists to study H7N9 when it first appeared in China back in 2013. I represented our country at WHO last spring. This virus is very infectious and has mutated. We were protected during the summer because of the heat, but that is over now. We have significant evidence that an outbreak is rekindling in Europe. R0 above five, maybe.*

Peri texted that he was returning home. Not much else he could fit in the van. Her front door buzzed. The garden shop driver was asking on the camera where to unload the soil bags.

Tina ran down the stairs, gave him a twenty. "Half on the front door, the other half by the garage door, stack them next to the garage door."

He declined. She made it a fifty, and he rolled up his sleeves.

"We need an isolation room," she said to Peri.

"What?"

"The storage room in the basement," said Tina. It has a tall window so we can look inside, it is perfect. She checked her phone, doing three things in parallel. Her Facebook post had four likes. She didn't know much, but she guessed that it wasn't good. "If you get sick, you isolate in there, Peri. We store food and water now. First cough or sneeze, you run down, and you stay in there. You don't come out unless I call an ambulance."

"What if *you* get sick?" asked Peri.

"I can't. I caught this three months ago. I have immunity. You don't go anywhere near Demetri if you have the slightest symptom. Chills, headache, fever, cough, anything. Get your tablet, so you are not bored. Put a mattress in there. Got it? Swear to me."

He didn't. He was shaking his head again.

"What are all these bags outside the front door?" Peri asked.

Niki was calling her, Melissa too. Both moms from Demetri's class. She had no time to answer.

"In case we need to barricade," she said.

"Have you gone mad? Maybe we should get an AK47 and a grenade launcher too? I'll call your mother to come by and talk some sense into you. All you need is some stress pills."

"Did you buy food for her, too, as I told you?"

"I'll go now. The stores don't close for another two hours," Peri said.

*There won't be a later,* Tina mumbled between her teeth.

Lucia was calling and asking for her FB password.

"YOU JUST SEND ME THE TALKING POINTS. I'LL POST IT," texted Lucia.

Niki was calling again.

"Good thing you didn't come," Niki said. "Two kids were throwing up. Food poisoning. Catering. Can you believe it? They had the magician, three-layer cake, unlimited game passes for everyone, and the catering failed her. She was purple with rage."

"Send me the moms' numbers," said Tina. "Yes, the moms of the poisoned kids. I want to make sure."

The doorbell rang again. When she stepped into the kitchen fifteen minutes later, Peri was eating pizza from the box. Too late. She had a lot of educating to do. She washed her hands for two minutes, sat down and ate a slice, then rushed back to her PC.

*What's on your mind, Tina?*

Her previous post had sixty-five likes, three shares.

"Sorry, doc, you come out too dry and dull," texted Lucia. "'R0 probably five.' Every word is wrong, starting with 'probably.' Might as well write in Chinese. Try a shocking photograph. The social media algorithms are toxic; they feed on panic, rage, not moderation and low-key. Try again. We need to get viral with this virus."

"What do I do?" Tina asked, but she knew the answer.

"Lie!"

Alexi was on TV, "there is nothing to be concerned about," he said. "The government council is meeting tomorrow."

They had postponed for one day.

A CNN alert flashed, reporting a mass vaccination campaign starting Monday in the Northeast US and China. Germany and Austria were ready with their own programs.

"We are getting some traction," Lucia said.

Tina checked her profile again. Lucia had posted without her permission. She fell on her chair, frozen. Thirteen shares already. Tina knew that her career was over the moment she started reading.

*Dr. Walker Update H7N9 Oct 8:*
*From my friend, the top epidemiologist:*
*YOUR GOVERNMENT IS HIDING THE TRUTH. Hundreds of cases of infected*

*patients in Greece already. They arrived during the last 48 hours by plane, ship, train. Most of them don't even know they're sick, BUT THEY MAY BE NEXT TO YOU. Self-isolate. Do not go to work, do not go to school. I repeat. DO NOT. Do not go to church or to the game tomorrow. Return to home now. Isolate. Stockpile food.*

Tina deleted the message from her profile, but a copy was still in Lucia's profile, mentioning Tina's name. It had about eight hundred and fifty likes, two hundred and twelve shares. Lies and bullshit were selling and, to her dismay, had the intended effect. She wrote her own version.

*My Suggestions to the Greek Government. Dr. Tina Walker, Ph.D.*

*PANIC NOW.*
*If I am wrong, we'll miss a week. If I am right, we'll save thousands.*
*SHUT DOWN SCHOOLS AND UNIVERSITIES.*
*MASKS EVERYWHERE. EVERYONE.*
*Cancel all inbound flights, trains, and ships.*
*Test and quarantine everyone arriving immediately.*
*Contact those who came from abroad last week and test them too if they report symptoms.*
*Shut down all social gatherings and non-essential shopping places for two weeks minimum.*
*SHUT DOWN SCHOOLS AND UNIVERSITIES.*
*Cancel games, concerts, church gatherings, weddings, baptisms, anything, everything. Stop all office work and non-essential production for two weeks until we know how it is developing here and we trace effectively.*
*Designate specific hospitals for H7N9 treatment only. Use a different three-digit emergency number, retaining the old 100 and 166 fast-dials for all other health-related problems.*
*Online ordering for supermarkets and pharmacies only. Deploy the army and get all professional drivers on conscription to deliver supplies. One order for each apartment building only.*
*GET VACCINES. AT ANY COST. NOW.*

It was 10 p.m. almost; she had spent another hour fighting with Peri, who was determined to go out for a drink with his buddies.

"Have a drink here," she said. "Please, don't go out." She said it in a way that suggested that she'd change the locks if he didn't comply.

"I would stay, darling, but you are no fun. Stuck on your screen," he said. "What's to do here?"

"Demetri is at grandma's tonight. We're alone." She winked.

Sex. Lipstick, anything. Sex was convincing and draining. Just keep him in the house. An hour later, an exhausted Peri got up from their bed and succumbed to examining his Netflix options.

Lucia texted: *OH YEAH BABY. NOW WE RE ROCKING!!!*

The picture on Lucia's message showed twenty-three hundred likes, sixteen hundred shares. For a ten million people country, that was big. Messages started coming by the tens in everything that Tina could be reached. Messenger, WhatsApp, Viber. She kept denying that she ever wrote that post. But it was viral now, and her name was on it, growing unstoppable in numbers, ahead of the virus.

"Whose idea was it to split the one messaging inbox we used to have into five?" texted Tina.

The call from her young and crazy friend came immediately.

"You are a celeb now," said Lucia on the other side.

"Please tell me you bought food and medicine for your parents."

"I did. Went with Yara, she helps a lot. She is talking more and more to them, to me. All good here. Keep writing and posting, you need to keep the content flow going now that you got the audience's attention."

"I am not trying to be famous," said Tina. "I wrote all I had to write."

"You are stubborn, doctor. Just listen to me. And goodnight," Lucia said.

"Fat chance I'll have a good night," Tina replied.

She gulped a valeriana and melatonin pill and slept till 5 a.m. again. She got up and slogged to her garden. It was unseasonably chilly for Athens. The virus would love this weather.

*"When I grow up, I am going to save them all,"* Tina had said to her mother back in Boston, referring to the flowers. More was at stake now and more had to be done.

She had swallowed her pride and sent an email to the Minister of Health last night, but he didn't reply, and he wouldn't; it was too dangerous for him to do.

Lucia's post had reached thousands; Tina had hundreds of new friend requests. On Sunday, supermarkets were closed but everything else that shouldn't be, churches and football stadiums were open. Tina spent the day answering messages, reposting news on H7N9 from abroad, preparing the basement room in case—knock wood—Peri got infected. What if Demetri got infected? What then? She couldn't dare think about it.

The Lancet paper on children's reaction to the virus once they got infected was more than alarming. Most flu viruses were lethal for the very young and the very old, but each virus was different.

Niki called for the third time, one of the two kids that were supposedly poisoned from the catering had tested positive.

Niki: *THEY TOOK LITTLE ANABELLA TO THE HOSPITAL. EVERYONE IS GOING MAD. RU SENDING KIDS TO SCHOOL 2MORROW?*

It was the last message Tina received Sunday night.

Tina: *NO. NOT THIS WEEK. NOBODY SHOULD.*

Peri was watching the football highlights. A packed stadium. Fans queueing, packing shoulder to shoulder. Hugging. Celebrating.

Monday morning came, but Tina hadn't put an alarm. The 7 a.m. phone call from Lucia woke her up.

"Oh, oh, oh. Doctor. Are you watching this? Turn Delta Channel on. They're reporting fifty-five cases now. Thirty-two from the airplane in Salonica."

"There are hundreds more that they haven't traced."

"Is this?" A long unanswered pause. "It?" asked Lucia.

"Yes. It begins."

# 46. Ella: Virgin Mary would Never Burn a Church

Athens, October 11, 2022

Dr. Tina Walker, the former head of Epidemiology at the Ministry of Health, was arrested today in front of the Private School of Aristotle, where, as we have been informed, her son is enrolled. A second woman named Lucia Maas (or Masoura) was also arrested. The duo organized a blockade of the school's bus entrance, abandoning their cars and using a homemade spike strip to disable a school bus. Police were deployed, and hundreds of parents rushed to the school, creating traffic chaos. Dr. Walker and her accomplice distributed fliers, calling for the school to shut down to protect children from the imminent, as she insisted, outbreak of the virus. The pair were released after the school bus driver declined to press charges. Upon her release, Dr. Walker was asked if she had any regrets for her actions. She replied. "Yes. I regret that I couldn't block more schools. It's only two of us, you see."

Athens, October 11, 2022

Earlier this afternoon, the Head of the Emergency Health Taskforce, Dr. Alexi Vardis, briefed the nation. According to his statement, there are twelve new confirmed cases of H7N9 and three deaths in the country today. Except for one, all other cases were diagnosed in Athens, and patients remain under observation at the Salvation Hospital. According to Dr. Vardis, the government is doing everything in its power to keep the situation under control, and there is no reason for alarm. The Emergency Health Taskforce will evaluate the situation and decide on further social distancing and potential school closures by the end of the week.

Athens, October 13, 2022

Chaos erupted today at all four special-purpose H7N9 hospitals of Athens as hundreds of patients of all ages were transferred by ambulances or reported to the ER by own means, as it appears that the virus is spreading out of control in the city. The doctors are pleading for the state to increase beds, supplies, and ventilators immediately. More than fifteen doctors and nurses have been infected, while the Left Front has called for a strike of all medical personnel tomorrow.

Athens, October 13, 2022

In an unprecedented turn of events, more than twenty-five thousand cases of H7N9 were reported worldwide just yesterday. The mortality rate is estimated at nine percent, while fifteen percent of the patients worldwide are underaged. Back in Athens, police forces have been deployed at the gates of supermarkets to enforce orderly access to food and medicine. Four pharmacies, twelve bakeries, and an electrical appliances store were raided last night, and more than two hundred home intrusions were reported.

Athens, October 14, 2022

A crosstown bus covering the X96 (Piraeus to Athens International Airport) Route crashed and killed four pedestrians waiting at the Olympieion bus stop. The driver was found unconscious and bleeding from the mouth on the wheel. Colleagues who interacted with him the same morning at the station reported that he seemed fine, and he had just complained of a headache. All sixteen passengers were rushed to the hospital, and eleven of them, including two high school students and brothers, have already tested positive for H7N9.

Athens, October 14, 2022

Dr. Walker, a renowned scientist and the former head of EHT, appeared on Delta Channel today and talked to Mr. Kokonis via Zoom teleconferencing.

The doctor, who is a close collaborator of the World Health Organization, suggested that the H7N9 virus is spreading rapidly via aerosols (particles suspended in the air for an extended period) rather than just by droplets. This creates a completely different risk profile for closed and poorly ventilated spaces. Dr. Walker asked for an immediate lockdown of all essential or not buildings and services for an indefinite period of time. The doctor has been the vocal de facto leader of an anti-government protest movement that has called for a severe lockdown. The EHT is expected to reconvene later today and issue guidelines for school closures next week.

```
On 14 October 2022,
the National Ministry of Health (MoH) of Greece notified
WHO of 2,129 additional laboratory-confirmed cases of
human infection with avian influenza A(H7N9) virus,
including 354 fatal cases.
Of these 2129 cases, 1345 (63%) were male, and 301
involved children under the age of 18. The majority (1809
cases, 85%) were linked to a previous known case. The
government of Greece has declared a state of national
emergency, shutting down all buildings and services while
access to food stores and pharmacies will be limited by
name at one day per week starting tomorrow.
```

Transcript of Dr. Walker's Interview to the virtual Burning Bush Talk Show.

"Joining us, now from Athens, a few kilometers from the studio is Dr. Tina Walker. You might remember that I was the first one to invite her to this show two weeks ago. Doctor, welcome. Unfortunately, today we'll conduct this interview via video conferencing."

"As I had *unfortunately* predicted."

"Doctor, everyone is searching for answers, and the government has not been able to provide any. The Prime Minister has left the country, some say, to avoid the consequences and the riots. Officially, he is visiting the European

Union Council headquarters, calling for a pan-European vaccine policy."

"I don't want to make this political, Mr. Kokonis, but we are too late. This is past the 'Let's hold hands and do policy' stage. It is about survival. No German, Austrian, Dutch, or whoever has secured vaccines for his own citizens will give away his stock. This virus kills children, nine percent of infected. You understand."

"So, when do we expect to have vaccines, Dr. Walker, and moreover, will they be safe?"

"Variants of the H7N9 vaccine have been produced for years though this is a new one. Therefore, we have some good indications that the vaccine is safe."

"You are not 100 percent certain."

"No, I don't use 100 percent for anything referring to a pandemic."

"When can we expect to have vaccines in our country?"

"The world needs a total of eight billion vaccines. Production started three months ago at an unprecedented record pace, and more than 2.4 billion vaccines are already in the hands of the countries that preordered them. Given China and the G7 nations that control production, there is no stock left at this point for anyone else. At best, we can expect 800 million vaccines per month, and by my estimates, we should have them hopefully sometime in February. The WHO will coordinate a rationing policy for the rest of the world, meaning that vaccinating the entire Greek population won't be feasible before May. At best."

"The government denies that."

"I know, and I hope they know something I don't. They deny it because the repercussions are immense. If the pandemic is not controlled by Christmas, we'll see human caravans heading for Europe, but this time *we* will be the refugees."

"Do you have an estimate?"

"Do you really want to know my estimate, Mr. Kokonis?"

"We all do."

"We already have 25,348 cases detected within our borders. My best guess is that the actual cases are ten times more, and there are hundreds of people who died before seeing an ambulance or a hospital."

"Yes. We have reports of the police being called to remove bodies from apartment buildings. Neighbors complained about the smell. We have lockdown in two army camps and the Naval Base at Salamis. Most of the public services, Police, and Fire Department, including, cannot muster adequate forces due to massive infections. Supermarkets are the next front."

"Mr. Kokonis, it is too late. We will reach more than half a million cases, no matter what we do. At nine percent mortality, which I am afraid will be much higher given that we've run out of hospital beds, you can do the math."

"But, we have ordered a lockdown already."

"It is too late, sir. And this is assuming that the immediate lockdown we are in will lead to a sigmoid epidemic function and significantly suppress the outbreak."

"Are you predicting more than fifty thousand victims? Doctor, is it true that one in six of them will likely be children? How did the virus spread so fast?"

"I am afraid so, and this may be much higher if we cannot get vaccines. You understand people will need to go out, shop, report to essential services. If they don't, we'll run out of food and face mass death from secondary causes."

"Doctor, I am sure you are aware of many theories flying around. I don't condone them, yet one has to wonder how can a virus that is supposed to have R0 below 3 and a mortality rate of nine percent has led to twenty-five thousand cases and more than four thousand deaths in a matter of days while other countries are reporting a handful. One has to wonder."

"No, he doesn't. Our EHT agency allowed thousands of fans to return from Spain and didn't quarantine them. They let the schools, metro, and public buildings remain open all week. One patient in a school, a metro, a flight might infect fifty. On average, the R0 is 3, but it is an irrelevant average for an aerosol-transmitted virus. In our case, the growth is exponential. We think we have twenty-five thousand cases now. I can tell you that we'll unavoidably have more than ten times that next week."

"While, as I said, other countries have a handful."

308

"But, but, Mr. Kokonis, I am not sure what you don't understand. Other countries shut down their borders earlier. We still haven't. Officially, we might tomorrow morning. It is too late. The deck is flooded. Too late."

"You have heard the counter-arguments."

"Conspiracy theories are not counter-arguments. What do you want me to answer? If the virus is teleactivated via 5G? That they do this to sell a vaccine? The global economy will take a hit of twenty trillion dollars for someone to sell a ten billion dollar vaccine? How does a ten billion interest win over a twenty trillion one? Or do you want me to answer why the Jews are not dying or getting infected? Because Israel ordered vaccines when our government called the virus a ploy of foreign powers to sabotage tourism. We were here, Dr. Vardis was here, why don't you ask him?"

"In fact, he is my next speaker."

"Oh really, you understand if I don't stay in the call to greet him. I hope you turn on the pressure on him."

Athens, October 15, 2022

A mob of unidentified individuals attacked Dr. Tina Walker's residence earlier tonight, throwing stones and breaking a window. Dr. Walker and her family are all in good health and didn't suffer any injuries. An anonymous phone call made earlier tonight claimed that the True Faith Revolution Party had taken responsibility for the attack. The group indicated that Dr. Walker is a co-conspirator of the New World Order pharma companies that exploit the crisis to sell overpriced vaccines to the Greek people.

In a potentially related incident, a petrol bomb attack against a church took place earlier on Friday morning. The church suffered severe damages just as the congregation gathered past midnight to join the mass prayer that the bishop organized. Witnesses reported a young woman wearing a cream shawl and a blue cloak that struck an uncanny resemblance to the Virgin Mary, throwing the Molotov cocktail before disappearing. The True Faith Revolution Party, which leans toward ultra-nationalism and the far-right based on its manifesto, later denied any responsibility for the Molotov incident, insisting that Virgin Mary would never burn a church.

# 47. Yara: Healing

*Athens, October 14, 2022*

I draw my sister's face, smiling and playing with her dolls, so I never forget. I won't lie. At times I think of what she might look like now, her remains deep in the inky sea, the fish removing all skin and meat. Breaking news: "Flesh-eaten seven-year-old washed ashore." Next to the sandcastles. This image is a purple elephant; once you say the words, it becomes imprinted in your mind. *Purple elephant.* I use those two words as an antidote so that my mind switches to purple elephants. I was walking by the bookstore the other day and saw a children's book featuring a colorful elephant. It is a story about refugees, Lucia told me, and though I couldn't read it, the eyes of the little fella said it all.

I don't feel like a refugee. I don't feel anything, more like an aberration, a creature that is not supposed to be still alive unless life itself is her curse. I have serious doubts that I am. The last week was the first that felt normal. Nobody cares to interview me anymore. Brits and Greeks are now consumed, quite an appropriate word, by the H7N9 epidemic. I have become an irrelevant backstory. Frankly, my only publicity value stems from the fact that I was in Moria camp during the cordon sanitaire.

I can't eat much these last weeks since I came here to Athens. The food is oily, cooked with oil, raw virgin green oil on salads, oily desserts and cookies, and a few bites fill me up. I've lost my trademark pitta-puffy cheeks and most of the muscle that I built through years of swimming. A newspaper article described me as scrawny, with hollow cheeks and skin barely darker than most of the locals—they actually put that skin-tone fact on paper, like it is supposed to be a positive thing or a relevant fact.

I live with Lucia and her parents in an immigrant neighborhood, and there are so many folks from Pakistan, Central, and Western Africa here. Frankly, nobody here cares about the color of my skin. Nausea and vomit come naturally whenever I eat or think of my sister. Lucia took me to the doctor last week—when one could still find a doctor—and he put me on some probiotics and a special diet.

Lucia is still searching for my parents, spending hours on the phone and her laptop all day. She switches from Greek to English, started an online campaign for information, and hired a P.I. out of Istanbul to help us. I am not convinced my parents are dead, I know my sister is, that sense deep in my gut, but we have no definitive evidence about my parents. Some people saw them in a boat that later sank. What if they made it back to Turkey? Maybe my mom is stuck in some camp or hospital. It is possible. Not probable.

There is special software now that allows one to see what a person would look like years in the future if you feed it some pictures. Lucia got the embassy to send us a few Nahla pictures from her early-stage school in Manchester. When I look at them, I remember things that I was close to forgetting already. The dreadlock curls on her left side seem longer than those on the right, maybe because she always tilted her head that way in a mischievous smirk. My favorite is her picture on the schoolyard's swing, the happiness painted wide on her face as she is looking up at the sky. No help came from there.

I use the Face Aging App to project what Nahla will look like next year. I do it almost every day. But deep inside, I know that she is gone. The soot-eyed djinn snatched her, and a djinn is too shrewd to let such a treasure escape.

Lucia's parents are nice, working-class people, simple, they can sense and smell pain. They don't ask me much or get annoyed by my presence, not even by the odd publicity that fell upon their daughter. They put an extra single bed in Lucia's room for me, and we all four share one bathroom. I talk to my grandparents in Latakia once a week, primarily to my grandpa, grandma weeps and wails, and that can be tolerable only for a few seconds.

It would be unfathomably awkward to reunite with my parents, especially my father. How am I going to explain? What am I going to explain? I was raped. I let my sister drown. I am married to a girl, though this is not really a thing; Lucia told me that it doesn't have to mean anything, and we can get a divorce later. I don't know why she had to say that; I thought it was redundant. Still, it would be devastating for my father. Not to mention the tight black jeans and the black sweater with the chemical symbol for titanium I am wearing every day. Other than that day they took me to see the Prime Minister and the First Lady, it has been the same clothes, different underwear.

I love Lucia. Not in that way, the romantic one, more like a kid loves and admires Spider-Man. She should have been back in school, studying in Portsmouth now, but she has postponed it until I get better. She said that we could even go back together once I felt like it, I could go to school there. I've enrolled at the British School here, which happens to be fifty minutes each way by bus. The Embassy intervened, so I didn't have to pay any tuition. I went for three days, vomiting back and forth each way. I sat alone on the school bus, not by choice. One of the kids was complaining that they make a full fifteen-minute detour just for me. Maybe that, and not the way I smelled, is the reason everyone gave me those icy stares. That thing about the detour makes sense, though. I am the only kid attending the British private school from this neighborhood of Nigerian and Pakistani immigrants, low-income Greek pensioners, hookers, waitresses, drug addicts, and Antifa anarchists. On the fourth day, I told Lucia that I didn't want to go anymore. The psychologist lady I see, someone who used to see Lucia way back, suggested that I take a two-week break.

I was supposed to return to school yesterday, but this virus is here, and Lucia insisted that I stay home. I don't understand why since I am immune already. About a month ago, Dr. Tina took us to a lab, and all three gave blood. They said we all have antibodies. Safe. Bulletproof. Not from actual bullets.

Lucia says that no one should go to school; it is a crime to send children there now that the virus is spreading in the city. She was arrested two days ago, trying to block a school with Dr. Tina. I complained that she should have taken me as well. We are supposed to be a team. That's what she said when we were at Moria, at the Prime Minister, at the lab giving blood.

Dr. Tina took us out to a nice little restaurant by the sea in early September when it was still warm at night. We got there long after sunset, and I suddenly realized that we were next to the vast blue; it was angry and growling after an autumn rain. I begged them to leave, go anywhere else; I was shivering. "I don't have a jacket," I said, "Can't sit outside."

Lucia understood, and she suggested a windowless hole in the wall pizzeria not far away. We ate a colorful veggie pizza. Dr. Tina was telling us that she has lost most of the colors. She can't see blue, green, yellow after she fell ill in Moria. That must be terrible! I lost my mother, Nahla, baby Omar. At least I have the colors, and I can draw.

Dr. Tina said that she could see only black, red, brown, gray. Do you know what the sad thing is? I only use these colors when drawing. I never draw sea, sky, trees, sunflowers, or Nahla's green t-shirt, the one from the school photo. My sketches are vampires, skeletons, blood, steel, and abandoned post-apocalyptic buildings and landscapes. To avoid water and blue, I draw ice. Ice comes naturally to my mind.

The virus got here, in downtown Athens, a few hours ago. Like a rabid hound that has gotten my scent and won't let go, it hunts me around the globe. The TV people caught up fast, and they figured that H7N9 would be the only news for a while. The name takes forever to say on TV or radio, so people have started calling it "79" in brief. Two little children died two days after they got sick, and then everyone knew what they were in for. I've been through that, the fear of survival escalating and making me numb, but I was alone in my journey—this is collective panic. Locals were stoic when they thought that only old diabetic smokers were in danger—"Well, everyone has to go sometime"— but the children's deaths changed everything. I can't understand a word on the news networks, but I can see the fear. I've been there.

I hate to admit it, but my spirits have been high and alert since 79 arrived. For a while now, since my father decided to move us back to Latakia from Manchester, I had the constant feeling that I was the doe in the leopards' feast, the lamb in the wolves' den, etc. It's been the other way around as of yesterday.

I am bulletproof now. Immune. It all came together with that song. Lucia has CDs, can you believe it, actual CDs from the old days in her room and even a CD player. I browsed through them—I like using the player—it kind of ritualizes the music. No wonder that people still love those bands from the past; I think they had a more religious relationship with music back then. Now everything is instantly available, like breathing air, you never think of it. Among her CDs, I discovered this DJ beat tune, "I'm bulletproof, nothing to lose. Far away, far away." Actually, it is "fire away, fire away," but I always sing it as "far away." I am bulletproof, and I am far away. Yeah!

I started going out at night. Yesterday was the first time. There are people here roaming the urban streets at 2 a.m. Lucia came with me; I told her that I was suffocating in our apartment. We passed by the late-night "dirty" canteen, as she called it, a truck serving spicy hot dogs. I ate three bites; it felt like a brick in my stomach. A couple of dimly lit bars, one playing music loudly, but we didn't go in. A hay-blonde Rasta guy offered pot to Lucia, and they talked, but she didn't buy. "High-school buddy," she whispered to me.

It's around 11 p.m. now, and Lucia asked me if I could go out again. She's been missing all afternoon, roaming the empty streets to find a pharmacy that carries her father's pills. She called and said she tried eleven of them already, but they all ran out. Two were raided, shop windows smashed. She is calling pharmacies ten miles away to see if any is open twenty-four hours. Ironically, the one around the corner from our apartment just called her back, and they carried the pills. She emailed them over the prescription, and I need to pick them up and pay.

"Mr. Mazur, I'll be back in a minute," I say to the old man. Lucia forbade me from telling him that she was out searching for his pills. He has been watching the news for the last twelve hours nonstop, and he can hear the shop windows getting smashed when he steps out of the balcony. Lucia doesn't want to send her mom; the 79 is out there and might take her.

As I walk down the street, it feels completely different from a night ago. The bars are locked, the Rasta guy is not at his spot, the hot-dog truck is gone. The pharmacist wouldn't open to let me in, even though I could see her inside. I show her the prescription through the iron-bar window and plead in pantomime. When I get in, I have to video conference with Dr. Tina, Lucia is not answering, to convince the pharmacist to let me pick up the pills. "Drug addicts. They come at night with knives. Very dangerous," she says. Her voice is hushed and dramatic, the accent harsh; it feels like a scene from an ancient theater tragedy. She locks fast behind me once I step out.

A stray dog crosses the avenue; a Vespa swerves so that it won't hit it. Men are shouting in some foreign language one block away; they're heading the opposite way. I see a glowing fire rising from the bakery shop across the street and three slender hooded figures running away. I should be running as well, this is no place for a seventeen-year-old, but instead, I cross the avenue; no taxis, no cars. My birthday is on the 28th, the avenue is named October 28, after the date Greeks stood against the Mussolini invasion; quite a coincidence. A heavyset bald man is outside the bakery fighting with the portable extinguisher, but it's too late. The flames are consuming baguettes, sesame rolls, and sugar-dusted pastries. He falls on the pavement; I see now that he'd been clubbed or something; his white apron is stained with blood. It doesn't look like a knife wound or a bullet.

"Sit down, sit down, sir, please," I say. "I'll call an ambulance."

He is burbling on, cursing, wipes his forehead with the back of his palm. His eyes dart between the flames, the bloodstained apron, and my face. I pull him away from the shop and the fire, and we rest on the wrought iron fence that separates the pavement from asphalt.

I am dialing 100, the number for emergencies Lucia has given me. He is talking to me now, angry eyes and lips, protruding jaw, and I can pick a few of the words. "Lathro." I know that means "illegal." I am the illegal, I guess. "Lesvia." I know that too, I am the lesbian, I guess. It seems he knows me, he has recognized me from TV, and we've bought sesame rolls a couple of times with Lucia from his place. I hold his hand between mine; I can sense pain and fear, and his words aren't hurting me. His balding head is burning, and I don't think it's the fire. He is coughing a dry abyssal cough from the bottom of his lungs. I call 179, the new emergency number they've set up to report suspect virus cases. That was one of Dr. Tina's first suggestions, "Have two different numbers. Separate hospitals."

I wait for "efharisto," but he whispers, "Esi! Lesvia." "You. Lesbian." His button eyes are not any softer on me. In his mind, I am the "illegal" who has infected everybody. Lucia said that our downstairs neighbors at the apartment building had complained, demanding that they see the tests that prove I am clean. They didn't want me to use the elevator. "The stairs. It is only four floors."

He can't hurt me or infect me. I am the one with power calling the shots, watching the flames consume the bakery, arguing with 179 in English that this is an emergency. I weep for the stains on his white apron and the sesame rolls that we won't buy again, and I embrace him softly.

"Ssshhh, ambulance. Coming. You'll be okay."

The heavyset body heaves with silent sobs inside my embrace. My dark hair heavy and wet against his sweating temple. Our pain is one and the same. He is infected with my suffering. I am healing. I know what I must do now.

# 48. Lucia: Madonna of the Streets

At first, Lucia didn't recognize him. She queued behind the man at the corner kiosk, waiting to pay for her water bottle. The task of finding a pharmacy open past midnight had proved impossible. She heard his gravelly voice before she saw his face. "Two packs of filters and the blue tobacco," he said. Gray thin hair so oily, almost glued to his scalp. His short neck hiding inside the worn-out leather jacket. He didn't say "thank you" to the kiosk clerk. As he turned, the glassy gray eyes measured Lucia head to feet. She felt his lupine stare working down her body like a knife carving her in half.

If she had not frozen in a pool of rage, fear, and shame, she would have punched him instantly. He was not as big and strong as she remembered him. How had he managed to molest her? True, she was just thirteen back then, and he was pressing the end of a screwdriver on the soft of her neck, right above her collarbone. She hadn't resisted at all. Shame. She had never seen him again since that day when he put his hand in her pants, for what was it? Nine seconds? Nine years. She had dreamed and devised any form of revenge, just, sick, or brutal possible, but she was not prepared for a face-to-face chance encounter. After the assault, her mom enrolled her in a school two miles away— the twice-a-day bus ride serving as punishment and penance. He was also transferred to a different school and then to another. Her mom continued sending anonymous letters to any school to which he worked, and she would remember his name. As for Lucia, she had erased it, buried it in her shame, though with some effort, walking through the alphabet, it would come back to her.

It was him, no doubt. 00:46 am. The streets were still busy with a few cars and pedestrians, but everyone was moving fast like they had some serious shit to take care of. Policemen, two on each motorcycle, were repeatedly passing up and down the avenue. The downtown smoggy air was electric with a nocturnal jungle aura, all two-legged animals around her scurrying, some preying, most of them heading for a shelter. She followed him, keeping her distance. *Where are you going, asshole?* The evening news two hours ago had terrorized even the most thick-skinned and the conspiracy theorists. "Sure, this is all fake news; there is no virus, but let's go and stock up on milk and flour because all others will do."

The autumn rain had turned the asphalt into a mirror, a thousand hues of neon lights reflected on its wet black. Lucia had walked for hours in this maze of twenty-foot-high cement buildings, each one uglier than the next in its own unique way, corn-yellow and lettuce-green tents covering the two-yard max-width balconies, wooden grilles shut completely or three quarters, senseless lazy graffiti on the walls, narrow pavements blocked by illegally parked scooters and mopeds, overflowing garbage bins. All she had escaped from was still here. Suffocation and misery—yet the whole neighborhood exhaled and inhaled very much alive, a Blade-Runneresque jungle of screaming colors and divergent beings struggling to survive, breathe, draw attention, procreate, revolt, and overcome the doomsday weight of the city and the 79 plague.

She was sacrificing herself big-time, missing her semester at Portsmouth, to help Yara, to protect her parents against the outbreak. She'd kill to leave this neighborhood and never come back. Kill him with zero remorse. She had trained for years, precisely for this purpose, for this night, and she was strong now. A knee on his crotch, two punches on the ribs, and then her boot smashing down on his face until it was a face no more. Purple pulp. She had seen it so many times, only with her eyes shut. Her only tattoo was two words: "PurPle PulP" on the inside of her left forearm, the Ps drawn as Grim Reaper sickles. A few had asked, but none of them knew the band. There was no band, just a vow of revenge.

He crossed the avenue, and Lucia followed fifty yards behind. She shifted her gaze off him only for a brief moment when she saw the ambulance stopping a few yards away and the masked nurses carrying the stretcher outside the bakery store. Case 2,130 or something, she thought. It looked like her favorite sesame roll bakery had caught fire, and someone was hurt. He made a left on Ithaki street, and Lucia hoped that Ithaki would be his final destination. St. George's church was two blocks away.

*Don't tell me you're going to the church, you filthy hypocrite.* Lucia was whispering to herself like a madwoman. He had ruined her forever if forever was a thing. She had not felt another body on hers but only for a few moments all those years. Every time she tried, it was more traumatic than the previous. The thought of touching a man intimately disgusted her. Before reaching the church, he stopped at the square, an oasis of green and open space, souvlaki, meze shops, dessert stores all open until 2 a.m., tables outside among the last of the city's trees. On that night, it was completely different, filled with dark shadows carrying candles, like a starry sky spread in front of her feet, hundreds of them stars, flickering in the darkness next to each other. He mingled with the old ladies, the mothers, the children, and became one of the candle flames. Children. So close to each other. About two hundred people in open space yet packed closely. He rested his back against a tree and rolled a cigarette without looking at it, all the time ogling the little girls wearing their Sunday dresses, their pigtails, and their shiny shoes. She was too far to see his eyes, just guessing.

What were all those idiots doing here? Why were the girls wearing Sunday dresses on a Friday night? She knew what they were doing. Praying. The Archbishop had gathered the faithful on an all-night prayer. "Hail Mary, full of grace the Lord is with thee." She'd seen it earlier in the news. Tina had posted on Facebook, asking for the police to prevent this lunacy of mass prayers from taking place, but you cannot send police against the children and their grandmas.

*This can't happen. Stop it now, Lucia. Don't be a coward this time.* This is her neighborhood. If she doesn't protect them from monsters and saints, then who will?

She mingles with the crowd, most of them old or very young, those who shouldn't be here; she walks among them, gets closer to him. Has he recognized her? The wool-haired woman who owns the souvlaki place at the corner—best souvlaki in Athens, by the way—is holding hands with a little girl. Probably her granddaughter. Lustro Sunday shoes and pigtails.

"What is this?" Lucia asks her. "Why are all these people so close together?"

"A miracle," the old lady answers, crossing herself three times as she explains. "The icon of our Virgin Mary wept. We are all waiting for the priest to open the doors to see and pray."

"Have you seen the news? The virus, Mrs. Martha?" asks Lucia. "This is not safe for you or her." Lucia points at the little girl. The fucker is five yards away, eyeballing them.

"Yes, we saw the news. We know. That's why we came to pray."

Icons of the Virgin Mary suddenly weeping tears or blood are a rare yet recurring phenomenon in Orthodox Churches. When it happens, the crowds amass to kneel and witness—there are no actual tears to witness usually, just some scratches on the oil wood canvas and an overzealous deacon watching with a devious smirk behind the candelabra. But it is human, after all. Lucia realizes now that more and more people gather—the crowd has probably doubled within a few minutes. A death trap for old and young. The hell-demon of 79 is rubbing his hands with joy. But who can she convince about a weeping icon of the Virgin Mary?

Here are some other stories. Changing Bear, the Navajo maiden, suddenly grew a full belly, and the shaman blamed the poor Coyote. Calchas, son of Thestor, the famous soothsayer, saw a snake devouring eight birds and her mother before the Greeks sailed for Troy, an omen of a long and bloody war. The statue of baby elephant Ganesha swallows the offered milk magically in a Hindu shrine in New Delhi. Capillary action, but what teenager pays attention during science class? Santa eating his cookies and Rudolph gulping a billion carrots to compensate for the stick of the speeding old man, the duo delivering Playstation Shoot Em Up zombie games to countless naughty children on the most sacred night of the year. Who is to argue? Miracles happen. Unbelievers burn in hell.

Believers believe, they gather. All of them, singing, exhaling, inhaling, so close to each other. He changed targets now, so close to the little girl with the black locks, almost rubbing himself on her.

This was her neighborhood, still is, and it needs a caped defender from all villains—rapists, fascists, and false saints. It is now or never. There used to be a cute Antifa ammunitions apartment on the basement floor two blocks away; she hopes it's still "operational." Lucia leaves the square, pushing through the singing crowd, and heads there. She is now facing the doorbells of the apartment building, the one she knows all too well. Press the no-name doorbell below the one saying "Doorman." Press it three times fast. Pause for two seconds. Two more times. Pause one second. A final time. The code. The door opens, you walk downstairs. The doorman is there waiting, eyeing Lucia.

Full face masks for tear gas, hoodies, even a motorcycle helmet. Molotov bombs. "Do it yourself," but cut cloth, bottles, and petrol neatly arranged. Bricks, but she won't need them, clubs. The apartment is still fully equipped, serving as an ammunitions station—she knows the ropes since her brief Antifa days.

"You haven't been here for ages," the Doorman says. Lanky and dressed in black, hair messy rather than long, a cigarette below his ear. "Still good?"

"Burn the establishment," Lucia says.

She makes two cocktails, shoves them in her hiking backpack side pockets, where the water bottles are supposed to fit. No helmet, that's too obvious; they'll stop her right away.

She runs out of the building carrying her backpack, hiding under the white skull hoodie, which covers most of her orange hair. *A wig. I need a wig.* She calls her friend Rita, the neighborhood hairdresser and childhood friend, who dyed Lucia's hair orange.

"Rita, sorry, hi. Do you have wigs? Are you here? Can you come down?"

"What? It's midnight, Lucia. What's wrong? Where are you?"

Rita doesn't sound like she was sleeping but rather alarmed. Not many people are sleeping early tonight; the 79 is spreading fast.

"I am downstairs, outside your hair salon. Please come. I need to borrow a wig."

Rita hangs up without replying, but Lucia knows that this means "on my way." At least, she hopes so. Rita comes out of the building wearing a pink robe with little white hearts and matching slippers, a wet towel on her hair.

"Are you nuts?" she asks.

"I need to borrow a wig. It is urgent." Lucia replies.

Rita's slippers are getting dirty on the wet pavement, but she rushes ahead of Lucia, heading for the hair salon. She unlocks, lifts the metal shutters, turns on the lights inside. She closes the shutters again.

"I am not opening tomorrow. It's crazy! My God, have you seen what's happening on TV? Tell me you're not sick."

"I am not sick," says Lucia. "You know I got this thing months ago, at Lesbos. You know, everyone knows. If you get sick, call me. I am not afraid to get infected again. I can help you."

"Here, Lucia, wigs. Why the hell do you need a wig at 1 a.m.?"

"I can't tell you. You don't want to know." Lucia picks a short blonde one. Everyone will remember the blonde.

She looks at herself in the mirror. He saw her at the kiosk twenty minutes ago, but he won't recognize her with this wig. He may remember the clothes, though. Her white skull hoodie was screaming for attention, especially among the church crowd.

"Do you have a coat?" asks Lucia.

"Sorry, no. The robe."

It is white elephants on pink, not white hearts.

"No, thanks," says Lucia.

"I can go upstairs, get you a coat, might be two sizes big for you."

"No, no time."

A linden wood icon of St. Fanourios hangs over the hair salon mirror, the saint who supposedly reveals in a girl's sleep the man whom she'll eventually marry. He is one of the most good-looking saints of the Greek Orthodox church, boyish, slender with a Duran-Duran hairdo and no facial hair. Rita's mom or grandma gave the icon to her, no doubt. Next to his icon hangs a print of the Madonna of the Streets, the famous Italian painting by Ferruzzi. The Virgin Mary is looking skyward, serene, but sorrowful. A chubby blond baby Jesus sleeping on her shoulder. She has a young, pale, innocent face, reminiscent of an unwanted teenage pregnancy mother rather than a virgin one, wrapped in her Egyptian-blue shawl and the beige headscarf, a few dark brown tufts of hair visible.

Would she ever burn a man, no matter what he'd done to her? Not her. Not the Madonna.

Lucia has a revelation.

She throws the blonde wig and goes for the brunette one, covers it with her skull cream-colored hood.

"Do you still have that doll I brought you from Selfridges?

"The FAO Schwarz one? Yeah, back there. You want to borrow the doll too?" asks Rita.

Lucia is nodding as she is fixing the wig on her head. "Dammit, I really need a coat," she says.

"Blue, white, black?"

"Stop joking, Rita."

"Blue, I guess."

The missing piece. Rita opens a drawer of supplies, takes out, and rips open a plastic bag. She clips the blue haircut-gown around Lucia's neck. It covers her from neck to knee, like a Madonnina shawl, makes her look three times her size.

"Please, be careful, Lucia, whatever you are doing."

"You be careful, girl. Stay inside, I beg you. If you want food, I'll go get it for you. I've seen the 79 at Moria. It is the shit. Keep your parents inside. Lock them in. I'll be okay."

Her arms are hiding inside the hair gown as she runs down the street to get back to the church. On the one hand, she is holding the backpack with the Molotov cocktails on the other, the baby FAO doll. A drizzle. It wets her nose; her hair is protected. She is back at the square; it is about 1:30 a.m., the priest is talking. What is he saying?

"We'll open the doors in a few minutes. Everyone is welcome to come inside to pray and kneel in front of the icon. You are in no danger under God's roof."

*Did he really say that? All ye children come inside? Sure, go ahead, children, women, all come inside the little church. Oh, those people, I wish they had seen videos from the deathbeds of Moria.*

Here goes nothing. A Hail Mary.

Now, before the drizzle becomes a storm if it does, they all die. She lights up the cloth-wick and throws the bottle against the wall before the plastic hair-gown catches fire. It explodes with tongues of flames flying out of the hell's bowels next to the side entrance of the North Transept. The effect is spectacular, flames cover the wall instantly.

*I hope there is no priest or deacon in there.*

Screams and panicked shouts come from the main entrance steps and propagate down to the square. Grandma Martha of the souvlaki shop was climbing up the stairs with her pigtailed granddaughter, but she retreats now. There he is again, that monster, right behind the little girl.

Lucia pulls out the second Molotov cocktail and lights it up. The first wasn't that effective. She hurries to throw it against the front entrance, the middle one of the three front doors leading to the church's narthex. Fortunately, the deacon has run out of the church. He shouts, "Fire, fire! Run Christians," hopping down the steps with a surprising swiftness like a Hogwarts mage in his dark black robes.

Against the raging blaze, in front of the main entrance, standing eleven marble steps taller than all the faithful, Lucia embraces the "sleeping Jesus" FAO Schwarz doll. She is wrapped in the Egyptian-blue hair-salon gown, her brown wig covered by the skull hoodie, but it might as well be a flowery shawl; the crowd is too far away to notice the pattern, a few tufts of brown wig hair visible. A Molotov throwing rebel, the perfect image of divinity.

"For once in your life, Christians. Do something Christianlike. Go home, and don't bring your children here until the plague is over. It is not safe!" she shouts. "God is where you find him, and he will forgive you."

She turns to escape before they come closer, running in the opposite direction from the shocked crowd. She shoves the gown in the first garbage bin she sees, the wig in her backpack. Her picture will be in the front of all newspapers the next day, but no one will recognize her, not even her mother, the girl with the brown hair and the cream-colored headscarf, the girl with the blue shawl, the girl who burned the church carrying the fire of the Archangel. Or something. Too many tabloids, one more creative than the other. No one was hurt, though, yet another miracle. She saved so many—now archbishops, politicians, and epidemiologists can agree to stay the fuck out of the church until the plague is over. She saved so many, even him. The monster she had sworn to kill. No one will recognize Lucia, not even herself. Everyone talks about the Madonnina of the Streets.

# 49. Tina: Before the Devil

*Athens, November 2022*

"Before the Devil came for our children, he made sure that God had abandoned us first," said the nation's top TV host burying his gaze to the table, to sum up the collective sorrow.

Kokonis was broadcasting from the studio all alone, interviewing remote guests and experts, anyone who still had the heart to talk to him. He was all drama and solemnity now, his voice slow and deep as if God and Devil had appointed him spokesman to the masses.

The 79 had been raging for more than a month now, devouring life by the thousands, razing all hope. Children. Old men. Parents. Children. Tina had barricaded with Peri and Demetri in her home since day one, no shopping, no walking, nothing. By Athens standards, their house was a mansion, four thousand square feet, Mediterranean style, three-level, one-family, its own porch, backyard, and a basement garage in the most upscale suburban neighborhoods. There were even a swing and a slide in the backyard where she could trick Demetri for a couple of hours into believing that life was still normal. The vast majority of Tina's friends lived in four or five-story apartment buildings with balconies wide enough to fit two chairs. They were fortunate, thanks to Peri's mother's fortune.

Once a week, four weeks in a row now, she drove before dawn downtown to her mother's new apartment. She lived on the second floor now. Lisa lowered a basket, and Tina put supplies in there, canned food mostly. No entering the building, always looking over her shoulder for anyone approaching. She would lift her tight fist toward her mother in a slow move to give her courage, to get some in return, to say all that she couldn't.

Kokonis had inquired twice about her appearing on TV to shed some light on the vaccine situation, but Tina had figured that it was a waste of time and lately dangerous for her family. Athenians didn't need opinions, they needed vaccines, and they were not coming any time soon.

The Kokonis TV card was brutally clear:

Period: Oct 13-Nov 20

Infected: 118,357

Deceased: 14,676 (Children: 2,099)

Half of the deceased were under fifty years old.

During the last few weeks, the city had become a ghost town. Everything except supermarkets was closed to the public, and even those would deliver only essential supplies to families and the elderly. You'd think by now everyone would get it, "stay home." Yet, there was a massive number who claimed that fifteen thousand deaths were not something unusual. She had argued with them over Facebook, replying, "but it's only fifteen thousand because we shut down, else it would be fifteen times fifteen if we didn't." No. "You are only safe because most of us stayed home. It's like saying you're not afraid of jumping from an airplane after I force-strapped a parachute on you." No. It was pointless, explaining to the thick-headed.

Tina became a doomsday celebrity overnight in early October, appearing on TV five and six times a day.

"You're going to regret it," Peri had warned her.

"You'll have your pick, any party to join the next election. You'll be elected hands down," Tina read her father's text aloud.

"Unless you're assassinated first," said Peri. Dead serious, not even the slightest grin on his face.

"I am doing this because it's my civic duty," she said. "I should be at the Ministry of Health, planning countermeasures, working on securing vaccines, but I am no favorite of the government. The least I can do is warn the common folk."

The 79 had nothing to do with previous milder versions of pandemics that had spread around the globe. It was spreading fast; it had a mortality of nine percent. Moreover, it attacked children. Mostly boys like Demetri. She didn't know why. It didn't take long for her to convince people to stay inside. Twenty-one hundred children, six times as many adults, more than two thirds of all those victims in Athens. Every family knew someone who knew someone. The government's attempts to calm down the people during the first days, to downplay the spread, were disastrous. If only they had acted five days earlier, the victims would be a mere fraction of what they were now.

By the third week of October, nobody was going out anymore, but that had created other problems. No grocery shops, supermarkets nearly empty, operating with military personnel to load and stock. No delivery, hospitals badly hit, and understaffed. One of the five million Athenians were people who survived on obscure unstable jobs, mostly related to tourism and the night scene. Black money, always cash. It was not a matter of losing their job; nobody cared about that. They had not stocked up on food or medicine.

By the end of October, the government had switched its tune to "all stay inside," yet this was once again outdated because some simply shouldn't. Policemen, nurses, army, security, drivers, blue-collar, so many people had to go to work; else, the deaths would be a lot more than the ones the 79 brought.

Even Tina had pleaded on TV and social media that people on essential security jobs should return to work, taking all necessary precautions. It hadn't worked.

*"I am not going anywhere to pack meat or stock beverages on shelves and risk the life of my child back home. Fire me."*

They were right.

It took only a couple of TV appearances, and she was instantly attacked by religious extremists, nightclub owners, and anyone who thought that he knew better. Threats, verbal mostly, a couple of phone calls. It had made her extremely uncomfortable and sad, the stupidity and the self-interest resembling a stoning from fanatics for a crime she hadn't even committed. In some other country or time, she could have been stoned or beaten to death for her other "crime," adultery. But this was uncalled for; she had blockaded a school with Lucia for the world to know, for the parents to grasp the seriousness of it since day one. The moment that the bus tire burst on camera with a thump, it was news, and it was early. She had saved a thousand lives, two hundred children probably with that one tire.

The first to call, plead, beg, bribe, and threaten were friends who had a friend in trouble, then relatives, then random callers she didn't even recognize. She had not anticipated it, but they were right on their guesses.

"Oh, come on, Tina. Don't tell me that the WHO or your friends from the pharma industry didn't send you some vaccines. I know you have vaccines. I only need two for the kids. One for me, if you can spare a third."

"My dear Mary, no. I don't have a single one." How on earth did she not think of it? She could have had a box if she had planned with Garnett months ago. She was confident that it wouldn't get this bad, that the government would somehow, in the end, take care of them.

"I don't believe you, Tina. If my kids get sick, their blood is gonna be on your hands. Yorgi died from this thing, the kids are asking me every day if they are going to die."

"I don't have vaccines, Mary. They don't send them via mail."

Her friend shut the phone abruptly. People started calling from everywhere.

"Damn you, bitch. We know you have them, and you sell them to the highest bidder. We'll come and make you sing."

A picture of her with Demetri came via email.

On the night of November 13th, Tina and Peri jumped from their bed at three a.m. as their bell started ringing. Two men were shouting under the lamp post, and one of them threw a stone at the window. Peri called the police and grabbed his baseball bat— he kept one near even though he had never taken a swing as a kid or adult; it was not a Greek sport. He had bought it on that Disney World trip years ago. Tina woke up Demetri and locked themselves in the basement room. They slept there cuddled in the tiny bed, telling him that the heat wasn't working upstairs.

In the morning, they found their front yard carpeted with flyers. She was accused by the Guardians of the Greek People— not that she had heard them before—of quite a lot of things. Apparently, she was a co-conspirator of the New World Order's plan to wipe out the races and sterilize the ones who didn't comply. They had engineered the virus and kept the vaccines for themselves, planning to exterminate half the world population—imagination at the level of copying an Avenger's movie plot. The Greek race, with its two extra genes of superiority—that was actual wording from the flyer—was mainly targeted. No Jews had been infected. How could anyone explain that? According to the flyer, it was simple; the Jews had planned the whole thing.

Kokonis called the next day asking the same questions, more or less, and Tina decided not to appear on his show ever again. Debating the obscure was a lost battle. Showing her face was simply throwing kerosene to the fire.

Calls, begging, threatening, screaming to give them the vaccine were multiplying, some of them cursing her to eternity. She got off social media, disconnected her phone, changed her mobile number, giving the new one to a handful of people she cared about.

"Can you please go by your sister and get two mannequin dolls from her boutique?" she asked Peri.

He didn't ask why and came back an hour later with two hairless, faceless, genitalia-less beige mannequins. Tina wrapped them, each one separately, using duct tape and black garbage bags and left them outside her door, visible through the iron gate that circled their yard. "Bodies, dead, DO NOT ENTER," message was clear and effective. She added a poor little mouse that Peri found dead next to the manhole for the smell.

It was the latest guideline from the Emergency Health Taskforce that Alexi was heading.

"To all citizens: If a family member dies in your apartment, wrap the body in any suitable material, call 1999, an extra nine, to report the name of the deceased and address. Or you can fill a form online. Army units will be collecting the bodies from the address given as soon as possible. Please, do not call private burial services. They are all overwhelmed and cannot handle your request. You also have the option to transfer the deceased to the closest mass-cremation sites, on Western or East Attica."

Funeral homes had been looted across all major cities. Coffins and body bags were being sold on the black market for ten times their price. Good thing that temperatures had dropped to 12°C.

She marked her front door with "DO NOT CROSS" yellow tape that she had ordered months ago when she was still planning Demetri's first Halloween party. It was supposed to be the event of the kindergarten year, no one else was having Halloween parties in Greece. Halloween had passed, in true horror, unplanned, and Thanksgiving was coming soon.

They didn't use their front door anymore, just the garage entrance. There were no more incidents. The whole house seemed abandoned; its front façade, windows, and drapes shut firmly. They'd let some light and fresh air come from the backyard doors into the rooms, waiting for the days to pass by.

She had made almost daily inquiries to Dr. Garnett and to anyone she had met at WHO. "No vaccines, nothing to be done. Please coordinate efforts through your government." The Israeli Ministry was kind enough to provide her with their whole operational plan for vaccinating a country within a day—from landing the airplanes with the vaccines to one hub, what aircraft and trucks were needed to serve the secondary cities, temperature and equipment to store them, everyone reporting to a voting center or school of their neighborhood with ID, training ahead of time personnel that would perform the vaccines in each town and city. It was a nose-spray vaccine. Even a monkey could do it after watching a training video.

Tina had shared the whole plan with Alexi; she had called him after a long time and pleaded with him to put it into action and be ready. When, if the government managed to procure vaccines, they shouldn't lose another day on planning.

On November 19, Alexi informed the public on TV that a nationwide vaccine program was underway. All he needed to do was press a button, and the whole process would automatically begin with a nationwide mobile phone emergency alert informing personnel and the public where to report. Last names starting with A would queue at 8 a.m., B at 9 a.m., and so on, until Ω at 7 p.m., the next day. Drivers and pilots were already allocated on specific assignments and waiting to receive the message. Refrigerators would be placed in all vaccination centers ahead of time, awaiting the vaccines.

Alexi never mentioned Tina's name or thanked her.

A day later, riots erupted in multiple cities. Thousands of people refused to leave their dead on the street for a military truck to transport them to a crematorium.

"I failed," she mumbled as she served Peri a greasy omelet.

She kept the effort on, inquiring everywhere, from the Chinese black market to the US government and with anyone in Brussels who'd pick up a phone, but to no avail. Her only hope was that Alexi and his pathetic government would fare better.

The streets had slowly morphed into a post-apocalyptic landscape. Police and ambulance sirens had gone silent, and that silence was more piercing than the screams of the days past. Keeping Demetri busy was the other task. What do you tell a six-year-old locked in the house for a straight month? He asked when he'd go back to school, to the neighborhood Titans soccer practice, or buy a chocolate from the kiosk. What excuse does a mother have not to buy a chocolate bar for a whole month? We are all going to die if we go out to buy candy? There is no kiosk open? He wouldn't believe any of them. Bad for your teeth.

She had promised Peri that she'd cook a roasted bird for Thanksgiving, even if it were a chicken. It was far past midnight, and Tina was digging to the bottom of the deep freezer, searching for a whole chicken, when her mobile phone rang.

"Tina, I need your help. Pack for one night," said Lucia on the other end of the line.

"Lucia, how are you? How is Yara?"

"Yara is volunteering at the 79 hospital downtown, haven't seen her in days. But she is fine. Everyone is fine. I need your help. I got the vaccines. But we need to go get them in person."

"What do you mean, 'got vaccines'? Got them from where?"

"I got them. Enough. Papalias came through."

"I'll need two. Maybe some more because people with kids are calling me? Can you hold these for me?"

"No, Tina, listen. I got them. Ten million. A cargo ship. We fly to Roberts Airport tonight."

"What? Ten million? How? Where is Roberts Airport?"

"Freeport."

"Freeport, Maine?"

"Freeport, Liberia."

# 50. Ella: Fake News

*Athens, November 2022*

The Prime Minister Addresses the Nation on TV:

"My fellow citizens: I stand here today with deep sorrow and humility to address you on the pandemic crisis that has devastated our country and the entire planet. Since the beginning of the year, our government was one of the first to identify the danger. Epidemiologists from our Emergency Health Taskforce, led by Dr. Vardis, forged the WHO action plan in Geneva back in March. They were instrumental in suppressing the first wave in June and the outbreak that erupted on the island of Lesbos. We were the only country to face a refugee camp crisis and managed to contain it virtually unscathed. A few weeks ago, I invited Ms. Yara Halabi-Masoura. We discussed her experience in Moria and how our local authorities and doctors were essential in stopping the virus outbreak.

"Since June, we have hired two thousand and three hundred medical workers and increased our ER capacity by 30 percent. We managed to keep tourism open during the summer though fears and scaremongering resulted in an unprecedented economic decline and budget shortfall.

"Alas, the virus returned, and despite our efforts, the global powers have restricted vaccine production to the numbers *they* needed. A so-called 'Paneuropean' Vaccine Alliance led by Germany and its neighbors secured vaccines, but we were excluded from this agreement. I have repeatedly warned you that the European Union is crippled and serves only the major countries' interests. I stand firm now more than ever on my belief that we must exit the Union and seek real allies that will support us in the worst of times.

"The situation has been devastating, especially in the capital of Athens, with thousands of our citizens succumbing to the virus. Medicine, vaccines, and essential supplies are not arriving in the country. Moreover, fake news overstating the number of victims and the spread of the disease has rendered the civil government incapable of maintaining essential services. Under these circumstances, I have no other option but to declare new measures. All medicine, food, essential supplies, and services will be under the armed forces' control and distributed in an orderly and just fashion to prevent black market and overstocking phenomena. Media, print or digital, distributing fake news, especially relating to the number of recorded deaths, will be shut down immediately, and the perpetrators will be punished.

"Our country has suffered such crises repeatedly in the past. With the help of God and the determination of our defiant people, we will prevail again.

"Secretary of Press Mr. Gerou will answer questions from the press now.

Reporter 1: Mr. Gerou, did the Prime Minister just announce that supermarkets will be closed, and the army will distribute food and medicine based on a coupon list?

Secretary: We will have more details in the next hours from the relevant Ministers.

Reporter 2: Deaths reported in the last thirty days exceed those of the previous year by twice that number. What is the deal? Are you hiding the deaths, or are you failing to record them?

Secretary: We are not hiding anything. I warn you: this is the last fake news statement we are going to tolerate.

Reporter 2: Victim names directly reported to our paper's website are not in your official list or appear as other causes. Is it true that bodies brought to the mass cremation sites are not recorded as H7N9 victims but rather as "cause unknown?"

Secretary: I have replied. This is too serious a subject to be left to extreme partisanship-driven questions. Someone else, please?

Reporter 3: The current predictions of the Oxford University model show 750,000 cases in Greece until May and around 90,000 deaths, almost one percent of our entire population.

Secretary: I know our population.

Reporter 3: Of which 13,000 will be under eighteen years old.

Secretary: That prediction assumes that we will have no vaccines until then.

Reporter 4: So, your government agrees with the prediction, but you hope to have vaccines earlier? When? Reports by the WHO state that vaccine capacity is exhausted globally and tightly controlled by the countries producing them.

Secretary: You have to realize what is happening here. We are squeezed by certain interests to accept their global agendas in exchange for vaccines. We will not fall for that.

Reporter 5: So are you claiming that Austria, Romania, Netherlands, and Portugal, among many others who have secured vaccines and are recording one-tenth of our incidents per capita, have accepted some global agenda that we don't agree with? What is that agenda?

Secretary: I am not here to discuss Romania or Portugal. Our government has done everything possible and more. We have a comprehensive "Vaccine 24" program, where we will be able to vaccinate the entire country within 24 hours.

Reporter 1: Is that the one that Dr. Walker submitted to you?

Secretary: I am not familiar with her. It is the official program of the Emergency Health Taskforce. We are ready to vaccinate everyone within 24 hours after vaccines arrive at the airport.

Reporter 2: When?

Secretary: When we have the vaccines.

# 51. Yara: White Knights

*Athens, November 20, 2022*

They rotate me. Early morning, I work in the elderly hospital wing, at night in the juvenile ward. It is kind of fortunate, the light is dim, and you don't get to see the details of the suffering. This virus has mutated and returned stronger and more violent since the days I caught it at Moria. There are kids and adults, healthy, athletic, who come when I start my night shift and are dead before I can see them again the next day, twenty-four hours, rapid cytokine storm. A doctor explained to me in English, the immune system of the patient overreacts. The white blood cells attack the vital organs to kill the virus and don't stop. White knights to the rescue, bringing death. It explains why young people—the average age of the dead is forty-three years—die within a day. That's one in five, and it is random who lives or dies other than the fact that boys go faster. More boys than girls, I don't know why. I've never had so many boys, not even one to be exact, hold my hand with such affection as the last week here. I will never have in the future, either.

We should be able to save nine in ten, they say, but the actual numbers are closer to eight in ten. That sounds close, but in fact, it means that the dead double. We lack basic supplies for the last few days, that's the main reason. It is not about some miracle vaccine or drug that will cure them all. The doctors need simple stuff like ventilators, Nitropress, heparin; one is a blood thinner, the other hypertension, I confuse them. We've run out.

I am not a nurse, of course, just a volunteer, so I don't give drugs, injections, or do any serious stuff. I print lists—they are in Greek, and I can't even understand the alphabet—with names, hospital rooms, date of birth, and then a number next to it, indicating severity, one to five. Fours and fives, we don't even deal with; they are people over sixty or with severe health problems. They are in the elderly wing; we just bring them in one day, out the next. I am overly dramatic; about half of them against all odds and with minimal treatment get better. It's just the flu, after all! Half survive. The battle is to select which of the ones, twos, threes should prioritize medicine and ventilators.

I've seen some ugly stuff. We had to take a ventilator from a mother to treat her eleven-year-old son, whom we kept in the same room. I wonder what happens to survivors? Do they recover mentally? Do they love, kiss, drink wine, eat souvlaki on pita, sing at a wedding, bathe in the sea, or are they just zombies that have gazed at all that lies beyond the river Styx?

I had to reassure a frail white-haired lady as she was dying that her granddaughter was getting better. They had arrived in the same ambulance. I wiped the tears, shut her eyes, rolled her bed out to the trucks. On my next night shift, I rolled her granddaughter's body out of the room. Different truck, they fill up too fast and run back and forth to the mass cremation site.

I smoke, one a day, around midnight. I have a smoking date or something like that with a university student, a boy who drives the wee-hours truck. He got sick on the first days but recovered and stayed in the hospital, his mom died here, and he had nowhere to go. He volunteered, the same way I did, and has food and something to do here. His name is Michail.

"Like the Archangel," he said.

"I can draw angels. I can draw you," I replied.

"My mom was one of the first to die. They even did an autopsy," he said. "The doctor said that her lungs were soaked with blood, like red *patsavouria*."

"What is a *patsavouria*?" I asked.

I google-translated it later; it means mop.

You'd think, I'd think, that I'd be falling apart by now, same as the patients, doctors, nurses, soldiers, policemen, all who work here. Yesterday, a doctor about Dr. Tina's age jumped out of the window. Michail told me that she was treating her eleven-year-old nephew and couldn't save him; a nurse said she was recently divorced and depressed. Both can be true. Exhaustion and lack of sleep are the worst counselors.

I find some corner in the supplies storage room to doze off in the afternoon. There is always something to eat, too many patients can't swallow a bite. I haven't gone back to Lucia's apartment for days now. She was acting weird, and all, and I needed a break. And though I have no nursing skills and barely speak Greek, I have one thing to offer: I am immune to the virus.

They keep asking me to do hard-core nurse work, between uniforms and masks, no one can tell who is who. A couple of the nurses freaked when we rolled over a man with crackling back skin; I had to explain to them from my Moria experience what those air bubbles were. "But I am not a nurse," I must always remind them, so they put me on mundane duties. Roll the dead out from room to elevator to truck. Bring their bed charts to the admin to record them. I brought eighty-four yesterday, and that's just at my hospital. There are many more dedicated 79 hospitals around the country.

So, no, I haven't collapsed. In fact, I can breathe for the first time. You see, eighteen months ago, I was a kid with a family in Manchester. I had hobbies, school, a swimming team, a sister. I hadn't been raped or thrown into a container to be sold as a sex slave or left abandoned in a Moria deathbed to rot. No, none of that. And then it all went downhill like an evil god grabbed me by the hair and pushed me down into a filthy toilet bowl to drown. Again and again. The only scenario that made sense from all that was that I descended into some hell where every construct and being simply existed for the purpose of torturing me.

After the night I helped that baker who was trying to save his shop from fire, things started making sense for me. In the hospital, I found clarity; the surreal became real. It is not just me. This is the Year of the Reaper. Everyone hurts, everyone bleeds. I must admit that I get a bit stronger with every cold body I roll out to the truck; I heal a tiny bit more at the touch of their pallid skin. Watching them gasping for oxygen with their dying breath, exhaling their stolen life into me, "Life is so precious, so beautiful, you cannot roll over and die, Yara. No matter what."

My greatest shock came on the morning that I started caring for an eighty-eight-year-old woman. The sun was blazing outside the window, and she told me to lower the shades and read to her. She was a retired English teacher from the States working at the American High School of Athens. She had brought a massive book by Carlos Ruiz Zafón, and she loved my British accent. She couldn't communicate well with the other nurses. Her dreams and nightmares were in English; she felt closer to me than the other patients. We were both scared for different reasons, and we sheltered forgotten in her room.

When I saw her again late that evening, she was panting, twenty-five per minute, holding on just to see me one more time, it seems. Mulberry lips and eggplant color hands from the cyanosis. You'd think a person her age dies peacefully, she had enough of life, pain and love, but no. That shocked me. She was making me promise her that they'd save her. "I have things to do. Finish the book. It's Thanksgiving next week. Every Friday, we go for coffee with the girls," she whispered to me secretively. The "girls" were the rest of the widowed octogenarian coffee co-conspirators.

"Don't worry, Mrs. Anna. The doctors are excellent here. I'll come back tomorrow. Sleep now," I softly caressed her palm.

"Yes, tomorrow," she said, and her eyes seemed to believe me.

She wouldn't accept death; life is so sweet and hurried. She died Thursday, one day before Friday coffee, one week before Thanksgiving.

Now, whenever I wash in the bathroom, staring at the mirror, my garbled thoughts start unfolding into a clear message. "You are so lucky to be alive. Remember all those children you and Michail pile up at the truck. You two, so lucky, like playing with Barbie dolls in a slaughterhouse."

Nurses and doctors are bound to the Hippocratic oath, cure those who need help, yet I am taking advantage of my volunteering to heal myself. Life will tell you how it is; it will give you the what, the when, the how, whether you want it or not, but you rarely figure out the whys. "Why me? Why Nahla?" Finally, I have some "whys" here.

"It is not just me. Not my color, my passport, my father, my youth, my sex, my luck. No, they all bleed the same. It is a godforsaken year, as Dr. Tina said, the year to survive. If you are religious, you look up to the sky and say 'thank you, God' if you are not, 'I beat you, whatever you are.'"

Of course, one thing I know for sure, after all, I've been through and witnessed. There is no God. And if there is one, he is a sadistic asshole.

Gotta go. My shift in the Children's Wing starts in five.

# 52. Lucia: Mr. Fortunate

*Monrovia, Liberia, November 23, 2022*

"They won't fit. We need at least five planes," said Tina. She wrapped herself in the blanket and leaned forward on her aircraft seat to repeat the words for the umpteenth time. "They won't fit."

Yangos stood tall above her on the isle, shaved head, Dwayne the Rock goatee, offensive tackle build. He was packing, and that made Tina even more uncomfortable. Tina, Lucia, and Yangos' eight-strong team had all boarded the first of the monster planes. They were criminals smuggling vaccines of all things out of a faraway country. Two more 777s were flying right behind them.

"Listen to me, lady," Yangos said. "Twelve years now, my job is to load ships, cargo planes, and containers. I know what we can fit in what. The containers are 8x7x4. They'll fit."

"No, they won't," Tina insisted, pleading with him to order two more 777s to Monrovia. "The Israelis used two planes for five million vaccines. We'll carry twelve million, so we need five planes. Three won't be enough."

The 777s were specially designed for cargo with just three rows for passengers in the front. The interior cabin was refrigerator temperature, six Celsius, the coldest plane Tina had been in her life. She rubbed her runny nose and watched her warm breath cut through the dry air.

"Where can I find two more 777s, doctor? In a Happy Meal box?" Yangos asked as he grabbed another burger from the fast-food paper bag. "Do you know what we had to do to commission three 777s to Monrovia on a day's notice?" He shook his head dismissively, gulped down the other half of the burger in record speed, and wiped the ketchup-stained stubble with the back of his leather jacket.

"What did you have to do?" asked Lucia.

"Ha, ha. Now that you ask, not much." He chuckled. "Almost all planes are grounded. Pandemic."

Panos, the second in command, who looked like Yangos' twin brother, went over the plan again. "We land at Roberts midnight after the airport shuts down. I have arranged with Mr. Fortunate, yes, that's his name, to have local cargo crews ready. Trucks are ready at Freeport—the ship docked six hours ago. We load the vaccines on the planes by 6 a.m., before the airport gets busy again, and fly back to Athens. We should be back home by 6 p.m., Wednesday."

*The evening before Thanksgiving,* Tina thought. She'd have twelve million reasons to celebrate.

"Does Mr. Fortunate know what we are loading on those planes?" asked Tina.

"Are you nuts, doc?" Yangos replied, his index finger revolving in mid-air next to his skull. "They know about mangoes. And even when we mentioned mangoes and plums, we had to bribe them more than they make in five years."

"Have you kept the vaccines refrigerated? Else all this is for nothing," she said.

"C39 Poseidon has refrigeration. At least for a few more hours. And these planes, as you see, they're damn cold. Six degrees, right?"

"Five," Tina said.

"Okay, we'll take them down to five, but it's tough. We're landing in Africa, you see. Most dangerous mission of my life. If they figure out that we are smuggling vaccines, we're all dead."

"But they are not *their* vaccines," said Lucia.

"Does it matter? Be careful with your words once we land there. Never say 'vaccines,' 'doctor,' even in Greek, or we're done for. Mangoes. Man-goes, ladies. Say it loudly fifty times to get it in your head. You are stewardesses. We carry mangoes."

"Isn't it strange that we land in Monrovia for mangoes?"

"Not these days. Another month like this and mangoes will be more valuable than vaccines. You know most meat factories have shut down throughout the world?"

Alexi sitting next to Tina, figured that this was an appropriate time to hold her hand. Lucia lifted her eyebrows wide-eyed in "a what the heck" expression, and Tina slowly but gently pulled her hand away. Alexi was the key unwilling participant of this plan; without him, they had nothing. Tina had played all her cards, including the "missed you, let's get together, baby," to get Alexi to the airport last night. She had lured him into a mystery-sprinkled rendezvous, claiming that she was lonely and needed company. "Meet me at the airport hotel," she had texted. Papalias' men abducted him as he was about to enter the hotel, shoved him into the plane, and confiscated his phone, allowing him only a misleading "off to Brussels" message to his wife.

The wheels touched the warm runway of Monrovia at midnight, and everyone rushed out in the open air, frozen and stiff-legged from the long flight. Local men in civilian clothes approached on a jeep, and Yangos started giving directions. Tina took off her wool coat, and Lucia stripped down to her tank top at the thirty Celsius night heat. One of Yangos' guards stayed with Tina and Alexi and warned him not to open his mouth. An exhausted Tina stretched the blankets on the runway next to the plane to sleep for a few hours. Alexi spooned around her, and she allowed it, despite her disgust—she had to keep him close for the next few hours.

The gods of Monrovia permitted them to sleep until dawn, keeping the African sun pale and shriveled behind wine-dark clouds. She opened her eyes only to see Lucia and a local man talking next to her loudly. Alexi was still sleeping or pretending to do so.

"This is Titus. He is the only one from the crew speaking English fluently," Lucia introduced him to Tina. She made a sign to Tina to shush and not say a word to him, yet Titus turned his gaze to her as she was the older one of the two.

"Seven a.m., the latest, you are wheels up, no matter what," he said. "Mr. Fortunate said that if your plane is still here at that time, it will be grounded.

Cargo confiscated." The sweat shone on his face capturing the dim airport light.

"Titus, please tell Mr. Fortunate that we need more time," said Lucia with hands crossed in a Virgin Mary praying position in front of the young man.

"I am sorry, Miss Lucia. Mr. Fortunate says that it's too dangerous. You should have left already."

Papalias's security team and the local cargo crews were completing the second truck trip from the Freeport port of Monrovia to Roberts International Airport, bringing the temperature-controlled mini-containers. Yangos was measuring a container and cursing a few yards away from them.

Alexi was up. He put his arm around Tina and shook his hand dismissively.

"You know, you are a pawn here, girl. This is all organized by Papalias's son, who wants to get into politics. They try to sneak the vaccines back to Athens, to strike a blow against our government."

"I don't care about your governments," she said. "We just need to land the planes to Athens and inform the people. I know you can give the order, and you will do it. You send the emergency alert on every phone. Tomorrow around this time, we start vaccinating."

"I am sorry, I won't. If I do, I am as good as dead. This here, is treason and highly illegal. How do you even know these are legit vaccines?" Alexi asked.

"I've seen the batch numbers and checked with the production company."

"Ever wondered how Papalias got his hands on them? You are part of a criminal organization."

"I know exactly how he got them. Else I wouldn't be here."

Lucia approached the couple and threw a dismissive glance at Alexi. "Is this asshole bothering you, doctor?" she asked.

"No."

Alexi repeated the question about Papalias, and this time it was Lucia who replied. "We are part of a crime organization only if you are still alive after we land to testify. You don't need to know how we got the vaccines. Your story is that the Greek government procured them, and your Prime Minister will agree. That's the plan."

"The Prime Minister is never going to accede to this. You are pirates trying to overthrow the government, breaking all international laws. You are lucky we don't execute criminals in Greece," said Alexi.

"And you are lucky that we must send the emergency alert after we land in Athens, else you'd spend a few years in one of these freezers before they found you," said Lucia.

"It's okay," said Tina. "Everything will be fine, Lucia."

Tina knew exactly how Papalias had gotten the vaccines. His ship had made three deliveries in Spain, Brazil, and Moroccan ports already, stock held by private companies who had been sold to the highest bidder outside the official government channels. More than a hundred and fifty million vaccines were transported illegally. Always count on a Poseidon cargo ship from Poseidon's homeland to break an embargo for the right price. Papalias had demanded and secured his payment in vaccines. Whether it was his own or his son's political aspirations, pure patriotic duty, or philanthropic impulse, the media-shipping mogul had a plan, and Tina knew that she was a pawn. She didn't care, as long as the vaccines landed in Athens. They'd probably go to jail or have public squares and elementary schools named after them, or both, in that order, but those possible endgames didn't mean anything anymore. Two of her best friends had been texting and calling her frantically for days now. One had a son, the other a husband at the 79 hospital. Peri had texted that mobs were gathering again, throwing rocks at their house, and their new phone number, even his email, was flooded with threats.

"Lock Demetri in the basement room," Tina said. "Tell him to keep quiet, and you stay guard. Can't you get the police to come?"

"You're joking, right? There is no police. It is a ghost town here. Don't worry. I have the gun and the baseball bat," Peri replied.

"Please, be careful. And lock the kid in the basement, tell the kid to keep quiet."

She was counting every minute until their landing in Athens. The crew was loading the third and last plane.

"Almost done," Lucia said.

Yangos and Panos, riding an off-road Jeep, hit the brakes in front of the two women.

"They won't fit," Yangos said.

"I told you," said Tina shaking her head. "We needed five planes."

"They messed up. I was pretty sure the RAP e2 containers were 8x7x4, and they verified it, but that's the interior dimensions. Exterior is 10x7x5 feet."

"Yeah, *they* messed up. Whatever," Tina said coldly. "It's fine, let's get out of here."

"What do you mean 'get out of here'? We have four million vaccines left unloaded. We need to send them back to the ship."

"Won't do you any good. They are probably going to go bad with all those temperature changes. Just get on the plane. We have eight million vaccines, they'll do."

Lucia had intercepted Titus, who was signaling from the second Jeep. She tried to keep him away from the Tina-Yangos discussion.

"How is eight million enough for eleven million people?" asked Yangos.

"One million of them is infected already or cannot be vaccinated. Two million won't get the vaccine unless you put a gun to their heads. We'd have to hunt them down in each building and drag them in chains. Won't, can't happen. We'll never vaccinate every single person. Eight is enough. Between the infected and the eight, we'll get to herd immunity."

"And what do we do with the other four million? Do we leave them here?"

"Exactly," said Tina. "I am relieved, actually. Should have told you earlier." She had that sick feeling in her stomach since they landed. Liberia didn't have vaccines either. They were five million locals who needed them as much as her compatriots. She approached Lucia and Titus.

"Hey Titus," Tina said. "We'll leave the rest of the mangoes here, but you keep them in the fridge trucks."

"Mangoes need no freezer," said Titus.

"Shut up and listen to me if you want to make money. These ones do. You keep them cold, no matter what, and we'll send you directions on what to do with them. I'll call you soon, and you will carry my words and orders to Mr. Fortunate."

Yangos would never agree to this, but two jeeps were coming their way, one of them painted with yellow and blue squares, clearly airport security.

"Got to stop them," said Titus and turned his back to Tina and Yangos. "Get on your plane now. Go!"

"I'll call you soon," Tina shouted at his back as he was running toward the airport security jeep.

The three planes were ready and loaded, and it was becoming clear under the 7:30 a.m. sun that Monrovia had exhausted its hospitality. It was their last chance to leave.

Yangos was on the phone, signaling them to get back on the plane, repeating what he was hearing.

"Our man can control air traffic for another fifteen minutes. Shift changes then, and we are stuck for good. We're off."

Everyone had boarded the aircraft, sweating and freezing at the same time. The 777 slowly rolled on the runway. Yangos face was stuck on the window ordering by phone the other two cargo planes to queue behind them.

"Now, now, you don't stop. No matter what they say or do. Yes, even if they fire at you."

"There's a yellow-blue jeep blocking the runway," said the pilot.

"Run him over. Or pretend to," said Yangos and pulled his gun out, pointing to the pilot. "I am not fucking joking."

Tina's heart was pounding with the weight of eleven million lives. She shut her eyes and held Lucia's hand, waiting for liftoff. It was the most triumphant, almost orgasmic liftoff of her life.

"I'll be home soon," she texted Peri.

"I need you," he replied, just before all communications went silent again.

An hour later, when they exited Liberian airspace, Tina got Yangos' sat phone and started making more calls. The first to Papalias, the second to Titus, the third to the Liberian Consulate in Athens, the fourth to the Liberian News Agency. Keeping everybody honest. Monrovia was saved. Athens, Salonica, Crete were still at risk.

Lucia shook a coke bottle to imitate a champagne cork-fly celebration and then high-fived everyone on the plane.

"We got them! We got them!" she hugged Tina, still in her tank top, in the freezing cabin, impervious to cold or dangers.

"We got them," Tina whispered, exhausted and sobbing. Eight million vaccines. Out of nowhere. A miracle.

By now, Tina had serious doubts if the girl she'd first met on the boat to Lesbos a few months ago was human. An angel, a superior being from another planet, or a time traveler. Choose your myth.

"Thank you," she said, holding Lucia in her arms. "Wear something, girl. It's cold."

"And it's not over," Yangos said. "You better get some rest. The toughest job is still ahead for you, lady."

"Wake me up two hours before we land," said Tina and crashed on her seat.

She always had trouble waking up in the cold; air-conditioning worked better for her than any sleeping pill. But this time, her sleep was not deep. She got up twice to pee and drink water, to interrupt the weird dreams that invaded her nap, each time feeling the cabin colder than before. The cold reassured her that the vaccines were okay. She kept dreaming of Demetri, not of the vaccines or all they've been through. The third time she slept for a long, dreamless stretch until Lucia shook her up.

"Two hours to Athens," Lucia said, giving Tina a cup of hot coffee. "Black, right?"

Tina nodded and shook Alexi to wake up as well.

Alexi rubbed his eyes, yawned, and stretched his arms. He ignored Tina and gazed outside the window, showing no interest in joining the conversation.

Lucia knocked on the glass window with her Glock to draw his attention. "Hey, pretty boy. Eyes and ears to me," she said. "This is what is going down," Lucia said, turning to Alexi, holding the gun in hand. "We land at 6 p.m. One hour before, you'll go online and give the order. You launch 'Hippocrates 24,' the vaccination program. Everyone gets vaccinated tomorrow."

"Who is this stupid kid? I've seen her before. Moria, right?" said Alexi turning to Tina but pointing to Lucia. He was shaking his head.

"You have fourteen hours to deliver the vaccines to every town and island," Lucia continued. Order the trucks and the planes to be ready. It is a small country, I am sure you can do this. I'll connect you with TV, Kokonis. You say it loud and clear on TV, so you cannot take it back. We vaccinate tomorrow."

"My dear, Dr. Walker," said Alexi. "I am really sorry for all that will follow, but you brought it on yourself. I'm not gonna help you."

Tina tried a different angle than Lucia. She put her hand on her ex-boyfriend's forearm.

"We got the vaccines, Alexi. Please! People are dying, this is not a game."

"I got the vaccines too, Tina. I am sorry you are late. And you, you, and you," he pointed to Lucia, Yangos, and back to Tina, "are all going to jail. And you'll probably stay there for the rest of your lives."

"What do you mean you got vaccines too?" asked Tina.

"The Prime Minister. He got them. He cut a deal with Germany," said Alexi, snickering.

"When? Where are they?"

"They are on their way."

"When?"

"December the 22, they'll start delivery. First vaccinations on December 24. He will announce it Sunday, on a National Address on TV."

"You are organizing a Christmas fiesta?" asked Lucia.

The expression of a triumphant know-it-all was on his face.

"I'm watching this charade of yours since yesterday. Always good to have more vaccines, though. We'll find something to do with them. Might reduce your jail sentence if you behave from now on and give me the satphone."

He crossed his wrists, miming to Lucia the handcuffs that awaited her.

"Alexi, that's one month from today."

"Yes."

"But." Tina stopped. She clenched her fists and felt her jaw tightening, her tongue pushing behind her teeth, almost breaking them. She bit her lower lip so hard that it should be bleeding, but it didn't. It takes more than anger for humans to bleed.

"What the heck, asshole," Yangos interjected. "A month wait?"

"He hasn't even gone to university," Tina said to Alexi, but pointing at Yangos.

"How many?" asked Lucia.

"The way 79 is spreading the last two weeks? Eighty thousand minimum infected, maybe more than a hundred," said Tina.

"Total or more?"

"That's the difference between using our vaccines tomorrow and waiting for the Prime Minister's."

"But that's like twelve thousand deaths," said Lucia. "Are you serious? The Prime Minister will go for that? Kill another twelve thousand people for the right to claim the credit?"

"More than two thousand children."

"No one will order a country-wide vaccination from an illegal batch you obtained, God knows how. Can you vouch for these vaccines?" asked Alexi.

"I can. I traced them with Geneva before we even departed," said Tina. "But it wouldn't matter, would it?"

"I am sorry, ladies and gorillas," said Alexi, "but you cannot escape what's coming. What on earth did you think would happen when you kidnapped me, Tina? You have a kid. You are all done for."

"I guess it's either all of us or just you. Hmmm, that's a tough one," Lucia said.

"Damn you! This is all politics," Tina said. "You don't give a shit if this plane carries vaccines or mangoes."

Alexi sneered with arms wide open but only for a second. Lucia landed a straight punch on his jaw and pounced on him, ready for more. Yangos locked her arms and pulled her back as his sidekick Panos restrained Alexi.

Tina sank in a window seat as far away from Alexi and spent the rest of the flight there brooding and cursing. Going by the book, any book, Alexi was right—no government could just accept the vaccines. She expected that they'd go through a validation process, there would be a delay of two-three days. Not a month. But the truth was that he wouldn't even try. It was not the smart political move. They'd bury this shipment and probably everyone on the flight if they knew now. They'd shoot them off the air, or even better once they landed to avoid the theatrics. The default plan had failed; it was time for improvisation.

There was a Plan B, but it was as good as a shot in the dark. Moreover, he was right; she'd probably spend the rest of her years in jail, away from Demetri and Peri. For the first time in her life, she realized that she could kill someone without remorse or second thought, and in the case of her ex-lover, it could be a calculated murder or an act of rage. Outside the oval cabin windows, the twilight was fading fast.

"I'll kill him," Tina whispered to Lucia.

"I know," she answered, nodding. "I'll help you."

"Twenty minutes to landing," the pilot announced.

"What's the weather like?" Lucia asked and leaned over Tina to gaze outside.

The sky was clear of clouds, and out of the window, the Attica Road and the other big traffic arteries were dissecting the city like flaming swords against the belly of a dark beast.

"Good. Clear," said Tina and wiped her nose.

"Are you crying?" Lucia asked her. "Please, doctor, no. We'll make it."

Tina tried to recollect herself, but the sight below wasn't helping. "Come see that," she said, motioning to Yangos. "Look out there." She pointed at a vast wide area glowing brighter than anything else, in the middle of an uninhabited industrial region northwest of Athens.

"Are these the bonfires?" asked Yangos.

"Yes, the cremation sites."

"Come here, you snake," said Lucia. She jumped off her seat and grabbed Alexi by his jacket. "Come count, twelve thousand bodies." She loaded a magazine into her Glock and pointed it straight to him.

"You can't shoot me in here," he said. "It's over, little lady."

"No, I can't shoot you yet, because the chamber is empty," said Lucia pulling the Glock's slide backward. "Now, I can."

"You won't," said Alexi.

"Not yet, not until we land, and you send the emergency alert," Lucia said.

"Five minutes to landing. Five minutes to landing," the pilot repeated. "Fasten seat belts."

Tina got up and embraced Lucia, pulling her back away from Alexi. They felt each other's hearts pummeling hard.

"Plan B," Lucia said. "Don't go soft on me, now, doctor."

"Yeah, Plan B," Tina answered.

# 53. Tina: Plan B

*Athens, November 23, 2022, the evening before Thanksgiving*

Plan B starts with a gun in the mouth. His mouth. The three monster planes have landed one behind the other. They roar on the tarmac like dragons awaiting the commands of their master. It is unclear who the master is, Tina or Lucia, though no one will have any doubt before the night is over. The airport is an abandoned desert of doom; only one flight from Brussels has landed all day.

"Crews and airport officials are on their way for inspection," says Yangos. "Plan B it is!"

They are out of the freezing cabin and on the runway again, carrying Alexi to a bus Yangos' team has secured.

"No one is coming for you," says Yangos pushing Alexi down to one of the bus seats.

"Please, we need you to authorize the emergency alert. Now!" Tina pleads with Alexi for the last time. The engine is off, and there is no driver, no lights, just the glow of a cell phone illuminating his face.

He is staring at her, silent and cold, like a bronze statue on a bench.

Yangos pushes his gorilla-sized fingers on Alexi's face between the two rows of teeth, making him open up his mouth wide. He sticks his gun in the shocked doctor's mouth. Alexi's eyes change instantly to a picture of despair as they try to find Tina's. There are tough-guy words, and then there is the taste of metal. She turns away; she is not prepared for things to get that violent.

354

Lucia is biting on her lip with arms crossed next to Yangos, wishing *she* was the one holding the gun. But Yangos is more effective when it comes to threats.

"One of two things happen here," Yangos says in an icy low confident voice. "You play ball and do as the lady doctor orders you. Then you're a hero, and we let you go. We *will* let you go—it helps our story. You live, and we say that we brought the vaccines as per your orders, government orders. But if you refuse, we have to end this here. They will never find a strand of hair." Alexi's lips around the gun barrel are full and stretched as a fish's, his eyes wide and watery. He signals with his hand that he wants to speak. He takes two deep breaths and then shakes his head slowly.

"It won't work, Tina," Alexi says, and this time his voice is that of a scared and exhausted man.

"Whatever. We'll try it," she replies.

She motions to the bodyguard behind Yangos, and he hands her a laptop. She enters the web address of the govsec site that coordinates the pandemic response effort.

"Log in, Alexi. We're down to minutes. Plan B is very simple. We call Kokonis at Delta TV, and the radio networks, we announce that we brought vaccines at AI Airport, without the government's okay. We force the Prime Minister's hand. The only one who is redundant and incriminates us in this version is you, so they," Tina points to Yangos and the rest, "get rid of you if you don't cooperate."

"They'll kill me anyway," Alexi says.

"No, they won't. I won't let them. They promised, and it was my one term."

"Bullshit! *You* lured me here. *You* will kill me, you have the most to lose," he says, yet he seems dejected rather than panicked. "If I testify to the police, you won't see your child again."

"The only one dying is twelve thousand people, two thousand children if they don't get these vaccines. I beg you!"

He logs into the govsec site, enters the page for the emergency alert setup. The message reads:

Civil Protection Agency of the Hellenic Republic:
Campaign Hippocrates 24 Commences tomorrow, Thursday,
November 24, at 8:00 a.m. Report for vaccination to your
designated center at the specified time with a photo
id. If you don't have this information, use your tax-id
to log into the 79vac.gr site. Do not report earlier
than the already specified time, or you will be sent to
the overflow one day later. Vaccination is mandatory,
regardless of age.

Tina is the one on the laptop now; she doesn't trust Alexi. "I am setting it up for 6 a.m.," she says. "Not now, else it will be panic and thousands of rumors till morning." She looks at her watch. "We have eleven hours to deliver the vaccines to every voting center and school." She turns to each face around to get their silent ok, her hands trembling. "Here goes nothing!" She sighs and clicks the button.

Thank you. Awaiting second authorization.

"Second authorization?" she asks.

Alexi smirks, "Well, the system needs a second Level-5 or above government employee to verify this. In case I went mad, or someone put a gun in my mouth. You know we copied this protocol from the Israelis—there are some elementary safeguards."

Tina exhales, defeated. Yangos steps away from the rest and calls someone his eyes peering at Alexi.

"Tina, you were a top-level gov employee," says Lucia.

"But I am not anymore!"

"But they haven't fired you, right?" asks Lucia. "It is impossible to fire a government employee in this country."

"You're right," says Tina and turns to him.

"I can reinstate you," says Alexi even before he is asked to. It seems that Yangos' body language is making him very cooperative. "Give me the laptop."

356

It takes a few more clicks for Alexi to reinstate Tina.

She logs in and gives the second authorization.

```
Emergency Alert scheduled for dispatch: November 24, 2022,
06:00a.m. Estimated Messages to be sent: 15,453,821.
Delivery window: 06:00am-07:30am.
```

"Fifteen million?" Tina asks.

"There are a lot more SIMs than there are people," says Yangos.

"What happens now?" asks Lucia.

"Now we wait," says Tina. "This sets up the whole chain. This airport was the original dispatch point in the plan, so once we initiated the process, everyone was informed. Airplane crews have been alerted to get the vaccines to the islands and anywhere farther than two hundred kilometers. Cargo crews should be here in the next hour. Right?" she turns to Alexi.

She is confident, having read the plan a dozen times, and she just went through all these screens, checking the boxes to verify everything. There is nothing on TV or the radio about a vaccination tomorrow, but that is the protocol; there should be no communication until 6 a.m. Lucia paces out of the bus, waiting, talking to the men. The November sky is mostly clear, and the breeze light and refreshing, keeping them awake. One of Yangos's men offers a chocolate-nut energy bar, and Tina downs it in small bites; she can't swallow from the stress.

Time passes slowly, with nothing happening. It's almost 9 p.m., and no sign of anyone. Tina, Alexi, and a guard are still on the bus. Silence is not good, a validation of something gone wrong.

Yangos enters again.

"They're not coming," he says. "We checked. We have people in the crews and patrolling Attica Highway. No sign."

"Was this all a hoax?" Tina asks.

"He is bullshitting us all this time," says Lucia. "Waste of time! Told you."

Alexi has dropped his face between his knees, laughing hysterically, enjoying the trickery, feeding on their despair. "My God, Tina! You should have known this government will never trust electronic systems and processes. This is all a charade! The moment we demoed the whole emergency alert system to the Prime Minister, he made it clear that he'd have the final approval on everything. Only he has the authority to send a nationwide message. Your plan is a dead duck," he laughs hard.

Yangos is threatening Alexi again. "Last chance."

"Go to hell," says Alexi.

Yangos brings the gun handle down on Alexi's head, and he falls straight forward like a chopped timber. The first love of her college life, they shared wine and bed so many times. She kneels over him, and her hand feels wet with thick dark blood as she holds his head.

"Oh no," she says.

"Get this piece of shit out of here," Yangos orders his thugs.

Tina goes with him, locking elbows and refusing to let them take him away all alone. She wants to make sure that they won't kill him. Murder was a step too far. Not even to save twelve thousand people. She'd never commit murder—famous last premonitions.

"Please, we need to get him at a hospital," Tina says.

"We're done here. It's either him or us, now," says Yangos. "Do you want to see your kid again? He is the only witness to what happened the last two days."

"We need him," she says. "He must call the Prime Minister. It's our only hope."

"It's over, doctor," says Yangos. "We failed."

Alexi is unconscious as they drag him from the armpits to a black Mercedes next to the bus. Tina gets in the Mercedes, refusing to let him go. They are in the back seat, and she wraps his head with the driver's undershirt to stop the bleeding.

"Get us to the hospital," she says to the driver, who buttons his shirt back on.

"Awaiting orders, ma'am," he replies, pointing at Yangos outside the car, not even looking at her.

The TV on the center of the car panel shows scenes from the hospitals, tallies of the dead. It is 9:33 p.m. the night before Thanksgiving, in the tiny country of hers.

Infected: 145,324. Recovered: 47,214. Deceased: 18,456.

For a ten million population, that's a lot, all dying in one month, and there is nothing to stop it except for the vaccines.

Lisa Walker texts: *YOUR FATHER IS VERY SICK*

Tina can't do much now other than watch the TV and wait. She has to drop Alexi at a hospital, then check with Demetri and Peri, then maybe try to help her dad.

Tonia Boura, everyone's favorite pop idol, and Costas Alexandrou, the most promising left wingman of the national football team, are among the dead. Greece is a tightly knit, family-driven society. Twenty thousand dead means that everyone knows someone. Doctors, nurses, mothers, taking their own life. It is not just the dead. The loss is bigger. Dreams, colors, songs, faith. Bodies abandoned next to the garbage bins. Too many stray cats in their neighborhood roam garbage bins at night.

*It is over,* she says.

The RAPe2 containers with the vaccines will be useless in a few hours.

A dark slim figure knocks on the Mercedes back row window. Tina opens to see a brunette giving her the thumbs up: "We are still on. Plan C!"

It takes a full three seconds for Tina to register that Lucia is the one talking, wearing a wig. What on earth is Plan C?

Plan C is simple. All it takes is the brute force of a twenty-two-year-old refusing to lose. Plan C is Lucia running to meet the Inspection Crew Head, who has just arrived, asking for explanations. Pleading to him, explaining, shaking him by the shoulders. She knows this land; it is not one of rules and regulations, always ruled by humans playing gods, inventing gods.

"You have children, sir?" she says, holding him by both shoulders, her hands against his yellow vest.

"My wife is pregnant. I have two nieces. My sister works at the hospital," he replies.

He understands. Rules are good, but in a pandemic, they are shit. He makes phone calls to gather any crew members on shift or living nearby.

Plan C is Lucia hitting everything from Twitter to Instagram. "Need trucks and drivers at AI Airport. Matter of life and death. We're paying thousand a shift." Refusing to lose. She is a brunette now, wig and all, as she charges ahead down the tarmac, calling Papalias. She shouts into the phone and signals to Yangos at the same time. "Nope, that was two favors, sir. You owe me the third one." She runs to a handful of yellow vests that have appeared out of nowhere. Airport crew or something. They are five of them. Tina and the driver are out of the car, watching Lucia and the airport coming alive as night falls.

There are more than a dozen yellow vests now next to Lucia. More keep coming like insects crawling out of their holes at night. Count them thirty. Baggage trucks and cargo loaders sprint to the planes. Twenty minutes later, they start unloading the bellies of the 777s.

Yangos has come to get Tina.

"We need you, doctor," he says. "Get his computer. Tell me how many vaccines to each prefecture."

"How?" Tina asks.

"Crews will be here in thirty. The planes were ready and filled anyway."

"Pilots? How?"

"Papalias and the Apollo Airlines owner are buddies. We'll launch twenty-five planes in the next three hours. The rest by dawn."

That's it. The longest flight within Greece is barely an hour. Fifty-four prefectures. Fifty airports, if you include even the small islands. Doable. Brute force.

"But the vaccines need refrigeration. Now."

"There is refrigeration storage in each location we'll deliver. Schools, centers, everything. That's in place, they followed the plan you gave them. We just need to deliver them."

"This girl!" he points to Lucia, "she is really something. Amazing!" Yangos says, and Tina notices that it's the first time he broke a smile on the two days they've been together.

Lucia is shouting directions to crews and men, who listen and obey. She hangs from the top of a yellow-white metallic pallet loader, a dual platform, hydrostatic drive beast, next to their main deck cargo door, screaming orders into the loudspeaker. She is the Valkyrie Brünnhilde, and nothing is over until she sings.

"We need numbers, by prefecture," Yangos says again. "Lucia said it is not as simple as population."

Too many prefectures. Too many islands. It won't be easy.

"Yes, no, it isn't," says Tina and is punching numbers on the computer. She gives her phone to the driver. "Read me, these," she says, and she enters the deaths per prefecture on a spreadsheet as he reads prefectures and the current number of deaths. It will take an extra fifteen minutes, but that's ok. You can't make a mistake. Divide deaths by nine percent mortality rate, estimate infected, subtract from prefecture's population. They don't have abundant vaccines, she needs to spread them smartly; some districts have been hit much harder than others.

"Do not unload the third plane," Tina says. "This flies straight for Salonica, as is. It will cover Northern Greece. One-third of the population, one-third of the vaccines."

Lucia jumps in. "And don't leave without me. Once we are done here, I am coming with you to Salonica. Need to mobilize there, too. "Panos," she says to Yangos' look-a-like, "you'll take Crete. Call Papalias's assistants there to help you."

There is still an impossible problem, delivering to Athens and anything around it less than two hours drive. That's almost half of the population. No airports are so close. There are at least a hundred vaccination points in the extended Athens territory, and Lucia needs trucks to deliver to all of them.

"What are we doing for that?" Tina asks.

Plan C. They'll do Plan C.

Another hour passes until 11 p.m. when a convoy of trucks light up the Attica Highway speeding one behind the other toward the airport. Lucia and the crew are directing them in as close to Cargo Plane 2 as possible, shouting loading numbers for each district and giving them coordinates.

The girl on the brown wig has managed to mobilize hundreds by social media, but most were useless, she only needed to get to four people in the trucking business, and they got to a few dozen of their drivers. Some of them woke out of their sleep, others from their stupor. One had just delivered his mother to a 79 emergency hospital. They run out their doors and to their trucks, not asking, calling more of their buddies. They drive with one hand, call buddies with the other, a cigarette hanging on their mouth unlit. The Attica highway is filled with empty trucks coming down one way toward the airport. AI Airport is bright like a radiant star with streams of truck lights beaming out and into it like rays. Queuing and honking, they drive their trucks right into the runway, loading four in parallel.

Tina is biting her thumb now, watching close by, and giving numbers and coordinates, but she is second fiddle to her young friend. If it were not for the November breeze, she would have collapsed. Her belly is hurting, and she has no Motrin with her. For a moment, she thinks that Lucia is waving at her, then she sees the girl holding two fists up in the air. A victory sign. Another text message. Peri. And another. No one notices her trembling and panic, no one feels her heart pounding. Tina gathers her strength to go unnoticed and backsteps to the Mercedes. The driver is gone, bathroom, or something. She checks Alexi's pulse, he is still alive, she is not sure if that's a good or a bad thing.

Lucia, Yangos, and a crew lady in a hard hat are hugging and high-fiving each other. Lucia is making the victory sign again to Tina. Tina slides smoothly on the driver seat, shuts off the headlights, and slowly makes a stealthy U-turn. A few minutes later, she is on the highway, speeding one fifty an hour, passing the honking trucks that have already loaded, and heading for the vaccination points.

Ten minutes past midnight. She hopes to be back in a couple of hours to help Lucia if she hasn't left for Salonica, the second-largest city. They might need her help—someone needs to call Kokonis and the media to explain. TV is the key. There is no emergency alert going out— the people will get the news from TV.

That call between Tina and Kokonis won't happen until 5 a.m. That's when Papalias himself calls and connects her to his employee, Kokonis, the TV host, who will be the first to announce the vaccination kickoff. By 5:30 a.m., all other channels and radio stations rebroadcast after verifying with the

Civil Protection Agency. Most people are not awake to listen to the news firsthand, but they get phone calls from relatives and friends. Millions of phones chirping and screaming early at dawn. Word of mouth at lightning speed. The Prime Minister calls her more shocked than mad.

"It is all over, sir. We did it, but you'll take the credit! The vaccines are nearly at every school. By noon, they'll be in the North too. Congratulations! Please, get on TV. Most people need to hear you say it."

Endgame, his hand is forced. He can be a cooperating embarrassment or a fifth columnist to the end.

"Send the emergency alert out now, sir," Tina pleads. She is resting on her muddy garden, alone, oblivious to cold or exhaustion.

Cities and villages, islands, and farmlands light up alive at 6:00 a.m. when the government's emergency alert is finally out, screaming a constant loud buzz on each cell phone. Athenians rush out in the streets to reach the closest vaccination center. Pandemonium, she has awakened the demons and the harpies.

There is a gap, a mystery that will remain unsolved for thirty-six years. What happened to Tina and Alexi between midnight and her 5 a.m. call with the TV host?

At the first breath of dawn, Tina is lying in the gluey mud of her garden, next to the angel flowers she planted. The rains watered them and kept them alive. "No one, God, Nature or Witch, has the right to kill them all." She is panting hard as the Prime Minister ends the call. He even thanks her for her services to her country, but she can't trust a snake. If they found Alexi, they'd have the evidence to burn them all, even conjure up enough excuses, Monrovia, etc., to stop the vaccination. But they won't find him. He is gone forever.

Her heart is pounding like an alien beast trying to rip out of her chest. She is spent for life. Everything that she used to be, dreams and colors, virtues and morals, have been drained out of her.

She knows that the police will be knocking at her door any minute now, and she'll have a lot to explain, starting with how she got those vaccines and ending with the mysterious and rather permanent disappearance of one Dr. Alexi Vardis.

# 54. Ella: Walker Memorial

*Athens, November 28, 2058*

If you ever decide to stroll up to the Walker Memorial, located at Attica Hill Park, I would advise opting for a mild autumn evening. The Memorial is shaped like a flight of pigeons, spreading their wings to ascend. Their bodies are created out of 46,798 pebbles, one for each life lost. For the visitors, the pigeon symbolizes peace and love; for the scientists, it is known as the intermediate host responsible for spreading the virus to humans back in 2022. Next to the Memorial, there is a little museum, the coldest place you'll find in sunny Athens. If you spend time within its gray, windowless, forged cement walls, you'll be able to verify everything I told you, browse the archives, the photographs, and read the official numbers. Most people know a lot about what happened after that Thanksgiving night but not much about the backstory.

My grandmother was prosecuted for the next twelve years—in the beginning ferociously, later out of the habit of a bureaucratic system that once it gets its jaws around flesh, can't let go. She was eventually found innocent of all charges. Most of those years, she managed to be out on bail and even to spend time between Baltimore and Geneva, raising my father, Demetri, away from the chaos that followed. In a prominent example of Kafkaesque justice, she was never accused of the crimes she committed, smuggling the vaccines out of Monrovia, and no one ever managed to connect her, or anyone else, with evidence to the disappearance of Alexi.

The accusations were quite mind-boggling and much worse, though she had predicted it all along. Close to six and a half million people were vaccinated with a flu mist vaccine in Greece during the last week of November, 2022. One hundred and eighty-five of them died within hours, and another six hundred and some caught the H7N9 and died within December. Of course, that was to be expected, any twelve-year-old in my class can explain it now, but our grandparents' generation seemed to be math-challenged in a massive fashion. You see, three hundred in a ten million population die every day, even if it is the sunniest, no flu, no vaccine, no pandemic day of the year. As for those who got infected despite being vaccinated, it takes three weeks for the vaccine to bring full immunity. Back then, people relied on slow-paced books and fast-action movies for their education, and that can give one a false sense of how time works, especially when it comes to biology or climate change—another mess. Alternatively, I have a nagging suspicion that people even back in the '20s knew their math sufficiently, but they just chose to ignore the facts to fool themselves and the easily manipulated.

In my day and age, science has spoken, and the truth is carved in stone in numbers and facts on Walker Memorial next to the names of those we lost. About a month after the vaccination, the effects were clear and dramatic. By the end of January, the number of new H7N9 cases across the country fell to single digits. By summer 2023, the pandemic worldwide was a bad and painful memory of the past. Vaccine companies made billions in revenue rather than profit; the devastating global economic effect was trillions. No matter how big a business vaccines are, the no-pandemic business-as-usual economy is much bigger.

The actions of Dr. Tina Walker (ex. Damianou) and Lucia Maas (ex. Masoura) prevented at least thirty thousand more H7N9 deaths in Greece alone. My grandma, Tina, received most of the credit, primarily because she also suffered most of the unfair punishment and persecution and because she was the one with the Dr. prefix on her name.

In the year 2058, when I complete this story, my grandma is seventy-four years old, and today's Memorial ceremony is special. The word is out, just to the organizers and the Mayor, that she was diagnosed with brain cancer, and though the prognosis is favorable, she may have problems speaking or seeing next year. Her colors never returned after the H7N9 infection; she has lived all those years in washed-out red, brown, gray. Black and white. I still haven't chosen the cover of this book, but I know its colors. They want to make sure that she speaks for the last time, and she promised herself it would be the last.

It is a brief speech, and her voice is steady and rather icy, except for her last sentence. These are Dr. Walker's final words about the year 2022:

"Thank you for coming here once again, to remember and honor those we lost. I find myself among you for what will be the last time, trying to describe, especially to the young people who didn't live through this, what we had to overcome.

"These days, the world has evolved and is driven by math and science. The 2022/79 pandemic is something a kid reads together with the Iliad and the Odyssey. But we ought to remember that this path to rationality was paved with thorns and gravestones. In my old age, I realized that when you live your life year by year, the world seems to head to its doom, and all is lost. I imagine that if there were a giant or a naiad out in the woods or in a cave, some mythical creature who wakes up every fifty years, she'd perceive our progress very differently. Every time she'd rise again from her long slumber, she'd marvel at how our worst moments, our most definite demise, became our salvation and propelled us to the next stage of prosperity and development. Watching our society evolve in fifty-year increments, rather than living through its daily brutality, wouldn't that be a completely different perspective? Like watching an image at the wrong Hertz frequency, you switch to a different one, and it becomes clear.

"But we are not that creature that wakes up every fifty years— that would be a totally different and quite interesting story—we evolve in our peculiar crab-like pace, three steps forward two back.

"You'd think that a pandemic would be an instant wake-up call of global proportions, jolting us out of our highway to hell, sleepwalk to doom one-way trip. But no. It took a lot more until the 2042 floods changed everything for good. Ignoramuses and hierophants shut up after that, and we scientists took over. It was long due. It didn't happen overnight, though.

"Soon after 2022, people became hugely irrational. Religious fanatics and nationalist champions grew stronger, feeding on the anger, the inability of the many to comprehend the catastrophe. Opportunists cultivated our narcissistic, self-centered nature, puppeteering us toward bogus theories. You see, it is unfathomable for a human to accept that a pandemic can occur out of nowhere, that it is simply what nature does. They want to believe in a powerful villain. 'I am so self-important that only foreign scientists and evil tycoons with supernatural powers could plot my demise. What do you mean we were almost extirpated by a lifeless parasite that is not even aware of our existence? That cannot tell us apart from a duck or a pig and just calls us all *hosts?*'

"The idea that a virus outbreak just comes, like the cold wind that blows away the grains of sand at a north-facing beach, is incomprehensible. A pandemic is so natural, like photosynthesis, germination, or a moonbow, and yet it doesn't make any sense—it has to be witchcraft.

"I would dare say that the immediate aftermath of 2022 boiled down to abhorrent cynicism. Those who lived through it unscathed whispered in front of the mirror with some guilty pride: 'We were the strong, the chosen.' But even those who lost someone didn't suffer from inconsolable guilt: 'It's not like I was driving drunk or could have prevented it. It was the damn plague! What could I do?'

"You see the difference: in a war, you die by the Devil's spear, in a pandemic, by God's hand.

"And that's why we forget pandemics. When it comes to historical events, we still make a hundred movies a year about WWII, and rightfully so, but no one ever will watch a film about the Spanish Flu. Midway, D-Day, and Hiroshima—those are film-worthy—we marvel at our own ability for good or evil. But if it's a virus, a lifeless parasite, how could it dare ask for a movie or a book? Or even a Memorial.

"As you know, there were more pandemics that followed the 2022/H7N9, and we acted swiftly and globally on them, though each one brought different challenges. We epidemiologists will tell you to read history and immediately ignore it. Each virus is unique, one will affect only the aged and the obese, another only the strong as the 1918 did, the third will be so deadly that it doesn't spread widely as it kills its host before he ever makes it to any airport, or it will be insidious and infecting through asymptomatic carriers. It is a different fight every time. A virus has no other goal in life than to multiply and keep spreading. But so do we. And in the end, the virus is no match for us.

"We humans will always be the most resilient and cunning virus, and we'll prevail over all others. Not because we are stronger, but because we don't even know how strong we are when it comes to the ones we love. Whatever sacrifice it takes, we'll make it. We'll kill for life, we'll die for love."

And thus, Tina Walker concluded her speech. I learned a lot writing this book about my grandma and my two aunts, though it is clear now that I cannot publish this story or even submit it as a term project unless I edit out everything that incriminates the famous Dr. Tina Walker and my "aunt" Chief Inspector Lucia Maas.

How could these two women, the best of the best, be capable of committing a murder and concealing it for so long?

I've watched hours of footage of what followed the night of Thanksgiving of the year 2022, some of it with newscasters talking about Alexi's disappearance, as there was political foul play suspected. The Prime Minister's office diverted the suspicions, citing strong evidence that Alexi had an affair with Tina, but no one could prove that she was somehow involved with his disappearance.

Most footage is about wailing relatives of those who died shortly after being vaccinated. It takes a few weeks for the body to produce antibodies, but grief overwhelms logic. My grandma was kept in a maximum-security prison for a few weeks until the global scientific community intervened. By Christmas, when the number of new cases came down to zero, the tides turned, and she had her own supporter base, the educated and the thankful. Finally, twelve years later, she won.

You can't hide from the truth. No matter how many years pass, she'll find you, reveal herself, naked and savage.

# 55. Yara: Alpha to Omega

*Athens, November 24 - December 1, 2022*

They will parade for the next seven days in front of me, and I'll be here, for every minute of it, helping the vaccination crew, taking the packages out of the freezer, unwrapping them. When the nurses take a bathroom, lunch, or smoke break, I take over, holding the head and injecting the flu mist up a nostril. I sleep on a thin mattress on the floor of the vaccination center for a few hours; by dawn, I'm up again.

Alpha to Omega. Antonia Avrami the first at 8:00 a.m., Thursday, to Fotini Oreopoulou a week later—spelled with omega this last one, nothing to do with cookies. The Greek alphabet is weird for me, but I memorize it fast as the days progress. We are stationed at the 17th Gymnasium of Athens, on Cynisca Street, right across from the big cemetery. None of the nurses knew who Cynisca was; I had to google it. Some of the folks who come to get vaccinated are immigrants, and they don't speak a word of Greek, not that they speak much English either, but I try to talk and give them courage. A little girl from Ethiopia was crying, she was afraid of needles. I told her there was no needle, but she didn't believe me.

"Be brave!" I said. "We are on Cynisca Street. She is the first woman to win a gold medal in the Ancient Olympic Games!"

Cynisca was a princess of Ancient Sparta and a breeder of horses. The only way a woman could enter the games was if she owned the competing horses. Cynisca won the *tethrippon*, four-horse chariot racing. Quite gutsy.

369

"Everything will be fine," I say to the little girl. "What's your name?"

"Nyala."

Nyala will live, unlike my Nahla.

The days are mild and sunny; that's the norm throughout the year. We are out in the courtyard, not in a classroom, to limit contagion. Most of the people are behaving, queueing silently, four yards apart. The line must be stretching for miles. Hundreds of lines like this all week across the country.

I am power and light. I am the life-giver and the shield, the sorceress who delivers a spell of immunity. You abandon me, you torture and rape me, but I will give back life. That's my revenge and my healing mantra.

Lucia called me on the first day, she said she was in Salonica, organizing the vaccine delivery there, but she had tons of help. I can't keep up with her energy and her surprises, but I miss her. She is my only family, my new family.

As we make it to the last day of the vaccination, a week later, eighty-five percent of those in the catalogs have showed up. There was a fear that the antivaxers would be a lot more, but those children dying saved more adults. I heard some of those conspiracy theorists were gathering all week outside Dr. Tina's house, protesting. What madness! I tried to call her, but she didn't answer.

Michail, my friend, promised that he'd come by to pick me up once I was done. At Friday's early dawn, they let me go—only a handful are still queueing—and I see Michail waving to me.

"I brought you breakfast," he says. "The hospital variety."

"How are things?" I ask. "Out there."

"Nothing changed yet. People are dying, the streets are empty. Fear, you know. They got the jab, but it will be a couple of weeks until it makes a difference."

"Please, tell me a good story. Something to cheer me up."

He offers me a smoke, but I have no use for it or craving. I dream of pancakes. Lucia took me to a place downtown when we first settled here, chocolate chips and strawberries. He still tries to think of a cheer-me-up story.

"Well," he starts, "it seems that this vaccine is effective worldwide. In any country people got it, the cases drop like that," his hand motions a downhill slide, "after a few weeks."

"Yeah, I know that. Anything else?"

"I heard a crazy story on my way here. There is a billionaire shipping guy, Papalias or something. Apparently, he bought millions of vaccines in a secret auction, and he donated them to an African country. Liberia, I think. Can you imagine?"

A billionaire buying vaccines for a poor country that would never get ahead in the queue! Wow! There is still hope for us humans if we are capable of such acts of selflessness and goodwill. I hope all this brings us closer, regardless of race and religion. The gods never came to our rescue, only the humans.

The years will pass, and we'll celebrate this day with Tina and Lucia over and over. Thanksgiving will become a Memorial Day in Greece to commemorate the dead, honor the scientists and thank the vigilantes who came to our rescue defeating all odds. In the morning, we go to the Memorial. In the evening, we head to the football game, all four of us, with young Ella joining as well. We have season tickets. Tina loves football, and we make it a regular pastime. We all four go to the game every second week; it's our thing. Yeah, we copied all American traditions, though we mean soccer when we say football on this side of the Atlantic. On Thanksgiving, I always think of Nyala from Ethiopia, who was saved by the kindness of strangers, and Nahla from Manchester, who was stolen by the moon-eyed djinn of the sea.

# 56. Lucia: Virgin Mary Burned a Church

*Athens, December 3, 2022*

Friday afternoon, a week after Thanksgiving, Lucia finally made it back to her parents' home. She had completed the vaccination mission in Northern Greece but hadn't slept for days and nights except for a few hours. She collapsed at 7 p.m., waking up twenty-two hours later. Her mother checked her pulse a few times to make sure that she was still breathing.

She crawled out of her cold bed and crashed on the couch next to her dad, who was, as usual, watching the news. Her mother, helped by Yara, had made spanakopita; the smell of olive oil and phyllo dominated the small living room. They brought Lucia two warm pieces and a double cup of tongue-burning Greek coffee. She asked for a blanket. The apartment was freezing, the same story every year. The condo tenants could never agree or collect enough money for heating oil until temperatures reached January levels.

"Look at her," Mr. Mazur, said, pointing to the TV. The amateur video was blurry and very low-quality. Still, you could see under the foggy lights a dark-haired girl shouting instructions to the crew at Athens International Airport from a top of a loading platform. "They say she is the same one who saved those people last month on that church here."

"Yeah, they believe that's the 'Virgin Mary' who burned the church of St. Georgios last month," said Nora.

Her parents were both squinting hard and trying to see if the two brunette faces looked alike as the videos played, again and again, one after the other.

Nah, it was too far away and too blurry. Nobody, not even her parents, would recognize Lucia. From the posture and her confident moves, it was evident that this brunette was something special, and Mr. Mazur wished deep inside that his orange-haired daughter would grow up one day to be someone that important.

"You did get the vaccine, dad, mom, right?" asked Lucia for the tenth time.

"Yes, Lu, we did. You think it will work?"

"It'd better," Lucia said and gulped another sip of coffee to wash down the spanakopita.

With body reenergized, her brain quickly shifted to action mode again. She called Tina's number three times, but there was no answer. "Tina, pick up. I'm back. Wtf, you're not answering a week now? Where is he?" she left a message.

Lucia rushed downstairs and got in her car to drive to Tina's house. In the five-mile distance between their downtown neighborhood and the suburb, she came across a handful of cars, none of them police or ambulance. Garbage was piling high in every corner, windows and doors were shut and dark. A block away from Tina's house, while driving by the playground, she saw an empty swing swaying all by itself—no soul, no wind—and felt goosebumps rising up her spine. She hit the brakes as a black cat crossed in front of her Fiat. The eerie silence was broken only once—she couldn't tell if it was a wailing woman or a catfight.

Lucia got out of the car to ring Tina's doorbell. Thirty yards across the street, two hooded figures were standing under a flickering lamppost. The taller one was holding a sign: "*AGENTS...DEVIL...BURN.*" She couldn't read it all clearly, but instinctively backstepped and pressed her back against the iron gate.

"Go away," Lucia shouted at them, but there was no reply or move. She grabbed the only thing she could find, a rock, but they made no move, just kept staring in her direction. As her eyes adjusted to the dusk, she saw three more figures standing further back, among the pines and the elms, and felt stupid for being unarmed. She rang the bell again, non-stop now, but there was no answer. The iron gate was an easy climb, and without a second thought, she was inside the front yard. Two bodies were lying outside the front door wrapped in black garbage bags. She put on a second mask and a pair of gloves, gathered her strength, and opened the first bags with her fingers. To her shock and amusement, it was a plastic mannequin. Same for the second bag. *Smart girl*, she thought, still surveying around for her friend and the threats. She rushed to the backyard—there was a light on in the kitchen, but no one there. The cabinet panels were ripped apart down to the last one, and that put her in panic mode. Why would anyone rip out kitchen panels? She broke a small window leading to the basement and slid down into a dark room. No alarm, no sound. She used the phone's flashlight to see around her: a small single bed, a kid's pair of worn PJs, a half-eaten donut. She passed that room and then found herself in the garage. There she was, Tina on her knees, a flashlight in one hand, washing a car seat with the other—the chlorine odor invading Lucia's nostrils.

"You, of course. Who else!" said Tina even before turning her head.

"What happened? How are you?" asked Lucia.

"Nothing happened," replied Tina, still scrubbing the passenger car seat.

"Where is Alexi? I called Yangos, he says they don't have him. He is missing a week now, since airport night."

"How would I know?"

"Didn't you leave with Alexi? From the airport?"

"I don't know what happened to him."

"Come on, Tina, please, they'll come for you, let me help you. What's this stuff you're washing?" The towels were a faint pink. "Is this? Blood?"

"You had to come, huh?" said Tina, shaking her head left and right in a disapproving gesture. "Help me wash the car. We need to get rid of these," she said and pulled a charcoal floor mat out of the XC90. "I've been washing and scrubbing for a week now, and it won't go away."

"Where is he, Tina?"

"Who?"

"Fuck off. Why are you doing this? I am here to help. I don't care if that asshole is dead. Where is the body? And what are these people outside? You need to get out of here."

"Don't know, haven't gone out."

"Are you here all alone? Where is your family, your kid?"

"Grandparents," said Tina and rested with her back against the wall. She grabbed a Hendricks bottle, took a swig, her stare blank and fixed at the red-white cement floor.

"Look, Tina, I get it. Was not your fault, he was bleeding badly already. You didn't hit him, you don't have to take the fall. Is Alexi's body still here? I'm thinking, here's an idea—"

"Too late for that!"

"—best thing to do is take him to the cremation site. I heard they don't ask anything, they just pile them in trucks and into the fire. We'll give them a fake name, he disappears forever. No body, no crime."

Tina took a second swig. For a few seconds, her head fell heavy as if she had passed out and then started laughing half-mad. It was a sad, sick, and silent laughter that went on and on.

"Gee, that might work, huh? Oh, bravo, to you," Tina clapped in a faint mocking way, her palms barely touching each other, "you save the day, little girl. Again!"

"Can you let me help you?"

"Get out of here. You've done nothing and know nothing."

"You can't do this all alone, Tina."

"Shut up. You never again ask me anything about this. Just wash," said Tina.

"Tell me where is the body, and we go together. You have no clue how to make a body disappear. I can help."

"What body? I don't know what you're talking about."

"Tina, please!"

"It's too late. Just wash. The blood."


And so ends our story of the year 2022. The invisible army of a quadrillion virus invaders lands in Athens, the city known as the Cradle of Democracy, and is defeated by a twenty-two-year-old girl who will not back down. No one will know anything about Lucia or her role for years, except for Tina,

Papalias, his crew, a hairdresser who will keep her mouth shut, and one P.I. investigation office in London that gives her a job every summer and winter for many years to follow.

Because let's face it, Tina is a heroine for all that she did and mostly for what she suffered and sacrificed, Yara is a heroine for surviving through the nine gates of hell, but it is Lucia who tips the scale, Lucia the Luminous, who rises above any skill, education, or stature she has achieved at that age, to be the savior of the millions.

Tina was burned—some of the airport crew had recognized her from TV—but no one knew the identity of the girl with the brown wig. It will take another twenty years until Lucia's role is revealed. Tina will protect her friend forever and claim that she was the only one giving instructions that night.

It will be the year 2041 when the deceased shipping tycoon leaves behind a detailed account of events. In the beginning, no one pays much attention as the floods and the "drizzle" that devastates Northern Europe overwhelms all other news stories. Slowly and steadily, though, the story regains the deserved spotlight, and Lucia becomes the person whom young rebels and aspiring public law enforcement men and women, what an impossible combo, look up to. As Papalias descends to Hades, Lucia ascends to the top of the law enforcement hierarchy, first of Greece and then across the whole of Southern Europe, or whatever is left of Europe, after global warming proved that there is more than one type of invisible enemy out there, and one of them could be so formidable that it may have already defeated us.

It will be almost a happy—though the heroine never gets the girl—ending because, yes, I might be focusing on the girl who drowns or gets raped in every chapter, but deep down, this is a triumphant tale, where the few perish, but the millions are saved, where evil, whether that's a Prime Minister, a sex-slave trade, or a virus parasite, is defeated wholly and swiftly.

As Lucia rises to the top of the law enforcement pyramid, she continues to be hands-on and a great administrator and reformer, but she will not be able, though she'll try in any possible way, to solve three cases.

"What happened to Dr. Alexi Vardis?" is the obvious one. She knows very well what happened to him, but she will protect Tina. No matter the cost.

Case closed, Tina will be safe forever. Lucia will ask again and again where that body is, she doesn't want a surprise, but Tina will just reply. "What body?" She'll refuse to accept any help.

The second case is the most ludicrous, but Yara insists. Do monsters exist? Was there really a djinn with eyes of soot on that refugee boat to Lesbos? Yara still claims that she has seen him again and again in other videos with dinghies crossing years before her ordeal. Lucia has watched the videos too, and, yes, she can spot the man, but what could that mean? A busy smuggler, what else? "The djinn," Yara repeats. But that's Yara, the artist, after all—Selene's shadow always fell heavy on her.

And finally, who were the killers of Pericles Aggelou? Yeah, this is not a happy-ending story, but you kind of guessed it after the first page. We never talk about that, how fate paid Tina back for all the good that she did. We never talk about how Lucia failed her friend, leaving her all alone that night among those fanatics who had surrounded her house. Pericles was stabbed to death a hundred yards from their door, among the elms and the pines, only one night after Lucia's visit to their house. They never caught the killers or found a weapon, but there were so many death threats, phone calls, even after they murdered him. That mob of the hooded bastards killed him, that much was certain, but they got away with it.

Lucia owed that to Tina at least, and she pursued Peri's case with all her powers. But still, she cannot find a single lead for that horrible, senseless crime. Lucia has been the heroine of 2022, a celebrity inspector worthy of her own TV series, but she is zero for three when it comes to helping her friends. Zero for three. Until the year 2058.

# Act 3: The Boat Rider

# 57. Tina: Lan-tra

Nothing is more awkward for a child than watching her grandma cry. Tina's eyes had welled up in the air taxi, and Ella was struggling to ignore it, humming a tune, staring out of the window and down at the colorful roof gardens. It was a short flight from the Walker Memorial to the Union and Solidarity Stadium, less than thirty minutes non-stop. The football game was not on for another three hours. They planned for late lunch, mingle with the fans, watch the full pregame, the works.

The other two passengers, within the spacious cabin, a teenage boy with purple pigtails and a girl with a spider-patterned fire-red crewcut, were staring at Tina from the couch across.

"It's the Walker Memorial, Ella," said Tina to break the unbearable silence. "We built it there for people to go and cry. Old couples stroll up that hill every day; they would be parents to forty-year-old sons and daughters now. Instead, they have a pebble, and they don't even know which one."

"You didn't keep any of the bouquets they gave you. We could have sent them home."

"I always leave them there for your grandfather, Peri. After all, that's his grave, too."

"But he didn't die from the virus," said Ella.

"Regardless, his only grave is that Memorial."

Ella replayed in her d-glasses the two-hour-old video of her grandma placing the bouquet of angel flowers on the monument. Tina was wearing a charcoal kimono top, inwrought with a carmine floral print and an asymmetric tunic, held together with a matching belt top and boots. Her chestnut hair was done in a Chinese empress style held up with black buffalo horn hair sticks. As Tina knelt in front of the pebble-made dove, the crowd broke into deafening applause that lasted for four minutes, a unique hair-raising moment. Eight hundred had come to pay homage in person, but another eight million broadcasted their applaud live over the network. There was a notable absence, Tina's son and Ella's father, Demetri.

"Dad never comes to the Memorial," said Ella.

"Demetri was a little boy back then. His father's death was a terrible shock for him. He didn't recover for years, not until *you* were born, maybe. The Walker Memorial brings him no solace, it's just a sad reminder of our struggles and what he lost."

"I'll check on the game. Maybe they posted the starting eleven," said Ella and pushed the frame of the orange-tinted d-glasses to the bridge of her nose.

Tina gazed out as they were flying three hundred yards higher than the tallest buildings. She couldn't tell if it was the gray organic photovoltaic coating of the glass that made the sky so gloomy or another one of those storms coming. The Attica sky reminded her more and more of her college years in New England lately. If she asked Ella, she'd tell her that the glass was a radiant lime color, not gray.

"Thunderhead!" shouted the spider-haired girl across from them, pointing out the window.

There it was, a cumulonimbus cloud, rising taller than the Parthenon hill, wobbling toward them like a walrus-fat ballerina in white tulle. The sky had turned to the ominous gray—or was that green—of a hail-carrying storm.

"Weather alert! Emergency descent in two minutes. Please gather your belongings," said the toneless sex-neutral voice over the speaker.

"One thing I always hated about this city. *Lan-tra*. Landing traffic every day," Tina mumbled, agitated, staring down at the hundreds of blinking orange stop-lights of the other air taxis.

"Hailstorm again. Wake me up when we land," said the teenage girl, ending her words in a yawn. She laid her slender body on the couch, her head resting on her palms, her fishnet-covered legs over the boy's jeans. A glare illuminated from her hoodie, and she journeyed to another v-dream. The boy imitated her languor, shutting his eyes and diving into fantasy worlds. Little dolphin holograms were hovering in front of his eyes, a clear "do not disturb" sign. Carnivorous droseras were eating out the girl's eyeballs in a hologram trick.

"We'll be stuck here for a while, Ella," Tina said.

"Are we going to miss the game?"

"In all my years, I've never missed an opening whistle. I won't miss one on a playoff game," said Tina.

The hailstorm started pounding the sturdy shatterproof glass of the air taxi.

"Grandma? Will they postpone the game?" Ella asked.

Tina didn't reply.

"Grandma? Is the game still on?" Ella repeated.

Septuagenarian. It happened more and more, the cancer taking over her brain functions, her mind going blank, unable to answer a granddaughter's simple question.

"I hope not. Forecast says that the hailstorm will stop in thirty minutes. I am sure they prepared. Don't fret about it. So what were we saying?" Tina said.

"I have something to tell you, grandma. I finished. The memoir. You, Lucia, Yara. What should I do with it?"

"Burn it? I mean, erase it. Or publish it. Whatever!"

"It does incriminate you, even Lucia maybe. That Alexi doctor. He is dead, right?"

"I didn't kill Alexi."

"Yes, that you said, but he is gone. Since that night. You got in the car with him, and no one saw him ever again. What would the police say? I can't publish the story."

"Have you been talking to Lucia? Did she say so in her story? I told you, stirring the ghosts is a bad idea, Ella."

"Lucia didn't say anything, other than you two washing the car, together, but that's enough. There was a body—"

"I didn't kill Alexi." Tina shook her head left and right in denial. "There is no body."

Ella stood awkward and silent, her grandma's lie was more shocking than the deed.

"Everyone assumed I did, but they had no evidence," Tina continued. "They had no evidence. No body. But it all went to shit today."

"Why? What happened today?"

"Today, today," Tina hesitated, "I'd better show you." She flipped her app-sleeve and popped up one of the event video clips from earlier that morning—the camera passing from the Mayor to the officials and other esteemed members of the State watching her final speech. "You see this guy?" said Tina pointing to a wool-haired balding man with a cream white suit and an amaranth-colored shirt. He was sitting at the end of the second row. "It's been thirty-six years, but it only took one look for me to recognize him. He returned to Athens a few days ago, hiding in Montevideo all those years."

"Who is he?" asked Ella in full anticipation.

"That's Dr. Lautaro Santiago de León," said Tina. "Once upon a time known as Dr. Alexi Vardis."

"What? Are you sure?"

"Well, he came to reintroduce himself after the ceremony. And to ask me out on a date," said Tina, exhaling with a scornful look at her face.

"What did you tell him?"

"Have you ever read 'Love in the Time of Cholera', Ella?"

"No, what's that?"

"Well, you will when you grow older. It is a novel about a persistent ex-boyfriend who won't give up."

"Is that what this doctor Alexi is to you?"

"Nah. He is the cholera, not the love. I told him to go to hell."

"Then all is fine!" Ella's face lit up. "I can publish the story as is. The truth."

"The truth? No. I told you, all went to shit today."

"I don't understand, grandma. If Alexi is alive, then all is fine."

"You don't understand. But Lucia will. Any minute now."

The glass air taxi cabin hovered like the tear of a giant among the raindrops that pounded it persistently, questioning, seeking. Unlike the rain, Tina remained silent, gazing out. One thing they all had insisted on when they started telling their stories to Ella was not to lie.

Ella had many more questions but didn't dare ask them. Nothing is more awkward for a child than watching her grandma cry.

# 58. Ella: Probability 98.6%

*Athens, November 28, 2058*

Young and old, parents and children, a cheerful swarm filled the streets, wearing the home team's red and green striped football shirt. Under her isovest, Ella was wearing one too. She held Tina's hand as they swerved through the crowds. Buy hot-vegs, soda, a souvenir, a pencil, or something equally antique and useless—they went through the same ritual every time.

She was too young to realize how ludicrous, even sacrilegious, her shirt looked to any of the old folks, signifying the club merger of the two biggest Athenian rivals, the reds and the greens. Occasionally, they dropped the green to wear red and white, or the red to wear green and white, to appease the old gods and elderly season holders.

It was the same everywhere in Europe, what was left of it south of the Alps. The Chelsea Gunners of Puglia had descended to Italy, the Celtic Rangers of Macedonia, Bayernlona, the Ajax of Troy, Het Legioen of Fenerbahce. Unity! A common fate. Embrace your old enemy. Even sports had succumbed to the new universal doctrine, not to mention that it made business sense as well. At least Tina's compatriots didn't have to abandon their country, immigrate, and rename their teams two thousand miles south.

"There's Lucia," shouted Ella, already greeting her aunt from afar with a crazy dance move. Aunt Lucia had donned a red-green Mohawk wig, a gray Steampunk Bolero jacket over an eggplant tank top and black Ninja pants. Her real hair was a short boyish brown— she had to maintain some thread of dull appearance for her day job. "I don't see Yara with her." The two "aunts" lived close by and always shared a ride to the game.

"En messaged that Yara might be late today," said Tina.

"En spooks me out," said Ella, referring to the virtual holo-agent who took care of all of Yara's chores and schedule.

Lucia waved to them to follow her to the seats, but Tina stopped them.

"Ella, Lucia, the football channel wants to interview me today. It is *that* special day of the year, you know, when everyone remembers who I am. You girls go inside. I'll be thirty minutes tops," said Tina, pointing to the stadium that was quickly filling up with the "in-fans." Today's attendance was fifteen million eight hundred, but in-person fans who made the ballgame trip instead of watching from a virtual seat at home were somewhat less than a hundred thousand.

Lucia and Ella went up the stairs, chanting along with total strangers and some familiar ones, hopping, breaking a sweat, getting in the mood. When they made it to the concession stands and queued for soda, Ella took the chance.

"Aunt Lucia, you didn't come this morning at the Memorial."

"Actually, I did. I was way at the back, dark hair wig, white jumpsuit, you can find me in the video. I didn't want to steal Tina's glory. It was her day. But I always honor the dead, I come every year. Reminds me of my youth, makes me feel fearless again."

"Did you ever meet grandpa Peri? Did you bring flowers for him too?"

"No, I never met him. I bring flowers for everyone."

"I have great news, aunt Lucia. I finished, you know. The story!"

"Wow, girl! Bravo! None of us had the guts to write it all these years. I didn't even try."

"It was hard. Thinking, until now, that you and grandma covered it up."

"Covered what up?"

"The Alexi thing."

"Oh, that," said Lucia. "I didn't kill anyone. Neither did your grandma, as far as I know. Shit happens."

Lucia didn't know. That much was obvious to Ella.

"Grandma said I should tell you because you will soon find out anyway," said Ella, keeping her eyes down.

"Tell me what?"

"You see, I don't understand what's happening anymore. I've been struggling for weeks now, since I finished the story, trying to figure out how could grandma and you kill a man, any man, I just couldn't believe it. Gut feeling, And guess what, I'm right. Nobody killed Alexi. He showed up just today."

"Who? What are you talking about?" Lucia's eyes were darting around, probing to see how long this queue was. Their conversation was on autopilot, she wasn't paying much attention to Ella's words, didn't think she had much to learn from a twelve-year-old.

"That doctor, Alexi. Showed up today. At the Memorial. Alive!" said Ella one word at a time, loud and clear.

"Did what you say?" asked Lucia, turning slowly to face Ella for the first time instead of the slow-moving queue. She lifted both eyebrows and widened her eyes, demanding Ella's full attention. "Showed up where? Bullshit! You're confused, kid."

"Here, watch!" said Ella and replayed the video.

"Are you sure that's him?" asked Lucia.

"Grandma verified it. She told me. They talked."

"Did they? Looks like him," said Lucia, checking her app-sleeve for travel data. "Airport records show that a foreigner looking like this man in your video reentered Greece six days ago." She checked the police records. Dr. Lautaro had been interviewed by the police four days ago, right after his arrival. Fingerprints and everything, it was clear who he was. But his disappearance was an irrelevant case by now; she had been alerted with low priority, they hadn't even sent her a direct message.

Lucia took off her mohawk wig. Her mind switched from football fan to investigator, and that wig looked ridiculous.

"Grandma said that you'd know."

"I don't know shit. But then how? What?" Lucia was talking to herself, processing, ignoring Ella. "I'll get you a soda later," she said and pulled Ella's hand to exit the queue. She needed some space and clarity to think. They walked to the edge of the open concourse, where they could gaze at the sea barrier that protected the city from the floods. The walls were covered with broadcasted images of a calm sea to remind them of what was once and could be again.

Lucia opened a private window to the AICE HQs and started inputting. She sucked her lips back in her mouth, struggling to make sense of it all, waiting for a response. An incoming message appeared on her d-glasses. Names, numbers, data. Lucia turned to Ella. "Why did you ask me about your grandfather?"

"Oh nothing, I'm just curious if you knew him. Grandma said that she considers the Walker Memorial his burial site. He died a month later, huh? December, right?"

"Not really a month, it was early December," continued Lucia avoiding Ella's eyes, thinking. "Right, it was. Just one day after I visited her. The car. That night. Shit!" Lucia was talking to herself, processing data through her glasses, ignoring Ella and everything around her.

"Is everything alright?" asked Ella.

The teams were just making their entrance into the field, and the ear-splitting cheers made it impossible for Lucia to collect her thoughts. First, she had to get rid of the young one.

"Ella, I'll need to take you to gate 12. Are your twin friends here today?" asked Lucia.

"Faye and Freedom? Yeah, they are," Ella said, checking their location.

Faye was Ella's classmate, and their dad had box seats. They always had an extra seat for Ella, soda, and mountains of popcorn. The girl would have more fun with them, especially today.

"We'll do that. Meet us here at halftime. I need to talk to your grandma."

"Is everything okay?" asked Ella, trying to read her aunt's worried face.

"Uh, yes," mumbled Lucia, clearly signaling "no." She turned on the noise cancellers, entering for a moment a completely silent bubble. Her app-sleeve was flashing, an eyes-only alert was repeatedly streaming in her d-glasses.

AICE: Artificial-Intelligence Investigation Central.
Serious Crime Alert: Immediate Action Required.
Unsolved Case #7181.
Murder of Mr. Pericles Aggelou, December 4, 2022.
Based on data submitted by Chief Inspector Lucia Maas,
November 28, 2058.
AICE points to a new primary suspect: Probability 98.6%.
Suspect name: Dr. Mathilde (Tina) Walker, wife of
victim.
Recommended Action: Locate and arrest immediately.
Dispatch P-Drones?

# 59. Yara: Bloodletting

*Athens, November 28, 2058*

*I met Yara Zed at her bare-bones, b&w, work-fight-no-play apartment overlooking the Acropolis. The secluded artist of Syrian descent works out daily— no Friday, Sunday, or other religion interrupting her routine. Judging from the sleeveless dress, the bare triceps, and the effortless catlike walk, I'd say that she maintains a stunningly ripped and lean body, though no one has ever seen her in a swimsuit.*

*She always dons her trademark crescent-moon sterling earring on the left ear. 'The other one, I threw in the sea, to honor the one I lost,' she says with an inapt steely voice. The celebrated graphic novel creator is a black-belt master and not an easy candidate for small-talk. It is not just her shoulder-high anime-heroine hairdo, the hollow cheeks, and the coin-sized creepy oval data-glasses that intimidate you. The moment you meet her, the air becomes thick with her stories' brutality and pain.*

*Despite the emptiness of her studio, you can taste it just by sticking your tongue out as if it emanates from her work. Her hovi, the mysteriously named En, pronounced 'N,' asked me right away: 'What do you smell?'*

*'Brine, a vague scent of metal and oil next to my nose, probably blood, burning fat—pork, man, idk—coming from that corner,' the words that came to my mind. I guessed En had programmed those scents into the room before my visit, but still. Yara Zed is a survivor, and those scents define her work more than anything else.*

"So that's the profile they wrote for your interview with RILM Immersive," said En, staring at Yara, who was sipping down a cup of black coffee. "Do we approve?"

"Whatever," said Yara.

"It's 5 a.m. You worked all night. Can you please go to bed now?" said En.

"Play some music. I'll get some exercise. Still not tired," Yara replied. She was already putting the kickboxing wraps on.

"How about a sleeping pill?"

"Music. Send it on," Yara said, and En streamed the sound and then the visuals to her boss'—though she never called her that—d-glasses, altering the surroundings. The experience turned to 3D as the music became a rushing river that flooded the minimal studio, ricocheting off the black walnut floor, embracing the single bed and the desk that also served as a dinner table for two. Inky ocean water rose around them and soon reached the ceiling; water Yara could see but not feel though En altered the room temperature and humidity to approach 4D. Yara was inside it, still kicking the bag, the music blasting on a continuous repeat of the same mind-numbing throbbing rhythm. She could have opted for earphones, but she wanted the echo to make it feel real. All apartments around hers were renovated with noise-cancellers; nobody ever complained.

Kickboxing was Yara's ritual and the cure to her insomnia. Bleeding ankles, white tape soaked in blood. Bloodletting. The ancients believed that bloodletting could cure anything from the Bubonic Plague to the common cold, even though the evidence was clear across centuries that it simply led to a faster death.

It was Yara's own way of facing her fear and pain— bloodletting worked for her. The ordeal back in 2022 was still a dagger twisting in her belly, but she was alone in her grief; nobody else was willing to commiserate for a few refugees drowning in the Aegean Sea thirty-six years ago. Just another insignificant tragedy, a prelude, a puppy-hound of Hades' Cerberus tooting a timid warning, an oboe leading the tuning of the doomsday orchestra, that the 21$^{st}$ century turned out to be.

After the 2022 pandemic, she moved back to the UK, went through university, and then a number of odd jobs in marketing and media. But she was not a career woman, staying up until dawn to draw, being half-asleep during the morning meetings. She became a mean machine of graphic novel production, though, and soon that was her only career.

Yara had lived in London, going through two brief failed childless marriages until it all started that April of 2039. The *Drizzle*. It was merely annoying in the beginning, a constant drizzle almost twenty-four hours a day. It lasted until October 2039, and then it changed to egg-size hailstorms. Then torrential rains, snowstorms. A different monstrous offspring of Poseidon attacking the island every month. People thought it would end sooner or later. They were quite brave, the Brits, the whole "we shall fight on the seas and oceans" heritage thing came out strong. They persevered, but it just wouldn't stop. Kids couldn't go out to play—football, cricket, horse racing, Wimbledon all was getting canceled. They did try. So many have stayed there, living almost underground, in subways and buildings, but the soil is gone, it is impossible to live a normal life, not many flights in and out either. It is evident now that the region is becoming Central Canada and Siberia. The Gulf Stream has lost its juice.

That's when Yara went back to sketching vampire armies on the ice-covered Thames. And then it moved south, Paris, Berlin, east to Stockholm, Amsterdam. Everyone north of the Alps became a refugee, moving south. She decided to return to Greece; she had a passport from her marriage to Lucia.

Yara continued working on the graphic novels, adopting them for short RILMs (Reality Immersive Films)—the first half of the century provided boundless inspiration. The gods had stayed thirsty for blood and misfortune, just like the first half of the 20th century. "No more," they said, watching from Olympus or somewhere. "Maximum occupancy exceeded. At first, those humans were funny with their roller skates, milkshakes, rock'n'roll, and drive-in theaters, but now we had enough of their plastic junk, toys, lives, jobs, dreams, and boobs flooding our beaches. Stop this, whatever it takes, Gabriel, or whatever they call you in your strange-strange land. Fire, flood, or plague." It took all of those and the Archangel's rage, bloody red rage as a cherry on top, to stop the party from getting overcrowded.

"You overdid it again today, Yara," En sighed. "Don't have to bleed yourself. This is real, not some VR shit. And I can't help you with the wounds."

"You can't cook, clean, band me. Not much of an assistant, are you?"

"I can do about everything else."

Hovis, short for holographic virtual assistants, had become as common in the 2050s as ironing boards or cooking pots were back in the 20th century. When it came to appearances, though, En was a one-of-a-kind hovi, an avatar that Yara had designed from scratch; she had personally drawn every feature of her and updated them every year to age together. Mass-market hovis, with their impeccable facial features, looked and felt plastic after a while. En's hologram was aging at the same pace as Yara; she was the one that would never abandon her.

En was Yara's personal assistant, travel agent, lawyer, banker, retirement planner, a buddy to watch a movie with (she always made the best choice), personal trainer, graphic novel editor and collaborator, literary agent, multi-channel marketing agency, library, grocery, and everything else shopper, dietician, a registered nurse approved to prescribe medicine, her emergency contact, and security guard. But there were some things even a hovi couldn't do, like boil an egg, make a smoothie, have sex, or bandage Yara's wounds. Oddly, twenty-first-century technology had replaced most brainy functions, but the human flesh was still real and aging, a prison, and a reason for pain, joy, sanity, madness, existence.

"Quick shower and off to bed you go now," En said. She shut the drapes and dimmed the lighting with a flick of her wrist.

"Are we on a schedule?"

"You are! You have a visitor at 1 p.m., so you need to get some sleep before she arrives."

"Who?" Yara asked, getting undressed to hit the shower.

"A lawyer, she is coming here in person," said En.

"Why would I meet a lawyer in person?"

"I vetted her. She reached out a few days ago, and she insisted on meeting you face to face."

"Are you asking me to meet with a stranger? In my apartment?"

"I am pretty sure this has to happen face to face, Yara."

# 60. Lucia: Bayernlona

*Union and Solidarity Stadium, November 28, 2058*

Opening whistle. The game was on. The concourse had emptied of fans, and only a handful of those arriving late were rushing past Tina and Lucia to take their seats in the football arena. The chanting of a hundred-thousand strong enfolded the two women as if they were drowning inside the belly of a roaring dragon.

"This kimono top of yours, it's something," Lucia said, but Tina didn't reply, signaling, pointer in ear, that she can't hear her.

The two women synchronized their sleeves, and all noise around them subsided, allowing only each other's voices to come through. Lucia waved her arm, and the concession stands were replaced with full 360° images of an olive grove, bathed in bright moonlight, silvery leaves swaying on an imaginary breeze.

"This may be easier," Lucia sighed. "We need to talk."

Tina sat on the bench and peered at her friend for a few seconds. "I'd rather go watch the game inside," she said. "Tonight is do or die."

"*Our* games are always do or die," said Lucia.

"It's Bayernlona, playoffs. Can't this wait?"

"Tina, I know. About that Thanksgiving night. AICE knows too. I haven't authorized the drones yet, I ran the data pretending it was a hypothetical scenario. You see, I am the only one who washed that car, in the garage with you. They don't know anything. I'm the sole witness."

"You had to make a mess, again," said Tina with a sour grimace.

"I just need some answers, you're not in danger. You know, Peri's murder remained unsolved for so many years. The bots refused to close the case. Do you know who the prime suspect was according to the machines?"

"I can guess."

"Yep, you, 65 percent probability. Not enough for an arrest. I always thought they were messing up, typical AI bots that can't see what I could. I've seen the eyes of too many criminals and liars, and you could not fake the devastation you showed the days after Peri's death. No one could, no matter how good an actress, but you are no actress, to begin with. I've been using your case as an example of what bots need to improve on in my biannual reviews. Every time. But still, they stuck with their prediction. A deadlock, but I didn't care, as long as they had no evidence. No weapon, no autopsy, just your testimony a few days after you saved millions. His body cremated. 'Conveniently.' The bots used that word in their report. But you are *the* Dr. Tina Walker, of course, the one of the Walker Memorial. You are the Mother of Science and Resilience, uniting Southern Europeans and Anglo-Saxons— we needed that after the migration. Nobody would doubt you, nobody with a heart."

"But the bots did," said Tina.

"Heartless. A few minutes ago, I gave them a hypothetical piece of evidence. Blood on your car, no DNA test done, just blood. I'd never given them that before because I knew, I thought I knew, that was Alexi's blood. Plus, Peri died almost nine days after Alexi. Or so I thought. I fed them a second fact, Alexi being alive, which we know it's the truth, and you jump at 98.6%. Done deal, *you* did it, they say."

The olive groves disappeared instantly as the frenetic cheers surrounded them. A board flashed in front of them.

*1-0 Olympians. Would you like to watch a goal replay?*

"Later," said Lucia, and the two of them returned to their moonlit grove.

"That's what I hate about this century. No privacy. All is revealed. Nothing stays hidden," said Tina gazing at the olive trees, avoiding her friend's eyes.

"I am sorry, Tina."

"Don't be. And don't worry. We never pay for our true crimes, only for the ones that irritate our enemies."

"I'm here for you. Just give me the truth."

"You have to know, huh? You're mad that you didn't see it yourself? Feeling betrayed."

"Kinda. I just need to know. Nothing to worry about," Lucia chuckled, tilting her head to the left. She tried to make this as casual as possible—the image of an arrested Tina was too much for her to handle.

"So, what gave me away today?" asked Tina.

"I mean, a husband is missing, and there is blood all over the garage. I just browsed through Alexi's testimony from a few days ago, and he said that you drove him in a black sedan and dropped him at a hospital. You left with Alexi from the airport on a black Mercedes. A week later, when I came to your house, you're cleaning the blood out of a gray Volvo SUV. Why would you move him from one car to another? I never understood that. But you didn't, didn't you? That wasn't *his* blood. The bots have analyzed every case in the world, counterfed it to US, Australian, and Japanese bots in minutes for cross-verification. 98.6 percent probability and up everywhere. And there is that other thing that still doesn't make sense. You called a hospital that night, twice."

"And?"

"But, see, you called a 79 hospital. You called an ambulance to your house and then canceled it. Why would you call an outbreak hospital for Alexi's head wound? After all, you were the one who had made the hospital protocols, you knew they'd never admit him."

"I need something to drink, Lucia. Give me a minute," said Tina. She turned her back to Lucia and walked into the virtual olive grove, heading for the soda stand.

By the time she returned with two ice teas, it was halftime, and they were surrounded by hundreds of fans who had left their seats to stretch their legs and get a drink. Ella, Faye, and Freedom ran toward them. The kids were animated and hyper, arguing everything about the game. Tina played along and pretended that she had watched the first half.

"We are one up. We *must* win this one," said Ella showing two tight fists to her grandma.

"You can't win all games, Ella. Sometimes a tie is good enough. Even a graceful defeat," said Tina, winking toward Lucia.

"What? Don't jinx it! You are more of a pessimist than aunt Yara. By the way, where is she?" asked Ella.

"Some emergency meeting, she messaged me," said Lucia. "Won't make it."

Ella pouted her lips, but soon she followed Faye to the ice-cream stand. A few minutes later, the fans rushed back to their seats, and Tina with Lucia were left alone at their virtual grove, continuing their conversation.

They were interrupted a minute later by the flashboard and the updated score. The stadium was swamped by a long sigh. They knew. *Olympians-Bayernlona 1-1.*

"Why are we always numb after halftime?" Tina asked. "It happens in life too, you reach forty-five, and suddenly you want to throw everything away, don't care about wrong and right, marriage, friends. You try to go through the motions one more day, but they don't make sense like you are sick of your own skin."

"It's called a midlife crisis."

"We start so strong at home. I hate halftime, we deflate, second half we are a different team," Tina said.

"Please, Tina. I've searched for Peri's killers for thirty-six years. You fooled me, and you owe me."

"I owe you nothing. There is no need to twist the facts around, Lucia. There is nothing as brutal as the truth."

"I deserve it."

"Nobody deserves *this truth*, Lucia. I didn't deserve it. He didn't."

# 61. Tina: We Survived

"Before we get to the facts, you need to understand the science, Lucia. You see, we humans are prone to make accusations and pass judgment on those we know or don't, but at the end of the day, we are just chemical machines. Our minds are cauldrons that witches, nature, storytellers, and nano-sized parasites enter and mess with our moral compass if such a thing even exists. We think we do because we are, but in fact, we do because we cannot not do. We are preprogrammed, once we are triggered, we execute. Organic puppet robots.

"Let's get to the point, though. I like facts because they are real, and I hate 'feelings' because they're just the exhaust pipes of our chemical machines. Back in November 2022, people didn't have enough data to assert that the H7N9 virus would wreak havoc across the whole body and even the brain. Blood clotting, liver damage, psychosis, neurotoxic reactions. We verified most of these later; the number of unexplained suicides among the infected was extreme. They say forty thousand died in Greece alone, but they don't count those who lost kidney function or lived the rest of their years in depression. Didn't make the news. You remember that policeman at Lesbos who tried to jump out of the second-floor window and thought we were flesh-eating Sirens?

"I had a hunch, a strong one, because the Spanish Flu had caused exactly the same symptoms. Even a hobbyist—not many pandemic hobbyists out there—had enough data from 1918. I am not talking about the high-fever passing delirium; that's normal. I am talking virus-induced psychosis. Every country back in 1918 had reported dementia, hysteria, insanity, maniacal frenzy; all the words in the dictionary were used. Brain swelling, meninges overflowing with blood to the point that a man could lose his hair in a few hours and his mind in minutes. It is important to remember all this as I continue.

"That night at the Athens Airport, when we were just back from Liberia, it was the closest I've come to witnessing the divine. You, Lucia. *You* were the divine. The way you saved all of us, them, the mission, gathering the airport crews, calling in the trucks, the airplanes from Papalias, I was trembling with despair one moment, then with awe, as I watched you up in that loading platform shouting from the bullhorn. Let's face it, I have to admit it today, and I said that to the Mayor, it should be called Mazur, not Walker Memorial, but I am an American-Greek epidemiologist, and you were a Polish-Albanian student.

"As I stand at that runway, watching you directing and the trucks go their way, Peri calls me. I kept this out of my story to Ella. I am surprised she never asked where Peri was when I came back. Floribeth, our housekeeper, had left us to stay with her daughter since the beginning of the quarantine, and those antivaccine nuts had come earlier that night shouting and throwing rocks at our home. Peri had locked Demetri in the basement, as I told him. Keep him safe. Demetri was seven years old, the kid had freaked out, but we had coached him to shut up and put a phone there, to call his grandma if we didn't reply for whatever reason.

"Peri had sent some crazy messages earlier when we landed at the airport, calling me 'bitch' and to 'go to hell,' which I didn't reply to. That was not Peri-like, he'd never call me names, especially in messages. Any other time I'd have called him right back asking for explanations, but that night, well, you remember, we had to save the world. He didn't sound right.

*ARE YOU WITH HIM?*

*HIM WHO HONEY???*

*DONT U HONEY ME BITCH. THAT ALEXI GUY FROM WORK. I KNOW U R TOGETHER. I SAW THE TEXTS.*

"I mean, shit! He never suspected anything back when I did have the affair, and then he finds at a synced tablet the messages I sent to Alexi to lure him to the airport. Don't shake your head, yeah, that's bad luck, Lucia. But that wasn't the worst. You see, I knew my husband. That was not him, cursing and threatening. Peri was what you'd call an *archon*, in Greek, meaning *gentleman*, not *ruler*. He'd never, no matter what. He orders me: "Turn on the camera, show me where you are."

"And I am like in the Mercedes, a bleeding Alexi unconscious at the back seat, so I step out of the car, sit on the tarmac against the driver's door, so he can't see, and there he is. Peri. The camera is on. In the beginning, I couldn't see clearly. He is in the kitchen, best guess, most of his face is just a dark shadow.

"'Peri, can you please turn on the light,' I say.

"He is cursing, ordering me to come back home now, or he'll take Demetri and abandon me forever.

"He turns on the light.

"Sorry, I need a minute, Lucia."

*The screen is flashing Olympians-Bayernlona 1-2. Defeat is imminent. Tina continues.*

"Peri is in the kitchen, his hair is all messy, and as he brings the camera close to his face, his eyes are red-rimmed. He is bleeding, Lucia, he can't speak, the cough is ripping him apart. He is bleeding from the nose, on the table, holding a kitchen towel soaked in…"

"'What's wrong, Peri?' I ask, but I know already.

"I get back in the car now, speeding out of the airport, going a hundred and fifty on the open highway. 'Where is Demetri?' I ask him. Is he with him, is Demetri infected too? When did this happen? My heart is pumping so hard it is almost blocking my throat now, I can't breathe. Fifteen minutes to home. About halfway, I stop on the sidewalk next to the Hygeia hospital, and I throw Alexi out of the car, half-conscious. 'Come on! The hospital, Alexi. Check in.' I see him crawling, and I speed away. Don't ask me what happened after that. Until this morning, I never saw or heard from him again.

"I am at home. I unlock, I rush in. 'Where is Demetri? Please, Peri.'

"'Oh, now you care about us? Where have you been? Two days now.'

He is holding and shaking me with both hands. Sweating, burning, I touch his forehead, 103, I don't even need a thermometer.

"'Where did you go? When did this happen? I need to get you to a hospital.' I beg.

"'I read the messages,' he answers.

"'There is nothing going on, Peri. Please, listen to me. Forget Alexi.' He is unsteady on his feet, crawling and grabbing the kitchen island. 'Is Demetri downstairs?' I turn to rush downstairs, I am going mad myself, do I grab Demetri and run, or do I drive Peri to the 79 hospital? 'When did this happen? How long have you been like this?'

I was with him two nights ago, he sneezed once, but that was all. We laughed.

"'How long have you been fucking him? Is that kid downstairs even mine?'

"He is holding a glass, ready to throw it at me.

"'Christ sake, Peri. Yes, Demetri is yours. He is your spitting image, a stranger can tell you that. Please, honey, we need to get you to the hospital.'

"He grabs me by the arm as I head for the basement, and he pulls me up the stairs. I hit my head on the door frame, and he pushes me down on the kitchen island, his weight on top, he tries to rip my shirt.

"Sexual excitation, psychosis, it just dawns on me right there that I am dealing with someone who is out of his mind. It is not about Alexi or the messages. He doesn't rape me, tries for a few seconds, and then collapses on his knees with a splitting cough. It is around 1 a.m. when I call the hospital, they say they have only one ambulance, and it will be at our place "maybe, in a couple of hours." I scream at them, shut the phone, and drag him to the elevator to get to the basement. We have the SUV there, I'll take him to the hospital myself.

"He is a big guy, it is not easy, he is not very cooperative. Demetri is locked in the basement's isolation room, a bed, a tablet, and the quarantine supplies, he can't see us unless he climbs to reach the small window on the metal door, but he needs a chair or something. I am pretty sure he can hear us because he calls me, 'Ma, ma, are you here? Ma, let me out!'

"I can't go inside. He needs to stay away from Peri. I'll come back, disinfect everything, then open, which is what I'll eventually do, hours later.

"'It's me, baby. I'll come soon. Need to drive your dad somewhere first. Do you feel sick, baby?'

"'No.'

"'Please, do you feel warm? Are you coughing?'

"'No, ma, I am fine. Please, open the door, ma.'

"He figures it out himself, sacks, chair, something, and he climbs. I see his face and his tousled hair, a little Pericles jr., through the door's window. He seems fine, no bleeding, coughing, sweating. I am all in tears, but I need to keep the door shut and him away from Peri.

"I still don't know how Peri got infected, he knew better than to go out— I'll find out months later that two of his friends, were also infected. They were together days before, when he went to help one of them out.

"I change to a t-shirt because his blood is all over me, a sparkling white t-shirt I pull from the laundry, along with some towels that I soak in cold water to place on his forehead.

"He is delirious, eyes half-shut and mumbling obscenities. When I start the car, Demetri is crying, 'Ma, please don't leave me here,' but I cannot risk him getting sick, not this, and Peri hears him, and he comes to his senses again, pulls the keys from the ignition. He gets out of the car, rushes to the driver's side, opens the door, and pulls me from the hair, throwing me on the floor, calling me a whore and a bitch.

"I am taking Demetri, and we are out of here. Stay with your boyfriend," he shouts. He zombie-walks to Demetri's door holding the keys.

I grab his arm with both hands and pull him, but he turns and punches me on the jaw, and I fall on the forged cement. I am dizzy and angry, mad and desperate, down on my knees, begging him, palms crossed. "Please, Peri, no, don't open the door. You'll kill him. Let's go to the hospital. Now."

"'I am fine,' he says as the coughing tears him apart. 'Aha,' and he is finally holding the right key in his hand, showing it to me, the cement is painted a red and white chessboard, a tribute to his favorite football team, and there is pink froth from his coughing on the white squares. His ear is bleeding, his back is turned on me, and he tries to unlock the door, and then it is all over, Demetri's life is over, and we are chemical machines, have I told you that, I did, we are programmed for survival, especially offspring survival, I'd walk into the fire before I let my kid get infected with this shit, I smuggled vaccines out of Liberia, lost my job and threw my Ph.D. in the toilet, destroyed my career in two nights, just to make sure Demetri is safe, there is no way that door opens, and we are chemical machines, yes, we are, and Peri is as good as dead, I've seen a few H7N9 cases and I know that Peri is done for, too late for any hospital to save him, do I know it, yes, probability 98.6 percent as your bots would say, and the baseball bat is right there resting against the wall, the one he used to "arm" himself against the mob a few days ago and just a split second before he unlocks the door, his back is on me, I said that, right, I swing it hard and it lands on his skull, that sharp cracking sound.

"He drops on one knee with eyes staring me open for two full seconds, and then he is down at his back. For a moment, I think I see Demetri's shocked face looking through the window, though I'll never know because we'll never talk about this again. I seriously still don't know what my son knows about me killing his father, I didn't mean to kill him, that's what I say to myself, but why did I swing so hard, Papalias' thugs hit Alexi on the head, but he survives, but me, I've never swung a baseball bat before, but he is not moving. 'Peri, baby, Peri, love, please honey, we need to get to the hospital, sorry hon, you can't open this door,' but he is not moving, he is resting peacefully on the red and white cement, a pool of black-purple gooey liquid runs out of his head, and I am all over him, sparkling white shirt blotched red, and I go to the basement sink to bring some water to give him, but he won't move, he fell like a tree.

"It takes all my strength and my sanity to pull his body, his head like that, on that passenger seat. I have to get him to the hospital. I cover his face with towels, he doesn't move. And only then do I finally accept the truth, that he is dead, I killed him, and I am going to jail, and Demetri will lose both parents and may not even survive this plague. Where, who will take him? He mustn't know. There is Demetri's old cradle down abandoned in the basement. I leave the kid there locked, may whoever made this world forgive me. It is around 2 a.m. when I enter the kitchen with a crowbar and a claw hammer. I need a coffin. Kitchen panels. The second call to the hospital is to cancel the ambulance. I work a straight two hours. Panels, nailing. You'll see tomorrow when you go dig him up.

"I push the cradle up the hill. You know that hill next to my old house, the path among the cypress rows where we walk your Charlie, Lucia. Yes, I go there often.

"I come back to the house and make the call to the Prime Minister. In the morning, I take Demetri to the vaccination center, a farewell present from his father, last name starts with 'A,' you see. He is silent, except when he is asking where dad is, and I say he left to take care of grandpa and grandma. Fortunately, they are at their second home in the village, and they will not come by. Does Demetri believe me? I drop him at my mom's. Yangos calls and comes by, three of them on bikes, to get rid of the Mercedes. 'Alexi has disappeared,' he says. 'He never checked in at the hospital.' The police will be at my door any minute, or so I think, but Alexi being a coward and all, never goes to the police; he disappears at Montevideo, where his brother has been living for years. That Saturday evening, you come by the house as I wash away the blood from the car and the floor. I'm shocked you didn't figure it out right then, I was quite certain that I'd be arrested way before you came, for Peri, for Alexi, for the airport thing, but nobody came. The whole country is on lockdown until the vaccines kick in, another two weeks, the dead are more than ever before. Those were the worst days mortality-wise.

"The whole week until that evening you came, I was washing the blood and the basement, not to get rid of evidence but because I had to. And then you visit, you have an idea, you said and, bingo, it dawns on me. It was all you, you see. Saved me, once again. Cremation site! Your idea. That's it! I may be able to get away with it—worth a shot. I start photographing those people who had surrounded our house. I have the death threats, messages, fliers dropped. Next night, I grab one of the garbage-bag-wrapped mannequins that play scarecrows on our front entrance, and I drive it to the cremation site. If you didn't go there back then, you still don't understand what we've been through.

"There is smoke and darkness, commandos with machine guns guarding the entrance, and a crew of men wearing full snorkeling style masks working the night shift. A landscape of Hades in rotting flesh, charred bone, and fire around me. Two men are loading bodies on a truck. I give them a fifty, and they throw the garbage-bag-wrapped mannequin in a pile. One of them takes off his mask, Pakistani, maybe Bangladeshi, looks at me perplexed—he senses something is wrong—so I take out another fifty. 'Write name here, lady.' There is a Department of Health logbook—I recognize the seal—but the clerk is long gone. Not paid enough to spend the night in the New Hades. *Pericles Aggelou, died of stab wounds, December 4, found murdered.* I sign my name. Cremated. The police buy my story, they didn't even ask me to testify for months, as they were completely overwhelmed with other matters, even *you* bought my story back then, because I cried, god, I cried, I am *the* Dr. Tina Walker, after all, bearer of the vaccines, who would doubt my words, but I am also a machine programmed to die or kill if my child's life is in danger. Do I regret it, you ask?

"Tell you what. There is duty and there is peace, but you can only serve one of these goddesses.

"Do I suffer?

"Every day.

"I hoped Demetri would confront me one day—does he really know, we'll find out tomorrow, finally. I am not keeping any secrets for the afterlife. All ends here.

"I still wonder, though, I fight the killer inside me. Did I do it because I lost the colors because I was left only with red, black, and brown after I got infected? My mom used to say that 'You can't save them all, Tina, you must sacrifice the old for the young to live,' though she was talking about roses back then.

"I still don't know, Lucia. Sometimes I doubt myself. You know all those murder mysteries, they say 'she did it for the money,' but you see that she hated him too. 'He killed her because he was jealous,' but it's evident in his eyes that he is also a psycho. Two motives always, one everyone buys, the second that not even the killer acknowledges, lurking deep inside. How did I find the strength to swing the bat so carelessly, so fast, with more power than was necessary, maybe I didn't love him, why does he have so few words in my story, maybe I was subconsciously trying to get rid of him, what if I am a monster, and I cannot even see that in the mirror? And what if those two seconds after I hit him and before he shut his eyes, what if? What happens to the brain as it shuts down? Is it an instant on-off switch or a slide to hell? Does it suffer from thoughts for a few more seconds, still that chemical machine bubbling, wondering. 'Why are you murdering me, Tina?'

"Every time we sit at a family dinner, Demetri, his wife Anastasia, my dear Ella, her brother Yanni, I know that if I don't swing that bat, none of them exists, none of them would be with us today or ever born, there would be no beautiful Ella, the only reason I am still alive, and I feel the burden of duty but can't find a crumb of solace, we are breaking bread and raise the glasses and exchange wishes for health and happiness, and wisdom, oh yeah, wisdom, but I am grieving, because he is there on every dinner with us, he is my empty chair and the clean fork, the plate on the kitchen cabinet whispering 'why am I not on your table, Tina?'

"That's it, Lucia. I have no more words.

Under the cold moonlight, surrounded by the olive trees, Tina panted hard, exhausted as if she'd run a forty-year marathon. Lucia embraced her. The illusion of their surroundings was shattered as the arena erupted again in cheers that pierced their grief, almost mocking them.

"If all this is true, a Collective Intelligence Judge would acquit you. Self-defense," said Lucia.

"It would. In most villages, they'd have stoned me to death a century ago."

"But the CI Judge would be right."

"Nobody is right. And unlike a robot judge, I have to live with it."

"The dates threw me off. I always assumed Peri died the following night after we washed the blood off your car. That was some clever trick. So, you took him up the hill to bury him that same Thanksgiving night?" asked Lucia.

"First, I had to push the cradle there. Then I drove him up. Yes, the cradle is still there. He is still there."

"Twice? You made that trip up the hill twice in your condition."

"Cradle wouldn't fit in the car."

"And, didn't you worry about getting caught? Someone seeing you?"

"I was almost certain I'd get caught. That same night, a day or two later. I just wanted to bury him and then get Demetri for his vaccine and then to my mother. And wash away the blood. Had to."

"So, why?"

"Why what?"

"Why didn't you just take him for cremation right away?"

"Two reasons. If he was cremated, I could never prove he was infected. I thought it would help my story, that when the police caught me, and his mother, our friends, my mother, saw the effort I made to save him, bury him, to honor him, they might actually understand, maybe they'd believe that I didn't mean to kill him that I loved him."

"And the second reason?"

"I did love him."


Final whistle. The fans were exiting from all gates, rushing toward and past the two women down the stairway. An ocean of jubilant faces surrounded them, a roaring song of triumph. Tina spotted little Ella hopping up and down, making a 360° turn, radiant with excitement.

"Unbelievable, aunt Lucia, huh! Did you see that last-minute header? We got the tie." Lucia just nodded to the girl, chocked up for words. "Rematch is next week at their place. Will you come to grandma to watch with me? Please come!"

"Sure thing," said Lucia and quickly put her glasses on to hide her eyes.

"Have we ever saved a playoff game on stoppage time before?" Ella asked. "Oh, grandma, you were spot on. We didn't win."

Tina passed her fingers slowly through Ella's long brown hair. "No, we didn't win. But we survived."

# 62. Ella: Caryatids

*A year later*

"Thank you," said my dad, Demetri, after reading the memoir. He said it was healing to learn that his mother did everything to save him, that his father was dying anyway. It means even more to him now that my grandma has passed away. "It's funny, though," he continued. "Tina (from Mathilde), Marcella, Lucia, Yara, who they thought was spelled Gianna, huh, back at Moria? Mathew, Mark, Luke, and John. Weird, huh?"

"I don't get it," I replied.

"Mathew, Mark, Luke, and John. But they are all women."

When I think of the four women, the ones who used to go every Sunday to the football game, I don't think of Evangelists. The picture that comes to my mind is the Caryatids, the draped marble maidens that are the pillars of the Erechtheion, the most sacred temple of ancient Athens. The Caryatids have been standing guards next to the Parthenon for the last twenty-five centuries, white-washed basket-bearers that have lost their colors, just like my grandma did, arms broken, noses chipped, and eyes hollow white. They have endured countless foreign invaders and local-born tyrants but are still standing tall, pillars supporting all that is sacred, serving their ancient purpose. Symbols of hope and perseverance; they carry the weight that men defeated in battle couldn't.

Most photographs show four Caryatids, those in the front row of the temple, but at a closer look, there is a fifth one further back—maybe she represents those who fought away from the spotlight. The archaeologists will tell you that there is yet another one, one more maiden, lost but not forgotten, who has been taken away from her sisters. But one day, she'll come back.

# 63. Yara: By the Sea

*Athens, November 28, 2058*

"Time to get up!" said En, clapping her hands. "Your 1 p.m. will be here in ten."

"Give me a minute. I had the same dream again last night," said Yara as she slipped out of bed.

"Night? You went to bed at 6 a.m., my dear. You slept through a bright sunny day and a brief hailstorm," said En.

"I need coffee."

"It's ready. But take a rhodiola too. And tell me about your dream. I'll pass it to Thera-Net tomorrow."

Yara dragged her feet to the kitchen and filled up her cup.

"It's almost real, most of it has happened, En. It was years ago, I am at a big-deal, BBC-Al-Jazeera-JV-Athens-HQ, post-awards, artists event, a cocktail party by the pool. First time I try to overcome my fear of water in public. A waiter, a Caribbean dreadlocks man, brings me a blue-curacao-vodka-lime-dry-ice cocktail with a little stevia-soluble-not-really-plastic-yellow-monkey-stirrer, the ones with the long curving tail. Everyone around me talks about the floods rather than the awards, the millions of refugees descending from Northern Europe to find shelter south. Water has become a word of horror and pain for everyone as if their grandmother had bequeathed them the same shred of wisdom mine did: *"Fear the water."* This is a true story so far.

411

But in my dream, the tiny monkey comes alive as she is hanging from the lip of the glass, suffocating from the dry-ice smoke, fighting for its dear life. The monkey slips and falls into my drink. I stare at her, slowly drowning in the pool, can the monkey swim, no she can't, I try to pull her out and save her, I don't even see her under the smoke, but my hand trembles, I break the glass and cut myself badly. The monkey drowns in my blood, its fake-sugary flesh deforms and melts in front of my eyes. I faint next to the pool and unwillingly hit the water. The water remembers me. 'Here you are! So many years. I was waiting for you, Yara!' and they drag me out of there, soaked, shivering."

"You're safe, Yara," said En. "No water here. Pop a pill. Your visitor is here any minute."

"How serious is this? A lawyer? Are we in trouble?" Yara asked.

"I don't think so."

"Who is this woman?" asked Yara. In her fifteen years living with En, watching her age to a face of forty-three years, her hovi had never allowed anyone to enter their apartment without being screened and intro-ed through a holo-call. The only reasons for anyone to come in person were dinner, sex, and therapeutic massage. "I can't do a face-to-face with a stranger. It's creepy. I have to leave for the game. Tina, Lucia, they are expecting me."

"I'm afraid you need to meet her, Yara. If you still care to go to the game after your meeting, I'll arrange a private air taxi to land you at the VIP parking. But I don't think you'll go to the game today. Oops, she is buzzing us. Get dressed, please."

"Are you for real today?"

"I am not real, she is," said En smiling and then "Elevator, third floor, only apartment," talking to their visitor.

"But who is she?" Yara asked, visibly agitated now.

"I believe it's…me!" said En beaming a radiant smile of mystery.

Yara watched the female figure entering the elevator, then pressing floor four. The woman's curly black hair hid her face, and she only lifted her gaze to stare at the camera for a brief moment, enough for Yara to know.

Moments later, En let their visitor in the apartment, and Yara watched with eyes wide and heart racing the two identical women greeting each other,

En faking awe and their guest expressing it genuinely. Their hairstyle was different, as En had opted to switch instantly to a straight dark olive-green cut, while the woman standing opposite from them had an impressive curly hairdo like blackberry-colored snakes had grown out of her head. She was in her early forties but looking much younger, wearing a black sleeveless wrap knee-high coat over a gray knit sweater and instapump ankle boots.

Yara stared at her, her body frozen like struck by lightning in a videogame, refusing to ask or to guess. She knew. For years, she had created En's image, drawing the hovi's features from the computer-generated images—those images projecting how her sister Nahla was supposed to grow and age every year if she were still alive.

"Who, what are you?" asked Yara. She didn't dare to offer a handshake, touch her. She could be a hologram, but going through the ordeal to create one and have it ring the bell, come up in the elevator, was something that En had no reason to do.

"Yara. You look different than the professional pictures, different than what I had in mind." said the guest.

"Worse?" En interrupted.

"I remember her warm. More flesh. She is metal now. Steel."

"You remember me from where?" said Yara.

"It's me, Yara. Nahla."

Yara took two steps back, protecting herself, protecting everything she knew and suffered for thirty-six years, and rubbed her welled-up eyes, hoping the image would fade to dust.

"What's this shit, En?" she turned to the hovi, who was stepping further away, trying to become invisible.

"Yara, love," said En, "this is your sister, Nahla. Goes by Nadia now. She got in touch with me a few days ago, but I had to run a thorough background check. DNA and all. She accepted. It's all here," said En and the white wall filled with data, files, sibling DNA matching results, and more.

Yara took a step forward, her eyes darting between the data and their guest.

"You've known for days?" she asked En.

"I had to check, Yara, to prep her. I knew how devastating this would be

413

for you, whether truth or lie. Had to protect you. I am afraid it's the truth."

Nahla raised her arms, palms facing Yara as if approaching a wild animal. She had a soft but confident voice; she was prepared for this meeting. "I am sorry, Yara, for not reaching out all these years. My father said you had all drowned, and I am not into reading comics or watching immersive reality films. I've never come across your name or your work. My old name, Nahla, has been lost to me. At sea. Two weeks ago, my teenage daughter was watching a RILM, and she runs to me all excited: "Mom, you gotta see this, this anime actress in the VR is like your spitting image. Even her expressions." She was."

En interfered. "That's the one they did with the enslaved sea maidens and the cephalopod monster."

Yara made a gesture toward En, signaling her to remain quiet.

"But I watched you drown. Did you say 'your father'?" asked Yara.

"I watched you drown too," said Nahla. "There was a man in that boat. Not our father. The one who raised me. Sorry, I call him that. I mean, you are too young to remember, he had his eyes covered with dark shadow."

"Surmah."

"You remember?"

"I never forgot. The djinn."

"The what?" Nahla smirked, and that did it for Yara. That smirk belonged to her sister. "No, that man saved me, he raised me. He was a father to me. I'll tell you all about him."

Yara took another couple of steps toward Nahla. "May I?" She took Nahla's hand between hers, hoping that she wouldn't break or turn to mist. Flesh, not digital; even the fingers were familiar.

"The man in soot?" asked Yara.

"Musa, his name was Musa. He was making the boat trips back and forth, saved so many of us. I grew up with six brothers and sisters, all thanks to him."

Yara wanted to say that she grew up all alone, but then her mind went back to Lucia. That would be unfair. En was right; she was not going to make the playoff game tonight.

"This is too much, Nahla. I feel I have inhaled something I shouldn't," said Yara.

"Do you mind joining me for dinner? I've booked us at Ithaca fish taverna by the sea. Also, can you please call me Nadia?" Nahla replied.

"By the sea?"

"Ooops!" En interjected again. "You know, Yara, never ventures—"

"That's okay, En. By the sea, it is. Nadia, it is Nadia right, could you give me a couple of minutes to change?"

En altered the studio's lighting, creating a virtual curtain, a temporary cocoon of privacy. Yara hid there, sat on the floor, eyes shut, panting hard, learning how to breathe again.

"This will do," said En, projecting a silver-black jumpsuit on the wall.

"I don't like you watching me when I dress," said Yara to the hovi.

"I am not real, Yara. This woman is. And she is your little sister."

"We'll see. It is too much to take in. Did she really find me from the comic book drawings?"

"Funny, huh? In some way, *you* found her."

"And you've checked her story about that man in surmah."

"That's quite a story, I'll let her tell you," said En. "I've double-verified everything, Yara. She is the one."

"Why did you say 'I am afraid'?"

"What?"

"Back in there, you said, 'I am afraid, it's the truth.'"

"Oh, don't worry about that, girl. Personal stuff. See, I'm gonna need a nose job, maybe gain some weight or lose a couple of inches, probably a radical 'plastic' surgery. I always wanted sparkling blue eyes. You'll need to rework me starting tomorrow. I can't look like a spitting image of your newfound sister. Even a new name. En, after all, comes from, well, N, we both know that."

"I see."

"Yara, I know it is a shock for you, but it is a shock for her too. Please, open up, she doesn't want anything, she is actually quite wealthy and not in any trouble."

"You triple-verified that," nodded Yara with a blank face.

"Right. Look, you need to warm up to her. Let her approach you. You were too cold in there. Some wise person once said, 'we don't fear pain, we fear love.'"

Yara checked the outside temperature; it was a balmy eighteen Celsius in November. She could even wear sandals, let her toes kiss the sea. She didn't have to worry about Nahla—her little sister seemed dressed for any weather. She didn't have to worry about anything. Yara waved her palm for the curtain to disappear, greeted Nahla with a warm smile, more flesh, less metal, and then turned to En.

"Whoever said that, my beautiful En, has never felt true love or true pain."

# 64. Lucia: The Boat Rider

*A year later*

The Boat Rider, who sails between the Turkish and Greek coasts, is a figure of legend. Stories have been spoken about him since the beginning of time. He is the ghost of a defecting Myrmidon warrior, an undead Byzantine prince who awakes every fifty years to fulfill his oath for revenge, a barbarian chieftain of an archer tribe, guilty of filicide, cursed never to set foot on land again.

Nahla said that the Boat Rider, Musa, the one who raised her, was an Afghani man who had first tried to cross in an overcrowded dinghy with his family back in 2006. He lost his wife and older son at sea, found his four-year-old lying dead at the beach where the waves brought him. The Boat Rider, who Yara named in her story as the Man with Eyes of Soot, was very rich, almost royalty back at his land until the local leaders turned against him. He escaped and became a refugee—alas, he'd always regret that he did—only to watch his sons and wife swallowed by the waves.

Musa settled in downtown Athens, a shadow roaming the streets, unable to commit suicide, waiting for death to liberate him. One night he stopped at an electronics storefront window—all the TV sets were broadcasting the news, the rescue of a boy at sea. Lesbos, a rocky beach, orange vests, twenty screens repeating, a nine-year-old boy, the same age as his, a hug, a mylar blanket. And in that one moment, he knew—they are all children, after all, ours, theirs. Innocent.

For the next fifteen years, he crossed the same straits to Lesbos and back

417

hundreds of times, on the most dangerous of boats, with one purpose. To save those who wouldn't be saved, the children traveling alone. Once they were ashore, he'd take them back to Athens, where he had set up an illegal but very decent orphanage. He raised the children alone until they were of age, making sure they eventually got European passports and an education. He died a year ago, a few weeks after my friend Tina, having raised seven boys and girls. Three became scientists and teachers, one musician, one OD'd on heroin, and one went into trade. Nahla, the youngest one, became a lawyer and a human rights activist. She is the one who took over Tina's football season ticket, so we all four still go to the games, though she is not much of a fan.

I miss Tina.

The Boat Rider brought balance to my life too. Our storylines, Yara's, Tina's, mine, were one-sided, women the victims and heroines and men resorting to crime, stupidity, and rape. It would be comical was it not so painful—until the Boat Rider. There is war, hatred, viruses, death, but there is also man. Oftentimes, he is the worst of those plagues, but once in a while, he is kind, even brave.

Tina, Yara, myself, we are all Boat Riders, survivors who found the strength to carry on.

It would be selfish to lie down, let grief overwhelm us, and wait for death. This earth was never meant to be some park purposely built for our amusement, it doesn't owe us anything, not even a smooth sail. We owe to the world, at the very least, to help those who can't help themselves. Even if the sacrifice required is unbearable, we will protect the life of the young, their future. It is our nature, we are like a virus ourselves.

We survive and multiply, harness the sun and the wind, conquer the seas and set sail for the stars. We expand.

As my late friend, Tina, a stranger I once met on a boat to hell, once said: "We'll kill for life, we'll die for love."

# About the Author

Back in 2018, I started writing a novel about a pandemic based on the H7N9 influenza virus, a very real and documented global threat. About the same time, I started working for a clean energy startup that aims to make diesel generators obsolete in developing countries, and I was raising four children. On the one hand, I was worried about their future; on the other, I kept reading world news about civil wars, refugees, and child exploitation. Somehow, all this messed together to create a novel about four women, a story that I hope is more about resilience rather than tragedy.

I was born in Athens, Greece, and lived in New England for almost twenty years, including 2018, when I started writing *Cradle*. This is my second novel, following the epic fantasy series *Drakon*. *Drakon*, which I highly recommend, is another variant of the same story that I write over and over again: man is the most dangerous monster, and the hero (or heroine) has to pay a price so high that it is worthy of a song and a story.

# Afterword

Fortunately, "all the characters and events depicted in this book are fictitious. Any resemblance to a person living or dead is purely coincidental".

Unfortunately, all the nightmares that this book may give you are based on actual events. The dead children washed ashore at the coasts of Europe. More than we dare to count. Millions of underaged children exploited by the global sex industry. Even the broomstick with the lemon and the chili powder. It is real. A pandemic that starts in Asia and spreads globally to a completely unprepared world, causing millions of deaths. It happened. It will happen again. The antivaxers and the conspiracy theorists. A flu virus causing an eye infection that makes the infected color-blind or mentally disabled, both reported symptoms of the 1918 influenza.

The H7N9 is a very real and dangerous virus. According to the CDC website, *"H7N9 virus is rated by the Influenza Risk Assessment Tool as having the greatest potential to cause a pandemic, as well as potentially posing the greatest risk to severely impact public health if it were to achieve sustained human-to-human transmission."* The WHO reports referring to H7N9 incidents and victims appearing in this book and dated before 2018, when I started writing, are all real, word by word. Yes, I did start writing "Cradle" long before I heard of Covid; I have one too many Facebook posts with draft passages to prove it.

When Covid19 hit, I was in the middle of the book, and I had no intention to change the story at all. I believe that every pandemic will be quite different than the previous, and it will be dangerous to always think in Covid19 terms. What would be the global effects if we were unlucky enough to face a pandemic that would seriously endanger children? Or if Covid19 had a 5% mortality? None of the global or local effects and reactions would be the same. We must learn a lot from the Covid19 pandemic, and we must forget it and move on, preparting for the next. Because, make no mistake, there will be a next one, there is one always.

The climate crisis is very real, though I cannot predict which parts of the world will be affected and by when. I do hope I am not always that prophetic.

The following books (added to countless online articles and documentaries) proved quite helpful in my research:

- The Great Influenza by John M. Barry
- Flu by Gina Kolata
- The Coming Plague by Laurie Garrett
- Deadliest Enemy by Michael T. Osterholm, Ph.D., MPH and Mark Olshaker
- Viruses, Plagues, and History by Michael B. A. Oldstone
- Pale Rider by Laura Spinney
- Sex Trafficking Inside the Business of Modern Slavery by Siddharth Kara

I've heard from experienced book industry folks that this novel is "too complex," that there are "one too many stories," maybe I should "cut one character." I heard that I should make it the ideal 323 pages and reduce it to a sellable medical thriller. It would mean dropping the refugee stories or the climate crisis mess. I thought hard for a long five minutes. Cutting a character felt like cutting one of my limbs to lose those fifteen pounds I have to. And so I did the stupid thing. After all, my stories, whether the fantasy series "Drakon" or "Cradle," are about heroines and heroes who never play it safe.

You can reach me at www.caskabel.com

# More Books by the Author

The Drakon series:
Drakon Book I: The Sieve
Drakon Book II: Uncarved
Drakon Book III: Firstblade
Drakon Book IV: Butterfly
Drakon Omnibus: The Complete Story Books I-IV

More about the book: https://caskabel.com/

Follow the Author on Amazon:
https://www.amazon.com/C.A.-Caskabel/e/B01ITDR0V6

and Goodreads:
https://www.goodreads.com/author/show/15559320.C_A_Caskabel

Made in United States
North Haven, CT
01 June 2022

19717590R00257